ABOUT

Janet O'K_____ _____ 'A literature, so
she went s_____ _____ Enid Blyton to what her Mum liked
reading: crime novels. And despite occasional dalliances
with other types of fiction, that's where she has happily
stayed.

Her career before turning to writing fulltime included
selling underpants to Roger Moore in Harrods and
marketing nappies for Boots. It was when she helped run a
GP surgery that she decided a doctor would make an
excellent main character for a crime novel

Janet lives in the Scottish Borders with her stonemason
husband and two cats, two dogs and far too many
chickens. She is now working on the sequel to *No Stranger
to Death*.

www.facebook.com/JanetOkaneAuthor

Janet O'Kane

NO STRANGER TO DEATH

To Mum

ONE

Zoe Moreland saw her first dead body at the age of twelve, and had seen many others since. But that morning, for the first time ever, she could not tell if she was looking at the remains of a man or a woman.

The blackened form lay in the ash of Westerlea's Guy Fawkes bonfire, surrounded by smoke-stained, metal debris and charred pieces of wood. Coated from head to foot in a thick layer of what looked like melted plastic, it seemed barely human, more a grotesque department-store mannequin which had been posed with elbows and knees flexed, fists clenched. Wisps of smoke rose from the torso.

It was still burning.

Zoe took a step back, glad that the worst cold she'd had in years currently prevented her from smelling anything. If only Mac had been similarly afflicted. She turned to the dog who had led her there. 'So this is why you wouldn't come when I called.' Mac wagged his tail.

Minutes ticked by. Zoe knew what she had to do, what any normal person would have done already. But most normal people had no real-life experience of the police, did not know that getting mixed up with them meant answering questions, giving statements, being asked more questions. She had only found this out when Russell died.

She considered her options. They were alone, just her and Mac and that poor soul on the ground. Only the pub overlooked this part of the field and its curtains were

1

still closed. She could walk away this time, feign shock when someone eventually told her the news.

Apart from the rumble of an occasional vehicle passing through Westerlea it was very quiet, yet another unsettling aspect of her new life in the country. Then the sound of high-pitched voices reached her, and she remembered the primary school only a short walk away. *What if the next person to come across this horror was a child?*

'You're a hard-hearted bitch.' Those words had echoed inside Zoe's head during the months since they were spat out at her, and they returned now. *Perhaps they were true.*

No, they weren't.

She reached inside her coat. Plastic bag, dog biscuits, tissues, no mobile. Usually she would no sooner have left without it than forget to put on boots. This cold must be affecting her brain as well as her nose.

Zoe sighed then started to lead Mac towards the village. Rather than knock on a stranger's front door, she would go a little further and ask Brian at the shop to call the police. But they were already there, a car with yellow and blue markings parked outside a grey-rendered bungalow on the other side of Main Street. A brass plate told visitors the drab little house was called Horseshoe Cottage, although the rusty horseshoe nailed above its front door did nothing to help it live up to this folksy name.

After tying Mac's lead to the fence separating the bungalow from its neighbour, Zoe rang the doorbell. Getting no response, she let herself in. 'It's Doctor Moreland. Is anyone home?'

Her attention was caught by a group of framed photographs on the hall table which tracked the transformation of a blonde, smiling child into a blonde, sulky teenager. In pride of place at the front was a snapshot of the same girl, face flushed and hair tangled, cradling two tiny babies wrapped in white towels.

'Morning Doctor.'

Zoe turned with such a start she knocked over one of the photographs. A young man, barely out of his teens himself, with bum-fluff sideburns and a rash of acne across his chin, smiled at her from the other end of the hall.

'They didnae tell me you'd been called,' he said, indicating the radio attached to the front of his black uniform. 'Come on through. He's in here.'

'It's you I need to speak with,' Zoe said, 'Constable er . . . '

'Geddes. Aye, but you'll be wanting to see your patient first?'

The policeman opened a door to reveal an elderly man in striped pyjamas sitting with a Jack Russell terrier on his lap. It was Jimmy Baird, one of the few villagers Zoe could put a name to, who used to run the pub. His dog lay quietly while he plucked at the hair on its neck with a trembling hand.

Zoe went over and crouched down beside him. 'Hello Mr Baird. I'm Doctor Moreland.'

He stared at her and opened his mouth, but seemed unable to form any words. Before Zoe could explain she had not brought her medical bag so would telephone the surgery for another doctor to come out straightaway, the constable spoke again.

'He's upset because his wife's missing. She was supposed to be visiting her daughter in Newcastle but she never arrived.'

Zoe stared at the terrier, unable to remember what she had been about to say.

'Doctor, are you all right?' Geddes asked.

'Yes, of course. But we need to talk. Alone.'

Out in the hall, Geddes blanched when Zoe told him what she had found in the remains of the bonfire. *He really was much too young to handle this on his own.* To his credit, though, he took control of the situation, fetching a neighbour to sit with Jimmy then accompanying her to the bonfire site behind The Rocket. After scrutinising the corpse he stumbled backwards, pale and perspiring, the reality of what, he had confided on the way there, would be his first dead body far worse than anything he could have imagined. And he did not have the benefit of a blocked nose.

Zoe led him upwind from the smoke still coming from the body. 'Deep breaths,' she instructed, anxious to prevent him from keeling over or heaving up his breakfast.

Geddes did as he was told and, with youthful resilience, quickly regained some colour. He moved away to use his radio, too far from Zoe for her to listen in. She stamped her feet and pulled her woolly hat down as far as it would go, while Mac sat patiently next to her.

When Geddes returned he seemed almost cheerful, ready perhaps to enjoy the prestige of being first on the scene of a serious crime.

'Can I go home now?' Zoe asked. Mac, sensing they were about to make a move, started to wag his tail.

'Not yet.'

'Why not?'

'I've been told to keep you here until a senior officer arrives to take over.'

Chilled and resentful at being trapped in a process she had no control over, Zoe could not help responding with words she knew would hit home. 'All right. As long as I don't have to be around when it's taken away.'

She paused, giving him just enough time to dread what was coming next.

'They won't have taught you this at police college, but bodies burnt that badly need extremely careful handling. Or else, when they're moved . . .'

Another pause. Geddes went grey.

'The flesh just falls off the bones like an overcooked chicken.'

TWO

The number of crime-scene professionals clad in white coveralls steadily increased at the bonfire site during the next hour, although not as quickly as the flock of inquisitive villagers restrained by crime-scene tape and Constable Geddes. Instructed to stay within the cordoned-off area, Zoe could not hear the onlookers' words but they had to be speculating about her part in the drama. *So much for keeping a low profile.*

Hanging around with no active role to play, no established procedure to follow, gave her time to brood. The fun everyone had at last night's party took on a different hue when she imagined what was happening, unseen, only a few metres away. While they swirled sparklers and exclaimed at fireworks exploding overhead, was someone trapped inside the bonfire, aware of the mounting heat and struggling to breathe through the smoke?

Unable to bear standing idle any longer, she gathered up Mac's lead and was about to slip away when a uniformed sergeant deigned to come over. He looked curiously at the dog, took Zoe's details and told her to go home. An officer would be in touch.

Which was precisely what she had wanted to avoid.

Her mobile lay on the kitchen worktop next to the kettle. A text was waiting. *What's up doc?*

Zoe texted back. *Fancy a coffee?*
On my way!

Keeper's Cottage was freezing. Given the promise of their size, its storage radiators gave off a pathetic amount of heat. Zoe fed Mac and the cat, then pulled a Supertramp CD out of the Pickfords' box in the hall and put it on, singing along as she lit the woodburning stove and brushed hair off Mac's armchair. Like most of the furniture in the cottage this had seen better days, but she saw no point in bringing her own out of storage yet.

'Hiya!'

Mac ran into the hall, throwing himself at Kate Mackenzie while she pulled off her shocking-pink hat and unwound a matching scarf. As her visitor entered the sitting room, Zoe rushed to turn off the CD player.

'Don't do that on my account,' Kate said, laughing. 'And don't look so embarrassed. It's great that you forget. I wish everyone else would.' Her voice retained the soft Borders accent she'd had at the age of twelve when meningitis had robbed her of her hearing. 'You've no idea how irritating it is when people speak verrrry sloooowly because they don't think I'll keep up otherwise.'

'I expect I did that when we first met. Most of us aren't used to talking to a person who lip-reads.'

'You didn't, but I take your point. Anyway, how are you?'

'Fine. How are your parents? I really enjoyed lunch with them the other day.'

'Still fighting over Dad's diet. As you saw, good food and lots of it is Mum's answer to everything. She can't get her head around cholesterol levels and calorie-counting.'

'I loved that story of her posting you potato scones when you lived in London. That's another Scottish delicacy I must try. Do you think I'll like them more than haggis?'

Kate said nothing but stood, hands on hips,

staring at Zoe.

'What?' Zoe asked. As if she didn't know.

'I'm waiting for you to stop blethering and get on with the interesting stuff.'

'What do you mean?'

'Aunty Phil rang to tell Mum the police were at Horseshoe Cottage first thing, then you took them to the field behind The Rocket, and now nobody's allowed in there and a tent's been put up over last night's bonfire. And Chrissie Baird's missing.'

Kate's voice became overloud sometimes, when she was excited or annoyed. This was one of those times.

'Do you want coffee?' Zoe asked.

'Not as much as I want to hear what you've been up to. But I see I'm going to have to prise it out of you. As usual.'

Kate strode towards the kitchen, Mac and Zoe following. 'Tell all,' she said, as they sat down. 'Don't leave anything out.'

Zoe took her through the events of earlier that morning, then got up to make the coffee but felt so light-headed she had to sit down again.

'You okay?' Kate asked.

'I must have stood up too quickly.'

'You look a bit peely-wally. Have you eaten anything?'

'No.'

Zoe watched Kate make toast and a cafetiere of coffee, then bring them to the table along with plates, mugs, butter and a pot of strawberry jam.

'I can't believe the police kept you waiting for so long and then made you come home on your own,' Kate said, buttering a piece of toast. 'You could be suffering from shock.'

'I've seen more dead bodies than most people, remember. Although they're not usually in that state, thank goodness.'

—

7

'There can't be much of her left. The Young Farmers excelled themselves this year – it was the biggest bonfire Westerlea's ever seen. Except for when the old garage accidentally went on fire, of course.'

'Actually I think it must have been covered over or wrapped in something which stopped it from burning up.'

'Really? So we're talking Chrissie en croute.' Kate laughed at her own joke, adding when Zoe failed to join in, 'Don't look so shocked. If you knew Chrissie Baird, you'd understand why I'm not heartbroken. Very few others will be either.'

'That's a bit harsh. And we don't know yet if it is her.'

'Who else could it be? No one would make a special journey to a wee place like Westerlea just to shove a dead body in our Guy Fawkes bonfire.'

'All right, let's say it is Chrissie. Tell me what you've got against her. I only met her once and she seemed harmless enough, maybe a bit nosy.' The slim, middle-aged woman in a pastel-blue tracksuit had proved difficult to escape, quizzing Zoe about her plans for converting the coach house and wanting to know what breed Mac was. *As if anyone would produce a dog like him on purpose.*

'Harmless? I won't repeat the mean things she said about me when Ken left. Luckily Mum has plenty of friends who put her right on that subject.' Kate paused to lick the melted butter running down her hand. 'She threw her weight around in the pub so much, a lot of the locals stopped going there.'

Zoe shook her head. 'That's in a different league to hating a person enough to kill them.'

'Has she brought her tray of Remembrance Day poppies into the health centre yet?'

'I don't know. But even you can't hold collecting for charity against her.'

'Yes I can, when she does it for the same reason

—

8

she does all her other good works, like turning up with food and sympathy when someone dies. It gives her an excuse to nose around houses she would never normally be invited into.'

'Every community has its busybody.'

'People don't like how she appeared from nowhere and manoeuvred herself into The Rocket and Jimmy's bed. His first wife was barely in her grave.'

'That must have been a long time ago.' From what Zoe had seen earlier, Jimmy Baird was in no condition to have been seduced by anyone recently.

'Twelve years.' Kate held up a hand, acknowledging her friend's look of disbelief. 'People have long memories around here. It's different to where you come from. Forget about six degrees of separation, in the Borders it's more like one or two.'

'So I'm discovering. Margaret at the surgery gives me potted histories of every patient I see.'

'In which case it won't surprise you to hear I'm related to Chrissie. Well, sort of. Her daughter, Alice, used to be married to my cousin Tom.'

'And how does Tom get on with Chrissie?'

'He loathes her. He and Alice have twin girls – they'll be nearly four now – who live with him. Chrissie's been trying to persuade Social Services to declare him an unfit father and give her custody instead. Can you imagine? I know what I'd do if someone tried to take my bairns away from me.'

Zoe flinched as Kate banged her mug down on the table. 'If the body is Chrissie's, your cousin may find himself a suspect.'

'That's ridiculous. Tom wouldn't hurt a fly.'

'The police always look at the family first.'

'In which case let's hope it isn't her after all.' Kate leaned back and folded her arms. It wasn't hard to guess what was coming next. Zoe knew she was lucky to have got away with it for this long.

—

9

'Tell me what happened last night when we came back here from the pub,' Kate said. 'With Neil.'

Zoe gathered up their plates and screwed the lid on the jam pot. 'Nothing.'

'Did I ever tell you how much communication is non-verbal?' Kate wagged a finger. 'It's no use fibbing to me.'

'I'm not. We were chatting while I made the coffee.'

'You were gone for ages. And he'd been a bit twitchy all evening. He was plucking up the courage to ask you out, wasn't he?'

'He was talking about the kitchen they're going to make for me. You know what Neil's like. Once he gets started he's hard to stop.'

'Come on, Zoe, it's obvious he's attracted to you. Why don't you admit you feel the same way and do something about it? He's not your patient, is he?'

'No. But that's not the point.'

'So what is?' Kate's smile vanished. 'Sorry. I'm being insensitive, aren't I? It's probably too soon after losing Russell.'

'No, it's not that.' Zoe half-expected Kate to be shocked by this disclosure, but the only expression on her face now was one of curiosity.

'So what's stopping you?'

'I'm stopping myself. I can't simply let rip with the first good-looking man who shows an interest in me.'

'So you do find him good-looking?'

'That's not what I –'

The doorbell rang.

A well-built man with close-cropped grey hair stood on the step. He wore a navy cashmere coat over a grey suit; his plain shirt and patterned tie were perfectly coordinated.

'Doctor Moreland?' His right hand held up a leather wallet, inviting Zoe to look at his identification

---

10

rather than the silver cufflink her eyes were drawn to. 'Detective Chief Inspector Erskine Mather, Police Scotland.'

'Hello.'

'Can you spare us a few minutes?'

'All right.'

Mather stepped into the hall, revealing a pair of black patent-leather shoes which secured his position as the nattiest dresser Zoe had met since crossing the Border. Not that such stylishness made dealing with him any more welcome.

'This is Sergeant Trent.'

The squat man coming in behind Mather wore wellies and a too-tight raincoat. He nodded a greeting.

Zoe led them through to the kitchen. With luck, Kate's presence would make them hurry up with their questions and leave.

Mather halted at the doorway, staring at Kate.

Kate stared back at him. 'Skinny?'

She stood up so quickly she knocked over her chair.

THREE

'Hello Kate.' Mather cleared his throat. 'How are you?'

Kate scraped a hand through her cropped hair. 'Very well.'

The policeman bent down and picked up the fallen chair.

'You two know each other?' Zoe cringed. *Could she have said anything more inane?*

Mather's response did nothing to explain or dispel the tension which had sprung up in the room. 'We were at St Andrews together.'

Before Zoe could enquire further, Kate produced her car keys. 'I'll leave you to it. Text me later, Zoe.' She left without another word.

Mather turned down the offer of coffee, although Trent looked like he needed warming up. Zoe led them to the sitting room, remembering too late there were not enough chairs to go round.

'I'll stand,' Trent said, leaning against the door frame.

'We won't take up a lot of your time,' Mather said, removing his overcoat, folding it inside out and placing it over the back of the chair before he sat down. His mouth twitched briefly into a smile as he half patted, half pushed away Mac, who was sniffing his trouser leg. 'An unusual mix of breeds you've got there.'

'You won't find another dog like him, that's for sure.'

'I believe you're relatively new to the Borders, Doctor Moreland.'

'I moved up in the summer,' Zoe said. She started counting down to the inevitable question.

'To your job as GP at the Westerlea Health Centre.'

'Yes.' *Here it comes.*

'Were you already familiar with this area?'

'No.' *Why doesn't he come straight out with it?*

Mather remained silent.

Zoe's heart thumped. How ridiculous to be this nervous. She had nothing to hide. 'I came here because I lost my husband and needed a change of scene.'

This was usually enough to move any conversation along, and it worked now too.

Mather nodded. 'You don't think you'll be able to help, but that's not necessarily so. A police investigation is like a jigsaw puzzle – we need all the pieces to see the full picture. What you have to tell us about this morning will be a useful starting point.'

'Like a piece of outside edge, you mean?'

Behind them, Trent only partly managed to stifle a snigger.

Mather smiled ruefully. His eyes were the same grey as his suit, which was probably not a coincidence. 'I apologise if I sounded patronising. In my line of work it's all too easy to slip into a combination of clichés and euphemisms when talking to the public about matters they'd rather forget.'

'The medical profession's guilty of that too,' Zoe said. She must be on her guard; she was starting to warm to him. 'We try so hard to avoid upsetting patients with bad news, it's no surprise they walk out not having understood a word.'

'I suspect no doctor could have predicted this particular death,' Mather said. 'That person – we have to wait for confirmation that it is indeed the missing Mrs Baird – didn't get into Westerlea's bonfire by accident. It's my job to find out who put him or her there, and you may be able to help. First of all, could you talk me through the events of this morning, up to when you showed Constable Geddes the body?'

Zoe briefly described her walk from Keeper's Cottage to the field behind The Rocket.

'What took you to the bonfire site? Did something attract your attention?'

'Mac ran off towards it and wouldn't come back when I called him. I thought he'd spotted a hare, but now I realise he was drawn by the smell.' Zoe grabbed a tissue and blew her nose hard. 'Sorry, I've had a cold.' *God forbid they'd think she was getting weepy.*

'Did you touch anything?'

'I didn't need to. Even covered in that melted stuff, I could see what it was. Though I don't understand why it hadn't burnt up completely.'

'Sometimes fire isn't as destructive as people expect. And I believe heavy rain came on while the bonfire was still burning. Were you there yourself?'

'I wouldn't have missed it.'

Zoe could almost hear the fireworks going off as she cast her mind back to the previous evening. According to rumour, this Guy Fawkes celebration would be Westerlea's last, due to the need for prohibitively expensive insurance, so what seemed like the entire village and all of the families living in outlying farms had come along to make the most of it. The guy, dressed eccentrically in a blue boiler suit, a red cravat and a horse-riding helmet, sat on top of the fire until flames reached up and pulled him in. Rockets shot skyward; Roman candles hissed and exploded.

The occasion was cut short when heavy rain began to fall. Young children grizzled and older ones sulked as their parents took them home. Most of the remaining spectators fled into the cramped comfort of the pub.

Mather cleared his throat, bringing Zoe back into

the present. 'Kate tells me that apart from the New Year's Day carpet bowls tournament, Westerlea's Bonfire Night party is the best attended event in the village,' she said. 'You see people in The Rocket who don't go there any other time. It was bursting at the seams, although that's no hard thing, given its size.'

'Was the bonfire already burning when you arrived?'

'We didn't go out to the garden until the fireworks were about to start. It was roaring by then, although the guy was still on top.' Zoe paused briefly, as a horrible thought occurred to her. 'The guy. It wasn't her, was it?'

'That's not likely,' Mather said.

'Thank goodness. I couldn't bear to think we were watching a real person being burnt before our eyes.'

'You said "we". Who were you with?'

'Kate and her children. Well, they played with some of their cousins out in the garden while we sat inside and had our first drink with Neil and Peter Pengelly, the joiners from Larimer Hall.' *He probably didn't need to know that last bit.*

'Was anyone behaving strangely?'

No, that came afterwards. She hadn't known how to react then and was no surer now.

'Doctor?'

'Sorry. Not that I noticed.'

'And there was nothing unusual about the bonfire?'

'It was much bigger than I'd expected, but it looked like any other.'

Mather brushed his knee to dislodge a dog hair which had landed on it. 'What time did you leave?'

'We were in The Rocket until about nine. Kate's aunt and uncle took the children home with them when the rain started, to let Kate stay on. She doesn't go out much, being a single parent.'

An expression flickered across Mather's face

which was impossible to interpret, then he gazed out of the window as though their conversation had come to an end. Zoe released her tensed-up shoulders; it was almost over. She was surprised when he turned his attention back to her.

'Are you acquainted with Mr and Mrs Baird? They used to run the pub, I believe.'

'Yes they did, but that was before my time. I've seen Mr Baird there occasionally, but never to say more than hello. I only spoke to his wife once, not long after I moved here.'

'Did you form an opinion about her?'

'We just exchanged a few words, when I was walking home from the shop one Sunday with the newspaper. She introduced herself, asked me a few personal questions, then went on her way.'

'What sort of questions?'

'Mainly about why I wanted such a big house, what my plans were for it, that sort of thing.'

Mather looked around, obviously puzzled.

Zoe smiled. 'This isn't mine. It belongs to Douglas Mackenzie, Kate's brother. I'm renting it while I'm having the old coach house at Larimer Park converted. Anyway, Mrs Baird must have realised I'm not at all interesting because I don't think I saw her again. Although that doesn't mean she isn't registered at our practice.'

'We're calling on your colleague, Doctor Ryder, next,' Mather said. 'I have one final question. Were you involved in the construction of the bonfire?'

'I didn't help to build it, if that's what you mean, but I contributed some old timber from the coach house.'

Mather stood up. 'We won't keep you any longer, Doctor. Thank you. You've been very helpful.'

'Helpful enough that you won't release my name to the press? It doesn't do a doctor's image any good, being associated with this sort of thing.'

Mather smiled politely, obviously not taken in by

her feeble joke but with more important issues on his mind. 'We never share witnesses' details with the press.' As he put on his overcoat he ran a hand down its front, checking for dog hairs, oblivious to the ones which had transferred themselves from Mac's chair to the seat of his trousers.

Trent nodded a farewell as he scurried after his boss.

Zoe shut the front door. *Thank goodness that was over.* With luck she'd never have to see them again.

FOUR

Despite not being in the telephone directory and having given no one the Keeper's Cottage number, Zoe had received five calls by early that afternoon, all from people she hardly knew, all claiming concern for her wellbeing. It was obvious they were more interested in what she had found than how it was affecting her, and she got rid of them politely but speedily. The only conversation she welcomed was with Paul Ryder, the senior partner in the practice she had recently joined, who rang from the health centre after seeing Mather. Zoe assured him she was fine and would be at work the next morning, as scheduled.

She tried watching TV and catching up with the ironing but could settle to nothing. Even reading, her lifelong refuge from boredom and sadness, and a short walk with Mac, going away from the village this time, did not work. So she went out to the garage, Mac at her heels. It was a novelty to have somewhere to keep the car, and it was big enough that if she bought a padlock for the doors she could move some boxes in there too.

Mac leapt onto the passenger seat, his claws scraping its protective cover, and squirmed with excitement at the prospect of being taken for a drive. Crossing round the front of the car to get to her own door, Zoe ran her hand over the bonnet and frowned. *Must get that chip seen to before rust sets in.*

A few minutes later, driving cautiously along the rough track leading to Tolbyres Farm and wincing every time the bottom of her car scraped the ground, she wondered about Kate's history with Erskine Mather. What she witnessed had not been a reunion of acquaintances who had simply lost touch over the years. She would wait for Kate to raise the subject first, though. They enjoyed each other's company but had only been friends for a short time, since Kate had called in to meet her brother's new tenant. It was too soon to start sharing personal confidences.

A light came on automatically when she pulled up in front of Tolbyres Cottage next to Kate's ancient Volvo. As usual, Mac jumped across her lap and sprang out as soon as she opened her door.

She had gone to the wrong entrance on their first visit. Her friend's home had been built by the Mackenzie family more than a century ago as a pair of semis for their farm workers. More recently, the cottages had stood empty for several years until Kate returned to the Borders with two demanding toddlers, a baby on the way and a jobless husband. Her parents had hastily started to convert the building into a single dwelling. However, owing to baby Mhairi's early arrival and the departure soon afterwards of Kate's husband – bearing out her father's direst predictions – the remodeling had stalled, never to be completed. So Tolbyres Cottage still boasted two front doors (one nailed shut), two staircases (one leading nowhere) and walls in unexpected places. It was a home as individual as its occupants.

By the time Zoe entered the warm kitchen, Mac was already there, catching and bolting down biscuits thrown to him by Frankie, Eva and Mhairi. The family's outsized ginger cat, Bluto, sprawled in his favourite position along the Aga's pot rack, his tail hanging perilously close to the hotplates.

Wearing a faded pink apron bearing the message 'Mum's in charge', Kate straightened up from putting a dish into the oven and shooed the children away, telling them to change out of their school clothes.

'I hope it's okay to arrive unannounced,' Zoe said. 'I had to get out for a while. Here, I brought you something.'

Kate took the bag Zoe held out and peered inside. 'You know you're always welcome here, especially bearing food. Is this the sort of bread we had this morning? It makes lovely toast.'

'Glad it meets with your approval,' Zoe said. 'It's an old family recipe.'

'You made it? I thought you didn't do cooking.'

'Bread-making's more science than cookery. It's the only culinary skill I inherited from my grandmother.'

Kate put away the loaf then slid the kettle onto a hotplate, brushing aside Bluto's tail. As she turned back to face Zoe, she said, 'Sorry I rushed off earlier. I couldn't think what to say when I saw who your visitor was.'

'A shock for both of you, by the looks of it.'

'We haven't seen each other since university.'

'That's a long time. I'm surprised you recognised him. He's gone very grey.'

Kate shook her head. 'His hair was already like that when I knew him. It's a family trait. He's put on weight, but haven't we all?' She made a pot of tea, covering it with a hand-knitted cosy, then closed the door into the sitting room where the children were playing with Mac. 'I want to explain.'

'You don't have to.' Every day Zoe heard things – deeply personal, often sad or disturbing things – that her patients felt unable to share with anyone else. It was all part of the job. But she was never comfortable when people chose to unburden themselves outside the surgery, especially as they often expected her to do the same in return.

'I'd hate you to keep wondering what the big deal is.'

'My involvement with the police began and ended

20

with finding that body. It's not likely I'll see him again.'

Kate continued to speak, looking out of the window rather than maintaining eye contact like she usually did. Zoe could not have interrupted her even if she had wanted to.

'A friend introduced us. Although Erskine was a couple of years ahead of me she reckoned we'd get on because we both came from the Borders. Which was ridiculous – Kelso's nothing like Galashiels and I'm nothing like him. He deserved the inevitable nickname because he really was skinny then, not my type at all. I only accepted his invitation to go to a party because I had nothing else on that weekend.

'He told me afterwards he was nervous about how I would cope with all those people I'd never met before. But fairly early on in the evening he stopped telling his friends I couldn't hear. Being able to lip read comes in handy when everyone else is deafened by loud music.'

She turned round to pour the tea and handed Zoe a mug, meeting her gaze again. 'It got to the stage where we were talking about getting married. Our mothers became friends. They still are.'

'Which must have made it worse when you broke up,' Zoe said. She took a sponge from the sink to wipe something sticky off her mug's handle.

'Aye, you're right. Mum and Bette still meet up occasionally to swap news. I shouldn't have been surprised to see him, because I knew full well he was living in the Borders again.'

Zoe said nothing, watching Kate take a gulp of tea, letting her tell the story at her own pace. When she spoke again, the words poured out of her.

'I got pregnant and had an abortion. I couldn't tell him, he was in the middle of his finals, so I went ahead and did it. Then someone else found out and told him, and he said he never wanted to see me again.' Kate's shoulders drooped and she gazed down at her hands.

Zoe waited until her friend looked up again before speaking. 'He must have realised it wasn't an easy decision for you.'

'I can't blame him. It was his baby too.'

'And it was your body. He treated you very badly.'

'With hindsight, I see now it wasn't so much my having the abortion he was upset at, but the fact I shut him out and didn't share the decision with him.' Kate took another mouthful of tea. 'I never saw him again, until today. He joined the police, moved to Glasgow and married a lassie called Laura. She's a social worker.'

'No wonder it was such a shock for you, meeting him again without warning.'

'It was inevitable – the Borders isn't a big place. Though I never guessed our paths would cross as the result of a murder enquiry. Thanks a lot, Chrissie.' Kate raised her mug in mock salute.

It was a relief to see Kate's sense of humour starting to return, so Zoe refrained from pointing out again that the body had not yet been identified. 'Why is he here now?' she asked. 'I would have thought Glasgow's a better place for an ambitious policeman to be based.'

'Bette had a stroke about a year ago and Erskine came back to be near her. His father died when he was a child, so they're very close. Laura's still in Glasgow, but they're not getting a divorce.'

'You're well-informed.'

'Mum regularly tells me about his promotions and how Bette blames Laura for not making her a granny yet. But I try not to –'

The door flew open. Three children and a dog rushed in.

'Mum, is tea ready yet?'

'Mummy, I'm starving.'

Zoe felt a light touch on her arm. She had noticed on her first visit to Tolbyres how Kate's children did this to be sure they had their mother's attention before speaking to her. Mhairi often used the technique on other adults too. 'She'll grow out of it. Her brother and sister did,' Kate said when Zoe commented on this.

'Zoe, did you know it's my birthday soon?' Mhairi asked.

'I think you told me before,' Zoe said. 'It's Saturday, isn't it?'

'Yes, and I'll be seven.'

'That's very grown up.'

'When's Mac's birthday?'

'I'm afraid I don't know.'

'Hasn't he got a stifficate?' asked Eva, the middle child and usually the quietest. 'Granddad's dogs have all got stifficates.'

'That's because Granddad's dogs are pedigree sheepdogs,' Kate said. 'Mac is what's called a mongrel. He's a mixture of breeds, so he doesn't have one.'

'But he must have a birthday.' Eva sounded scathing. 'Everyone's got a birthday.'

'You're right,' Zoe said, 'but I don't know when it is. I wasn't there when he was born, and I never met the people who were.'

'Why not?' Mhairi asked.

Zoe looked at Kate. Unused to conversing with children except to ask where it hurt, she had no idea how much of the story she should tell. Kate grinned and shrugged.

'Well, the people who owned Mac didn't want to keep him, so they put him in a box and left him by the side of the road for someone else to find and look after.'

'Like baby Moses?' Mhairi asked.

Zoe admitted the similarity. She had expected her audience to be upset by the harsh reality of Mac's arrival in her life, but instead they were enthralled and wanted to hear more. They knew there was going to be a happy ending.

'It was a Friday, and I was driving home when I needed to stop and stretch my legs. I saw a cardboard box and it started to move. When I opened it up, there was Mac. He seemed hungry, so I took him home to give him something to eat. And then I decided to keep him.'

'Why did you call him Mac?' Eva asked. 'Is it short for Mackenzie?'

'Don't be silly. She didn't know us then,' Frankie said.

'Because I wrapped him in my mac – my raincoat – to keep him warm.'

The children were delighted with this story, and they all agreed that Mhairi should share her birthday with Mac. Then their mother told them to go and wash their hands because tea was nearly ready.

In the silence which followed, Zoe could not help thinking back to the day Mac came into her life. She had left a lot out. Like having to pull over on to the hard shoulder during the drive home from Russell's funeral because she was shaking, not so much from grief but shock at the hostility she had encountered from people who used to be her friends. And how Mac was not on his own in the box but standing on top of three siblings who had not shared his tenacious grip on life.

After settling the squirming puppy on the front passenger seat, she had put the box and its pitiful contents into the boot of her car. Once home, she officiated at the second burial of the day then telephoned a local animal shelter to ask if they would take the tiny creature which was now curled up on her lap. Despite assurances that young dogs were easy to re-home, she had made her first ever visit to a pet shop the next morning, returning with a *Puppies for Dummies* book, dog food, a collar and lead, and a bed Mac would never sleep in because he preferred to share hers.

Leaving Kate to serve up the delicious-looking lasagne she had taken out of the Aga, Zoe wandered through to the sitting room. Further talk on anything but the blandest subjects would have to wait until she and Kate were alone again. Despite their apparent concentration on a host of other things, she knew children always overheard what adults would rather they did not. She had learned this lesson the day Eva had told her grandmother to be extra kind to Zoe because she was still getting over having to put her hand up a man's bottom that morning.

Kate's sitting room would have been huge, had the abrupt curtailment of building work not left the remains of the original party wall protruding halfway across it. This marked a boundary between two separate areas, one for the children and one for their mother and her work. Zoe settled herself into a deep armchair on the adult side of the room.

A desk sat against the wall, holding a computer and printer, a pen pot made from a handle-less mug, and a set of stacking trays. An acrylic magnifying dome was close to hand on the mouse mat. Hanging above all this was a framed montage of family photographs, none of which, as far as Zoe could see, featured Kate's ex-husband. A pine shelf unit stood close by, packed with neatly-labeled box files, several large reference books and lots of smaller ones, and boxes of CDs.

The centrepiece of the children's side of the room was a three-seater sofa, its faded green cover partly hidden by a multicoloured throw. It faced a television with DVD player, satellite box and games console stacked beneath it. A stretch of storage units, taken from the house's redundant second kitchen, was piled high with boxed games, DVDs and books.

With the exception of an occasional stray toy, the children and their possessions generally respected the invisible line between their territory and that of their mother. Even Bluto usually found the extra energy required to bypass the good furniture and settle himself on an arm of the children's sofa. One of the few rules of the house was that nobody but Kate touched her desk and its contents.

A lull in the noise coming from the kitchen told Zoe the children were tucking into their meal. Kate joined her soon afterwards.

'That should keep them busy for a while, though there's bound to be a stushie later when Frankie serves the ice cream. He always takes extra for himself.'

'I suppose Mac's under the table waiting for dropped food,' Zoe said.

'He is, and I'm not complaining. Since you've been coming here I haven't had to sweep the kitchen floor nearly so often.'

'He has his uses.'

'He's certainly better at housework than Ken ever was. Perhaps I should have gone for a puppy rather than a husband.'

'Some women might agree with you.'

'But not you, Zoe, surely? It must be completely different when you're widowed. You'll wish you'd had more time together, rather than feeling all those years had been wasted, like I do.'

Zoe always found Kate's animosity towards her ex-husband difficult to respond to, and now she felt guilty as well. 'But the children came from your marriage. You wouldn't want to be without them.'

'Of course not. I'm grateful to Ken for siring them, but that's all he did. He might as well have sent his sperm through the post, like a prize bull, for all the use he was in raising them. My life actually became easier when he left, can you believe that?' Kate paused and frowned. 'You've done it again, haven't you?'

'What?'

'You've managed to dodge the question and make me talk about myself. Did they teach you that at medical school or does it come naturally?'

Zoe laughed, then asked, 'So what are you going to do about Erskine Mather?'

'There's nothing to do. It's ancient history. If we meet again, I shall behave in a much more grown-up manner, ask after his mother and comment on the weather, that sort of thing.'

'Good for you.'

'And talking about history, I have a new client.'

'Where from this time?'

'Phoenix, Arizona. He's called Noah P Reece the Third and he wants me to do a family tree for his father.'

'Mr Noah P Reece the Second?'

'How did you guess? He thinks they may be descendants of William Wallace. Frankly, he's more likely to be related to Mel Gibson, though I didn't tell him that, of course.'

'It must be interesting, poking about in people's pasts.'

'A lot better than poking about in their nether regions.' Kate grimaced. 'I could never do your job.'

'It's not all piles and warts. Often the only thing people need is someone to talk to.'

'Well they'll certainly be wanting to talk to you over the next few days. You've become a local celebrity, Mum says. She's been getting lots of calls from folk asking about you.'

Zoe groaned. 'That's the last thing I want.' She glanced at her watch and stood up. 'Whoever it was I found and however they got there, I wish I wasn't involved.'

'It'll die down eventually,' Kate said, 'Although I know a way of speeding up the process. You need to deal with everybody's curiosity in a oner.'

'How do you suggest I do that?' Zoe said, taking Mac's lead out of her pocket in preparation for dragging him away from the children's leftovers.

'Meet it head on. Come to The Rocket with me

27

tonight. Most of the village will be there, acting shocked and loving every minute of it.'

Zoe shook her head and said no, but Kate wasn't going to be deterred.

'I recommend you give them all a chance to hear at first hand what you saw. The more gory details the better. Then they'll lose interest in you and move on to deciding who did it. I'll drop the bairns off with Mum and pick you up at the back of seven.'

FIVE

They pulled into The Rocket's small car park at around seven-fifteen and bagged the space of a car just leaving. The vehicle which followed them in wasn't so lucky, and had to reverse out to park on the road.

Kate picked the remains of a boiled sweet from the leg of her jeans and got out of the Volvo. She leaned over the car's roof to Zoe. 'I can't believe it's only a day since we were last here.'

'It's certainly been an eventful one,' Zoe said. 'Promise me we won't have to stay long.'

There had been no public confirmation of the identity of the corpse in the bonfire, although media coverage made much of the police 'refusing to confirm or deny a link between this gruesome discovery and the disappearance of retired landlady Christine Baird'. Zoe was referred to in Police Scotland's official statement as 'a woman walking her dog', but it was only a matter of time before identification of that woman spread further than Westerlea itself. She had gone back to using her maiden name when she came to Scotland, but would that protect her against people whose job it was to dig up the past of anyone remotely connected with a sensational crime?

As they reached the back of the pub, Zoe halted. *Coming here was a stupid idea. Feeding people's curiosity would only make matters worse.* She was about to turn around and walk back to the car when Kate linked arms with her and said, 'You'll be okay. Come on.'

The two women walked along the side of The Rocket, past an open window out of which came the sound of classical music and the smell of frying onions. On Main Street, the pub's sign creaked, the black and white depiction of a steam train swinging to and fro in the breeze. The green tips of bulbs planted in the window boxes were already beginning to show, and neatly-trimmed conifers stood in tubs on either side of the small porch.

Zoe opened the door and peered into the bar, which was as crowded as it had been the night before, though now child-free. She stood motionless until Kate nudged her and told her to get a move on.

'Evening ladies.' Ray Anderson's voice boomed from behind the polished counter. Some people insisted on shouting at Kate, and he was one of them.

All conversation stopped and the throng of bodies parted to let the two women through. An open fire burned steadily, with a stack of logs on its hearth ready to be thrown on whenever it started to die down. Some of the piled-up logs were smouldering one evening, but when Zoe alerted Ray to this he simply grinned and told her it was always happening and not to worry. An entire wall was covered with paintings, photographs and sketches of steam trains, references to the new name the pub was given in the 1950s on the slim grounds that Robert Stephenson, inventor of the steam locomotive, may have passed a drunken evening there a hundred years earlier during the building of the railway bridge at Berwick-upon-Tweed.

'Red wine?' Kate asked Zoe as they reached the bar.

Straightaway several hands went into pockets and there were cries of, 'I'll get them,' and 'This one's on me'. Dod Affleck, the herdsman at Tolbyres Farm, tapped Kate's hand to gain her attention before making his offer.

Zoe's eyes met Ray's as he dried a pint glass that

———

30

looked like a tumbler in his huge hands.

'First drinks are on the house,' he said. 'You'll need something, Doctor, after the shock you had this morning.'

As soon as Kate and Zoe sat down on two hastily vacated stools, they were bombarded with questions. What had Zoe seen? Was the body Chrissie Baird's? Who did the police think had put her there?

In the end, Zoe gave an account of the morning's events to the room at large. While disappointed at her avoidance of a graphic description of the body, failure to identify it, and assertion that DCI Mather had not confided in her about anything, everyone seemed satisfied enough to start discussing the matter between themselves again.

No longer the centre of attention, Zoe sipped her wine, resisting the temptation to gulp it down and immediately order another. Dod was asking Kate's advice on what to buy his wife for Christmas, so Zoe studied the people around her. There were more unfamiliar faces than usual, several of them looking ill at ease, as if uncertain they should be there. The hubbub gradually diminished as people left, enabling her to pick out individual conversations.

'Has to be Chrissie,' a small, red-faced man said. 'Cannae be anyone else. Jimmy's no seen her since Sunday morning, when we left for Melrose. Said she was going to church then out selling poppies before driving down to see that daughter of hers.'

'I warned him she'd be trouble, that yin.' Zoe recognised this speaker, Eric Sibbald, who ran a butcher's shop in Kelso. 'Told him, I did, but still he went and married her. The age difference between them, how could he hope to keep her out of mischief?' Eric led a communal shaking of heads at the perils of taking a much younger wife.

Although itching to point out that Chrissie Baird was the presumed victim here, Zoe stayed silent.

The earlier speaker said, albeit grudgingly, 'Aye Eric, but you'll admit she looked after Jimmy well. A grand cook she was.' On this occasion heads nodded.

'Not a patch on Ellie, not even her cooking.'

Zoe had to crane her neck to see the dissenter, a thin, grey-haired man in a Fair Isle sweater at the back of the room. Dod leaned over and whispered, 'That's the first Mrs Baird's brother, Robbie Grant. He never spoke to Jimmy after he remarried.'

Ray cleared his throat. Coming from a smaller man this would have failed to gain anyone's attention that night, but the whole room turned to look at him. 'Can anybody tell me why it took so long to notice she was missing? Today's Tuesday, she left on Sunday. The lassie only lives in Newcastle.'

'Aye, but Chrissie wasn't expected there until last night. The daughter rang about midnight, and Jimmy was in his bed. He only knew Chrissie hadn't arrived when he got up to let the dog out early this morning and found a message asking where she was.'

This last piece of information was delivered by a soft voice from behind Robbie Grant. Zoe had not noticed the woman before, and was forced to lean forward precariously on her stool to see her now. The Rocket's usual clientele was predominantly male, and she and Kate were sometimes the only women in the place, but tonight the sexes were more balanced in number. It was as if the regulars' wives did not trust them to gather the very latest intelligence.

'Which must mean the rumour about her having a fancy man somewhere is true,' Ray said. 'Why else would she go off a day early?' He looked around, apparently waiting for someone to come out in support of his theory. Instead, the whole room went quiet. For what felt like several minutes, the only sound was an occasional click of dominoes.

Just as the silence started to become embarrassing, the door from the kitchen burst open. Everyone turned to look as it banged against the legs of a table, obliging the young couple who were sitting at it to grab their glasses to stop them from sliding to the floor.

Hazel Anderson came in carrying a bowl of steaming roast potatoes between oven-mitted hands. A good eighteen inches shorter than Ray, she wore blue-checked chef's trousers which emphasised her broad buttocks. Zoe studied Ray's face as his wife came to a halt, swaying slightly. She recognised a mix of emotions she sometimes saw worn by the spouses of dementia patients when they thought no one was looking.

The expression did not last long. As Ray placed a woven mat on the bar top and Hazel set the hot dish down, it was replaced by the neutral face he adopted when suggesting to a customer that maybe they'd had enough to drink and should consider going home. 'Thanks, love,' he said.

Hazel turned away from the bar, her face red and damp. 'Evening ladies and gentlemen. Help yourselves. You'll need these. Save me washing up.'

She pulled a clutch of paper napkins from her pocket, then fumbled and dropped them. They floated apart, each following its own trajectory, finishing up strewn around her feet. Ray must have known what was coming next, as his arrival beside his wife was swift enough to coincide with the loud wail she let out. Grabbing Hazel firmly by the shoulders he propelled her towards the kitchen.

Without a word, Eric moved behind the bar and started to refill people's glasses. A dominoes player got up to put more logs on the fire, while someone else picked up the napkins. The sound of voices resumed and gradually rose in volume. Zoe accepted the roast potato Kate offered her but declined an invitation to start their own game of dominoes. She was soon being entertained by Dod's reminiscences about Kate's grandfather, although every now and then she could hear muffled noises coming from upstairs.

Robbie Grant and his wife prepared to leave. The woman turned round as she reached the door and said, 'What you should all be asking yourselves is where that son of his has got to. Jimmy and Robbie think he can do no wrong, but he cannae fool me.' She hurried outside to join her husband.

There was a clamour of voices at this signposting of a new direction to take.

'Gone again, has he? I'm not surprised.'

'They two didnae get on at all. Hated each other they did.'

'He was lucky his dad took him in.'

Dod leaned over to Zoe. 'If Gregor – that's Jimmy Baird's son by his first marriage – becomes prime suspect, there's a few round here'll be right pleased.'

'Does he live in Westerlea?' Zoe asked.

Kate answered. 'He moved in with Jimmy and Chrissie a few weeks ago. Rumour has it that he'd done a spell in prison and had nowhere else to go when he got out.'

'Jimmy denied it, of course,' Dod said. 'Claimed he'd just had a run of bad luck and came back here to sort himself out. Chrissie wasn't happy about it.'

'Gregor and Chrissie didn't hit it off?'

'They fought like cat and dog,' Dod said. 'Gregor isn't the sort to be ordered around by a woman. Different to his dad. It's a funny thing, we all felt sorry for Jimmy because Chrissie ruled the roost, telling him where to go and what to do. But now it looks as if she's gone and he's completely lost without her. I went to see him this afternoon, and all I can say is thank goodness for that wee dog. It's all he has left, the poor old bugger.'

'So Jimmy thinks the body is Chrissie's?' Kate asked.

'He seems convinced, although they won't let him see it. You'll understand why, Doctor.' Dod lowered his voice. 'I reckon he thinks Gregor killed her.'

'No way,' Kate said. 'Jimmy dotes on him.'

'So why won't he let me try to find Gregor and tell him what's happened? It's not natural he doesn't want him here.'

Out of the corner of her eye Zoe saw Kate glance towards the door, but she did not look round until she felt a tug on her ponytail. Turning to protest, she found herself face to face with Neil Pengelly. His brother Peter was close behind.

Neil winked at her, pulled off his hat and swept a hand over his bald head. Kate often joked he was like an amputee who could still feel the limb he had lost, because of this habit of pushing nonexistent hair out of his eyes.

'Doctor Moreland, I hear you've been getting yourself into a spot of bother.' Neil removed his thick sweater and placed it on the back of Zoe's stool, forcing her to lean forward. 'Make mine a pint of Belhaven Best, please, Big Man. And one for Pete too.' Despite several years in Scotland, the singsong quality of his Cornish accent remained.

Zoe was appalled to feel her face redden. She looked at Neil and frowned. 'If anyone's going to find a body, best it be a doctor, don't you think?'

He stared at her for longer than she found comfortable, but did not respond. Eventually she broke free and said hello to Peter, who had moved into a space next to Dod. Resembling Neil in height, build and colouring, it was as though he had searched for a way of differentiating between himself and his elder brother and gone for the easy option: a head of thick, shoulder-length hair which he frequently tucked behind his ears.

Speaking to Ray but with a sidelong glance at Neil, Peter said, 'I'd prefer a whisky.' His voice was a deeper version of Neil's.

Neil nodded without taking his eyes off Zoe. 'This patient was beyond the reach of even your care, Doctor, from what I hear,' he said, then saw her stony expression. 'Okay, not funny. How's the cold? Still sneezing?'

'It's moved onto my chest now.' *Damn. She must sound like a teenager.*

Neil's gaze briefly fluttered downwards, then he looked her in the eye again. 'Sorry to hear that.'

'I suppose there's only been one topic of conversation in here tonight,' Peter said.

'How did you guess?' Zoe drained her glass and put it down on the bar, shaking her head at Dod as he indicated his willingness to buy her another.

'Have they identified the body?' Neil asked.

'Not officially,' Kate said, 'although everyone seems certain it's Chrissie Baird. She was last seen on Sunday, out selling Remembrance Day poppies. Did she come to Larimer Hall?'

'No, we're too far out of the village,' Peter said. 'Not even Jehovah's Witnesses can find us.'

'And anyway, she wouldn't have called on you, Neil, would she?' Dod said. 'For some reason she didn't approve of you. Something to do with young Alice, wasn't it?'

'I'm not to blame for her silly little daughter taking a shine to me,' Neil said. 'I didn't encourage her.'

'Maybe not, but she still ended up sitting in your lap here a few nights, didn't she?'

'Dod, if you drank as much as she did, you'd end up there yourself,' Neil said. He, Dod and Peter laughed.

Zoe wondered if Chrissie Baird's daughter had received more encouragement than Neil was admitting to. Not that she cared. She was about to suggest to Kate that they leave when Ray spoke, taking her by surprise. He moved quietly for such a big man, and had slipped back behind the bar without her noticing.

'That woman would go anywhere she could poke

36

her nose into other people's business,' he said.

Several heads moved in agreement.

Dod passed his glass over to be refilled. 'Been on the receiving end of it yourself, haven't you, Ray?'

'She may have left this place nearly a year ago,' Ray said, 'but she behaved as if she still owned it. I came down one evening last week and found she'd nipped in behind the bar and poured Jimmy a pint, rather than wait for me to come and do it. Trust me, I told her where to go.'

'Aye, and I heard her say you should treat her with more respect,' Dod said. 'She had a right nasty tongue on her sometimes.'

Ray's large face went red. 'My point is that Chrissie Baird loved snooping round where she wasn't welcome. Me and Hazel, we've nowt to hide, but maybe someone else has.' He turned to join in with a lively discussion about Scotland's chances in the forthcoming rugby international.

Kate raised her glass of orange juice to Zoe. 'See, I said you'd be a ten-minute wonder.'

'You were right. I'm glad I came out – thanks for making me. But can we go once you've finished your drink?'

'Of course.'

Neil was listening in and had other plans for them. 'You must let me buy you both a drink before you go.'

'Not tonight, thanks,' Zoe said.

Neil put on the little-boy face she was starting to recognise. 'Please don't go.'

'I'm exhausted. It's been a difficult day and I have to work tomorrow.'

'We need to talk about last night, don't we?'

'Not here.' Although red wine never used to have this effect, Zoe felt her cheeks burning again.

'But I've come up with some really great ideas for your kitchen, now I know what you're looking for.'

Zoe handed him his sweater and took her jacket off the stool. 'Another time.'

As she pulled the pub's front door shut, she glanced back inside. Neil had forgotten her already and was gesturing to Ray for another pint.

SIX

Despite feeling exhausted after a poor night's sleep and still suffering from flash-backs of her gruesome discovery the day before, Zoe felt her mood lift as she drove to work. It would be good to have some structure to her day, to be left with less time to dwell on things. She encountered a farmer on a quad bike moving sheep along the road with the aid of his sheepdog, but rather than fume with a city-dweller's impatience, she stopped the car's engine and watched in admiration as the black and white collie darted to and fro to keep the heaving mass moving forward. According to Kate's father, the shape of Mac's head suggested he had some Border collie in his genes, but she could not believe this of a dog who often failed to obey even the simplest command.

She drove into a space reserved for staff in front of the single-storey building which looked more likely to house a small manufacturing business than a health centre. It would have disfigured the old part of the village, but its red brick exterior and steel window frames were not out of place on the modern estate where more than half of Westerlea's residents lived. The front door opened automatically. Halfway in, Zoe paused then stepped back outside.

No, she had not imagined it. A shiny new brass plaque bearing her name, *Dr Zoe K Moreland*, followed by her qualifications, had been mounted underneath those of the partners. She sighed in exasperation. Margaret Howie, the practice administrator, was a stickler for doing things properly, which must be why she had ignored Zoe's request and made sure the plaque included the middle initial Zoe preferred not to use.

'Good morning, Doctor. How are you?' Margaret was sitting at the reception desk, sorting through repeat prescription requests. She self-consciously touched her hair, which was a few shades lighter than when Zoe last saw it.

Every GP's practice Zoe had known was blessed with a treasure like Margaret. Invariably female and usually nearing retirement, their familiarity with their patients' lives exceeded that of any doctor or database. Margaret was a useful ally; Zoe decided not to mention the plaque.

'Fine, thanks. That new hair colour really suits you.'

Margaret beamed. 'My Hector says it takes years off me.' She looked keen to chat, but Zoe continued walking towards her consulting room.

Once there, she switched on her computer to open up the GPASS system and read the list of patients she would be seeing that morning. As usual, only a few of the names were familiar, which was hardly surprising, given that she had only worked there a little over three months. A busy session lay ahead, so thank goodness she didn't have to wade through a tottering pile of buff folders anymore. The medical records of any patient registered with the Westerlea practice could be summoned at the click of a mouse.

She turned her head on hearing a soft knock on the door and saw Paul Ryder, the practice's senior partner. Aged about sixty, he had a neatly trimmed grey beard and wore one of his many tartan ties – reputedly all gifts from grateful patients – over a blue shirt. He clutched a plastic phial in his left hand.

'What a terrible experience for you, my dear.

Absolutely ghastly.' Paul came in and sat down, placing the urine sample on Zoe's desk. 'You sounded fine yesterday, but how do you feel now? The effects of shock can take their time coming, though of course I don't need to tell you that.'

In Zoe's experience, people often go overboard with expressions of concern to hide the fact that they don't actually give a damn about you. Paul's solicitude, though, was always genuine, something recognised by his devoted patients. Few of them chose to see Zoe, except if Paul was unavailable or the nature of the problem made consulting a woman doctor preferable. According to Margaret, if he ever decided to remarry, candidates for the post would fill the waiting room.

'It's not something I'll forget in a hurry. Although, to tell the truth, I didn't examine it closely. As soon as I realised what it was that Mac had led me to, I went for help.' The wriggle of guilt in her stomach reminded Zoe this wasn't strictly true.

'The memory will fade. But again I don't need to tell you.'

'It's still nice to hear.'

'DCI Mather was impressed with you as a witness.'

'I can't think why. I didn't know much, and he wasn't with me for long.'

'From what I hear he's very thorough, so your observations must have been useful. If this dreadful business can be resolved, Mather's the man to do it.'

'Do you know him?' Zoe asked.

'Only by reputation. I used to play golf with his predecessor, Bill Brady. Scored a hole-in-one the day before he died. And I've met his mother, Bette, on several occasions. She's a marvellous dancer, used to do it professionally. Her son must have inherited her show-business gene because I remember hearing that he plays the bagpipes to a very high standard.'

41

Zoe tried and failed to imagine this. 'Coming from the Borders should help him in his investigations,' she said. 'People round here will be more inclined to open up to him than someone parachuted in from Edinburgh, don't you think?'

'I'm not sure if that's necessarily the case. He's been away for most of his adult life.' Paul absentmindedly toyed with the urine sample. 'Even if he feels he still belongs, it's possible not all the people he has to deal with will accept him back as readily.'

'Were you able to tell him anything useful?'

'I told him what I could, general things like Chrissie's weight, height and so on. I didn't bother him with her nut allergy and wilful refusal to have any internal examinations, of course. I also suggested he contact Derek McCracken, the dentist, although these days Derek spends more time being a lay preacher than looking into people's mouths. But the police don't really need us any more, now they've got DNA testing. If they didn't have to wait so long for the results, we would never see them at all.'

'I'm not sure if DNA will be any use in this case. I read somewhere that it's destroyed by very high temperatures.'

'In that case they may be forced to fall back on her dental records.'

'Does he think the body is Chrissie Baird's? Everyone round here seems convinced of it.'

'Mather was much too circumspect to share that with me. And until the police inform me officially who it was you found, I can't tell them anything more.'

There was an intonation in Paul's voice which made Zoe ask, 'Is there more to tell?'

'Oh yes, my dear, although I have no idea if it's at all relevant. If anything it complicates matters rather than clarifies them.'

Unsure whether to press him to explain this cryptic remark, Zoe had the decision made for her by

Margaret looking round the door to tell them they both had patients waiting. Paul stood and yanked up his baggy chinos. He was scarcely out of the room when Zoe noticed the urine sample sitting on her desk and rushed after him with it.

Identification of Zoe as the 'woman walking her dog' had spread. Everyone who came into her consulting room that morning was eager to sympathise over her experience, and several patients openly questioned her about it. She dealt with them all in the same manner: a brief smile followed by a firm 'What can I do for you today?'. Given the time of year, coughs and colds were in abundance, the uniformity of symptoms broken up only by a throbbing toe, an infected boil and a case of chronic constipation. Just one patient presented with symptoms justifying referral to a specialist at Borders General Hospital.

It was all over by noon. Zoe had closed her briefcase and was rising from her chair when the door, left ajar to indicate she was no longer seeing patients, opened fully. On the threshold stood a young woman in her late twenties wearing a white blouse, a black, knee-length skirt and flat shoes. Her hair was cut in a neat but unflattering bob and she was unadorned by cosmetics or jewellery, bar a small silver cross on a chain around her neck.

'Hello Jean,' Zoe said.

'Doctor Zoe, can you spare me a minute?' The girl's voice was so soft Zoe had to strain to hear it.

'Of course. Come in.'

Jean shut the door and approached Zoe's desk, straightening her skirt as she moved. Instead of sitting down she placed her hands on the chair's back and remained standing.

Zoe did not know Jean Hensward as well as she knew the other practice staff for the simplest of reasons: they were both part-timers and their hours rarely coincided. Most of what Zoe did know was courtesy of

Penny and Margaret, and mainly revolved around the problems Jean experienced in caring for her elderly mother who had recently been diagnosed with Alzheimer's.

'How can I help?' Zoe asked.

Jean blinked rapidly. 'I hope you don't mind me coming to you, Doctor, but it's all very difficult and with you being involved I thought maybe you could tell me what to do.'

Zoe waited, expecting more, but nothing came. 'What's worrying you?' she eventually prompted.

'It's about Chrissie – Mrs Baird – being killed. They think my Tom did it. I know they do. But he didn't. He couldn't.' Jean released her grip on the back of the chair to wipe her eyes with her hands.

Zoe held out the box of tissues she kept on her desk and watched Jean take one then blow her nose. When the girl seemed more composed, she asked, 'Are you talking about Tom, Kate Mackenzie's cousin?'

Jean seemed surprised the question was even necessary. 'Tom Watson, yes. We've been seeing each other for more than a year now. He's ever so good with Mum, and I love his girls. We were so happy and now it's going wrong and it's all Chrissie's fault.' She dabbed at her eyes.

'We don't even know it was Mrs Baird in the bonfire,' Zoe said. 'And if turns out to be, I'm sure the police will discover who did it. No one's going to accuse Tom of doing something he hasn't.'

She knew this to be an absurd assertion but it was apparently what Jean needed to hear. The younger woman stopped sniffing and managed a wan smile.

'You're right. He can't have done it and no one will think he did. It's common knowledge how horrid Chrissie can be. Tom's an absolute saint to put up with her. He does it for his girls.'

'Did – do – you know Mrs Baird personally?'

'She used to visit a lot and sit with Mum, listening to all her stories. Mum loves talking about the old days, when she worked as a maid up at the Hall. But then she stopped coming.'

'Why was that?'

Jean's worried look was replaced by one of indignation. 'I started seeing Tom, and Chrissie didn't approve.'

'That must have hurt your mother.'

'It was awful. Mum's like a child, she doesn't understand things and hates her routine being changed. She kept asking where Chrissie was and looking out of the window for hours on end.'

'Did you tell Mrs Baird how upset your mother was?'

'Oh no, that would have made things worse. Even before Tom started seeing me she threatened to find a way to take the girls from him. She was determined they weren't going to grow up the daughters of a mere chimney sweep.'

'That's terrible.'

'And it got a lot worse when she found out about us. Even though Alice was the one to leave and she chose not to take the twins with her, in her mother's eyes she can do no wrong.' Jean stepped out from behind the chair. 'I know I shouldn't say this, but if that body is Chrissie's, I'm glad. And you're right – no one can possibly think Tom did it. Thank you so much for the advice, Doctor. It's really helped.'

'But Jean, I – '

Zoe was speaking to herself.

She had hoped to see Paul on her way out, but the door was closed when she went by his consulting room. Following up his mysterious remark about Chrissie Baird would have to wait until tomorrow. Perhaps the formal identification would have been made by then.

A few moments later, as she approached the

health centre's exit, she heard someone call her name. Half-expecting to be dragged back by Margaret, who still had not had a chance to grill her about yesterday's experience, Zoe looked towards the reception desk. Margaret was on the phone, but Walter was standing at his consulting room door, hands on hips.

Like Mather, Walter Hopkins favoured the formality of a suit for work, but his were usually brown and never fitted him properly. He had a fine head of hair for a man in his mid-fifties, although Zoe was suspicious of quite how dark it remained.

'Hello Walter.' As she went over to him, Zoe put on her most winning smile while inwardly cursing herself for trying too hard. Whatever she did, it would not prevent more pointed comments from Walter about the number of his patients who were asking to see her these days.

'I want you to take the ante-natal clinic tomorrow afternoon,' Walter said.

'I'm scheduled to do tomorrow morning's surgery.'

'Are you saying you won't change?'

'No, of course not. I'm happy to, if that's what you want. I just need to know if you want me to do the clinic instead or as well as.'

'Instead. And see to it that Margaret knows.'

Zoe could tolerate the Welshman's offhand manner and tendency to waive time-wasting niceties like please and thank you. Not long after she arrived at the practice, Margaret had explained he behaved that way with most patients and all the junior members of staff. But lately it seemed as though he was deliberately trying to make things difficult for her.

He had not said much during Zoe's interview, leaving most of the talking to Paul, except for challenging her to explain why she wanted to move to the Borders. She had thought him shy and was confident he would unbend once they worked together. Now, though, she was certain he had not wanted to give her the job, but had been overruled by Paul.

She took a deep breath and made for the reception desk.

Margaret put down the phone. 'You looked like you were going to rush off without telling me about yesterday.'

'I wouldn't dare,' Zoe said.

SEVEN

That afternoon, after sharing a cheese roll for lunch, Zoe and Mac set off on foot for the coach house. Zoe wanted to see what progress, if any, the builders had made. Given Gerry Hall and Son's track record so far, it was more than likely nothing would have changed since her last site visit, in which case she planned to deliver an ultimatum to them: get back on the job immediately or she would find someone else. Although Keeper's Cottage was available for as long as she needed it, she had not envisaged spending Christmas there. Now that seemed inevitable.

Their walk took nearly half an hour, although the journey could be made by car in a fraction of the time. But the route through Pender's Wood alongside the Blackadder River offered Zoe the chance to observe more wildlife than she had ever seen before. Granted, most of it was running away from her – squirrels vanished up trees, ducks flew out of the water – but she knew that as soon as she and Mac moved on, everything would return to normal.

A semi-derelict lodge house presided over the entrance to the Larimer Park estate. Mac, off his lead, knew now where they were going and ran ahead up the cracked and weedy driveway. Zoe caught up with him as the coach house came into view.

Their future home was being created out of the L-shaped remains of a Victorian quadrangle built entirely in hand-cut sandstone for people so wealthy they had seen no reason to economise even when stabling their horses. Its longest side faced the drive and featured a broad archway with a small tower above, giving access to what had once been a courtyard and was now a dense growth of brambles and couch grass.

The neglected structure had been on the market for some time when Zoe agreed to view it in the early summer, after the estate agent had enthused about its potential.

'The plans are drawn up and approvals granted. Unfortunately the owners separated before the work started. It's waiting for the right person to come along and make it into a lovely family home.'

As she was shown around, Zoe had tried to dismiss the idea of taking on a project of this size, while simultaneously experiencing mounting excitement at the prospect. It was the tower room, the building's only upstairs space, which had decided her. They had been standing in what the agent called 'public room number one' when Zoe had pointed to a door in the wall at the top of a ladder and asked, 'What's up there?'

'Storage space, I think.'

Ignoring the agent's protestations that she was not insured, Zoe had handed him Mac's lead and climbed the ladder. As she opened the door at the top, stale air had hit her in the face, making her gasp. The tower room had contained row upon row of saddles mounted on wooden staging and numerous bridles hanging from brackets around the walls. She had reached out and grasped a leather rein dangling near her head. It had felt dusty and brittle.

She had wiped many years' accumulated dirt from the hexagonal window and looked through it. The drive continued for a few hundred metres then widened out in front of a grand house built in a classical design with stone columns flanking its entrance. Several peacocks strutted their stuff on the lawn. Larimer Hall spoke of such wealth, no wonder its original owners had expected their horses to live in style too.

Zoe had made her mind up to buy the coach house before she reached the ground floor. The man in the suit had perked up considerably when she asked if its owner would accept an offer lower than the asking price.

Now, in November, the tower room still had to be accessed by a ladder, but it was cooler, cleaner and empty. Zoe's hopes of salvaging some of its contents – though with no idea what she would do with them – were dashed by years of neglect and extremes of temperature which had rendered the leather friable, causing many of the saddles to snap like folded cardboard as soon as they were lifted. Their removal had been a mournful sight and she had felt guilty for assenting to the destruction of the building's final link with its past life.

She stood now with her back to the window and tried to imagine the room full of her favourite possessions. *Would Gran's three-seater sofa fit up the new staircase and through the narrow doorway?*

In the room below, where she had left him contentedly chewing a stick, Mac started to bark. When Zoe looked down, the dog had disappeared, although she could still hear him. Then the tone of his bark changed from warning to joyful greeting. A familiar voice drifted up to her.

'Hello boy. Where's that mistress of yours?'

'I'm here,' Zoe shouted.

Neil appeared a few seconds later. His eyes traveled up the ladder and a smile spread across his face when he saw her.

'I was on my way down the drive when I saw some windows open. There were no vehicles parked outside, so I thought I'd be a good neighbour and check the place out.'

'Thanks for that,' Zoe said. 'As you can see, it's only me and Mac.'

'As soon as I heard the dog bark I knew it had to be. Is everything all right? There's been no sign of Gerry and his boys the last few days.'

'Their work seems to have come to a halt. Again.'

'It's lucky you've got someone reliable to do your kitchen.'

'So you keep telling me. I'll be down in a minute.' Zoe turned around and grasped the top of the ladder.

'No. Stay there and I'll come to you.' Neil had been crossing the room as they spoke and was now directly below her. He put his foot on the bottom rung and started to climb.

Deeming it unsafe to risk both of them on the ladder, Zoe retreated inside the tower and waited for him. It would not be the first time he had been up there, after all. He and Peter had helped her clear the old horse-riding tack in exchange for the saddle stands, which had turned out to be made of solid oak.

'You shouldn't be climbing ladders on your own,' Neil chided as he entered the room.

'I managed, thank you.'

'Well, I'm here now to make sure you get down safely.'

'I don't need any help.'

'Of course not. And if the ladder slipped and you fell, you're a doctor so you'd be able to put yourself back together again.'

'Now you're mocking me.'

'I'm just concerned.' He moved closer to her. 'Would it be an adequate defence to say that when you're the eldest child you're expected to look after the others? It's a habit I find hard to break.'

Zoe took a few steps back towards the window; Neil followed. Akin to a disobedient puppy, he managed to be maddening and appealing in equal measures.

'So,' he said, waving his arm to take in the entire room, 'what are your plans for up here?'

Zoe outlined her ideas. They were nothing fancy – window seat, waxed floorboards, white paintwork – but Neil listened attentively and made some suggestions of his own. She realised his response to the coach house was similar to hers.

'I never imagined owning a building this old,' she said. 'But now I'm beginning to understand why some people prefer them to new ones.'

'Living on a modern estate is my idea of hell,' Neil said. 'This place will make a beautiful home, with all the mod cons but still keeping its character. And it'll have a fabulous kitchen, of course.'

'You never give up, do you?'

'Neither in my professional or my personal life. And I never say anything I don't mean.'

Neil's face was uncharacteristically grave, dashing Zoe's hopes that his behaviour on Bonfire Night had been the result of too much red wine and he would be sufficiently embarrassed not to mention the episode in her kitchen. Or, better still, that he might not even remember it.

'I meant what I said the other night, Zoe. All of it.'

'And my response stands too.'

'In spite of that apparent rejection, I'm not going to apologise for how I feel, or for sharing it with you. Why should I?' He dug into his pocket and brought out a tobacco tin and a pack of cigarette papers.

'You can't do that here,' Zoe said, glad to change the subject. 'You'll be a fire hazard.'

'In that case, shall we go down?'

They returned to the ground floor in silence, Neil going first then holding the ladder steady as Zoe followed. She glanced down midway, ready to scold him for enjoying the view a little too much, but found him courteously averting his gaze. He rolled a cigarette while she shut the windows and made the building secure, and lit up as soon as they reached his mud-spattered Land

Rover, which was parked under the arch.

After a couple of puffs Neil said, 'Can we talk business again, or have I blown my chances of even fitting your kitchen?'

'I've already said I want you and Peter to do the work. I mean what I say too. And anyway, you come highly recommended. Kate's mother can't stop telling me what a wonderful job you did for them. She must have shown me inside every cupboard and drawer.'

'Still friends then?'

'Of course, as long as you understand that's as far as it goes.' Zoe reached down and attached Mac's lead to his collar. 'I'll be in touch soon about choosing a design.'

'Why don't you come over now and have a look at some of the options?'

'Weren't you on your way somewhere when you stopped?'

'Only to the shop to buy more tobacco. It'll wait. I'm trying to cut down like you told me to.' Neil grinned, dropping and stepping on the remains of his cigarette.

'It'll be getting dark soon, and I haven't brought my car.'

'Not a problem. If it's too dark for you to walk home when we've finished I'll give you and your funny-looking hound a lift back.' He opened the Land Rover's passenger door. 'Hop in.'

Although he was too big for either of them to feel comfortable, Mac sat on Zoe's lap for the short journey to Larimer Hall. Unable to put on her seat belt, she clung to the dog as they bounced along the pot-holed drive.

'How long have you lived here?' she asked Neil.

'Nearly eight years. Incomers tend to fall into two groups. Some, like me and Pete, take to life in the Borders straightaway and stay forever. Others can't hack it and leave not long after getting here.'

'I hope I'll be in the first group.'

'Me too.'

'Was it difficult to establish a business?'

'We were lucky,' Neil said. 'We fitted a kitchen for a guy with a big shooting estate the other side of Kelso, then a friend of his saw what we'd done and offered us work too. And so it went on, until we were here so much it seemed logical to stay. If you're good enough and you do a few jobs for the right people, your name gets known. Round here, word-of-mouth is more important than an ad in the Yellow Pages or a snazzy website.'

'Not everyone can afford a bespoke kitchen.'

'You'd be surprised. Borders folk aren't flash. They don't drive around in new sports cars.' He looked across at Zoe and winked. 'They prefer to invest in their homes, so the first thing they do when they move house or have some spare cash is order an Aga and build a new kitchen around it. And because of the lives they lead, they usually need a separate utility room fitted out to wash their wellies, store their chicken feed and keep their dogs.'

Zoe patted Mac's head. 'Sorry boy, I'm not giving you your own room. You'll have to sleep on my bed and like it.'

'I'm sure he's happy with that arrangement. I know I would be.'

Pulling up outside Larimer Hall saved Zoe from having to think of a suitable retort. Neil opened his door and Mac leapt across his lap, out of the vehicle and up the steps.

'He's in a hurry. Must realise his mate Pete lives here too,' Neil said.

'They got on very well the other night.' Zoe tensed, fearing he might pounce on this opportunity to raise again what happened between them. However, like when she climbed down the ladder, he proved unpredictable. 'Pete loves animals and they love him.' He pushed the front door open. 'After you.'

Mac charged inside, while his owner looked on helplessly. 'You'd never believe we went to obedience classes. I hope he doesn't give Peter too much of a shock when he finds him.'

'It's all right, he'll know we're here. A bell rings in the workshop when the front door opens.'

'You're very security-conscious.'

'A house of this size, if someone wandered in it could be days before we found them. We keep the back door locked unless we're loading stuff into the van.'

After mounting a further set of steps, Zoe found herself in the largest hall she had ever seen in a house that did not charge for admission. Eight doors led off it, and a balustraded gallery looked down from the first floor. Topping all this was an elaborate stained-glass skylight which took up most of the vaulted ceiling.

'Wow,' she said. 'Business must be good.'

Neil laughed. 'It's not ours. We rent it off a bloke who lives abroad. He charges us next to nothing because we're gradually renovating it for him.'

'Does it need a lot of work?'

'Nothing structural. We're mainly restoring fireplaces and patching up floors. See that?' Neil pointed to an ornate wooden fireplace. 'One of the philistines who used to live here covered it in white gloss. Took months to get that muck off.' He started to cross the hall. 'I'll give you a proper tour when we have more time. Let's find Pete and the dog.'

He opened a door on the right, revealing a flight of uncarpeted stairs. The rubber soles of Zoe's boots squeaked on the bare stone as she and Neil descended. She stopped to peer out of a narrow window; the grounds must have been impressive fifty years ago, but now it was impossible to tell where the lawns stopped and the flower beds started.

'You've yet to tackle the garden, I see.'

'That's someone else's responsibility. We don't do green.' Neil opened a door at the bottom of the stairs and warm air came out to meet them. The source of this was apparent as soon as Zoe entered the kitchen: an Aga so big it must have been custom built. On the floor in front of it was a basket containing two heaps of fur, one black, one ginger.

'You didn't tell me you had cats.' Zoe walked over to the basket.

'In a house as big and old as this you need them to keep the mice down. As you can see, those two are rushed off their feet.'

'What are their names?'

The cats stirred and looked up at Zoe. She crouched down and started to stroke them, one with each hand.

'Meet Bert and Tom.' Neil shrugged at Zoe's expression of disbelief. 'It's easy to shout when you want them to come in.'

'Not that we have to do that because they never go far from their bed except to eat,' added a voice from the other end of the room. Zoe looked round to see Peter, accompanied by Mac. The dog wagged his tail on seeing his owner but appeared disinclined to leave his new friend's side.

'Told you he'd find him, didn't I?' Neil said. 'Pete, I bumped into Zoe on my way to the village and brought her back to look at some ideas for her kitchen. Is the workshop in a fit state for visitors?'

Zoe straightened up from the cats' basket in time to see a scowl pass briefly over Peter's face.

'Sure.'

Neil, seemingly oblivious to his brother's irritation, took Zoe by the arm and led her towards the door Peter had come in by. 'Tea, Pete?'

As Zoe admired the kitchen under construction, Neil explained that two local men built the basic units while he and Peter did what he called 'the fancy bits', like the barley-twist carving on their current commission. Then he guided her to the desk where a set of plans lay, anchored down by a black leather belt. He slid the belt into a drawer, and described the process by which he had designed the kitchen's layout.

Peter appeared, carrying a tray. He walked straight past them.

'Looks as if we're going to the showroom,' Neil said, running a hand over his head. Zoe noticed for the first time a small mole above his left ear.

They followed Peter up to the ground floor via a different staircase to the one they had earlier come down. The showroom contained a series of small kitchens, all in different styles, fitted with tiling and sinks and accessorised with fake loaves of bread and plastic fruit.

'Most people don't see the workshop,' Neil said. 'We usually bring them straight here. The displays took ages to put together, but they help clients decide what they want.'

'They're all so lovely, I don't know how to choose between them.' Zoe ran her hand along a marble worktop, enjoying how smooth and cool it felt.

'That's why I'm here,' Neil said. 'If you're swithering, I know the questions to ask to help you decide.'

'It's strange hearing someone with a Cornish accent use a Scottish expression.'

'Swither's a great word, everybody should use it.'

They reached a pair of sofas on either side of a low table where Peter had left the tray. Neil invited Zoe to sit down then took the sofa opposite her. This time Mac stayed with them, leaning against his owner's leg, his eyes fixed on a plate of shortbread.

'Most English people think Scots is just an accent,' Neil continued. 'An eccentric way of pronouncing the same words. Stay here any length of time, you'll learn lots of new words and expressions and wonder how you ever managed without them.'

The next hour passed quickly, as Neil helped Zoe

---

decide what features she wanted in her kitchen and made some rough sketches of possible layouts. She was pleasantly surprised by his ability to be serious for once and impressed by his professionalism.

'You don't have to commit yourself today. Think about it, and when I've measured up and drawn a proper plan, you can come back and have another look.' He tucked his pencil behind an ear and grinned. 'That's business taken care of, so now let's move on to pleasure. How about a glass of wine? I've got a bottle of Bordeaux I think you'll enjoy.'

'I can't. I need to get home.'

'What's the rush?' Neil asked, feeding Mac a piece of shortbread.

Zoe shook her head in irritation. He was always challenging her. 'There's no rush. I just want you to take us back to the cottage, like you said you would.'

EIGHT

For once, Mac did not hear the front door open. He was too fixated on the spoonfuls of porridge veined with melting brown sugar moving between Zoe's breakfast bowl and her mouth.

Kate burst into the kitchen. 'Surprise!' The collar and cuffs of a cream blouse decorated with splashy pink flowers poked out from beneath her black sweater. 'I took the bairns into school this morning because they missed the bus, so I thought I'd drop by and see how you are.'

'You're lucky to find me home,' Zoe said. 'I wouldn't be here if my work schedule hadn't been changed at the last minute.' She told Kate about her latest clash with Walter.

'He seems to really have it in for you. What have you done to upset him?'

'I wish I knew.'

Zoe's half-eaten breakfast sat on the table. 'Ugh, is that sugar in your porridge?' Kate said. 'Don't let Mum catch you eating it like that. She'll have you repatriated to England.'

'I have tried eating it with salt, honestly.' Grimacing at the memory, Zoe put her bowl down to Mac.

'I forgive you, though only because you ate the haggis I served up, despite obviously hating it.'

'You didn't help by reading out its ingredients. Have you got time for a coffee?'

'Only if I'm not keeping you back from something important.'

'All I have planned for this morning is tracking down Gerry Hall and giving him another bollocking.'

'Things still not moving very fast at the coach house?'

'At a standstill would be more accurate. They haven't even –'

Mac started barking. 'Someone's at the door,' Zoe said.

'I hope it's not Erskine Mather again,' Kate said. 'He'll think I've moved in.'

Zoe hoped that too, for a different reason. However, she managed a polite smile when she saw the policeman standing on her front step. He must have recognised Kate's car this time, because he showed no surprise at her presence when Zoe led him into the kitchen.

'Hi, Erskine.'

'Hello again, Kate.' Mather folded his coat and draped it over the back of the wooden chair before sitting down.

'Do you want some coffee?' Zoe asked. Without waiting for his response, Kate poured a mugful and slid it along the table. She offered him neither milk nor sugar, and he did not ask for them.

'Would you prefer to speak to Zoe alone? I can go into the sitting room.' Despite this offer, Kate repositioned herself so she could see Mather's face as well as Zoe's.

'This is Doctor Moreland's home. I'm happy for you to stay if she is. I was just passing and remembered a few more questions I needed to ask her.'

No one just passed Keeper's Cottage. Zoe felt certain he had been hoping Kate would be there. 'Of course I don't want you to go, Kate.'

Turning her attention to Mather, she asked, 'The body – was it Chrissie Baird?'

'Dental records have confirmed that it was.'

'Told you,' Kate said, looking a little too pleased with herself. 'How did she die?'

Mather hesitated. 'I can only tell you what's going to be public knowledge.'

Zoe and Kate nodded in unison, urging him to continue.

'She incurred an injury to her head.'

Both women stayed silent, expecting more. Eventually, Zoe said, 'So she wasn't alive when she was put in the bonfire?'

Mather did not respond.

'You're not sharing everything, are you?' Kate said.

'Tell me there was no smoke in her lungs,' Zoe said.

'There was no smoke in her lungs.'

Kate and Zoe started to speak at the same time. Mather held up a hand. 'As I said, I can only tell you what we're making public. Please don't ask for more details.'

'All right,' Zoe said. 'But can you explain why the body didn't burn up? Even taking account of the rain, there was still a lot more of her left than I'd have expected. Nearly everything else was reduced to ashes.'

Again the response from Mather was unsatisfactory. 'She'd been wrapped up tightly in something.'

'What?'

'I can't say.'

'When did she die?' *It felt like they were playing some ghoulish parlour game.*

Kate broke in before Mather could reply. 'I've been thinking about that. Chrissie was seen going about the village on Sunday morning with her poppies. And they didn't finish building the bonfire until Sunday afternoon, although he wouldn't have risked putting her in during daylight anyway. I realise the site can't be seen from the road, but it's overlooked by the pub –'

'And is completely open to anyone walking across the field,' Zoe added.

'So she must have been killed after Sunday lunch,' Kate continued, 'then kept somewhere and put in the bonfire during Sunday night. It gets dark very early now, so that could have been any time from about four o'clock.'

'You've given this a lot of thought,' Mather said.

Kate looked indignant. 'Of course I have. This is my home. As I told Zoe, no one would travel to Westerlea just to hide a body in its Guy Fawkes bonfire. The murderer must come from around here, and as I know nearly everybody, I probably know him. It could be someone I drink with in the pub or speak to in the shop, or perhaps my children go to school with his.'

Her voice had become very loud. Mather made a slight downwards gesture with his left hand, and for the first time Zoe noticed he wore a narrow silver band on his ring finger.

Kate frowned but her tone became softer; their old signal still worked. 'I can't ignore what's happening in my own community.'

'I appreciate any ideas you can pass on to me, but that's where it has to end,' Mather said.

'You should be pleased we're trying to help.'

'I have a team of experienced officers working to find out who killed Mrs Baird. You can best help by reining in that curiosity of yours.'

Kate was not going to be put off so easily. 'Genealogy is very similar to police work. Every day I'm ferreting around in old records, trying to fill in the gaps and make connections between people. You should recruit me to your team, not scold me.' She grinned at the policeman and after a couple of seconds he smiled back. The pair stared at each other for so long, Zoe started to feel left out.

At last Mather said, 'I mean it, Kate.'

62

'I believe you had more questions to ask me?' Zoe said.

He turned his attention back to her. 'Kate's right, Mrs Baird was out selling Remembrance Day poppies on Sunday after church. She dropped into the pub at around one o'clock and told Mr and Mrs Anderson she was returning home for lunch. We don't know where she went after that. Did either of you see her?'

'It was a lovely day, so I put Mac into the car, drove to Kelso and took him for a long walk by the river,' Zoe said. 'Then I went straight on to Tolbyres Farm for a meal with Kate and her parents. I didn't see Chrissie, but I suppose she could have called round while I was out.'

'She definitely didn't come to see me,' Kate said. 'We were at home all day until we went to Mum's. And Mum didn't see her either.'

'Was she on foot or in her car?' Zoe asked. 'Perhaps she only visited places she could walk to.'

'That's where things start to get complicated,' Mather said.

'What do you mean?' Kate asked.

'Mrs Baird's car is missing.'

'Missing?' Kate shook her head. 'No, that can't be right, or she wouldn't have been put in Westerlea's bonfire. If she'd gone somewhere in her car, the person who killed her would have hidden her further away, not brought her right back where she came from.'

'It isn't where it should be.'

'You do know she kept it in a garage, not in front of her house like everyone else? It's at the end of the village, opposite the war memorial.'

'Mr Baird told us about the garage and we've checked it out. All that's in it is a large patch of oil.'

'He must know if his wife was intending to go out in her car,' Zoe said.

'She told him she was driving to Newcastle later in the day, but he has no idea if she planned to use it before

---

63

then. He returned home around four o'clock and, as he expected, she wasn't there.'

'Although, according to gossip, she wasn't due at her daughter's until Monday night,' Kate said.

'Apparently so,' Mather said. 'Another mystery.'

Kate and Zoe exchanged looks.

'It's only a rumour,' Kate said, 'but there's been talk of Chrissie having an affair.'

'In which case, the obvious reason for her lying to her husband must be because she planned to spend Sunday night away with her lover,' Zoe added.

'Do either of you know who this person could be?'

'Don't ask me,' Zoe said. 'I probably spent longer with her dead than alive. I only know about this lover theory because someone brought it up in The Rocket the other night.'

'That was the first time I heard anyone suggest it as well,' Kate said. 'I checked with Mum and it's news to her too.'

A mobile phone started to ring. Mather unfolded his overcoat and reached into a pocket. He answered with his name, listened, then said, 'I'll be there as soon as I can.'

He stood up.

'Has something happened?' Zoe asked.

'They've found Mrs Baird's car.'

'Where?' Kate asked.

The policeman concentrated on putting on his coat.

'Why won't you say?' Kate's voice had got loud again.

Mather sighed. 'You'll find out soon enough anyway. Behind an old barn at Heartsease Fields.'

Kate stood up. 'I'm coming with you.'

'No, I don't want you involved. Let me deal with it.' He strode out of the room.

'He must realise this means I'm already involved,' Kate told Zoe.

'In what way? Is Heartsease Fields on your father's land?'

'Heartsease Farm belongs to Mum's brother, Uncle Billy. He's Tom's father. If they already suspect Tom, this can only make things worse for him.'

NINE

Driving to work in the rain on Friday morning, Zoe practiced saying a phrase she had heard a lot since moving to the Borders: 'It's a dreich day'. But no matter how many times she repeated it, the Scots expression continued to sound phoney coming from her lips.

Despite the weather and her inability to describe it in the local dialect, she felt almost cheerful. A distinctive yellow van she'd seen speeding in the direction of Larimer Park gave credence to Gerry Hall's assurance last night that his men would be back at the coach house today. Her anxiety over Neil was abating too, although she kept warning herself not to misinterpret being flattered by his attention as the onset of other, deeper feelings for him.

The news headlines came on the radio as she pulled into the health centre's car park. Unsure what to expect, the discovery of Chrissie's car having been reported at length the previous evening, she was astonished to hear the words, 'A local man is helping the police with their enquiries into the death of retired Westerlea pub landlady Chrissie Baird'. Perhaps because the story was just breaking, or maybe in deference to legal restrictions, the report gave few details except that the man had been taken for questioning to police headquarters in Hawick. Whatever Mather had found in Chrissie's car, it must have been significant to result in an arrest so soon.

A medical practice is rarely busier than first thing

in the morning. Walter started his morning surgeries at eight-thirty, and the telephone would have been ringing since eight with requests for home visits, repeat prescriptions and urgent appointments. So Zoe was surprised to find the front desk unmanned and Margaret and Penny huddled together in the area where patients' old paper files were archived. Deep in conversation and facing away from reception, they only noticed Zoe when she stood behind them and cleared her throat.

Penny turned round, clutching a tissue. 'Oh Doctor Zoe, isn't it terrible?'

Zoe tried to think which patient had been ill enough to have died, but drew a blank. 'What's happened?' she asked, putting down her briefcase.

'It's Tom, Jean's Tom. They've arrested him. For the murder.'

Zoe's stomach lurched; Kate had been right to be worried about her cousin. She was about to ask more when the phone rang. Margaret pushed the younger woman towards the front desk to answer it.

Margaret was calmer than Penny, having worked at the same job for thirty-six years and dealt efficiently with the frequent episodes of sickness, disaster and death suffered by others throughout that time. Even so, she was obviously upset, her breathing laboured as she spoke.

'Haven't you heard, Doctor? It was on the news this morning.'

'I caught the headlines on the radio just now, but they didn't say who had been arrested. How do you know it's Tom?'

Margaret's breath rattled in her throat. 'Jean rang – in a terrible state she was. Penny had to fetch me, because she could hardly tell what Jean was saying. The police went round to Tom's house very early and searched it from top to bottom. Then they drove him to Hawick, after telling Jean to collect the twins.'

'What did they find that made them arrest him?'

'I couldn't get much sense out of her. I think she said they were taking away his clothes and some rubbish he kept in his shed. But I could be wrong. The lassie was crying that much.'

'Is there anything we can do to help her?' Zoe regretted being so positive in her reassurances to Jean a couple of days ago. Here was proof, as if she needed any, that she was the least qualified person in the world to advise someone when it came to dealing with the police.

'Doctor Ryder's going to stop by to see her when he's out visiting patients later on. She's had to take the girls home and her mum won't like them being there. She'll not understand.'

Penny rejoined them, absentmindedly clutching a piece of paper on which she had written a repeat prescription request. Zoe gently took the note from the girl and placed it in a box containing several others. She glanced at her watch.

'My patients will start to arrive any minute now, so we'd better get ready for them. I recognise how upsetting this is for everyone, but the best thing we can do is try to make it business as usual. Tom hasn't been named publicly as the person who's been arrested, so nobody will be coming in asking awkward questions.'

Penny and Margaret went their separate ways, Penny to open the post and Margaret to greet the patient who was approaching the reception desk. Zoe walked to her consulting room. She knew as soon as her first patient, an octogenarian with wispy hair and a surprisingly unlined face, started to speak that her confidence in Tom's arrest not being common knowledge had been misplaced.

'The other receptionist, that Jean, she'll no' be working th'day, what with the trouble her man's in, eh?'

'Now you know I can't talk about that Mrs Dalby. What seems to be the problem? Is your leg still painful?'

'Ah cannae understand your English accent,' the old lady said. 'Speak slower, won't you?'

Zoe spent much of the next two hours parrying attempts, some blatant, some more subtle, to discover what she could add to this latest development. The media may not have named Tom Watson as the man who had been arrested, but the local bush telegraph had no such scruples.

When her final patient took his leave with the comment, 'Tell Jean I was asking after her,' she leaned back in her chair, arms dangling over the sides, relieved the session was over.

The two partners were already in the practice's small kitchen when Zoe got there. Paul greeted her warmly; Walter wordlessly pulled out a chair.

'Zoe, my dear, let me make you a coffee,' Paul said.

'Thanks, I need it.'

She sat down next to Walter, who stared at a brown folder on the table.

'I expect the ladies have put you in the picture about Jean,' Paul said, as he stood waiting for the kettle to boil.

'Yes, thank goodness, or I wouldn't have known what most of my patients were talking about. Were yours fishing for information too?'

Walter met her gaze for the first time. 'Some of them were, but no doubt not as much as yours.'

'Why is that? You've both been here a lot longer than me.'

'That's not how it works,' Walter said. 'You're connected, see, what with finding the body. You're expected to be more clued up than the rest of us.'

'But as I keep on telling everyone, including the police, I don't know anything,' Zoe said. 'I hadn't even heard it was Tom who'd been arrested until I got here.' She smiled her thanks for the coffee Paul passed her. It would be weaker and far more milky than she liked it, but in common with everyone else faced with a drink prepared by him, she would swallow it down without complaint.

Paul returned to his seat. 'I hear you were interviewed by the police again yesterday,' he said.

'It was more of a chat than an interview. Who told you?'

'I saw Erskine Mather yesterday as well, after Chrissie's car was found.'

'And there was me about to rant about village gossip again.'

'I would certainly have found out that way if I hadn't heard it straight from the horse's mouth, so to speak. I asked him to call round again and he came straight here after going to look at the car.'

'You were about to tell me why you wanted to see him when Zoe came in,' Walter said. He made it sound as if she had interrupted their conversation on purpose.

'I can have this in my room,' Zoe said, picking up her mug.

'You don't need to go,' Paul said. 'You're one of the team now, isn't she, Walter?'

Walter shifted in his seat and nodded half-heartedly. 'So why did you need to see Mather again?'

'There was something I wanted to tell him about Chrissie Baird.' Paul said. 'I wouldn't normally have broken her confidence and there's still young Alice to consider. However, it was so out of character that I thought the police ought to be told, in case it has a bearing on their investigation.'

Zoe took a mouthful of coffee and suppressed a shudder.

'You won't find any reference to this in her notes,' Paul continued, 'but Chrissie came to see me some months ago. She wanted to talk about AIDS.'

'She thought she may have contracted AIDS?' Zoe asked.

'No, that's not what she said. But she asked a lot of questions, like how the disease is transmitted, what the riskiest sexual practices are, that sort of thing.'

'Without explaining why she wanted to know?' Walter sounded impatient.

'She claimed to be asking on behalf of a friend who'd discovered her husband was having an affair and was worried about the risks to herself. And while we're all familiar with patients who insist someone else has the problem which is actually their own, it's difficult to imagine that applies in this case. Poor old Jimmy hasn't been capable of having sex with anyone for quite some time.'

'There's a rumour going around that Chrissie was having an affair,' Zoe said. 'I heard it mentioned in the pub the other night. Perhaps she was worried about putting herself at risk.'

'You're starting to be a good source of gossip too,' Paul said. 'I hadn't heard that one. Had you, Walter?'

'I try not to listen to idle chitchat. Anyway, it sounds like the police have got their man.'

'I'll be very surprised if young Tom turns out to be the culprit,' Paul said.

'They must have compelling evidence to have arrested him,' Walter said. 'I haven't ever met the lad. He's your patient, isn't he, Paul?'

'And has been since he was a baby. He suffered from terrible acne as a teenager, but apart from that I've hardly seen him, though I know the family well, of course. In my opinion, the police are heading off in entirely the wrong direction if they think Tom had anything to do with this awful business.'

'Jean must be devastated,' Zoe said. 'Let's hope they see sense and release him quickly.'

'Pardon me for being old-fashioned,' Walter said, 'but I think we should trust the police to do the right thing.'

Zoe bit back what she wanted to say.

Paul stood up. 'Sorry to rush off, but I'm going to

see Jean. She's trying to be strong, for the girls and to stop her mother from realising there's something amiss, but this is taking its toll on her.'

Zoe tried to make conversation with Walter in order to fill the silence left by Paul's departure. She thought she had succeeded, as he launched into a spirited description of the work his daughter, also a doctor, was doing at a London hospital. Then he slid the brown file in front of him along the table to her.

'There's a backlog of these,' he said, his tone implying this was Zoe's fault. 'Deal with them, will you?'

Zoe opened the file and flicked through the pile of forms sent in by insurance companies requesting reports on patients who were either taking out new policies or claiming on existing ones. Some of them were dated several weeks ago.

'As quick as you can.' Walter was already on his feet, making for the kitchen door. As he grasped the handle, the door opened and Margaret rushed in.

'Oh Doctors, thank goodness you're still here,' she said. 'When did Doctor Paul leave? I've got Jean on the phone. Her mother's had an accident, and she doesn't know whether to call an ambulance or wait for him to arrive.'

TEN

Paul's directions were spot-on: take a left at the church, right at the hall, and it's the third bungalow on the left. Zoe saw Jean's anxious face at one of the windows as she parked the car, and the front door was open before she had locked up.

'Doctor Zoe, this is so kind of you. I've tried to phone Tom's parents and his sister but no one's answering. And I haven't got their mobile numbers.'

'Like I told Paul when he rang, I'm happy to help.'

'But you must've only just got home, and now you've had to come out again.'

'It's no problem. Mac's in the car. I thought the girls might like to play with him later.'

Jean led Zoe through a hot, stuffy hall, where a pair of walking sticks stood propped up against a radiator and a patch of carpet showed dark against the rest. Her nose no longer blocked, Zoe could smell disinfectant. She would open the windows as soon as Jean left.

They went into the kitchen, which felt slightly cooler. Its basket-weave cupboard doors and orange walls looked dated, but every surface was clean and uncluttered. Zoe heard a burst of childish laughter coming from one of the other rooms.

'Doctor Paul's keeping the girls busy in the lounge,' Jean said. 'Now you're here he's going to take me to Borders General to be with Mum when she has her x-ray. We had a terrible job persuading her into the ambulance when she realised I wasn't travelling with her, but I've promised to get there as quickly as I can. And I'll come back as soon as possible.'

'Take as long as you need,' Zoe said. 'But before you go, tell me what the girls like to eat.' A few minutes later, feeling a lot less confident than she tried to appear but bolstered by knowing she was capable of preparing the twins' favourite meal, she followed Jean to the lounge.

The room was dominated by a framed poster of Dali's Christ on the Cross hanging above the mantelpiece. The only other ornament was a photograph recording Jean's first communion. She had been a pretty child and resembled a miniature bride, dressed all in white, clutching a bible.

Paul Ryder was on his knees being pelted with cushions by two shrieking little girls. The game ceased abruptly as the twins, identical in every respect including their clothes, looked up at the newcomer. Paul got to his feet, tucking his shirt into his trousers.

'Angie, Maddy, this is Doctor Zoe,' Jean said. 'She's come to stay with you while me and Doctor Paul go out for a wee while. Say hello.'

The twins studied Zoe for a few seconds then both said, 'Hello'.

Zoe bent down and said, 'I've got my doggy out in the car. He's called Mac. We can play with him later, if you want.'

The little girls rushed to Jean and peered fearfully from behind her skirt. One of them asked in a voice not far from tears, 'Where's Daddy?'

'He'll be back soon,' Jean said, wrapping her arms around them both. 'Come on. Let's show Doctor Zoe where the biscuits are kept, shall we?'

Holding a biscuit tin made Zoe much less scary. She and the twins returned to the lounge while Jean and Paul drove away, and soon they were showing her the contents of their toy box. By three-thirty she had been let into the secret of how to tell them apart (a tiny scar on the bridge of Maddy's nose, the result of a fall when she was learning to walk) and at four o'clock she made them all tea. It was a long time since she had last eaten fish fingers and baked beans. After tea, exhausted by a busy afternoon in a warm house, dog and children slept on the sofa and Zoe relaxed drowsily in the armchair next to them.

She came to when she heard the front door open and a voice call, 'Jeanie, I'm back'.

Mac leapt from the sofa, his growl low enough not to wake the girls. He pushed open the lounge door and pelted up the hall. Zoe followed, coming face to face with a short, powerfully-built man wearing green camouflage trousers and a black polo neck sweater. His crew-cut hair was greying at the sides and he wore a gold stud in one earlobe.

Recognition spread over his face when he saw Zoe. 'Doctor Moreland. Is everything okay? Where's Jean?'

'Hello,' Zoe said. 'You must be Tom. I don't think we've met.'

'Aye, I'm Tom. Jean pointed you out in the Co-op one day, though you didn't see us. Where is she? And what about my girls?'

'The twins are fine.' Confirming this, two small bodies pushed past her and raced to put their arms up to Tom, shouting, 'Daddy, Daddy!'

'Come and sit down and I'll explain what's happened,' Zoe said.

Tom, with one twin balanced on his hip and holding the hand of the other, followed her into the lounge.

'Jean's gone to the BGH. Her mother had an accident,' Zoe said.

'She fell over, the old lady did,' Angie said.

'She cried,' her sister said. 'She wasn't brave.'

'When you're old things can hurt a lot,' Tom said. 'Now, you two haud yer wheesht, let the doctor finish.'

'Luckily, Paul Ryder was already on his way over,' Zoe said. 'He thought Mrs Hensward's wrist was fractured, so he called an ambulance, and as soon as I arrived to look after the girls he took Jean to the hospital too. That was a few hours ago, so I would expect –' She put her hand to her mouth. 'Oh God, I'd forgotten where you've been. Are you all right? How did it go with the police?'

Tom cast his eyes towards his daughters, saying nothing.

'Sorry, I wasn't thinking.'

'Girls, I'm going to make a cup of tea for me and the doctor. You stay and play with her dog. What's his name?'

'Mac!' chorused the reply.

'You play with Mac and I'll see you in a few minutes.'

Normality having been restored with the return of their father, Angie and Maddy were happy to let him go out of the room, on condition that he left the door open and promised to bring them biscuits. They restarted what had been the afternoon's favourite game, trying to roll a ball between them without Mac intercepting it.

'Thanks for looking after them, Doctor,' Tom said as he put the kettle on. 'Jeanie wouldn't have left them with just anyone. She thinks a lot of you, she does.'

'I've not had much experience with children outside the surgery, but the twins have been brilliant. They're a credit to you.'

Tom smiled briefly, then sank heavily onto a stool, his shoulder hunched. 'I know Jean spoke to you about the trouble I'm having,' he said. 'It's terrible for her. She's got enough on her plate with her mother.'

'It must be awful for you too.'

'The worst part was having the police arrive before we were even up. Why did they need to do that? Then I had to watch them go through our things. Not only mine, but the girls' too. I couldn't believe it.'

'What were they looking for?'

'Damned if I know. They took away a basket of clothes waiting to be washed, some pairs of boots, and an off-cut of carpet one of my customers gave me when I mentioned I was doing up the spare room so the girls can have a bedroom each. Oh, and a poppy they found on the hall table.'

'A Remembrance Day poppy?' Zoe felt guilty for asking all these questions, but Tom seemed keen to talk.

'Aye, like the ones Chrissie was out selling on Sunday. Dead excited they were when they spotted it. I'd already told them I didn't see her that day, so they reckoned they'd caught me out. I told them she's got a key so she'll have let herself in and left it there. Probably took money out of my change pot for it too, knowing her.'

Tom pulled out a packet of cigarettes. 'Jean hates me smoking in the house, but I don't suppose she'll mind this once.'

'I'm a doctor and even I wouldn't try to stop you today.'

He reached into his pocket and drew out a book of matches, its cover advertising an Indian restaurant in Berwick. He had to strike several before one caught without breaking. 'Free but useless,' he said, dropping the matchbook back into his pocket.

They both took gulps of tea.

'I suppose it's all over the village, me being taken in,' Tom said.

Unwilling to confirm this, Zoe said, 'The police haven't publicly stated it was you they arrested.'

'I wasn't arrested, just detained.'

'Sorry,' Zoe said. 'I didn't realise there was a difference.'

'No one does. I didn't until today. They don't arrest you until they've got enough evidence to charge you.'

'Did they provide you with a solicitor?'

'They offered to, but why would I need one? I didn't kill Chrissie, so they'll not find any proof that I did.'

'Even so . . .'

'I managed fine on my own. They were very polite. It's not the same as on the telly.' Tom reached for his cigarette and Zoe noticed that although his hands were well-scrubbed, there were dark deposits under the short nails. 'The bloke in charge – Mather – I knew him years ago.'

'From when he was going out with Kate?'

'I was forgetting you're friendly with her. Aye, me and Skinny Mather met several times back then, but he behaved today as though he'd never seen me before.'

'I don't suppose he'd do anything that could put you at ease. They might not have been banging on the table, demanding that you confess, but they'd still want you to feel under pressure.'

'They kept asking where I went on the day Chrissie disappeared, and who I saw. Just my luck the girls were at a party in the afternoon and Jean had taken her mum out, so I was alone.' Tom pulled off his sweater, revealing a blue T-shirt with short sleeves. His upper arms were muscular, the right one adorned with a tattoo of a crab. 'They laughed when I told them I stayed at home, catching up with the housework. I'm a single parent. Who do they think does it for me?'

'Kate reckons Chrissie's body must have been put in the bonfire during Sunday night. The twins were home by then, I expect.'

'Aye, but according to the police I could have gone out again later when they were asleep. As if I'd leave them alone in the house.' Tom laughed humourlessly. 'That bloody woman. She made my life a misery when she was alive, and she hasn't stopped now she's dead.' He took out another cigarette, studied it, then returned it to the pack.

'You know she was trying to take the girls away from me?' he asked.

'From what I've heard she didn't stand much of a chance.'

'Maybe so, but that didn't stop her from telling anyone who'd listen that it wasn't natural for a man to be bringing up two girls on his own.'

Tom fell silent. It was not until he said, 'Ugly isn't it?' that Zoe realised she was staring at his tattoo.

'Does it signify something?'

'Only that my mates got me drunk on my birthday one year and persuaded me to get it done. I'm going to have it lasered off.'

'It's not that bad.'

'Jean hates it. We've decided to get married in the spring, so maybe I'll have it done before then.'

'I hadn't heard that news. Congratulations.'

'With this hanging over me, she may be having second thoughts. I'm glad we didn't tell the girls. I'd hate them to be disappointed.'

'I'm sure it won't come to that.'

'Aye, well, we'll see.' Tom got up. 'I think I'll put the girls into Jean's bed. Will you come and say goodnight to them before you go?'

Appeased by the novelty of going to bed without the usual conventions of a bath, teeth-brushing or even pyjamas, the girls allowed themselves to be led away by their father after Zoe promised to bring Mac to see them again soon. Once alone, she checked her watch. It was later than she expected; Jean had been gone a long time.

'Thank you again for helping out,' Tom said when he reappeared.

'I'd have thought Jean would be back by now.'

'She refuses to carry a mobile, so I can't contact her.'

'Shall I try to find out what's happening?'

'No, really, you've done enough. I know my Jeanie. She'll be home as soon as she can.'

As if on cue, they heard the front door open. Tom went out into the hall. Zoe held back, but could still hear the anguish in Jean's voice.

'Oh Tom, thank goodness you're here. I don't know what I'd have done if you hadn't been. She's dead, Tom. Mum's dead.'

Jean wept noisily as Tom led her into the lounge and guided her onto the sofa. She acknowledged Zoe's presence with a raised hand, unable to speak. A few minutes passed, during which Tom held Jean and looked grim, and Zoe stroked Mac to distract him from trying to comfort the young woman himself. Eventually, in between blowing her nose and further bouts of weeping, Jean managed to tell them what had happened.

After being dropped off at Borders General Hospital by Paul, she had accompanied her mother to the x-ray department, where it was confirmed Mrs Hensward's right arm was broken in two places. Later that afternoon, exhausted by the ordeal and her pain subdued by medication, the old lady had dozed off, so Jean took the opportunity to get herself a cup of coffee.

At this stage in her narrative Jean once again burst into noisy sobs. She exclaimed, 'I should never have left her!' and buried her head in Tom's chest. Feeling superfluous, Zoe got up and took Mac outside, while Tom tried to comfort his despairing fiancée.

After its unpromising start, the day had brightened into one of those sunny, cold ones the Borders does so well. It was dark now, so the temperature had plummeted still further, although the sky was clear and Zoe found it hard to believe the dire warnings of snow on the teatime news.

As she waited for Mac to complete his circuit of the garden, her thoughts turned inevitably to the day she was summoned to receive the news from a white-faced teacher that her own mother had been involved in a serious road accident. No one would say if she was dead or alive, but even at twelve Zoe had realised no news must be very bad news. However, unlike Jean, she had not shed a tear, even when her worst fears were confirmed. Gran and Grandpa, well-meaning but virtual strangers to her, had rationalised this as 'being brave', never giving Zoe the opportunity to explain it was not a matter of choice. Bawling her eyes out would have been preferable to the solid mass of grief which had lodged in her chest for many months.

Anxious to escape these memories, Zoe let herself back into the house and found Tom and Jean sitting silently, their arms wrapped around each other. It was as if they were waiting for her return, because Jean immediately continued with her story.

Before leaving her mother's bedside, she had asked a nurse to keep an eye on her. The nurse went to check on Mrs Hensward a few minutes later, and had noticed straight away that something was wrong. Jean had returned to find the hospital staff battling to save her mother's life, but the heart attack had been too severe. Mrs Hensward was declared dead at around the time Zoe was sitting down with the twins to eat tea.

'I didn't know where you were, Tom,' Jean said. 'The nurses were ever so kind and they offered to call someone, but I thought you might still be with the police. I couldn't tell them that, could I?'

ELEVEN

The next morning, Zoe bolted down her breakfast, eager to discover what had been accomplished since her builders' return to work. She put on the thickest sweater she owned under her jacket. If the first snow of winter arrived while they were out, she was ready for it.

As she and Mac approached Larimer Lodge, she spotted someone walking ahead of them on the road. The slight figure was accompanied by a small white dog; both were moving very slowly. At that moment, a dark blue Volvo estate drove past. It was travelling at such a speed that Zoe tugged Mac up onto the grass verge beside her and shouted, 'Slow down!' after it. Her eyes were drawn to the car's number plate: LTM had been her mother's initials.

The Volvo braked sharply as it caught up with the second walker and his dog, and veered over to the other side of the road to avoid them, before disappearing round a corner.

'Lucky we weren't in a car coming the opposite way,' Zoe told Mac, as they started walking up the Larimer Park drive.

She found plenty of evidence at the coach house that the builders had been there recently. Cigarette butts were strewn outside the front door and an assortment of equipment, including a cement mixer and an old vacuum cleaner, had been left under the arch.

Her irritation grew into indignation then anger as she went from room to room, trying to find evidence of any actual work having been done. She kicked the new staircase lying prone on the floor and grimaced with pain. It may be Saturday but she was going to phone Gerry Hall as soon as she got back to the cottage and tell him to take away his tools and send her a bill for the meagre amount of work accomplished so far.

Zoe's imagined conversation with her builder was interrupted by a strange sound resembling a primitive wind instrument, accompanied by frantic barking. She raced outside and traced the noise to the far end of the building, where Mac had backed a male peacock against the wall. Both were engaged in noisy displays of fearlessness.

Unsure which creature she should be most concerned about, Zoe shouted Mac's name. Momentarily distracted, he backed off slightly and the peacock took advantage of this to make its getaway, initially running along the ground then soaring into the air, still protesting loudly. Undeterred by the bird's rapidly increasing altitude and ignoring Zoe's calls, Mac ran off along the drive in pursuit.

Zoe followed him and stumbled over a pothole, only just managing not to end up sprawled on the ground. Then she realised she could no longer hear barking.

Running faster, she rounded a bend and saw a car parked awkwardly, the driver's door open, its engine still running. Peter Pengelly was on his knees in front of the vehicle, leaning over a motionless Mac.

'Oh my God!' Zoe ran over and threw herself down next to the dog.

'I only clipped him,' Peter said. His hand shook as he pushed his hair off his face to look up at her.

'There's blood on your trousers. He's bleeding.'

'I always drive carefully along here. You never know when a rabbit or deer might run out. I'm sure I only clipped him.'

Zoe stroked her dog's head. 'Come on, Mac, wake up. Please.'

Mac opened his eyes and whined. Then he stood up and shook himself.

Zoe felt sick; her tea tasted metallic. Mac had had a lucky escape, his only injury a graze on one of his front legs. He had shown no sign of being in pain until Peter took a first-aid box from a cupboard and Zoe applied a dab of antiseptic to the leg, provoking a short yelp. His tail was soon wagging again as he gulped down every piece of ginger biscuit Peter offered him.

'Do you want to ring the vet and arrange for him to be checked over?' Peter asked. 'I can drive you there if they'll see him straightaway.'

'I'll keep an eye on him, but I don't think there's any need for a vet,' Zoe said. 'It would be good, though, if you could take us home when I've finished my tea.'

Bored now the supply of biscuits had dried up, Mac wandered over to Bert and Tom in their bed beside the Aga. When the cats stood up and spat at him, Peter and Zoe shared a smile, but Zoe could not think of anything to say. She was finding it difficult not to dwell on what might have happened had Peter not been driving so carefully. Less than a year ago she would have told anyone else in a similar situation, 'It's only a dog,' but today's mishap made her realise just how much Mac meant to her. She called him over and hugged him. He sat down, leaning against her leg.

Peter had not volunteered any information as to his brother's whereabouts, and Zoe was about to ask if he would be home soon when Neil sauntered in, his attention focused on pulling a packet of bacon out of the plastic shopping bag he carried. He looked up and saw Zoe, and his face broke into a broad smile.

'This is a nice surprise. Come for breakfast, have you, Doctor?' he said.

'I'm not here by choice.'

'I nearly ran the dog over,' Peter said.

'Shit. Come here, boy. Are you okay?' Neil bent over Mac and ran a hand along his back.

'I only clipped him,' Peter said.

'He was lucky – Mac, I mean,' Zoe said. 'Peter was driving slowly enough to be able to stop in time. He just grazed one of his legs.'

'Chasing a rabbit, was he?'

'No, a peacock, believe it or not.'

'Mac, you silly bugger.'

'I thought he was dead.'

'Poor old you.' Before she realised his intention, Neil pulled Zoe to her feet and put his arms around her. She stood immobile, feeling more comforted than she would have expected.

He released her and moved towards the Aga. 'I prescribe a bacon butty for the shock.'

'Thanks, but I had breakfast before I came out. I just need a lift back to the cottage.'

'What do you make of this woman?' Neil asked his brother in mock despair. 'She's always turning me down. I must be getting old. I never used to have this problem.'

Expressionless, Peter gathered up the mugs on the table and carried them over to the sink. His silence did not seem to bother Neil, who turned his attention back to Zoe.

'I can see you're upset, so I'll take you home. But promise you'll let me serve you up a bacon butty soon.'

Zoe did not answer. She was still trying to reconcile her indifference toward this annoying man with how happy that brief physical contact with him had made her feel.

As they bumped along the drive a few minutes later, she remembered leaving the coach house unsecured, so Neil stopped to let her lock up. On her way back to the Land Rover she glanced at the inert cement mixer.

'What's annoying you?' Neil asked, as they pulled away.

'How do you know I'm annoyed?'

'You shake your head and your ponytail swishes like an angry cat's tail. I've spotted it a few times now. You'd be rubbish at poker.'

'Oh really? You're obviously very good at it, seeing how observant you are.'

'There's no need to be touchy. I like looking at you, that's all. Anyway, what's the problem? I saw Gerry's men here yesterday. Haven't they done what they were supposed to?'

'They haven't done anything at all, except dump more of their crap. I'm seriously considering getting someone else to finish the conversion.'

'Do you want me to have a word with Gerry?'

Zoe didn't need help from anyone, and started to tell Neil so. He put up a hand to stop her.

'I know you can fight your own battles, but I've worked with these guys. At least let me try.'

'Oh, all right. What have I got to lose?'

'Nothing, I promise.'

Wondering whether to invite him in for coffee when they reached Keeper's Cottage, Zoe remembered she had used up the last of the milk at breakfast. 'Can we take a detour to the shop?'

She had heard from many sources how Lisa and Brian Mortimer had rescued Westerlea's general store and post office from almost certain closure when they took it over. Unable to compete on price with supermarkets in the surrounding towns, they gained the community's support by working hard to offer more choice than was usually found locally. They even sold taramasalata, one of Zoe's favourite foods.

Lisa was alone in the shop, saving Zoe from pretending not to notice Brian's inability to keep his hands off his much younger wife, even while she served customers. The girl shared her husband's slight build and pallid complexion; despite being surrounded by food all day they never looked well-fed. Today her skinny jeans and tight T-shirt made her seem positively malnourished.

Anxious not to keep Neil waiting, Zoe walked briskly past the delights of the deli counter to pick up a carton of milk and the local newspaper. She might come back later for a wedge of carrot cake. Lisa smiled shyly and took Zoe's money without a word. The silence was broken when a woman Zoe remembered meeting on Bonfire Night hurried in.

'You'll never guess what's happening,' she said. 'That's the police over at the Bairds' house again. Gregor came back last night. I expect they're here to arrest him.'

'Why would they do that?' Zoe asked. 'They're probably just talking to Mr Baird again.'

'Everyone knows it was Gregor that did it. Anyway, his dad's not there. He went out with his dog earlier and he's not home yet. They asked me if I'd seen him.'

Hearing this, it dawned on Zoe who it was she had seen on the way to the coach house: Jimmy Baird and his Jack Russell terrier.

Neil had turned the Land Rover around while she was in the shop, and as she got back in he pointed over the road at Horseshoe Cottage. 'They've caught up with Gregor Baird at last.'

'Not you too,' Zoe said, but she could not help looking.

It was easy to spot the distinctive figure of Erskine Mather as he led a group of men towards two cars, one a dark green saloon, the other in police colours, which were parked on the road. Two uniformed officers flanked a man wearing jeans and a check shirt, while Sergeant Trent walked behind them carrying a black holdall. As the uniformed officers guided the man into the rear of their vehicle, Mather dropped back and spoke with Trent, who looked cold despite his duffle coat and the red scarf wrapped high around his neck.

'I need to see Mather,' Zoe said, opening her door again. 'Sorry, but they've been looking for Jimmy Baird and I think I saw him earlier.' Without waiting for a response she got out and crossed the road. The police car drove off.

'Good morning, Doctor,' Mather said. Trent greeted her with his usual brief nod.

'I believe you're looking for Mr Baird. Jimmy, that is.'

'Yes.'

'I think I saw him a couple of hours ago, out walking his dog. I'm surprised he's not home by now.'

'Where was this?'

'Heading towards the water meadow not far from the Larimer Park estate.'

Mather looked at Trent, who shook his head.

'Can you show us?' Mather asked.

'Yes, of course.' Zoe cast a look over her shoulder towards the Land Rover and its occupants. 'But I'll need to tell my, um, friend first.'

Rather than take Mac back to Larimer Hall until she was able to collect him, Neil insisted on following them to the water meadow, so as to be on hand to drive Zoe home once they were finished. Disinclined to argue with him in front of Mather, she nodded, walked back to the police car and climbed in.

Less than ten minutes later, Trent brought the car to a smooth halt beside a gate a little way on from where Zoe had seen Jimmy Baird walking his dog. Neil's Land Rover pulled in behind them shortly afterwards. Mather got out and looked expectantly at Zoe. She realised he must want her to accompany them in case they found Jimmy needing medical attention, and wished she had brought her bag.

Mather took a pair of green wellies from the car's

88

boot and put them on, carefully tucking his trousers inside. Trent tried, unsuccessfully, to button up his coat, then caught his boss's eye and went to open the gate. They all three walked through it.

The rough grass was interspersed with patches of coarse brown spikes. A small stream emerged on the left from an adjoining field, followed the boundary fence a short distance, then started a meandering route across the meadow. Mather stared into the distance, then raised a pair of binoculars to his eyes.

'You think something bad has happened to him,' Zoe said, not expecting a response.

Trent strode off, shoulders hunched against the cold. His DCI followed, though at a slower pace, and Zoe walked alongside him.

'Is there a way out at the far end?' Mather asked.

'I don't think so,' Zoe said. 'But I've only been here a couple of times. We couldn't walk the full length because one of the wooden bridges has been swept away.'

Some distance ahead of them, Trent reached the first of the narrow bridges. He shouted, 'Boss!', pointed at something and rushed to the water's edge. Mather and Zoe hurried to catch up with him.

They stared at the macabre white buoy floating on the surface of the water. Immediately below, still clutching the lead which bound them together, its master lay face down in some reeds.

TWELVE

Zoe watched Trent uncouple the lead from the dog's collar, pull the animal clear of the water and lie it down on the bank. After removing his overcoat and handing it to his sergeant, Mather lowered himself into the water, which came up dangerously close to the top of his boots, and tugged on the lead.

Jimmy Baird bobbed to the surface and swivelled until he was floating on his back. A deep gash split his forehead and his cheeks were sunken, as if his dentures had fallen out.

Mather pulled the body towards him and bent to examine it, then he straightened up and wordlessly exchanged looks with Trent. Apparently deciding it would be a waste of time trying to resuscitate the old man, Mather returned to dry land, while Trent dug deep into his coat pocket and pulled out a mobile phone. He moved a few metres away and had a brief conversation with someone, presumably summoning the same team which had turned up following Zoe's discovery of Chrissie's remains less than a week earlier.

Zoe could not stop looking at the dog's corpse, its position a disturbing reminder of how Mac had first looked after being hit by Peter's car. She reminded herself its owner was also dead.

'Shouldn't we get him out?' she asked.

'No,' Mather said. 'He's beyond help. Strictly speaking, I shouldn't even have moved him.' He took

---

90

Zoe's arm and led her a few metres away from the water's edge.

'You don't seem surprised,' Zoe said. 'Did you expect this to happen?'

'We had no reason to believe Mr Baird was in any danger, but he'd been out for so long, I began to have my concerns. Most people wouldn't take their dog for a two-hour walk on a day like this, and certainly not an elderly man in poor health.'

'I wonder why he came here today.' Zoe gazed at the bridge, a grandiose term for a pair of wooden planks held together halfway by a metal bar. The one time she had crossed it herself, she had thought how easy it would be to slip and tumble into the water below. She shivered. The already bleak day was growing colder and darker as heavy clouds gathered. It looked like the predictions of snow were going to be proved right.

Mather stared over her shoulder and shouted, 'You were asked to wait in your vehicle'.

Zoe turned to see Neil approaching, bent awkwardly low and clinging to Mac's collar.

'Sorry. The dog was getting restless, so I let him out for a breather. It didn't occur to me he'd chase after you.' Neil released Mac, who rushed up to his owner, tail wagging.

'What's happened?' Neil asked.

'See for yourself,' Zoe said.

Neil started to move towards the stream. Trent, back from making his phone call, grabbed him. 'You can't go there.'

Neil wrested his arm from Trent's hold and glared. 'There's no need to get physical. You only had to ask.'

Trent's jaw clenched, but Mather intervened before his sergeant could take things further. 'Mr Pengelly, we've found a body, so this whole area must be treated as a crime scene. Could I ask you to escort Doctor Moreland back to your vehicle? I think she's feeling the cold. I'll join you there shortly.'

Neil shot a hostile look at Trent, then took Zoe's hand and led her to his Land Rover. He started the engine and switched the heater to maximum. Once her teeth had stopped chattering, Zoe briefly described what she had seen.

'Talisker too? Who would kill a defenceless dog?' Neil asked.

'We don't know yet if anyone killed them. The poor man may have simply slipped and fallen, dragging the dog in after him. Just because Chrissie was murdered, we shouldn't assume her husband has suffered the same fate.'

Neil nodded. 'An accident would make more sense.'

For once they were in agreement.

Very soon, more police cars and several unmarked vehicles started to arrive, lining up along the road in front of the Land Rover. Neil and Zoe watched as men and women pulled on their crime-scene coveralls, and Mac growled as the white-clad figures then passed by to check in with Trent, who stood at the gate like a head waiter directing diners to their tables. Last to appear was an ambulance from which no one descended.

Mather came over to ask Zoe what time she had seen Jimmy and whether she had noticed anyone else in the vicinity, pulling out his notepad when she recalled the speeding Volvo and the letters on its registration plate. Then he told Neil to take her home and strode back into the field.

'You'll be on his Christmas card list this year,' Neil said, steering his vehicle back on to the road.

Suddenly feeling exhausted and not trusting herself to reply, Zoe stared out of the Land Rover's smeary window and tried to push the images of the dead terrier and its owner's face out of her mind. When they reached

Keeper's Cottage, she only managed to send Neil on his way by agreeing he could ring her that evening to check she was all right.

However, being alone brought her little peace of mind, and halfway through making a long-awaited coffee she remembered promising to look in on Jean. She grabbed her coat, scarf and driving gloves and opened the front door, only to discover the snow which had started to fall gently while Neil drove her home was now coming down much more heavily. And settling.

Radio Borders was warning people to go out only if their journeys were absolutely necessary, but Jean lived so close this hardly qualified as a journey. Zoe drove towards the village at a fraction of her usual speed, the car's windscreen wipers working overtime to keep the glass clear. Although it was only mid-afternoon, what light remained was a sickly yellow and fading fast.

Coming up to the junction opposite Westerlea's graveyard, Zoe applied the brakes as gently as possible. Despite this, her car continued to move forward, unchecked.

Trying to remember what she had learned on the advanced driving course Russell gave her one Christmas, she fought the urge to struggle against the vehicle's momentum, instead steering into the skid. The car slewed across the road and Zoe braced herself for the impact as it glided into one of a pair of cylinder-shaped stone gateposts at the entrance to Westerlea's cemetery.

There was less noise than she expected, and the jolt was no greater than when she had to brake suddenly the other day to avoid a hare running along the road. Getting out to look, she could find no visible damage to the car's bodywork, although the front lights on the passenger side had imploded. This would definitely mean a visit to a garage and, worse still, she could already see the smug expression on Kate's face.

Back in the driver's seat, misery overwhelmed her.

Deep breathing failed to relieve the tightness across her chest, and so did a blast of Led Zeppelin. This stupid accident was the last straw. *Imagine thinking her life would improve by moving here. All she had achieved was to swap one set of problems for another.* Unable to hold in her despair any longer, Zoe repeatedly banged the palms of her hands against the steering wheel and howled, her breath steaming up the windscreen which snow had already started to obscure from the outside.

Headlights loomed in the rear view mirror. Zoe froze, gripping the wheel as a Range Rover slowly passed her and continued without hesitation up the road. So much for looking after each other in the country. She resented the other driver for not stopping to check she was okay, while simultaneously feeling relief at not being discovered with crimson cheeks and eyes puffy from crying. Nevertheless, the appearance of that vehicle out of nowhere reminded her it was now dark and still snowing, and she was parked at a junction with no lights on.

She blew her nose, then restarted the car and carried out a series of cautious manoeuvres until it faced in the direction of Keeper's Cottage. *No one could say she hadn't tried.*

Back home, she telephoned Paul to tell him about her abortive attempt to reach Jean's house. He sounded horrified. 'My dear, you must promise me you won't try to go out again tonight. It's stopped snowing now but that may only be temporary.'

'Don't worry, I won't. But can you give me Jean's number? I'd hate her to think I've forgotten my promise to visit.'

'I spoke to Tom a few minutes ago. Jean was asleep on the couch – she didn't have a good night. I've arranged for her to call me when she wakes up, so I'll give her your message then, if you want. It's not worth us both disturbing the poor lass.'

Zoe agreed, then asked if he had heard about

Jimmy Baird.

'Yes, Margaret called to tell me. What a terrible turn of events for young Gregor. Being taken to Hawick for questioning about his stepmother's murder, and then finding out his father's dead too.'

'Do you know Gregor? Do you think he could have done it?'

'What, kill his stepmother and then his father?'

'You're assuming Jimmy was murdered as well?'

'Even if he wasn't, it changes very little in my estimation. Is a person more evil if they're capable of killing two people rather than just one? I don't feel qualified to answer that, my dear. Do you?'

THIRTEEN

The sky remained overcast next morning, threatening yet more snow. It was Sunday, and not being a churchgoer, Zoe resigned herself to seeing no one. She had not experienced another deplorable loss of self-control since the previous day's incident at the cemetery gates, but her spirits were still low.

Kate turned up mid-morning unannounced, as Zoe was about to reward herself with a coffee for doing an hour's housework. It was the first time they had met since Chrissie's car was found on Heartsease Farm, although numerous texts had passed between them, particularly about Tom's experience with the police. Feeling as she did, Zoe would not have chosen to have a visitor at all, but if anyone could cheer her up it was Kate.

'I felt sure you'd be in. Bet you can't even get that car of yours out of the garage. Do I smell coffee?'

'The roads can't be too bad if you made it here,' Zoe said, not wanting to mention her prang quite yet. 'Or did you walk?'

'Dad lent me his Discovery to take Mum to church. She goes for a sherry with some old ladies afterwards, so I thought I'd look in on you, see how you're coping with your first taste of a Borders winter.'

'We do get snow in England sometimes. Though not usually this early, I admit.'

'Have you heard about Jimmy Baird?'

'Your mother's network of spies is slipping. I was

there when they found him.'

'No!' Kate stopped midway through unbuttoning her coat. 'Not again.'

Zoe gave a humourless grin. 'People will start to think I'm some sort of attention seeker.' Once they were sat down at the kitchen table she ran through what had taken place in the water meadow, Kate watching her intently.

'Poor little Talisker,' Kate said. 'Jimmy loved that dog. Which reminds me.' She pulled an envelope out of her handbag, followed by a small package wrapped in blue tissue paper. 'Here's Mhairi's thank you note for her birthday present. She loves it. And here's Mac's gift in return. We've saved you both some cake for next time you visit.'

The package contained three bone-shaped dog chews. Zoe gave one to Mac and put away the others with his food.

'Do you think Jimmy was murdered too?' Kate asked as soon as Zoe sat down again.

'I don't want to second-guess the post mortem. He could easily have slipped and fallen off that rickety bridge.'

'Will they be able to tell if he fell or was pushed?'

'It depends on the wounds he sustained, if there was water in his lungs, that sort of thing.' Zoe poured the last of the coffee into Kate's mug. 'Whatever happened, it's very sad. But there's one bright spot on the horizon.'

'What's that?'

'Your friend Mather has turned his attention to Gregor Baird. I saw the police taking him away, which presumably means they've ruled out Tom.'

'I hope you're right,' Kate said. 'But that was before they knew Jimmy was dead. Now they might reconsider and think Tom killed him as well.'

'You're not normally so pessimistic.'

'The whole family's very upset. Mum especially. I could hardly get a word out of her on the way to church. So I've come to a decision.'

'Oh dear. I'm not going to like this, am I?'

'We must find out ourselves who the murderer is.'

'Tell me you're not serious.'

'Of course I am. It's no joking matter.'

'You've been watching too much television and reading too many crime novels. What makes you think we can do any better than the police?'

Kate poured herself more coffee, then added another spoonful of sugar. 'There's no physical evidence, is there? If there had been, they'd have charged someone by now. So it all boils down to personalities – Chrissie's and the killer's. And the police don't know people round here like we do.'

'Like you do, you mean,' Zoe said. 'I'm still a very recent incomer.'

'But you're a good judge of character. That's what's needed right now.'

'I've probably never even met the killer.'

'You met Chrissie.'

'Once.'

'And you know the sort of person she was.'

'Only because of what you've told me. You may have disliked her, Kate, but you can't be suggesting it was her own fault someone murdered her.'

'No, of course not. But think about it. What made someone want to kill her? Murder isn't the same as a car crash. You can die as a result of a road accident just by being in the wrong place at the –'

Kate put a hand up to her mouth. 'Oh Zoe, I'm sorry. I was forgetting what happened to your mum.'

'You don't have to apologise. It was a long time ago, and you're right, being the victim of an accident can simply be rotten luck. Being a murder victim tends to be less random.'

'Exactly.' Kate nodded earnestly. 'If we assume Chrissie Baird was killed by someone she knew rather than some passing psychopath, which seems improbable, this being the Borders, that must mean it was something she did which led to her being murdered.'

'Such as?'

'Think about when you met her. What impression did she make on you?'

'I didn't like her, although I can't pinpoint why. She asked me lots of questions about myself, which is usually flattering, but with her there was something a bit off. Perhaps she was more direct than I'm comfortable with.'

For some reason, Kate found this funny. 'You don't say?'

Ignoring the jibe, Zoe went on. 'She made a big thing about me buying the coach house, wanting to know if I planned to run a business from it or have lots of friends and relatives to stay. At the time I thought she was worried I might start holding rowdy parties every weekend.'

'That was Chrissie all over.' Kate drained her mug and set it down on the table. 'She'd try to dig up things she could then bitch about. She hardly knew Ken, but that didn't stop her from pumping my friends to find out why he'd left us and where he'd gone.'

'I remember she was quite ingratiating as well,' Zoe said. 'She spoke like she knew all about life in a doctor's surgery. When I asked where she'd worked, it turned out she was only going on what a friend had told her.'

'See, I was right. Even after a brief conversation you had Chrissie Baird sussed. Maybe she snooped around once too often and discovered something so bad she had to be killed to prevent her revealing it.'

'It's a huge leap from recognising she was nosey to deciding that was why someone murdered her.'

'I've struggled to believe someone actually killed her and put her in Westerlea's bonfire, but we both know it happened. Once you can get your head around that, anything else seems possible.'

'Don't you think you should be sharing this with Mather?' Zoe said. 'I'm sure he'd find it useful.'

Kate frowned. 'I can detect sarcasm, you know, even if I can't hear it.'

'I wasn't being sarcastic, honestly. But whatever insight you have, we can't act on it.'

'We can talk to people, find out what they know.'

'And so can the police, Kate. What they don't know about Westerlea's inhabitants they have the means to find out.'

'People will talk to you much more freely. You're a doctor.'

'And because I'm a doctor, it's unlikely I could pass any of it on.'

'Even if they're not your patients?'

Zoe paused to think about this. 'You've got me there,' she admitted. 'Most of the confidentiality issues I've been faced with were pretty clear cut – underage girls wanting to go on the pill without their parents' knowledge, that sort of thing. But it would be wrong to use my position to invite confidences I have no intention of keeping.'

'So you're saying you won't help me prove Tom didn't kill Chrissie?' Kate reached for her gloves and stood up.

Zoe put a hand on her friend's arm. 'Please don't think I'm being unsympathetic. I recognise how awful this must be for your whole family.'

'At least come to The Rocket with me tonight.'

'I can't go anywhere. As you so accurately predicted, my car is useless in this sort of weather.'

'If that's the only thing stopping you, I'll pick you up. Must go. I have to collect Mum and relieve Dad of child-minding duties.'

'You're incorrigible. You've no intention of taking my advice and leaving well alone, have you?'

Kate marched out into the hall saying, 'Okay, see you around six-thirty.'

FOURTEEN

A rapid thaw had set in, so Kate and Zoe drove into Westerlea that evening along roads wet with dirty slush. The car park was empty except for a blue Volvo.

Zoe nudged Kate. 'Do you know who that Volvo belongs to?'

Kate stared at the car. 'No, but I wouldn't mind having it. It's a few years younger than mine.'

'It's the car which drove past me when I saw Jimmy Baird out walking yesterday. I remember the number plate.'

'Do you think whoever was driving may have seen something?'

'Probably not. It was travelling very fast and Jimmy hadn't reached the water meadow when it passed him. I expect the police have already been in touch with the owner and found that out. Brrr. Let's get inside.'

Tonight the view into the pub's kitchen was obscured by plastic blinds, although one of its windows was open. The metallic sound of saucepans being washed and stacked was accompanied by a low murmur of conversation.

Out of the blue, reminding Zoe of an enjoyable evening she once spent at a Greek restaurant in Nottingham, came the noise of plates smashing. Then silence. Then raised voices.

'Look what you made me do!'

'You can't blame me for your clumsiness.'

Zoe grabbed at Kate's jacket to gain her attention, pointed at the window and put a finger to her mouth.

Hazel's voice was shrill. 'If we'd gone to the police, I wouldn't be in this state. Look how my hands are shaking.'

'If we'd done that, we'd be in a lot more trouble. No one would've believed us.'

'Yes they would!'

'No, love, they wouldn't. Leave it, can't you? It'll be over soon enough, if we keep our heads down. I'm going to open up.'

The sound of washing-up resumed.

Ray looked startled to see them waiting at the door when he unlocked it, but his professional hospitality kicked in and he was soon pouring their drinks and asking Zoe what she thought of the bad weather. She still had not told Kate about her skirmish with the graveyard gatepost, so this seemed the ideal opportunity to mention it, playing the whole episode down.

'I told you to get yourself a proper vehicle,' Kate said.

Hoping that if she didn't argue, Kate would drop the subject, Zoe simply nodded.

Kate turned to Ray. 'Talking of cars, Ray, whose is the Volvo in your car park?'

'What, the blue one?' Ray asked, pulling open a packet of cheese and onion crisps. 'Like the look of it, do you? Sorry, but you're out of luck. It's ours, and we've only recently bought it.'

'In that case,' Kate said, 'you'll probably be hearing from the police soon. If you haven't already.'

Ray stared into the crisp packet, his face more florid than usual. 'Why would they want to speak to me?'

Wishing Kate had been more subtle in her approach, Zoe said, 'I think I saw your car yesterday morning, driving past me and Jimmy Baird, just before he went into the water meadow. When the police asked me if

I'd seen anyone else around, I told them about it. The letters on its number plate are my mother's initials, which is how I . . .'

Zoe's embarrassed smile became rigid as the silence in the room lengthened. Eventually, Ray said, 'You must have made a mistake. It wasn't our car. Hazel went to Kelso yesterday, which is in the opposite direction. Excuse me.'

The big man turned abruptly and went out of the bar, leaving his crisps untouched on the counter. Kate and Zoe made bewildered faces at each other, but before they could speak the door opened and several regulars filed in. After saying hello they started calling for Ray to come through and serve them. A note of impatience had crept into their voices by the time he reappeared, his face even redder than when he went out.

Elsewhere in the building, a door slammed.

Half an hour later, The Rocket was nearly full, the crush only lessening after Ray put up a board announcing the management's regrets that no food would be served that evening. Kate tried to engage a couple of elderly men in conversation, but apart from conjecture concerning Gregor Baird – who had apparently been released by the police without charge, his current whereabouts unknown – the chances of having a murderer in their midst was no longer a hot topic. It appeared everyone was putting Jimmy's sudden demise down to bad luck and the folly of going out alone when in poor health.

Kate and Zoe sat down at a small table.

'Now will you tell me what you overheard when we were passing by the kitchen?' Kate asked.

'It'll have to wait until we're somewhere more private,' Zoe said, looking around. 'Someone might hear.'

'No one need hear, silly. You don't have to talk out loud to me.'

Zoe self-consciously mouthed an account of Hazel and Ray's argument. Kate watched intently then asked, in an uncharacteristically soft voice, 'What was it all about?'

'Your guess is as good as mine. They're obviously scared about something they can't tell the police about.' Zoe was reaching for her purse to go up to the bar and buy another round of drinks when the front door opened and Neil rushed in. He surveyed the room; it didn't take him long to spot her.

'Zoe, thank Christ you're here.' Neil pushed past some drinkers who were trying to persuade their friend to take out his squeeze box and start a sing-along. 'I've been searching everywhere for you.'

'There's no need to shout,' Zoe said. She could tell the whole room was watching. 'What's happened?'

'I wondered why you didn't call last night like you said you would. Then my mate Gavin said he'd seen you out yesterday during that snow, slammed up against the entrance to the graveyard. I phoned you and there was no answer, so I went round to the cottage and you weren't there.'

'Which could be why I didn't answer the phone.'

'Then I thought Kate might be able to tell me where you were, so I went there.'

'And found her house deserted too, I expect.'

'Yes. So I came here.'

'Well now you've found me and as you can see, I'm safe and sound.'

'I'm glad about that.' Neil pulled his wallet from his pocket. 'What can I get you girls to drink?'

'Actually we were about to leave, weren't we Kate?'

Kate looked confused for a moment, then gulped down the rest of her Diet Coke.

'I can't tempt you to a quick one?' Neil asked, a broad smile creating deep wrinkles beneath his eyes.

Standing up, Zoe lifted her handbag on to her shoulder then leaned towards Neil to be sure only he could hear what she had to say. 'You rush in, speaking like you own me. And now you want us to sit down and have a drink? I don't think so. Give your mate Gavin a call if you get lonely.'

Once outside, Zoe strode towards the car park. Kate grabbed her friend's arm when she caught up with her. 'Hold on. What's wrong?'

Zoe swung round. 'He's behaving as though I should tell him where I'm going every time I set foot outside the house. I'm not having that.'

'He was worried about you.'

'He had no right to make such a fuss. People were watching.'

'I think it's sweet.'

Zoe turned away. 'Well I don't.' She continued to walk towards the car.

'Sorry, I didn't catch that,' Kate shouted after her. 'What did you say?'

Zoe stopped and took a deep breath. She turned back to Kate. 'No, I'm the one who should be sorry. I'm taking my annoyance with Neil out on you.'

'People often forget I need to see their faces when they're talking.'

'I didn't forget. I was being rude.'

It seemed like Kate was retaliating when she looked away as Zoe spoke. Then Zoe also spotted the figures approaching them.

The woman leaning on Erskine Mather's arm was nearly his height. Dressed in a camel coat and taupe trousers, she wore coordinating animal-print hat, gloves and scarf, and her handbag and boots were of perfectly matched tan leather. She dragged her right foot very slightly.

'Mother, this is Doctor Moreland, who I told you about. And you'll remember Kate.'

'Of course I remember Kate.' Bette Mather threw her arms wide like an opera singer reaching a high note.

Kate stepped forward to be hugged. 'Hello Bette.

It's lovely to see you again. I was sorry to hear you haven't been well.'

Bette released Kate and waved her hands, dismissing the idea that a stroke could be anything but a minor inconvenience. Mather smiled apologetically at Zoe as his mother positioned herself close to Kate and spoke to her.

'Etta tells me your eldest has reached double figures already. That must mean the girls are, what, six and eight?'

'Eva is nine and Mhairi was seven yesterday.'

'How time flies. Of course your mother hasn't brought any photographs round recently, so I've lost track.'

Mather cleared his throat and said, 'Speaking of birthdays, it's Mother's today, so I've brought her out for a meal.'

'I don't think they're doing food here tonight,' Zoe said.

'I phoned earlier and Mrs Anderson said they were.'

'She must have had a last minute change of plan,' Zoe said. 'I don't think she's even in now. Her car's gone, anyway.'

'It was Hazel's – Mrs Anderson's – car that Zoe saw yesterday morning passing Jimmy on his way to the water meadow,' Kate said.

'You're sure of this?' Mather asked Zoe, the dutiful son abruptly replaced by the diligent policeman.

'I was until Ray Anderson told us it couldn't have been.'

'You told him you'd seen it? I wish you hadn't done that.'

Kate said hurriedly, 'Blame me. I asked him who the car belonged to.'

'And when Ray said it was theirs and asked why we wanted to know, I saw no reason not to tell him,' Zoe added.

'Did he say why it couldn't have been their car you saw?' Mather rubbed his bare hands together against the cold.

'Hazel drove it to Kelso that morning,' Kate said. 'But we're not convinced he was telling the truth.'

Mather turned to Bette, who had just asked Zoe how she was enjoying life in the Borders.

'I think we should go inside, Mother. If they're not serving food we'll have to find somewhere which is, but at least we can warm up with a drink.'

'I'm not the one who's cold, Erskine,' Bette said. 'But if we're going in, will you join us, Kate? And your friend too, of course.'

'Thanks, Bette, but I need to go home. I promised Mum and Dad I wouldn't leave them babysitting for long.'

'I'm so pleased to have seen you again. Come for tea one day, will you?'

After extracting a promise from Kate to visit soon, Bette smiled goodbye to Zoe and allowed her son to lead her towards the front of The Rocket.

'Now I see where he gets his dress sense from,' Zoe said when the pair were out of earshot.

'Bette always dresses impeccably, and Erskine was never able to do anything else, however much he tried. At university he was the only one with creases ironed into his jeans.'

'He took his laundry home?' Zoe said. 'Typical man!'

'Oh no, he did it all himself. Come to think of it,' Kate said, smiling, 'he was the only one of us who owned an iron.'

'Will you visit her?' Zoe asked while they sat waiting for the car's windscreen to clear.

'I'm tempted to, but it might not be a good idea. What do you think?'

'If you do, just be sure it's Bette you're going there

———

to see.'

Kate looked in her rear view mirror. 'Uh oh, here comes Neil. I take it you don't want me to hang about for him to reach us?'

Without waiting for an answer, she put the car into gear and drove towards the car park's exit. Neil stuck out his arm as though wanting to flag them down, then must have thought better of it and waved instead. Zoe did not wave back.

What was she going to do about that exasperating man? Things were difficult enough, without Neil Pengelly complicating them further.

FIFTEEN

Penny put down the phone and waved excitedly at Zoe, who had been hoping to reach her consulting room unobserved.

'Doctor Zoe, are you all right?'

The telephone rang again. Mondays were always like this, the genuinely unwell joined by people seeking the slightest excuse to remain off work after the weekend.

Zoe had to wait while the young receptionist took another call before replying. 'I'm fine, thanks. Did you have a nice weekend?'

'Margaret told me what happened. How awful for you.'

'It was a bit of a shock.'

'But you didn't hurt yourself?'

Zoe stared at her, perplexed, then light dawned. 'You're talking about my car going into that gatepost, aren't you?'

'Of course. What else has happened?'

'You haven't heard about Jimmy Baird?'

'Yes, but –'

Margaret appeared at the reception desk. 'Penny, we'll never catch up if you keep gossiping.'

Penny traipsed back to the post she had been opening and sorting into piles before the rash of phone calls started.

'We're very behind,' Margaret said, 'what with Jean still being off.'

'How is she?' Zoe asked. 'I set out to see her on Saturday but the weather got the better of me.'

'So she said, when we spoke yesterday. She sounded a lot better, though there's still the ordeal of the funeral for her to get through.'

'When is it?'

'Wednesday afternoon.'

'Will you be going?'

'Yes, if Penny thinks she can look after things here on her own for a while.'

Penny nodded without looking up from her work, and Zoe was at last able to move towards her consulting room. Margaret followed, her thick tights swishing as her legs rubbed against each other.

'And you, Doctor, how are you after your adventure at the weekend?'

'As I was telling Penny, I'm absolutely fine. My car slid on the snow and hit a gatepost. It's damaged, but I'm not.'

Margaret shook her head, setting her chins wobbling. 'I was talking about finding Jimmy Baird.'

Wrong again. 'I didn't actually find him. I took the police to where I'd seen him earlier, and they found him.'

'And poor Talisker was killed too.'

Jimmy Baird's dog was getting more sympathy than its owner. 'Mr Baird was still holding the lead,' Zoe said. 'He must have pulled the dog in after him.'

'My Hector says it's all very peculiar and probably not over yet.'

Zoe sensed Margaret wanted to say more, but the older woman was distracted by a queue of patients which had formed at the front desk while Penny was taking another telephone call. 'Oh dear, I'd better go and help.'

Alone at last, Zoe went into her consulting room and checked through the list of patients she was due to see. A name at the bottom jumped out at her, but before she had a chance to open his file on the computer she was distracted by a knock on the door. It was Margaret again.

'Doctor, I meant to tell you that I've slipped an extra patient in at the end of your session. He insisted on having an appointment this morning. I think you'll understand when you see who it is.'

'I saw his name on my list. So he's still registered with this practice?'

'Never goes far, that one.'

'It sounds as if you don't like him.'

Margaret pursed her lips in disapproval. 'Thinks he's God's gift to women. Always has. He's losing his touch now he's older, but there's still lots of silly girls who welcome the attention of a man like him. As my Hector says, lovers fool awfy easy.'

Zoe called up Gregor Baird's medical records on her screen. 'It doesn't look as though he's a regular visitor.'

'No, but his conquests are.'

'Broken hearts?'

'Unplanned pregnancies. Gregor obviously isn't keen on using condoms. He's been the cause of at least three abortions and two bairns that I can think of. One of those is ten now and was the saving of her mother's marriage, mind, so perhaps some good came out of it.'

'Do people think he killed Chrissie?' Zoe asked.

'My Hector says it's unlikely, because he's not clever enough. But you'll not find many prepared to stand up and defend him.'

'I hear he didn't get on well with her.'

'If I'd had to share a roof with that woman, I may have been tempted to murder her myself.' Margaret pointed at the clock above Zoe's desk. 'It's gone nine. You don't want to be behind from the start.'

Zoe worked steadily through the morning's patients. It was all pretty routine, except for another adult presenting with the symptoms of chickenpox, making the third in a week. She would have to ask Walter and Paul if they had seen anyone else with it. They may have a mini epidemic on their hands.

She went out to the waiting room to collect her last patient of the morning. As she called his name, the practice nurse glanced up from pinning a poster on the notice board and an elderly woman nudged the man sitting next to her.

Gregor Baird followed Zoe silently along the corridor and slid into the chair she indicated, not once making eye contact. She studied his turquoise check shirt which hung outside a faded pair of jeans but could not entirely hide an incipient beer belly. Although his clothes were crumpled, probably thrown on without being ironed, they were clean and gave off a wholesome smell of fabric conditioner.

Then he lifted his head and looked straight at her for the first time.

Zoe felt a jolt of surprise. His eyes were a Mediterranean blue, blurred at the edges by thick blond lashes, while his lips were full, almost feminine. Gregor Baird had once been beautiful, and even now, in his late thirties, would need nothing more than his face to capture many women's hearts.

'Mr Baird, I'm sorry for your recent loss,' Zoe said. *Or should that be 'losses'?*

'It was you who found him, weren't it?' His voice was disappointingly high-pitched, boyish even.

'I was there, yes.'

'You found Chrissie too.'

'Yes.' Zoe paused. Unsure where Gregor was going with this conversation, she steeled herself for hostility, but he leaned back in the chair, stretched his legs and crossed them at black-booted ankles, and said nothing more.

'So, how can I help you?'

'You have to give me something.'

'What for?'

'To make me to sleep at nights.'

'I realise you must be quite stressed at the moment, what with –'

'"Quite stressed"?' Gregor uncrossed his ankles and sat up straight. 'I'll give you quite stressed. I go away for a few days and come back to the news that my stepmother's been killed. The police drag me over to Hawick. They put me in a room, leave me for hours, then tell me my dad's dead and kick me out.'

'It's little wonder you're having difficulty sleeping.'

Gregor snorted. 'Want to know the worst part?' Twisting his torso round and pointing at the door, he said, 'Half of 'em out there think I did it, the other half think I'm next. Dunno which is worse.' He sank back into his chair and gnawed at a fingernail.

'Do you have anyone you can talk to?' Zoe asked. 'You may find that helps.'

Straightaway he was on his feet, glaring down at her. 'Are you trying to do the coppers' job for them, make me confess when I haven't done anything?'

'Please sit down, Mr Baird.' Zoe glanced beneath her desk at the panic button Walter had demanded for every consulting room after being physically threatened by a patient. She wondered what would happen if she pressed it.

Gregor glowered but did as she asked. 'He was my dad. And Chrissie kept him happy enough.'

'What about your step-sister?'

'Alice? What about her?' Gregor was braced to leap up again. Zoe had touched another nerve.

'I only wondered if you've been in contact with her.'

'I told the police and now I'm telling you, me 'n' Alice haven't spoken for ages.'

'Not even to discuss funeral arrangements?'

'Who for? They're not releasing either of the

bodies yet. Not finished cutting them up, I s'pose.'

Zoe sometimes offered bereaved patients out-of-hours appointments to talk through their feelings without the time constraints of a normal surgery. Gregor would probably be suspicious of her motives if she made such a proposal to him, and she did not relish the idea of spending any more time with him than she was obliged to. *If he wanted drugs, he could have them.*

'I'll prescribe you a short course of tablets to help re-establish your sleeping pattern,' she said, skimming through his medical history, checking for contraindications. The only recent entry she could find was a routine notification from a hospital out of the area that he had been treated for a badly sprained ankle a fortnight earlier. She asked if it was still giving him any trouble.

Gregor tensed again, and Zoe readied herself for another outburst. She would be relieved when this consultation was over. 'I'm only asking in case you're taking painkillers for it.'

'No, it's fine now.' His shoulders relaxed.

Zoe pointed the arrow on her screen at the appropriate box and clicked. When the prescription whirred out of the printer behind her she signed it and passed it over to Gregor. 'These should do the trick, but if you're still having problems when you've finished them, come and see me again.'

Smiling at her for the first time, Gregor batted his eyelids. 'Thanks, Doc.' Seconds later he left her room without a backward glance.

Feeling she had been outmanoeuvred in some way, Zoe looked again at the scanned-in notification about Gregor's treatment for his sprained ankle. It contained nothing significant, and she was about to close his file when she noticed where the hospital was located.

Newcastle upon Tyne. Where Chrissie had been going. Where Alice lived.

Newcastle is a big place; Zoe remembered spending a weekend there with Russell before they got married and wishing for more time to enjoy it properly. Gregor and Alice could both easily be there at the same time without seeing each other. But his overreaction to the letter from the hospital piqued Zoe's curiosity. *If he was in touch with Alice, why lie about it?*

Zoe clicked her mouse to send the page to print. She did not go along with Margaret's husband's judgment. Gregor Baird seemed wily enough to have killed his father and his stepmother. And stand a good chance of getting away with it.

She swivelled round to the printer, picked up the copy letter and stared at it. Deep in thought and still facing away from the door, she had no idea Walter was in the room until he rapped his knuckles on her desk, making her jump.

'Surgery finished?' Walter asked.

'Yes. Is there something you want?' In case that sounded curt, Zoe made an effort to smile.

'Just a chat.'

Walter sat down. He didn't usually do this. *In fact, when was the last time he had been in her room?*

'Are your patients still more interested in you than their ailments?'

'Not everyone has heard about me getting caught up in the discovery of Jimmy Baird's body, thank goodness.'

'You do have the unhappy knack of being in the wrong place at the wrong time.'

'I hope the old saying about things coming in threes isn't true. If it happens again, DCI Mather will think I'm getting some weird kick out of killing people and pretending to find their bodies.'

Walter's laugh was more polite than comradely, but it was a start. For the first time in ages they were having a normal conversation.

'We'd understand,' he said, 'if it all got too much for you.'

'It takes more than a couple of dead bodies to upset me.'

'There you go, joking again. No one would blame you if you decided to call it a day.'

'What do you mean?'

'Relocating to a new job can be difficult in the best of circumstances. After losing your husband you must have hoped that by coming here things would improve.'

'And they have.'

'But you've been let down by your builder and now I hear you crashed your car in the snow.'

'"Crashed" is too strong a word for it.'

'All the same, Zoe, I think you should consider whether coming to Scotland was the best of ideas.'

Zoe stared at an ink stain on her desk, hardly trusting herself to speak. Then she looked him in the eye and said, 'All the same, Walter, you should realise that I'm not leaving.'

His mister-nice-guy approach having failed, Walter stood up and flounced out. The trembling in Zoe's legs when she got up a few seconds later forced her to admit how upsetting this latest spat had been, and when she passed Paul's consulting room she briefly considered confiding in him about Walter's hostility. *But what good would that do?* The men had worked together for eight years, they were partners. She was only the hired help. During her interview, Paul had mentioned a partnership 'further on down the line', but she realised now this was never going to happen. *Maybe Walter was right, and she should think about moving on.*

Paul's voice rang out. 'Leaving without saying goodbye?'

Zoe stopped in her tracks. 'Sorry. I was miles away.'

'Can I have a quick word?'

117

Oh shit, Walter's already given his version of their encounter. 'Of course.'

'It's naughty of me to hinder you like this,' Paul said. 'You must want to get away. But I'm curious to hear how you found Gregor Baird.'

Zoe sat down. 'He's having trouble sleeping.'

'That's hardly surprising. What did you think of him?'

'Margaret forewarned me about the bewitching effect he has on women, but I must be immune to it. Although my reaction to him could be tainted by the possibility that he's a double murderer.'

'If he's not, it's a terrible thing to be suspected of,' Paul said. 'I hope the police sort the matter out soon.'

'How well do you know him?'

'Hardly at all, although I knew his mother very well. I diagnosed her final illness and did my best to keep her comfortable through it. Lovely woman. An excellent cook.'

'So I hear.'

'But Gregor? You know what young men are like – they'd do anything rather than consult a doctor.'

They exchanged looks of frustration, after which Paul apologised again for keeping Zoe back and wished her a good afternoon.

She got up, relieved that was all he wanted, then sat back down again. 'Paul, can I ask your advice?'

'Of course.'

'This is about Gregor too. I've noticed something in his records that could mean he's been lying to the police.'

Zoe slid her copy of the form about Gregor's sprained ankle across Paul's desk. He read it and looked up, obviously puzzled. Zoe pointed out the address of the hospital then told him about her patient's insistence that he was not in touch with his step-sister, who lived in the same city.

118

'He may be telling the truth,' Paul said.

'I know.'

'But you want to tell the police about your suspicions?'

'What do you think?'

'I think, Zoe, that you should remember the GMC's guidelines. Confidentiality is central to the trust between doctors and patients. Without it, they won't seek our care. If you find something too difficult to deal with, confide in me or Walter. But share nothing with anyone outwith the practice.'

'You're telling me to leave it?' His response was disappointing, though not surprising.

'Even if you're right and he was lying, it isn't anywhere near being proof that Gregor killed anyone, is it?'

'No, but –'

'And he could simply have been in Newcastle and not seen Alice.'

Paul was talking sense, and if anyone had come to Zoe with the question she would have given them the same answer. But he hadn't spoken to Gregor, hadn't seen the man's unease. Gregor had lied to her, she knew it.

'You look frustrated, Zoe. Patient confidentiality can be such a burden. At the moment I'm struggling with a patient who's desperate to get pregnant. What she doesn't know is her husband had a vasectomy before they met, but I'm not allowed to disclose this. All I can do is try to persuade him to be honest with her.'

'I don't envy you that one.'

'Anyway,' Paul said, in the tone of someone wanting to get back to work, 'I expect the police won't simply go on what Gregor tells them.'

'You're right. So they won't need my information.' Zoe stood up to leave. She knew how much scrutiny Mather and his team would be putting Gregor under, but that wasn't the point. If she could help speed up their

---

119

investigation it was surely her duty to do so. Or was she motivated by a far less honourable sentiment, such as the antipathy she felt towards him?

'It'll come right in the end, my dear, you'll see,' Paul called after her as she left his room.

Even accompanying Roger Daltry in a loud rendition of 'Can't Explain' failed to stop Zoe brooding as she drove the short distance home. Regardless of what she had inferred from his medical records, it was hardly plausible that Gregor had conspired with Alice to kill their respective parents. Although, as Kate pointed out, once you accept the reality of a murderer in your community, anything else must be regarded as possible.

She puzzled over what motive the pair would have had. Horseshoe Cottage might fetch more than Jimmy paid for it, but that still would not be a great deal by today's standards. Of course, matters could be complicated by Jimmy dying so soon after the death of his wife, but a lot depended on whether they had left wills. *And what if Jimmy had formally adopted Alice?*

Zoe braked sharply. She had nearly missed her turning.

SIXTEEN

That afternoon, Zoe was pleased to see a yellow van parked outside the coach house when she and Mac arrived there on foot. The feeling did not last long. She discovered the van had a solitary occupant: Gerry Hall, champing on a sausage roll and reading *The Daily Record*.

Zoe rapped on the side window and Gerry looked up, startled. He thrust his half-eaten lunch back in its paper bag and tossed the newspaper on to the empty passenger seat before opening his door.

'I've been to check on progress, Doctor, and left you a note. Aye, a note.' He pointed towards the coach house.

'And what does it say, this note?' Zoe spoke in as pleasant a voice as she could muster. It was her own fault, after all. Gerry's habitually gloomy expression belied the optimistic messages he kept on delivering. She should have questioned before now his assertion that the work would take no more than eight weeks.

'I ken you're no happy with how we're getting on. We're right busy now, but I'm taking them off other jobs to finish yours. The men'll be here tomorrow. Aye, tomorrow.'

'How do I know they'll finish my job this time?'

He looked affronted. 'You have my word. As I promised that boyfriend of yours –'

'Who?'

'My good friend Neil. As I promised him, we'll no

121

stop until we're done. You'll be in for Christmas. Aye, Christmas.'

A little later, as Zoe walked up the drive to Larimer Hall, she absentmindedly tugged at Mac's lead every time he tried to follow a promising new scent. *How should she react when she caught up with Neil?* Her indignation in The Rocket last night had dwindled to the amused exasperation she seemed destined to feel towards him, no matter how badly he behaved. And she supposed she should be grateful for his apparently successful intervention on her behalf with Gerry Hall, although the appreciation she felt was tempered by concern about how it had been achieved. The last thing she wanted was to be portrayed as a feeble woman dependent on her man to get things done. *Not that Neil would admit to using such a tactic.* She could imagine his indignant expression if she dared suggest it.

Relying on the bell in the workshop to announce her arrival, she opened the front door and waited in the hall for someone to appear.

The disappointment which flared up when she saw Peter was reflected in his manner towards her. After a brief glance he turned his attention to Mac. 'Hello, boy. How are you after our little accident?'

'He's fine, thanks,' Zoe said. 'His leg was a bit stiff the morning after, but that soon passed.'

'Good, I'm glad.'

Zoe waited for him to say more. When he didn't, she asked, 'Is Neil in?'

'No, he's gone to see a customer.'

'Will he be long?'

'Shouldn't be.'

'Can I come in and wait?'

'If you want.'

Zoe followed Peter down to the kitchen, where Bert and Tom were out of their basket, batting a scrap of paper between them in the half-hearted manner of bored teenagers playing football in the street. When Mac approached them, tail wagging and eager to join in, the cats seemed relieved to have an excuse to stop and jumped in unison onto the windowsill.

'Tea?' Peter asked, approaching the Aga.

'Yes please.'

'Did you walk?'

'Yes.'

'Snow's all cleared now, at least.'

'Thank goodness.' Struggling to find something to talk about, Zoe told him about her mishap in the snow on Saturday afternoon. 'I'm beginning to think there's something in Kate's suggestion that I replace my car with a four-wheel drive'.

Peter's smile reminded Zoe how much he resembled his brother. 'Wait and see what the rest of the winter has in store,' he said. 'Whatever folk might tell you, snow like that is usually short-lived. I can only remember a couple of times when it lasted more than a day.'

He passed Zoe a mug of tea and pushed a newspaper across the table towards her. 'I must get back to work.' Having discharged his responsibilities as host, he disappeared into the workshop, shutting the door behind him.

Zoe glanced at the paper's front page then started to flick through it. She stopped at page five, her attention grabbed by the headline 'Borders body in bonfire: Another death'. A small photograph, obviously taken with a mobile phone, of Westerlea's Guy Fawkes bonfire lighting up the evening sky, was next to a larger, more professional image of a young blonde. The caption read, 'Alice Watson, daughter of the first victim'. For some reason, Zoe was surprised Tom's ex-wife had kept her married name.

The article told her little she did not already know. It scrupulously pointed out that the cause of Jimmy Baird's death was as yet unconfirmed, while still implying that with one murder in the family it was only a matter of time before this second death would be upgraded to the same status. Possessing little in the way of new facts to give its readers, the newspaper relied instead on the human interest aspects of the story. The interview with Alice was billed as an exclusive, a reporter and a photographer having been dispatched to Newcastle to record her feelings.

Alice could not shed light on who might have wanted to kill her mother, because she was 'such a good person, always helping others'. She suggested Chrissie may have been killed for the money she had collected selling poppies, a simplistic theory Zoe considered more suited to an inner-city, drugs-related crime. The journalist described Alice as being 'devastated at the loss of the woman who was her best friend'. The twins were not mentioned.

On the subject of her step-father, Alice was less emotional. 'Why would anyone want to kill him? He was just an old man.' She revealed the dog which died with Jimmy had been his sixth Jack Russell terrier, all named after whisky distilleries. When asked about her step-brother, she responded, 'We haven't spoken for ages'.

Weren't those the exact words Gregor had used in Zoe's consulting room a few hours earlier?

Zoe sighed, once more feeling the burden of knowledge she could not share.

'You sound like you need cheering up, and I know just the man for the job,' a voice said behind her.

Zoe jumped, knocking over the remains of her tea. Neil grabbed a tea towel hanging on the Aga's front rail and wiped the table, pausing for an instant as his eyes scanned the open newspaper.

'All gone,' he said.

There was a brief silence.

'Sorry if I pissed you off on Sunday night.'

'I shouldn't have left in a huff,' Zoe said. 'Though you're right, you did piss me off.'

124

'I was worried about you.'

'Why?'

'I heard about you crashing your car and wanted to make sure you weren't hurt.'

'As I keep telling people, it hardly qualified as a crash. I slid, very slowly, into a gatepost, that's all.'

'How was I supposed to know, when you didn't tell me yourself?'

'Make me another cup of tea and let's say no more about it.'

Neil put the kettle on the Aga. 'So what brings you here, apart from the opportunity to scold me again?'

'I was at the coach house. It seems as though you've done me a favour. Aye, a favour.'

Neil laughed. 'You've seen Gerry.'

'Oh yes.'

'And?'

'It seems that giving folk the impression you and I are romantically involved is the key to getting things done around here.'

'So he's putting his men back on your job?'

'Not only that. He's promised to take them off all their other jobs to be sure the coach house is ready for me to move into by Christmas.'

'You'll be pleased at that news.'

'I'm glad he's at last going to do what he should have done all along. But on the other hand . . .'

'What's wrong now?'

'I can't say I'm happy you used our relationship to persuade him to do it.'

'So now you're admitting we have a relationship?' Neil wore a broad grin as he lifted the kettle and poured boiling water into their mugs. 'In which case, will you give me your mobile number?'

'It's no good trying to change the subject.'

'What do you want me to say? You asked me to intervene with Gerry and I did.'

'Okay. Thank you.' Determined today's encounter would not end in a row, Zoe pointed at the newspaper on the table. 'Have you seen this? It's an interview with a friend of yours.'

'She's no friend of mine.'

'Sounds like she wanted to be.'

'Alice was looking for a way out of her marriage to Tom. She mistakenly thought I was it.'

'You weren't interested?'

'She's just a lass. That may be some men's idea of heaven, but not mine.'

'She's very attractive.' Zoe tapped her finger on the photograph.

Neil glanced down at it. 'They must have paid her to smile. In the flesh she's as hard as nails, with a face to match.'

'That's unkind.'

'True, though. She wouldn't take no for an answer. For a while I couldn't get away from her, she turned up all over the place.'

'Poor Tom.'

'He's a bit of a wimp if you ask me. Must have known what she was up to. And that mother of hers encouraged it.'

'In what way?'

'She made out Jimmy was going to treat her to a new kitchen at Horseshoe Cottage. I must have gone there three times at least, to measure up and talk about what they wanted. Alice was there every time, and they always made sure I ended up alone with her.'

'I can't picture you being unwillingly pursued by a woman.'

'Believe me, I was.'

'How did it end? Did she eventually lose interest?'

'Not before I had it out with Chrissie. The last time she rang me demanding yet another visit, I asked if Alice would be there. When she said, "If you want her to be", I told her in no uncertain terms that I didn't and I'd be happy never to see either of them again. She put the phone down on me.'

'And that was it?'

'Not likely. She spread a rumour that I'd planned to rip Jimmy off by designing a kitchen way more expensive than he could afford and bullying him into ordering it.'

'That's awful,' Zoe said. *Maybe Kate was right in her condemnation of the dead woman.* 'I didn't realise Chrissie was so ruthless.'

'When it came to Alice she was. They say she only married Jimmy to provide a home for the girl.'

'Had she been married before?'

'No one knows. From what I hear – it was before my time – she got a job in the pub and was soon running it and Jimmy's life.'

'Who do you think killed her, Neil?'

'Don't know, don't care. Let's change the subject. Does this relationship of ours stretch to going out for dinner?'

Zoe studied the man sitting next to her. The more time she spent with him, the harder it was to deny the warmth she was starting to feel towards him. Giving him any encouragement was a bad idea, but after the events of the past week, she deserved a night out. 'Maybe. When?'

'Saturday week? I'd prefer it sooner but I've got something on this weekend.'

'Where do you want to go?'

'A mate of mine runs a restaurant in Kelso. You haven't lived until you've tasted his haggis and mozzarella filo parcels.'

Zoe groaned. 'I was looking forward to it until you told me that.'

On the way home a short time later, while glancing at her mobile for texts from Kate, Zoe realised she had forgotten to give Neil the number. At least that reduced the chances of them falling out again before their date.

The cottage phone started to ring as she walked in the door, someone calling from Hawick with a message from Mather. He was in the area tomorrow and would like to call round to see her. Would ten o'clock be convenient?

He'd never made an appointment before.

SEVENTEEN

Mather arrived ten minutes early the next morning, making Zoe wish she had waited until later to prepare her weekly batch of bread. Her heart sank further when she opened the door and saw his spotless navy blue suit. He could not have worn a better flour magnet.

She sat him down at the far end of the kitchen table. 'You don't mind if I work on this while we talk, do you?' she asked, plunging her hands back into the dough. 'I've got to go out as soon as we're finished. It's my first appointment with my new dentist and it would be a professional discourtesy to be late.'

'I won't keep you long. I'm due to see someone in Duns later, which is why I thought I would call in rather than telephone.' Mather smoothed down his expensive-looking paisley tie. 'This is the first time I've found you here alone.'

He sounded disappointed.

'I haven't heard from Kate. But there's no guarantee she won't just turn up.'

'You're obviously good friends.'

'Yes. She's really helped me settle in.' Zoe reached for more flour.

'Her family's lived in this part of the Borders for a long time.'

'Even if she was new to the area herself, Kate would do her best to make me feel at home. She's that sort of person, isn't she?'

129

Mather made no comment. Zoe pummelled her dough.

'Anyway,' she said, 'I'm sure you didn't come here to discuss my friends. What can I do for you?'

'Now you've had time to think, can you remember seeing anyone else on Saturday morning during your walk?'

'Near where I saw Jimmy Baird, you mean?'

'Anywhere along your route.'

'I've gone over it in my head so many times, but I'm still certain there wasn't a soul around. And the only vehicle I saw was the Andersons' Volvo.'

'That's the main reason I'm here. Mr and Mrs Anderson are both adamant it couldn't have been their car because Mrs Anderson travelled to Kelso that morning. Is there any chance you made a mistake?'

'Over the letters on its plate? Definitely not. LTM was my mother's initials.'

'Could it have been another dark colour – black or green perhaps? You said it was travelling fast and your eyes were drawn to its number plate.'

'I don't think so. Perhaps Hazel's lying. To her husband as well as you.'

'Do you have any reason to believe she'd do that?'

'Their relationship definitely seems strained. I overheard them arguing in the kitchen on Sunday night, then my asking about their car seemed to spark off an even bigger row. Whatever it was about, Hazel drove off, despite knowing people like you and your mother were coming for a meal.'

While Mather considered this, Zoe concentrated on shaping the bread into a ball. Then she transferred it into a greased bowl and covered it with a clean tea towel. The woodburner kept the sitting room at a perfect temperature for dough to rise. It would be ready for a final kneading by the time she returned from the dentist.

The policeman took her by surprise with an

abrupt change of subject. 'There was an animal in the bonfire too. A sheep. Its flesh burned away completely, but we found bones and they've been identified. You've no idea who may have put it there, I suppose?'

'None at all,' Zoe said, running her hands under the tap. 'Is it important?'

'Probably not.'

Another pause. Zoe looked at the clock. She would have to leave soon to keep her appointment. First, though, she had some questions of her own. Mather would probably refuse to answer them, but it was worth a try.

'Have you had the results of Jimmy's post mortem?' she asked.

Mather thought for a moment, then lifted his briefcase onto the table, popped the locks and took out a sheet of paper. 'This is the summary. Your practice will be sent a copy of the full report eventually. It must stay confidential at this stage.'

'Of course.' Zoe took the sheet, studied the close type, then gave it back to Mather. He blew gently to dislodge the floury deposit she had left on it before returning it to his case.

'So the head wound I saw was the result of him falling against the bridge, rather than being hit by something,' Zoe said.

'That's one of the conclusions. The internal damage on the opposite side of the head to the impact –'

'It's called contra coup.'

Mather smiled briefly, acknowledging her familiarity with the term. 'The contra coup injury tells us that it was Mr Baird's head which was moving, not what it came into contact with. The question to be answered is why he fell in the first place.'

'You haven't ruled out someone pushing him?'

'Without a witness or a confession we have no way of knowing if that's what happened. As you've read, there was water in his lungs, so the fall didn't kill him. He drowned. As did his Jack Russell.'

Zoe shuddered, remembering the dog lying dead on the bank. 'You got a post mortem done on Talisker too?'

'It's called a necropsy.' Mather allowed himself another brief smile. 'According to the vet.'

Touché.

'If Jimmy was pushed, do you think it was by the same person who put Chrissie into the bonfire?'

'That's what I'm trying to find out.'

'May I see her post mortem results too?'

'No.'

'Kate's not here now and I'm a doctor. Can't you at least tell me how she died?'

The policeman frowned. Zoe interpreted this as meaning he had lost patience with her incessant probing, but then he said, 'It's important her injuries don't become public knowledge at this stage of our enquiry.'

'I won't share anything you tell me in confidence. Not even with Kate.'

'Especially not with Kate, I hope,' Mather said. 'Mrs Baird suffered a head wound, and then she was strangled.'

Zoe gasped. 'He certainly wanted to make sure she was dead.'

'That's one interpretation.'

'Was it manual strangulation or done with some sort of ligature?'

'That's less easy to determine.'

The tone of Mather's voice warned Zoe off trying to find out more. However, emboldened by his relative candour so far, she asked, 'Had the Bairds written wills?'

'Why do you want to know?'

'I'm curious.'

Mather stared at her. 'I think it's more than that.'

'Honestly, it's not.'

'All I can say is that Mrs Baird, being much

younger than her husband, would have expected him to predecease her.' He was clearly choosing his words even more carefully than usual.

'So Jimmy left a will but Chrissie didn't?'

'This isn't a game, Doctor Moreland. Someone in this community has killed once, maybe twice, and could be planning to do so again. We need to find him.'

Zoe glanced at the kitchen clock.

Mather rose from his chair, brushing specks of flour from the undersides of his sleeves. 'You have somewhere to go and so do I.'

On the doorstep, he repeated, 'We need to find him,' then turned to walk towards the road.

A few minutes later, Zoe swept some fallen leaves from her car's bonnet and slid into the driver's seat. As she emerged from the gateway and checked in each direction for other vehicles she saw Mather parked up a short distance away, talking on his mobile. She hoped she wasn't the subject of that conversation.

She had not travelled far when his blue saloon appeared in her rear view mirror. Zoe frowned. Sixty was perfectly safe for this stretch of road, but being followed by a policeman would make anyone nervous. Trying to forget the vehicle behind, she concentrated on enjoying the drive. Led Zeppelin had come on as soon as she started the engine; she turned up the volume.

As Robert Plant told her there was still time to change the road she was on, she sensed something wasn't right. Her car failed to respond to a light touch of the brakes as it started to descend the hill past Billiewick Farm. A harder push had no effect either.

Unchecked, the car gathered speed. Glancing in her mirror, Zoe saw the distance between herself and Mather become larger as he slowed in anticipation of the corner coming up and she didn't. She pumped at the brake pedal. Still no response.

She had only two options: try to take the corner

and probably end up overturned or embedded in a tree, or aim for the narrow entrance to a stubble field that lay ahead. At this speed, the second alternative would be a bumpy ride, but it offered a better chance of coming out unscathed.

The road took a sharp right. Zoe's car travelled straight on.

It screeched against the hedge. Grated along the uneven ground. Plunged into deep tractor tracks. Lurched violently from side to side.

The steering wheel wrenched itself from Zoe's grasp. Her handbag flew off the passenger seat on to the floor.

Just as the car felt like it was going to tip over completely, the ride became much smoother. Suddenly aware she was holding her breath, Zoe exhaled deeply. The car was still travelling at high speed but this field must be longer than the distance it could coast.

Then she saw what lay ahead.

A plough. And she was hurtling towards it.

Zoe grabbed the steering wheel. It felt slack. However much she turned it, she could make no difference to the car's course.

She pumped the brake pedal again. Still useless.

Robert Plant's vocals were replaced by Jimmy Page's guitar solo. That huge and shiny plough, the low sun bouncing off its metal curves, was much closer now.

At the last minute, the field's uneven surface made the car veer to the right, preventing it from hitting the plough head-on. Even so, blades designed to cut through the hardest soil ripped open the passenger side with the sound of a giant metal zip.

The vehicle juddered to a halt.

Zoe's chest took the full impact of her exploding airbag.

EIGHTEEN

Mather flung open the car door, leaned in and switched off the ignition.

'Smoke,' Zoe whispered.

'Don't worry, it's talcum powder from the airbag.'

She tried shifting her legs slightly. They obeyed the command, a good sign.

'Need to move my head.' *Not so good.* A wave of nausea swept over her.

'Zoe, you must stay still. Help's on its way.'

He had never used her first name before.

Pain spread up from her ribs to her shoulders. Her head was thumping too, and she felt very sick now. *Was she going to vomit all over his lovely shoes?*

'Brakes failed. Couldn't stop.'

'There's no need to talk. I saw it happen.'

'Steering went too.'

She managed not to throw up until she was in the ambulance.

Kate insisted on Zoe taking her arm as they made their way slowly to the hospital car park.

'You can't imagine how I felt when I opened the door and there he was. Straightaway I could tell something awful had happened, from the look on his face. My first thought was the bairns, or Mum and Dad.'

At any other time, Zoe would have joked what a relief it must have been for Kate to learn it was only her friend who had met with an accident. But she felt light-headed and shaky, and the painkiller she had taken was only just starting to make a difference. Despite no bones being broken, her body ached as if a large, angry person wearing hobnail boots had knocked her down and kicked her repeatedly in the ribs.

'I don't know what happened. I'm sure I wasn't driving too fast.'

'Try not to think about it.'

Kate drove even more slowly than usual, because Zoe could not do up her seat belt. A yeasty smell hit them as soon as they walked into Keeper's Cottage, and once Kate had settled Zoe into her chair, she retrieved the bowl of shrivelled bread dough from the bookcase and carried it away. Then she relit the log burner and took Mac for a short walk.

Zoe had not realised she was dozing until her friend's voice made her start.

'Do you want me to fix you some food?'

'Thanks, but I couldn't eat a thing.'

'Is it very painful? They should have kept you in overnight.'

'I'm fine, really. It's shock more than anything. I might have a nap when you've gone.'

'I'll come back later.'

'You've got three children to care for. You don't need me as well.'

'Shut up. You're my friend. Okay?'

'Okay. Take the spare key so you can let yourself in. It's hung up by the front door.'

Although she only expected to doze, Zoe slept until a little after six, when she was roused by Mac's barking.

Kate poked her head round the door. 'Have you slept?'

'Ever since you left.'

'Sorry, did we wake you?'

Zoe shifted cautiously in her chair and winced. The painkiller was wearing off. '"We"?' she asked.

Kate still didn't come into the room. 'Are you feeling any better?'

'Who's with you?'

Kate opened the door to reveal a sheepish-looking Neil holding two shopping bags.

'I'm here to make sure you don't shout at him,' Kate said.

'I couldn't, even if I wanted to.'

Leaving the bags in the hall, Neil came over and knelt down next to Zoe's chair. He looked gravely into her eyes. 'I've come to take care of you, and for once you can't say you don't need it.'

Zoe gestured at him to stand up, then pointed to the woodburner. 'That needs stoking, and perhaps you could bring in more wood.'

Neil stood and saluted. 'Yes ma'am. Leave it to me.'

Zoe pushed herself to her feet and groaned. 'There are some things I have to do for myself.'

From the bathroom she could hear other people getting on with her life: boiling her kettle, pulling her curtains and letting her dog out into the garden. She glanced into the mirror above the sink and let out another groan. Not even Neil could find that grey face surrounded by clumps of hair attractive. Lifting her arm to remove the scrunchie, brush her hair and then tie it up again was painful. It didn't do much to improve her appearance either.

By the time she returned to the sitting room, a small table had been placed next to her chair on which a mug of tea, a glass of water and the bottle of painkillers from the hospital waited for her. The room felt warm and someone had even plumped up her cushions.

Kate came in as Zoe was easing herself down into the armchair. 'I must go home now. I'll come round tomorrow morning after I've got the bairns off to school.'

Out in the hall, Neil and Kate spoke too quietly for Zoe to hear what was being said. Then the front door banged and he carried in his shopping bags and put them down in front of her.

'I didn't think you'd be up to eating much, so I've come prepared to make my speciality, roasted tomato soup.' He brought out two packs of tomatoes, a head of garlic and, with a flourish, a bunch of fresh basil. 'I can't believe Lisa and Brian can still get this in November. It makes all the difference. I assumed you'd have olive oil.'

Delving deeper into the bag, he produced a bottle of Merlot, a ciabatta loaf and two wedges of passion cake. 'I asked Lisa what I could buy you as a treat and she told me this is your favourite.'

'I can't drink wine,' Zoe said, holding up her medication.

'It's for me. This is for you.' A container of fresh orange juice appeared.

'What's in the second bag?'

'I noticed the other night that you've got a DVD player.'

'It comes with the house,' Zoe said. 'I've never actually used it.'

'Luckily I'm the owner of what is probably the best collection of films in the Borders.' Neil put the bag gently on her lap. 'Here's some for you to choose from while I put the tomatoes into the oven.'

When he came back a few minutes later, Zoe held up *Fargo*. 'This looks interesting.'

'Have you never seen it?'

'I don't watch many films.'

'Are you sure you wouldn't prefer something lighter? How about *Animal House*? It's one of the funniest films ever made.'

'They don't call comedies rib-tickling for nothing. It'll hurt me to watch if it's that funny.'

Neil's shoulders slumped. 'Sorry, I never thought.'

'Another time, perhaps.'

'So what happened?' He sat back and took a sip from his glass of wine. 'Kate only told me that you'd run your car off the road on the way to the dentist. Which is going to ridiculous lengths to avoid a filling.'

'It ran itself off. The brakes failed just after Billiewick.'

He gave a low whistle. 'You'd've picked up a fair speed coming down that hill. What did you do?'

'What could I do? There was an opening into a field directly ahead, so I aimed for that. I could never have made it round the corner.'

'Kate said you hit a plough.'

'It was parked in the field. I'd slowed down by the time I reached it, but was still travelling fast enough for my poor car to be a write-off.'

He reached over, grasped her hand and squeezed it. 'You could have been too.'

'I'm trying not to think about it.'

'You can't blame me for being upset. After all, how can I marry you if you're dead?'

Zoe tried to cross her legs. Even that hurt. 'Why is it that whenever you're here you insist on saying you're going to marry me?'

'Because I am.'

'If you keep this up, I shall have to ask you to leave. However good your roasted tomato soup is.'

'Okay, you win. For now. Never let it be said I'd take advantage of a lady in a weakened state.' Neil sipped his wine. 'So how come that policeman was first on the scene?'

'He'd been here asking me some more questions.'

'Are they any nearer to finding out who killed Chrissie?'

'I don't think so. We mainly talked about what happened to Jimmy.'

'Wasn't that an accident?'

'There's no proof one way or the other.'

'So why did Mather need to see you again?'

'He wanted to check if I was sure about the car I'd seen by the water meadow that morning. The owner reckons she was nowhere near there.'

'Does this owner have a name?'

Zoe said nothing.

Neil let out an exaggerated sigh. 'You're still so guarded. Even now, when you're drugged up to the eyeballs.' He rose to put another log in the woodburner and remained standing. 'Did a liquidiser come with the house too?'

'It's in the drawer next to the cooker,' Zoe said. 'And please don't be annoyed. I'm a doctor, I can't tell you everything.'

'I understand that, but there are some things you can share. It's as though the habit of keeping your patients' secrets has bled into the rest of your life.'

'We're talking about one, possibly two murders. It's a serious business.'

'You think I don't realise that?' Neil moved towards the door.

Zoe got out of her chair as fast as she could, crossed the room and put a hand out to him. 'Despite what happened earlier, I'm enjoying this evening with you. Let's not spoil it.'

Neil led her back to her chair. 'And I'm enjoying being here. Sorry the food's taking so long.'

'I'm sure it'll be worth the wait.'

'It will, I promise. Are you warm enough?'

'You'll be spreading a blanket over my knees next. Please don't treat me like an invalid.'

'I'm not. But your stove isn't drawing very well.' Neil bent down, grasped a handle on the side of the woodburner and moved it a few times. They both watched a small flame flicker behind the sooty glass then

———

disappear. 'I think the chimney needs sweeping.'

'I'll call Tom tomorrow.'

'You know him, do you?'

'He's Kate's cousin. And his girlfriend Jean works at the health centre.'

'Oh yeah, silly me. Everybody knows everybody around here.'

They ate off trays on their laps, Zoe with her feet raised on a pile of books Neil took down from the bookcase. She was surprised how hungry she felt, then remembered her last meal had been breakfast some twelve hours earlier. Relieved her enthusiasm could be genuine, she congratulated Neil on his soup.

'You should see me bake a cake,' he replied.

'I'll look forward to that.'

After clearing the trays away, Neil manoeuvred their chairs into a better position to see the television. He found the DVD player's remote control among a pile of magazines and put on *Fargo*, then sat down, his knee just touching Zoe's.

The film was punctuated by Neil asking Zoe if she needed anything, sharing snippets of information about the actors and directors, and alerting her to 'a good bit coming up now'. When it ended, she could truthfully say she had enjoyed it, although she had been mystified by Neil's laughter at certain scenes.

'You'll love it when you've seen it a few times,' he said.

'I don't think I've ever watched a film more than once. Knowing what's going to happen takes all the fun out of it.'

'No, that's where you're wrong. The anticipation of a good scene or a really clever line adds to the enjoyment. I've got films I watch regularly, and I never grow bored with them.'

Zoe remained unconvinced, but Neil vowed to

introduce her to more of his favourites, comparing the appreciation of a good movie to educating the palate to enjoy fine wine. She laughed at him, then hugged herself, grimacing. It was after ten and despite her long afternoon snooze she felt exhausted again.

Neil leant over and gently pushed away a strand of hair which hung across her face.

'I'm going to put you to bed. You look terrible.'

'Thanks. Just what I needed to hear.'

'You know what I mean. It doesn't matter to me what you look like.'

Zoe pointed at the empty wine bottle. 'You're well over the limit to drive home.'

'It's not far. I won't get caught.'

'That isn't the point.'

Neil looked around the room. 'I'd sleep on the sofa, but you haven't got one.'

NINETEEN

As she came to, Zoe was conscious of pain throughout her body, someone in bed next to her, and whines coming from the other side of the bedroom door.

'Your dog needs oiling.'

The room was still in darkness, so she could only see the outline of Neil's head against the pillow. 'This is usually his bed too.'

'I could tell that from the dirty look he gave me when I shut the door in his face last night.' Neil put on the bedside lamp and gazed at her. 'Why do women look so gorgeous first thing in the morning? All rumpled and bleary-eyed, but even lovelier than when they went to bed the night before.'

'You've seen a lot of women first thing, have you?'

'Given that I'm nearly forty, wouldn't you be worried if I hadn't?'

Zoe tried to raise herself into a sitting position while thinking of a suitable retort, but the pain which clenched her ribcage forced her to lie back with a groan.

Neil sat up, his shirt flapping open to reveal more chest hair than she would have expected.

'I'll fetch you a glass of water and your painkillers, then I'll make us some tea.'

'Thanks.'

'Can I ask one tiny thing?'

'What?'

'Would you mind if I put on your bathrobe?'

A few minutes later they were sitting up in bed drinking tea, Zoe propped up by both her own pillows and one of Neil's. Mac had reclaimed his rightful position and lay bolster-fashion between them. Neil still wore the turquoise towelling robe.

Pushing her hair out of her face, Zoe realised something was missing. 'My scrunchie's fallen off in the bed.'

'What the hell's a scrunchie?' Neil asked.

'The thing I tie my hair up with. I forgot to take it off last night '

'I thought you used a rubber band.'

'They cause split ends.'

He ran a hand over his head. 'I'll try to remember that.'

Zoe laughed then grimaced with pain. 'When did you start to lose your hair?'

'Are you suggesting I'm bald?'

'Aren't you?'

'It began to recede once I hit thirty, but no, this isn't my natural look. I thought you knew.'

'How would I?'

'Can't you tell it's starting to grow? Here, feel.' He lifted her hand and guided it to his head. Rather than polished and smooth as she expected, it felt slightly rough, like velvet.

'A few years ago I was sponsored to shave it all off for Comic Relief. Raised quite a bit of money, too. I kept it like this because everyone said it suited me.'

'It does. I can't imagine you any other way.'

'I'll grow it back again if you ask.'

'Don't be silly.'

Neil lifted a lock of Zoe's hair and held it up to the light. 'You have beautiful hair. Why do you tie it back all the time?'

'It gets in the way if I don't.'

'So few women have long hair these days. Even

the ones in James Bond films. It's a pity.'

'When I was a child I could sit on mine. My mother wore hers long too. We used to brush each other's every morning.'

Neil got out of bed and padded over to the dressing table, returning a few seconds later. 'May I?' he asked, holding up Zoe's hairbrush.

'If it doesn't hurt me too much to lean forward.'

Self-conscious at the start, Zoe began to relax as he ran the brush gently through her hair. It was, she realised, the most intimate act she had shared with a man for some time.

'This'll be something to tell our grandchildren about,' Neil said as he returned the brush to the dressing table.

'What will?'

'Our first night together. Nothing physical happens due to Granny's injuries, and Grandpa ends up wearing her bathrobe.'

Zoe laughed then clutched at her ribs. 'Ouch.'

'Still hurting?'

'The pills are beginning to kick in, but today will probably be the most painful.'

'You're not planning to go into work, I hope.'

'I wasn't due to anyway.'

'Will you be okay here on your own? I need to go home soon. Pete'll be wondering where I am.'

'Didn't you tell him?'

'He was out when I left.'

'You never did say how you found out about my accident.'

'You never asked.'

'Don't be irritating, Neil.'

'Promise not to be annoyed with Kate. Look how well it turned out.'

'You mean she came and told you?'

'Admit it, aren't you glad she did?'

Zoe paused for a moment then smiled. 'All right, you win – I am glad. You've cared for me brilliantly. The soup and cake were exactly what I needed and the film was, well, interesting.'

Neil looked worried. 'You must have sustained a head injury they didn't spot at the hospital. You're being nice to me.'

'Idiot. When do you have to go?'

'Trying to get rid of me now, are you?'

'No. But I was wondering if you'd take Mac out for a quick walk.'

Mac jumped off the bed the moment he heard his favourite word, trampling over Neil in the process.

'You did that on purpose.' Neil took off her robe and walked to the wicker chair where he had draped his clothes. Last night, once they agreed he would stay, he courteously waited outside the bedroom, giving Zoe time to put on her pyjamas and get into bed. She was already dropping off to sleep by the time he slid in beside her. The last thing she remembered was a kiss on her cheek and a whispered, 'Goodnight'.

Now, though, she was awake and able to appreciate the sight of Neil's neat backside in close-fitting underwear and his muscular legs. When he turned round she could see the slight paunch which testified to his preference for red wine over white, but the overall effect was pleasing.

'You're staring at me,' he said, making no move to pull on his jeans.

'You don't strike me as being the shy type.'

'With these legs, why would I?'

A few minutes later, Mac cast a confused look at his owner but nonetheless followed Neil out of the room. Zoe listened for the sound of the back door closing, then got up slowly and went through to the warmth of the sitting room, glad the cottage had no stairs to negotiate. On her way, she switched on the immersion heater. She would feel a lot better after a bath.

As soon as man and dog returned, Mac wolfed down his breakfast while Neil made toast and another pot of tea.

'Have you fed the cat?' Zoe asked. 'She gets very grouchy if her food's not ready when she wants it.'

'I didn't know you owned a cat.'

'I don't. She comes with the house. Lives in the airing cupboard.'

Neil leapt from his chair. 'Shit,' he said, rushing out into the hall.

'Just kidding,' Zoe called after him. 'I opened the door when I saw you'd closed it. I don't think she even noticed she'd been shut in. And I've fed her.'

Neil sat down again and swallowed a mouthful of tea. 'What's her name?'

'She hasn't got one. As I said, she's not mine. Kate's brother forgot to tell me until after I agreed to rent this place that I'd be sharing it.'

'Was she left behind by a previous tenant?'

'No, they took her with them when they moved to Duns, but she kept on coming back. In the end, Douglas decided she could stay. She's no trouble, as long as I feed her.' Zoe pulled up her sleeve, revealing three parallel scratches on her right arm. 'And don't try to pick her up.'

Neil concentrated on eating, while Zoe toyed with a slice of toast, eventually returning most of it to her plate. *A treat for Mac later.*

Putting down his empty mug, Neil asked, 'What time do you want me here this afternoon?'

'Don't you have work to do?'

'Nothing that can't wait. You're my priority at the moment.'

'Kate will be here soon. Why don't you call me later and I can let you know how I'm doing.'

Neil agreed to this plan with the enthusiasm of a man who'd been told to get lost for a week. He took the breakfast things through to the kitchen and Zoe heard water running into the sink.

'You're treating me like an invalid again,' she called. 'Please leave me something to do.'

'If you insist.'

A few seconds later he returned with his jacket on and Zoe got up to see him out. He gently guided her back into the chair and kissed her fleetingly on the lips.

As soon as he was gone, the house felt empty. Zoe watched a little breakfast television without taking any of it in, then made her way to the bathroom. What she saw when she took off her pyjamas to get in the bath made her gasp. Although less than twenty-four hours had elapsed since her accident, bruising from the car's seatbelt was already a wide, purple slash across her chest. And while medication had lessened the pain to a dull, persistent throbbing, it could not remedy the turmoil in her mind.

No longer befuddled by shock, what she had accepted in the upheaval of the previous day to have been a frightening mishap began to take on a more sinister appearance. That sort of catastrophic failure, especially in a car less than a year old, did not simply happen. The significance of this, when it came, felt like a punch to her stomach.

She grabbed hold of the taps and pulled herself up with such haste that the water ebbed and flowed, splashing onto the floor. The room was so small she did not need to get out of the bath in order to vomit into the toilet.

Someone had tampered with her brakes.

TWENTY

Zoe heard Kate let herself into Keeper's Cottage. She carried a bulging Sainsbury's bag, and after a cheery greeting and an enquiry as to how Zoe was feeling, she went through to the kitchen, returning soon after with a cafetiere of fresh coffee. Reluctant to play the invalid but recognising, as she often told patients, that she should accept help when it was offered, Zoe let her friend fuss over her.

Once Kate had stoked up the woodburner, plugged in Zoe's mobile to charge, and produced a plateful of ginger biscuits, she sat down herself. 'So, what time did Neil go?'

'About eight-thirty.'

'He wasn't here long, then?'

Zoe bit her lip, not answering.

Kate stared at her. 'Or are we talking about eight-thirty this morning?'

'He'd drunk a whole bottle of wine. I couldn't let him drive.'

'I hope he was gentle with you.'

'Kate! For goodness sake, look at me. Would I have any use for a man in my bed except as a glorified hot water bottle?'

'What a disappointment for you both. Still, it should make things easier when the time comes.'

Zoe opened her mouth to argue that a physical relationship between herself and Neil wasn't inevitable, and shut it again when she realised she would be lying.

Kate grinned. 'You're starting to like him, aren't you?'

'Yes, I admit it, I am.' Zoe held her hands up in mock submission. 'It was lovely having someone to look after me last night, and he did it so well. He made me soup – from scratch, not out of a tin – and brought me my favourite sort of cake. And afterwards we watched a film.'

'I've heard he's a bit of a movie buff. He's got a whole library of them, apparently.'

'He's got a nice backside as well,' Zoe said.

Kate clapped her hands together noisily. 'Hurrah! It's great to hear you talk like that. How strong are those pills you're taking?'

Zoe chose to ignore her friend's gibe. 'Why, if he's such a good catch, hasn't he been snapped up already?'

'During all the time I've known him he's never seemed particularly interested in a serious relationship. Don't get me wrong - he's been out with lots of girls but never for very long. I've not known him be as persistent with anyone as he is with you.'

'So why me? Why now?'

'Could be he's never met the right woman before. Or are you worried he could be gay?'

'No, I'm pretty sure he's not gay.'

'Peter Pan?'

'Are you referring to his brother?'

'No. I mean perhaps Neil has Peter Pan syndrome – he doesn't want to grow up, accept responsibility, settle down. I've met a lot of men like that.' Kate paused then added, 'Stupid me, I even married one.'

'So you don't recommend them?'

'It depends what you want from a relationship. Peter Pans are fun, there's no arguing with that, but if you're looking for long-term commitment? Forget it.'

Zoe shifted in her chair, unable to get comfortable. *Was it time for another painkiller yet?*

'I'm sorry,' Kate said. 'Once more I'm being tactless, assuming your natural instinct would be "never again". But of course, what happened to you was completely different to my experience.'

'I'm not looking for another husband, if that's what you think.' Zoe sought a new direction for their conversation to take. 'But I may need another car. Do you know what's happened to mine?'

Kate's raised eyebrows showed this clumsy change of subject had not gone unnoticed. 'Erskine said he'd take care of it,' she said. 'I expect it's at some garage waiting for your insurance company to assess the damage.'

'I was lucky to get out alive, wasn't I?'

'And to have a policeman on the scene straightaway.'

Zoe took a deep breath. Which hurt. 'You know, I don't think it was an accident.' She regretted her words as soon as she said them. It was obvious from Kate's reaction that this possibility had not occurred to her.

'You don't really think that, do you?' Kate shook her head. 'No, you must be mistaken.'

'There's no other explanation. The car's a reliable make and less than a year old. The chances of its brakes spontaneously failing are like . . .' Zoe paused, searching for the right analogy, 'like you dropping dead tomorrow from a heart attack.'

'Are you saying someone tried to kill you?'

'Maybe not actually kill me. It would've been hard to predict the exact outcome. But at the very least they wanted to give me a scare.'

'Who would do such a thing?'

'You tell me.'

'If you're right, it must be connected with everything else that's been happening here.'

Zoe frowned. 'I knew you'd say that, but it makes no sense. I stumbled upon Chrissie's body and was there when they found Jimmy in the burn. Hardly cause for someone to make me their next victim.'

'Perhaps you'd better wait to hear what Erskine thinks. He's sure to have someone check over your car. It will have been an accident, you'll see.'

'Either way, I can look forward to another visit from him soon,' Zoe said. *Not a comforting thought.*

'I'm sorry, but I have to go.' Kate stood up and Mac immediately retook possession of his chair. 'Noah P Reece the Third emailed me yesterday to ask if I can get his family tree done in time for Christmas. I've warned him I may not be able to, but he's paying me extra to try.'

'I've taken up a lot of your time, haven't I?'

'That's what friends are for,' Kate said, gathering up their mugs and the empty cafetiere. 'Can I bring you something before I go?'

'No thanks. I think I'll sit here quietly and watch some undemanding daytime television.'

Half an hour of watching a programme about buying properties at auction then doing them up for a profit was all Zoe could tolerate. The pain in her ribs was becoming difficult to ignore, and her neck and shoulders had stiffened up too. She rose to fetch another tablet, dismayed she could only walk stooped over like an old lady with osteoporosis.

Mac growled. The threat wasn't immediate enough to make him jump off his chair, but he was warning Zoe to be on her guard.

'What's up, boy?' She listened and could now hear footsteps on the gravel outside. It was almost certainly Neil, taking no notice of what she'd asked him to do. *As usual.*

The footsteps continued. Whoever it was had bypassed the front door and was making for the rear of Keeper's Cottage.

TWENTY-ONE

Despite being neither big nor ferocious, Mac took his protection duties very seriously. As Zoe went to investigate the footsteps which she could now hear crunching in the gravel at the rear of the house, he rushed past her, stuck his head out of the cat-flap and barked loudly. Yet this demonstration of pugnacity was unmatched by his tail, which continued to wag amicably. Zoe took this to be a sign that her unexpected visitor was well-intentioned and opened the back door.

Lisa Humphreys held a large bunch of flowers and a small white box. Without a shop counter to take cover behind, she appeared even more slight and pale than usual, and chewed her lip in apprehension, as if knowingly delivering the wrong order to a hard-to-please customer.

'Doctor Moreland, I hope you don't mind me coming to see you.' The wispy voice was that of a girl half her age. She stared down at the ground.

'Of course not, although you don't find me at my best. Come in.'

'I've brought you carrot cake.' Still not making eye contact, Lisa put the box down next to the flowers on Zoe's draining board.

'Thank you, that's so kind. Would you like some tea or coffee?'

After winning the now familiar tussle over whether she was fit enough to undertake this simple task,

Zoe made two mugs of tea which she allowed Lisa to carry through to the sitting room. Lisa expressed shock and sympathy over the accident and Zoe responded graciously, although all she really wanted was to be left alone to take another painkiller.

The room fell silent, while a bird sang in the honeysuckle outside the window.

'I'm told you and Brian have done wonders with the shop.'

Lisa picked at a hangnail on her left thumb. 'It was a bit run-down when we took over.'

'I imagine it must be tricky sometimes, working and living together.'

'Oh no, we enjoy each other's company.'

'Have you been married long?'

'Before we came to Westerlea.' The thumb started to bleed, and Lisa wiped it on her jeans.

Zoe could not work out if the girl was merely shy or being evasive, and did not feel up to the effort of finding out. Even Kate would be hard pushed to make conversation with her. She was considering feigning the need to lie down in order to get rid of this uninvited visitor when Lisa stood up, her pallor now a chalky white and her lips blue.

'Can I use your bathroom?' She headed towards the hall without waiting for a reply.

Zoe had no time to give directions, but the slamming of a door signalled that Lisa had found her own way. The sound of retching shortly afterwards indicated she had got there just in time.

Trying to keep her back straight, Zoe carefully placed a log inside the woodburner. Unasked, Neil had filled the basket that morning but it was already getting low. She wondered when he would telephone, then silently scolded herself for the thought.

Lisa reappeared, a little colour in her cheeks now but her lips still blue. 'Sorry about that. I must go.'

'I think you should sit down for a few minutes. Make sure you've finished throwing up before you set off.'

Lisa sat on the edge of the chair, poised to flee at any time. She started to chew her lip again and her eyes shone with tears.

'What's the matter?' Zoe asked.

When the answer to her question finally came it was no surprise. This was a scenario which had played out in her consulting room many times over the years. Only the names and faces changed.

'I'm pregnant.'

'Does Brian know?'

'He guessed.'

'You mean you didn't tell him?'

'No, I couldn't.' Lisa pulled a tissue out of her pocket and started to sob into it.

Despite having no religious or moral opposition to abortion and not being in the least bit maternal herself, Zoe hated moments like this. An unwanted pregnancy was such a reversal of what should be a joyful occurrence.

'How far gone are you?' she asked gently.

'Eight weeks, I think. I'm not very regular.'

'Have you discussed it with Brian, now he knows?'

Lisa nodded.

'Does he want you to have an abortion?'

Another nod.

'What do you want?'

Dabbing at her face with the tissue and leaving a small deposit of damp paper on the side of her nose, Lisa said, 'I can't have this baby.'

Zoe leaned back and rubbed her ribs. 'Why not?'

'Me and Brian, we agreed, no children. I don't know how this happened. We're ever so careful.'

'Does Brian feel he's too old to start a family? Or perhaps he already has children from an earlier marriage?'

Lisa laughed, a sad, high-pitched sound. 'We

agreed, no kids. Please help me, Doctor.' Her mind seemed made up or, more probably, had been made up for her.

'Who's your GP?'

'I haven't got one. Can't you arrange it for me?'

'You need to be registered with the Westerlea practice. Why don't you pop into the health centre and fill in the form then ask whoever's on reception to make an appointment with me at the end of the week?'

'Can't you send me somewhere?'

'If you want me to refer you, you'll have to be a patient.' Seeing Lisa shake her head, Zoe added, 'Don't you think you should be registered with a doctor anyway?'

Lisa swept a hand across her face, dislodging the piece of tissue from her nose, and Zoe watched it float slowly down to the floor. She was moved by the girl's plight but also starting to become impatient. They were, after all, in her home not her consulting room, and she felt in no fit state to counsel anyone.

'If you're worried people in the village will find out, I promise they won't.'

Lisa didn't reply.

Zoe sighed. 'I can give you the address of a clinic in Edinburgh, if you want to go privately,' she said, her words sounding harsher than she intended. Her ribs were really hurting now. 'Would you prefer that?'

Lisa sniffed and nodded.

'I don't have the information here.' Zoe made an effort to keep her voice as kind as possible. 'But I can drop it round to the shop in a couple of days. Would that be soon enough?'

The phone rang a few minutes after Zoe saw Lisa out of the front door. She put down her glass of water and groaned. *Would she ever be left alone long enough to take her medication?*

'Zoe, my dear, how are you?'

'Hello Paul. I'm all right, thanks. I've got painkillers to help me over the next couple of days.' She gazed longingly at the small bottle standing with its lid off.

'Why didn't you let us know what happened?'

'I was going to ring you later. Please don't worry, I'll be in tomorrow.'

'You must take as much time off as you need to recover. I'm phoning because Walter and I were terribly worried when DCI Mather told us your car had gone off the road.'

Thinking it unlikely Walter shared Paul's concern, Zoe asked, 'When was that?'

'He's just been here. I think he's on his way over to you now.'

'He's seen rather a lot of me recently. Still, I can't complain. It's a good thing he was there when it happened.'

'I got the impression he doesn't think it was an accident. I do hope he's wrong.'

'Oh Paul, you can't believe someone deliberately set out to make me crash my car.' Zoe's attempt at a carefree laugh sounded more like a witch's cackle to her ears.

There was silence at the other end of the line.

'As I said, I'll be in tomorrow.'

'Is there anything you need?'

'Nothing, really. Kate's made sure I won't run out of the basics. But I shan't be able to attend Mrs Hensward's funeral. Tell Jean I'm thinking of her, won't you?'

'Of course, my dear. Are you sure you should come back to work so soon? We can bring in a locum if necessary.'

They both knew this was untrue. Finding one at such short notice would be virtually impossible.

'I'll be fine,' Zoe fibbed in return. 'I'll have to come

in by taxi, of course. I'm hoping my insurance company will pay for me to hire a car, but I haven't been able to organise that yet.'

'There's no need for a taxi. One of us will come and pick you up.'

Before she could argue with this, Zoe was distracted by Mac barking. 'That must be Mather now,' she explained, hurriedly saying goodbye.

As usual, the patent shoes gleamed, while the navy wool coat had been replaced by a grey raincoat worn with a matching scarf. After greeting Zoe and asking how she was, Mather frowned as she let him in.

'I know the dog tells you when someone's about,' he said, 'but you really should be more security conscious. Look out of the window or ask your caller to identify themselves before opening the door.'

'Is that a roundabout way of telling me someone tampered with my car?' Zoe slowly led Mather into the sitting room. He did not reply until he had draped his coat over the chair and sat down.

'I would give anyone the same advice. But you're right. Its brakes didn't fail of their own accord.'

'Oh shit.'

It was one thing to speculate about the cause of her accident, quite another to have her worst fears confirmed by a policeman. Zoe's heart began to race. She tried taking deep breaths to stay calm but it hurt too much. She reached for Mac, who was lying beside her chair, and he licked her hand.

'That was fast work,' she said, when she trusted her voice to keep steady.

'I asked our collision investigators to phone through their preliminary findings as quickly as possible.'

'How was it done?'

'Do you know anything about how a car's brakes work?' Mather added hastily, 'I'm not being condescending. Most people don't.'

'And I'm one of them. I love to drive but I rely on others to keep my vehicle roadworthy.'

'In that case, I won't try to explain the technicalities of it. Our investigators found that your car's braking mechanism had been damaged – on purpose – so that it would fail the first time you tried to use it at speed.'

'My steering went too. The wheel felt loose when I tried to avoid the plough.'

'They didn't find any indication of that being meddled with. It was probably damaged by your car being jolted about over the tracks in the field.'

'Is it easy to rig a car's brakes or would the person responsible need specialised knowledge?'

'They definitely had to know more than the average car owner, but we aren't necessarily looking for a qualified mechanic. It was easy to spot. An expert could have covered their tracks better.'

'Unless it was more of a warning than a serious attempt to get rid of me. Though goodness knows what I'm being warned against.'

When Mather replied, it was with a degree of seriousness in his voice which surpassed any he had previously used. 'I wish I could say there was no intention to do you serious harm, but I can't. The result was so unpredictable that, at best, it must have been carried out by someone who didn't care what happened to you.'

Again Zoe had to pause to collect herself before asking, 'Do you think they'll try again?'

'If we accept it was a serious attempt on your life – yes, in all probability.'

This was beyond belief. The person who examined her car must have made a mistake. Then Zoe remembered Kate's dictum that once you accepted Chrissie Baird had been murdered, anything else could happen too. And Chrissie was dead, indisputably by someone else's hand.

'Why me?' she asked.

'I was hoping you would know. And be prepared to share it.'

Mather's expression had shifted from solicitous to stern. It was obvious he suspected Zoe of keeping back information which held the key to what had happened. Now he and his officers had a murder, a suspicious death and an attempted murder to investigate. *He can't have expected to see this much action when he moved back to the Borders.*

'How many times do I have to say this?' Zoe thumped her fist on the arm of the chair and winced at the pain this sent through her body. 'I know nothing about the Bairds' deaths and have no idea why anyone should be out to get me too.'

The policeman said nothing.

Zoe's exasperation abated as quickly as it had flared up. 'I'm sorry. You've every right to ask me anything you like. I know you're only trying to help.'

'Can you think of anyone who would want to hurt you? How about from before you came to the Borders, when you lived in the Midlands?'

Zoe tensed. He can't have been in touch with the police down there yet, but it was only a matter of time. She shook her head.

'In that case let's approach it from another angle. Do you ordinarily lock your car away in the garage or leave it parked outside the house?'

'I usually put it in the garage at night, but there's no lock on the door. I've been meaning to buy one ever since I moved here but never found the time. You know what it's like.'

Mather nodded, although Zoe doubted he ever put off doing anything.

'And before yesterday, when did you last drive it?'

She thought about this, tried to remember. *Why couldn't she remember?*

'Yesterday was Tuesday,' Mather prompted.

'I know. I didn't go anywhere that morning except down the road for a quick walk with Mac, and then I waited in for you. The day before – Monday – I drove to work in the morning, came home for lunch, then we walked to Larimer Park to check up on what the builders were doing.'

'Where was your car during this time?'

'Outside here.'

'And when did you get home from Larimer Park?'

'It was nearly dark, so that must have been four-ish. I put the car away soon after, but I didn't notice anything wrong with it then.'

'You wouldn't have, making a slow manoeuvre.'

'It felt perfectly normal to drive when I set off in front of you, or I would have pulled over. And . . . oh dear.'

'Have you remembered something?'

'I'm so sorry. I haven't thanked you for helping me after the crash.'

'I could hardly have driven past.'

'It was very reassuring to have you there. Thank you.'

'You're welcome.' He smiled. And suddenly it was easy to imagine him as a student in well-pressed jeans with a young Kate on his arm.

'So what now?' Zoe asked.

'Given the circumstances, you need to consider moving out of here for a while. Until we find out who tampered with your car there's always the possibility he may try again.'

'Even if I wanted to do that – which I don't – where do you think I'd go? I don't know anyone well enough to land them with me and Mac.'

'I'm sure Kate would take you in.'

'She's got enough to deal with. No, I'm staying put. I won't be driven out of my home by some vague threat.'

161

Mather did not look surprised. 'We could install a panic alarm.'

'No thanks.'

'Carry out a security survey.'

'Didn't you do that when you came in?'

He had little more to say, save a parting shot as Zoe showed him out. 'At least ask Mr Pengelly to fit a chain to this door.'

'All right.' She closed the door behind him. And turned the key.

Half-expecting another phone call or visitor any minute, Zoe gulped down a painkiller with an addict's fervour. Before settling back into the chair, she fetched her mobile.

She texted Kate, inviting herself to lunch at Tolbyres Cottage after surgery the next day. A response came back almost immediately: *CU then*.

Even looking on the bright side, the inescapable fact was that someone had wanted to frighten her. And if their intention had been more malevolent, they would probably try again. No one could say she was on the sidelines of whatever was happening in Westerlea now.

Kate was right. They had to do something.

TWENTY-TWO

For the first time in years, Zoe went to bed in the afternoon. She woke two hours later, still sore but in a better frame of mind. Going into work tomorrow was not such a bad idea after all.

Remembering one of her gran's favourite sayings, 'If you're bored, you're better', she roamed the cottage looking for things to do. Vacuuming and catching up with the ironing were out of the question, but she managed to make a new batch of bread to replace the one which had spoiled the day before. The phone rang a little after five o'clock.

'Does that log basket need refilling yet?'

'I was starting to think you're the kind of man who spends a night with a girl then never calls her again.'

'You're obviously feeling better.'

'But still in a sufficiently weakened state to appreciate a visit.'

'I won't be able to stay.'

'Did I ask you to?'

As soon as he arrived, without stopping to take off his hat or gloves, Neil replenished the log basket then took Mac for a brief torch-lit walk up the lane. By the time they returned, Zoe had poured a glass and a half glass of red wine from a bottle she kept in the larder. She handed the full glass to Neil.

'It's a bit cool, I'm afraid.'

He took the wine and cupped it in his hands, but remained standing. 'It'll warm up soon enough.'

'Please sit down. You look as though you're about to make a run for it.'

He did as she asked and they chinked glasses.

'To your speedy recovery.'

'Cheers.'

Zoe took a sip of wine. She warned patients about combining alcohol with strong painkillers, but it was only half a glass and she had no plans to drive or operate machinery any time soon.

Neil seemed more at ease now, leaning back in the chair with one hand stroking Mac's head.

'I'm going to work tomorrow.' She braced herself for the inevitable dissent.

'Are you up to it? You should take another day off.'

'I can't stay cooped up here any longer. I'll be fine.'

'Okay, but let me drive you in.'

'Paul's already offered to come and pick me up. But there is something you could do. DCI Mather suggested it.'

'Mather? Has he phoned?'

'No, he came round to see me.'

'Checking you're all right?'

'Partly. But mainly to tell me my car didn't go off the road accidentally or even because of what Kate considers to be my reckless driving. Someone tampered with the brakes.'

'Fucking hell.' Neil jumped up, spilling several drops of wine onto the carpet. He strode over to the window and glared at his own reflection in the glass.

'Your getting angry won't help the situation. And don't you want to know what he suggested?'

'Yes. Of course.'

'He thinks I should ask you to put a chain on my front door.'

Neil looked incredulous. 'That's the best he could come up with?'

'He made some other suggestions, but nothing I'm prepared to consider. I expect he thinks it'll make me feel more secure, even though a chain would hardly be much use if someone's really out to get me.'

'Why would anyone be out to get you?'

'I don't know. Mather didn't say as much, but I'm sure he's linking it with all the other things that have happened in the village.'

'Don't you keep the car locked up in the garage when you're not using it?'

Zoe shook her head. 'I've been meaning to buy a padlock for ages. So anyone could have got in when I was out walking with Mac, or during the night for that matter. I usually sleep very soundly.'

'The hound would have heard someone skulking around.'

'You'd think so, judging by the fuss he makes when people arrive during the day. But I've never known him bark in the night. The bedroom's at the rear, well away from the garage.'

'I know.' Neil smiled for the first time since he arrived, although the hand holding his wine glass shook slightly. He tugged at the curtains to close them, then returned to his chair. 'You'll be safe now, I promise. Nothing else will happen to you.'

'You can't be certain of that. If he's tried once, what's to stop him from trying again?'

'You're on your guard now and the police are involved too. Not to mention Captain Courageous here, who'll be looking after you.' Neil cocked his head to one side, trying to coax a smile from her. It didn't work.

'We don't even know why he went after me in the first place. It has to be connected with the Bairds' deaths.'

'Who can tell what goes on in other people's heads? Or perhaps the police have made a mistake and it was an accident after all.'

Zoe stared at him. 'Are you suggesting this has nothing at all to do with what happened to Chrissie and Jimmy?'

'Think about it. You don't know anything to help find out who killed Chrissie, do you?'

'No, but –'

'So what advantage would there be in killing you as well?'

'None that I can see, but there must be a connection. It can't be a coincidence.'

'You don't believe in coincidences?'

'I'm a doctor. I believe in science, in cause and effect.'

'If you were a vicar, would you put it down to God's will?'

'Now you're being facetious.'

Neil rose to pick up the bottle of wine from where it sat next to the woodburner. He silently topped up his glass and gestured towards Zoe's. She shook her head.

'I just don't want you to worry,' he said.

'Worry? I feel angry more than anything. And violated. Which is why Kate and I are going to find out who's behind all this and put a stop to it.'

Neil choked on his wine. When his coughing abated, he demanded, 'You're what?'

'Kate reckons that between us we can find out who's doing these terrible things. I wasn't keen on the idea at first, but now it's got personal.'

'Let the police sort it out, Zoe. That's what they're paid for. I won't let you get involved.'

'You won't let me? Who are you to tell me what to do?'

'Please be sensible. What can you and Kate do that the police can't?'

'Someone tried to kill me.' Zoe got slowly to her feet. 'Don't you think it would be a good idea to find out who that person is? He may have better luck next time, while I was being sensible and waiting for the police to do their job.'

She glared at Neil. He held her gaze for a few seconds then looked away. After a silence that seemed to go on forever, he said, 'This is typical of Kate, but I'd've expected you to see what a stupid idea it is.'

'I think you'd better go. My ribs have started hurting again and I can't be bothered to argue with you.'

'Promise me you and Kate won't get involved in things which don't concern you.'

'You don't understand, do you? I'm already involved. I won't promise you anything.'

TWENTY-THREE

Having fallen asleep more speedily than expected, thanks to the combination of painkillers and red wine, Zoe woke just after three in the morning with heartburn. She should have known better than to force down that cheese on toast after Neil left. There were no antacids in the house, so she would just have to wait it out.

Reading a book provided a temporary distraction but as soon as she put it down her mind started to race, replaying the accident again and again. *What would have happened if she'd tried to take the corner or that plough had been nearer the gateway?* Then she became consumed by trying to work out who had tampered with her brakes and what she could have done to deserve such animosity.

At five o'clock, despite feeling exhausted, she abandoned all hope of falling back to sleep and sat up more quickly than her ribs liked, although this was a lesser evil than having Mac jump on them. She pulled on her dressing-gown and went through to the kitchen to make a cup of tea.

Her discomfort lessened as she started moving about, which only added to the shock when she stripped off in the bathroom. The blue and purple markings, now tinged with yellow, had spread across her torso and the impact point where her airbag had exploded was clearly visible. She took a very quick bath, in a hurry to put those contusions back out of sight.

Paul arrived at eight-thirty, as she was on the

point of dropping off to sleep in her armchair. 'I'll drive very slowly of course, my dear, but you will need to put on your seatbelt. Look, I've brought this to make you more comfortable.'

Zoe held the red velvet cushion in place while Paul tugged at her seatbelt. She probably looked ridiculous but felt surprisingly comfortable as they inched their way through the village as though part of a funeral cortege. Drawing up in the health centre's car park, they were greeted by Margaret and Penny, who flapped around Zoe so much she was surprised they had not met her with a wheelchair. Once inside, they instructed her on a system devised to save her from having to fetch patients from the waiting room.

As the morning passed, she received many commiserations and heard several anecdotes about drivers who had also failed to negotiate that particular corner. One, faced with the same split-second decision, had been less fortunate than Zoe: the gate into the field had been closed. He had died at the scene.

Her final patient having left nervously clutching the container in which he was to submit a stool sample the following day, Zoe continued to wade through the pile of insurance forms Walter had unloaded on to her. She was signing the last one when Margaret knocked and came straight in, carrying a mug of coffee and wearing a knowing smile on her round face.

'Someone's been enquiring after you, Doctor Zoe.'

'Who?'

'Your friend Neil.'

'Neil Pengelly? You know him?'

'Of course I do. Him and his brother. Lovely boys they are.'

'They're not patients here, are they?'

'No, but when my Hector's mother passed and he sold her bungalow, he treated me to one of their kitchens.'

'What did Neil want? Do I have to call him back?'

'He said he was just checking you'd got to work safely, as he wasn't able to stay with you last night.' Margaret's eyes widened. 'I told him you were fine, and he said he'd see you this evening.'

'Right.' Zoe pointed at the pile of forms on her desk. 'Would you take these away please? They're ready to be scanned and sent off.'

Once Margaret had left the room, Zoe rose from her chair and, trying hard to forget this latest example of Neil's inability to be discreet, made her way slowly to the practice waiting-room. The local taxi firm's business card was pinned up on the notice board, and he arrived shortly after her call. Despite Paul's cushion, Zoe found travelling along the bumpy farm track to Tolbyres Farm a few minutes later so uncomfortable that she promised herself another painkiller before the journey home.

Over a bowl of home-made vegetable soup she told Kate about Mather's most recent visit. 'He confirmed what I suspected. Someone tampered with my brakes.'

Kate's spoon clattered in her soup bowl. 'Oh my God, Zoe. How can you be so calm about it? This means the murderer has set his sights on you now.'

'I'm not calm inside. Far from it. But getting upset won't help matters.'

'He might try again.'

'I doubt it.' Zoe found herself repeating Neil's words. 'I'm on my guard now and the police are involved.'

'Will they protect you?'

'What, by giving me a new identity?'

'Don't be sarcastic. I'm worried about you.'

'I know you are. Sorry.'

Kate looked so upset that Zoe decided to move their conversation on to a subject she knew would distract her. 'My other piece of news is that I'm finished with Neil Pengelly.'

The ploy worked. 'What's he done now?' Kate asked.

'He as good as told Margaret that he spent Tuesday night with me.'

'Well, it's true.'

'There's no need to broadcast the fact.'

'He's not as private a person as you are. Hardly anyone is, let's face it. I know you're finding this hard to accept, but people round here are used to knowing everyone else's business. And in return, everyone knows theirs.'

'I don't think I'll ever get used to that aspect of living in the country,' Zoe said. 'I've come to realise a city has benefits other than big shops and regular buses. Like privacy.'

'And don't forget he's crazy about you. Your relationship took a significant leap forward the other night and he'll be wanting to tell everyone. You're quite a catch, you know.'

Zoe laughed, then clutched her ribs as pain darted up her body. 'Ow. Maybe I need to take another painkiller.'

Kate fetched her a glass of water before asking, 'You're not really going to stop seeing him, are you?'

'Have I even started? It's not as though we've been out on anything resembling a date yet. We simply stagger from one crisis to another, with lots of arguing in between.'

'These haven't been ideal circumstances for starting a relationship. You need to take some time, get to know each other properly and then decide.'

'I didn't come here to start a relationship. The most important thing for me now is my job, and that's not going well either.'

'What's happened?'

Zoe described her latest altercation with Walter, and Kate sympathised by telling her that none of her mother's friends would see him if they could avoid it. Then Zoe asked how research into the American client's family tree was progressing and Kate showed her what she had discovered so far and explained the process by which she went about tracing a person's ancestors. It was nearly an hour later when Zoe looked at the time.

'This is all so interesting but I'd better go home. Poor Mac's been on his own for too long already. Will you drive me or shall I call the taxi company?'

'I'll take you, of course.'

Back at Keeper's Cottage, Zoe unbuckled her seatbelt and prepared to get out of the car.

'Do you want to come over to us again later, to avoid seeing Neil and having another row?' Kate asked.

'Yours is the first place he looks if I'm not here, remember.'

'In that case, we'll go somewhere he'll never find you.'

'I should get to bed early after sleeping so badly last night.'

'Nonsense, you can't stay home brooding about what happened and worrying Neil might drop in unannounced. I know the perfect place. I'll pick you up at six. Don't eat anything beforehand.'

Zoe didn't feel strong enough to argue. 'All right. But there is one more thing before you go.'

'What?'

'I don't want anyone else knowing about what really caused me to crash, okay?'

'Not even Mum?'

'Especially not your mum. You said yourself she's upset about Tom. Let's not add to her worries.'

The sky was darkening when Zoe went indoors and changed into her trousers and boots to take Mac out. Walking slowly up the lane she realised she had not told Kate about her change of heart. She doubted they would be more successful at identifying the killer than the police, but she already felt more in control of events.

As they turned for home an owl swooped across their path and plunged into the hedgerow. Shortly afterwards, Zoe heard several high-pitched squeaks, then silence. The bird flew away, bearing its kill.

TWENTY-FOUR

At just after six that evening, Zoe checked the cottage's front door was properly locked then got into Kate's car. Her foot slipped on a discarded crisp packet and she dropped, wincing, on to the passenger seat.

'Sorry. I must clean this out.' Kate reached down to scrape up the litter at Zoe's feet and tossed it behind her. 'We're going to Eyemouth. Have you been there yet?' She leaned over to help Zoe fasten her seatbelt around Paul's cushion, which she would probably need for a little longer.

'Not since I moved here. I went diving at St Abbs a few years ago and we had something to eat in Eyemouth afterwards.'

'Fish suppers, I expect.'

'Steak, more likely. That's what I usually eat when I go out.'

'You can't go to Eyemouth and not have a fish supper.' Kate looked genuinely shocked. 'We'll put that right tonight.' She started the car and needed to keep her eyes on the road, so they made no further conversation until they were parked beside Eyemouth harbour half an hour later.

'It's very disorientating to see the boats bobbing in the water, isn't it?' Kate said, as she released Zoe's seatbelt. 'Feels as if it's you that's moving, not them.'

Zoe looked past the boats towards an imposing building on the other side of the water. Lights shone in every room and a steady stream of people were making their way up the steps to its front door.

'That looks very grand,' she said, pointing.

'It's called Gunsgreen House. An eighteenth-century gentleman smuggler built it.'

'Does anyone live there?'

'No, but it's open to the public and used for functions. Someone must be having an early Christmas party. I'm afraid our destination's a wee bit more modest.'

A queue for takeaways stretched out of the restaurant's front door. Kate and Zoe sat down at the rear of the small dining area, the only people eating in.

'This is still the best place for fish and chips in the Borders,' Kate said. 'A bunch of us used to come over here when I was a teenager. Tom was the first one to pass his driving test, so he'd borrow Uncle Bob's car and we all piled into it. Of course the aim then was to drink as much alcohol as possible without our parents knowing.'

'Do you recommend I have the small or the medium fish supper?' Zoe asked.

'The portions here are so huge, even I struggle with the medium. And you'll want to leave room for a pudding.'

Their young waitress wore rings on all her fingers and both thumbs, and her left ear was adorned with a silver hoop nearly as big as Mac's collar. She showed little interest in her customers, writing down their orders without making eye contact or saying a word, but her head turned suddenly and the earring swung wildly when Kate asked Zoe, 'Does Neil have any idea who might have tried to kill you?'

Her earlier shock at the idea of someone rigging Zoe's car to crash had obviously abated. Zoe smiled weakly and waited for the waitress to drift away before replying.

'He doesn't believe it had anything to do with Chrissie Baird's death.'

'He can't think it's a coincidence.'

'That's exactly what I said. But because there's no obvious link between Chrissie's death and my car crash, Neil refuses to believe the two things are connected.'

'Three, if you assume Jimmy was murdered too.'

'We don't know that yet.'

'Hasn't Erskine told you anything?'

Zoe shook her head, expecting to be challenged, but Kate seemed satisfied. 'Maybe Neil's right. I'm no psychologist, but it's hard to believe all three incidents were the work of one person. They're too dissimilar.'

'We don't know what happened to Chrissie before she was put into the bonfire.'

Some of us do, Zoe wanted to say, but she had promised Mather she would not pass on what he told her about Chrissie's injuries. Instead, she said, 'Leaving her aside, knocking an old man into a burn and tampering with a car's brakes are two completely different approaches to disposing of someone.'

'They're both equally cowardly,' Kate said, 'but I see what you mean. There's no pattern, is there? You'd think two deaths and one narrow escape would make identifying the person responsible easier. Instead, things are more complicated.'

'Perhaps we should be looking for more than one person,' Zoe said, as the waitress approached them carrying two plates piled high with battered haddock and chips.

'"We"?' Kate said.

'I see what you meant about not eating too much. If these are small portions, how big is a large one?'

'"We"?'

'Can I get you anything else?' Their waitress looked disappointed when Zoe answered no, and moved away.

'You said "we".' Kate stared at Zoe. 'I thought you'd decided to leave any investigating to the police.'

'That's something else I argued about with Neil. He doesn't think we should get involved, but I already am. I can't just sit around waiting for something else to happen to me. It's in my best interest that whoever's responsible be exposed as soon as possible.'

'I'm glad you've changed your mind, though of course I hate the reason why. I can't imagine what it must feel like, being the target of such malice.' Kate speared several chips with her fork and put them into her mouth.

They ate in silence. This was definitely the best fish and chips Zoe had tasted. It was a pity she could not do it justice.

Her plate almost empty, Kate reached for a second piece of buttered bread. 'So, where do we start?'

'Perhaps by accepting there isn't a pattern to what's been happening.' Zoe was pleased at the excuse to take a rest from eating and put down her knife and fork.

'What do you mean?'

'It's tempting to assume the same person who killed both the Bairds also tampered with my brakes. But instead of trying to see the big picture and understand how things fit together, perhaps it would be better if we took one element and examined it closely.'

'You keep using the word "person",' Kate said. 'I agree it would have been easy to topple Jimmy into the burn with just a shove from behind, but surely it took two people to manhandle Chrissie into the bonfire?'

'Not necessarily. She was quite small, wasn't she? Anyway, however many there were, I suggest we ignore what happened to me and come up with the names of people who may have wanted Chrissie and Jimmy dead. Then we concentrate on establishing if they could have done it.'

'And once we've got the answer to that, the reason for what happened to you will become clear.'

'Exactly. Simple, isn't it?' Zoe said with a wry smile.

Their waitress returned several times, ostensibly to check if they had finished eating, each time forcing Kate and Zoe to suspend their conversation until she went away. As soon as they both put their cutlery down for good she appeared once more and slowly cleared the table. Her serving of fruit sorbet to Zoe and a knickerbocker glory to Kate was equally protracted as she fussed around them, fetching fresh paper serviettes and mopping up a spillage of vinegar. However, her customers did not return to the subject of murder until they had turned down coffee and asked for the bill.

'Now we know what to do, I can't wait to get started,' Kate said. 'What's first?'

'I've got a couple of provisos before we go any further,' Zoe said.

'Which are?'

'Firstly, we tell no one what we're doing. We have to stay safe.'

'I can't argue with that. I've got the bairns to consider, and I certainly don't want Mum any more worried than she already is.'

'Good. Secondly, you must agree that if we find out anything definite, anything at all, we go straight to the police with it. We can't confront a killer ourselves, however much evidence we have.'

'Okay.' Kate set about scraping the remainder of her icecream from the bottom of the glass.

Zoe pushed one of the balls of sorbet to the side of her plate.

When they had finished their meal and paid for it, Kate preceded Zoe out of the front door and then surprised her by speeding off in the opposite direction to where the car was parked, towards a large white building with striking black window surrounds. Aware she would be wasting her time calling to someone who could not hear her protests, Zoe followed as quickly as the ever-present pain in her ribs allowed.

The only other people in the pub's lounge bar were an elderly couple with a Scottie dog in a tartan coat sitting docilely between them. Kate led Zoe to a seat by the window.

'This was our favourite haunt when I was a teenager with nothing to worry about except boys and spots,' Kate said. 'Just one drink and I'll get you home.' She crossed the room and peered over the counter into the adjoining public bar, looking for someone to serve her. A few seconds later she hurried back to Zoe.

'You'll never guess who's sat on the other side!'

The elderly couple stared at Kate and whispered to each other.

'Who?'

'Alice, that's who. With a bloke in leather trousers. Come and see.' Kate practically dragged Zoe over to the bar. 'Look, in the far corner under the darts board.'

At first, all Zoe could see of the young woman was a curtain of very fair hair obscuring her features. But when she threw back her head and laughed, Zoe recognised the face from the newspaper article she had read in Neil's kitchen.

'Who's that with her?'

'No idea. Her latest conquest, knowing Alice. She –'

Kate stopped speaking as the door leading to the pub's toilets opened and another figure ambled into view. Gregor Baird paused to check his flies were properly done up, then walked over to Alice and her companion and sat down.

Before Zoe and Kate could say anything, the barmaid dragged herself away from the conversation which had been more interesting than serving customers. She positioned herself squarely in front of them, obscuring their view into the other bar.

'What can I get you ladies?'

Kate let out an exasperated sigh and looked ready

to shove the woman aside. Zoe had to tap her on the arm to gain her attention. 'Half a lager, Kate?'

Her friend nodded absently.

'Make that two, please.'

The barmaid bent down for glasses, temporarily restoring their line of sight. Alice and the two men were deep in conversation, their heads close together.

'Excuse me,' Kate called to the barmaid, 'we've decided to have our drinks in the public bar. We'll see you on the other side.' She dashed to the table, seized her handbag and made for the door.

Zoe caught up with her outside the building. 'What are you doing?'

'This is the only way to get into the public bar.'

'And why are we going there?'

'They're huddled too close for me to read their lips. They don't know you, so you can go in there, sit down near them and listen. I'll wait here for a while then come in myself.'

'That won't work. I met Gregor recently. He's bound to recognise me.'

'Damn. Oh well, the only alternative is direct action.' Kate wrenched the door open and strode into the public bar. Zoe initially hung back, then followed.

Kate halted in front of the table in the corner. Alice and the two men stared up at her.

'Hello,' Kate said. 'Fancy seeing you here.'

TWENTY-FIVE

Kate was clearly enjoying herself. After offering condolences to Alice and Gregor on the deaths of their respective parents, she introduced Zoe and pulled over two stools from the next table. Zoe sat down, wishing she had her friend's ability to barge into awkward situations unchecked by self-consciousness.

The looks on the faces of Gregor and his stepsister changed rapidly from surprise to unease and, in Alice's case, outright hostility. She bore little resemblance to the grieving daughter pictured in the newspaper. Zoe stared at the girl's piercings, which were halfway up one ear and through her nasal septum and lower lip. She had certainly looked more sympathetic without those. *Had it been Alice's idea, or the photographer's, to remove them?*

Kate chattered on, pressing for an introduction to the one person she did not know.

'This is Terry,' Alice said. Her voice sounded a lot older than she looked.

'Hi Terry.' Kate stuck out her hand. 'Alice used to be married to my cousin. I'm deaf by the way, but you needn't shout. I can read lips, as long as you don't all speak at once.'

Terry looked sideways at Alice, as if seeking her permission, then unenthusiastically grazed his hand against Kate's. He heeded her request not to shout, instead mumbling a few words which communicated little to Zoe other than he was a Geordie. She doubted Kate was able to interpret what he said either, but her friend had already turned her attention back to Alice.

'Are you up here to make arrangements for the funerals?' she asked.

Alice swallowed a mouthful of Guinness before responding. 'Police won't release the bodies yet.'

'Will it be a joint ceremony?' Kate directed her question at Gregor this time. He sat next to Alice, their shoulders nearly touching, while Terry faced them on the opposite side of the table. 'I'm sure it's what they would have wanted.'

'Dunno,' Gregor said. Apart from fixing those blue eyes on her, he was not wasting any of his charm on Kate.

As her friend struggled to keep the conversation afloat, Zoe realised her own embarrassment had been replaced by antipathy towards the sullen threesome. *Kate wasn't the only one who could be unsubtle.* 'I met Angie and Maddy the other day, Alice. They're lovely girls.'

Alice flicked her hair out of her eyes. 'They ill?' she asked. So she knew that much about Zoe.

'No, I babysat for a short time.'

'Round at that Jean's I suppose.' Alice wagged her finger at Zoe. 'You can tell her she won't get my kids, even if she does marry Tom. Not after what Mum told me about him.'

'What was that?'

Gregor nudged Alice. She lowered her hand and put it around her glass. 'He'll find out soon enough.'

Even Kate had no response to this.

Alice finished her drink then stood up, pulled on her denim jacket and looked down at the two men. Gregor rose first, and a couple of beats later so did Terry. All three trooped out through the door into Harbour Road.

'The pied piper and her rats,' Zoe said.

Kate laughed. 'Terry must be the boyfriend Chrissie told everyone Alice had settled down with. I wouldn't be happy if that was the best one of my girls could do. Those trousers aren't even real leather.'

'I wonder how he gets on with Gregor.'

'Alice and Gregor look like they're still very comfortable with each other. Poor old Terry's definitely the odd one out.'

'But she'd look upon Gregor as her big brother, wouldn't she? They must have lived in the same house while she was growing up. I wouldn't know, of course, but I don't expect that familiarity ever disappears.'

'Or *over*-familiarity,' Kate said.

'Are you suggesting what I think you are?'

'I can remember Mum telling me she wouldn't trust Gregor Baird to live in the same house as anyone's teenage daughter, let alone one like Alice.'

'You mean there were rumours of something physical going on between them?' Zoe had assumed that if Gregor and Alice conspired to murder their parents, they were motivated by greed. But here was another possibility.

'I lived away at the time and had my own problems, so I didn't take much notice. What Mum said has only just come back to me.'

'If you're right, perhaps Chrissie found out what they were up to. That would explain the animosity between her and Gregor.'

'I'll ask Mum if she knows anything.'

Zoe was on the point of reminding Kate to be circumspect with her questions when she saw movement up at the bar. They had forgotten their drinks, and the barmaid was pointing at the two halves of lager, untouched and not even paid for. Zoe went to fetch them.

'Do you know much about Scots law?' she asked when she sat down again.

'I've picked up a bit during my work,' Kate said. 'Unfortunately most of it dates back to the eighteenth and nineteenth centuries. Why do you ask?'

'It would be interesting to know who inherits

Horseshoe Cottage. Jimmy was a lot older than Chrissie, so he probably left a will but I wonder if she did.' There was surely no harm in discussing this, given that Mather had not told her anything definite.

'I remember when Auntie Louie, Dad's sister who stayed up near Aberdeen, died unexpectedly a few years ago. Nobody could find her will and there was a terrible stushie about who got the house. In the end, it had to be sold and the proceeds shared out among her children. Her husband had died years before, and his children from an earlier marriage got nothing.'

Zoe sipped her drink. 'So Chrissie dying intestate would mean that Jimmy inherited everything, although he didn't live to collect it. And even if his will named Chrissie as his sole heir, because she was already dead the estate might revert to his nearest living relative, Gregor.'

'Unless Jimmy formally adopted Alice,' Kate said. 'Knowing Chrissie, he may have had no choice in the matter.'

'I wondered about that too. But maybe money's not the motive. We're not talking about an estate worth millions, are we?'

'Aside from what Horseshoe Cottage, which he bought years ago, is worth, Jimmy sold the pub outright to the Andersons. The profits from that must be stashed away somewhere. He's unlikely to have spent it. The only indulgence he allowed Chrissie was getting her hair and nails done every week.'

'Which means even if Alice and Gregor have an entirely normal relationship, it could have been profitable enough for them to get together and bump off their parents.'

'You've convinced me.' Kate took a mouthful of lager and put her glass down on the wooden table. 'This has been a good evening's work, hasn't it? We've solved a double murder that was baffling the police.'

Zoe laughed, despite being unsure if Kate was

actually joking. 'Don't you think we should consider some alternatives?'

'Why? Gregor and Alice have a motive, maybe more than one. Finding them here proves they've got something to hide.'

'No it doesn't. It's perfectly natural for them to meet up and discuss what's happened.'

'But why come here? Why not go to The Rocket?'

'Perhaps they want to avoid village gossip. I can't say I blame them.'

Kate sighed in exasperation. 'Okay, but who else is there?'

'That argument I overheard between Ray and Hazel Anderson suggests they're hiding something from the police, and there was definitely bad blood between them and Chrissie. Remember Ray telling everyone about how she still treated The Rocket as though she owned the place?'

'That wouldn't be a strong enough reason to kill someone.'

'By itself, no, but I think there's more to their relationship with Chrissie than that. Ray was very disparaging about her, and he's usually so affable.'

'Aye, you're right,' Kate said. 'I've never known him utter a bad word about anyone before, and there he was suggesting she had a lover. Hearing interesting stuff and not passing it on is one of the rules of running a successful pub. Much like being a doctor.'

Zoe ignored this dig. 'Their marriage was definitely under strain even before I mentioned having seen their car the day Jimmy died.'

'I still can't imagine Hazel sneaking off for a torrid sex session with a secret lover while Ray thinks she's shopping in Kelso.'

'Why not? She's only in her early fifties. That's not nearly past it these days.'

'I'm not suggesting she's too old for a fling, only

that it's very unlikely. She hasn't recovered from their son's death yet. You saw how drunk she was the other night. That's been happening a lot lately.'

'When did the son die?'

'Less than a year ago – just before they moved here. He'd been ill for a long time apparently, some sort of cancer.' Kate shuddered, her usual exuberance briefly stifled. 'It must be unbearable to lose your child, even when they're grown-up. You'd do anything to make the pain stop.'

Zoe remembered how her grandparents dealt with the loss of their only daughter. They hid their own heartache and never spoke about what happened, a well-meaning attempt to spare Zoe further distress which left her feeling even more bereft. She could date her curiosity about her father from those days. Until then she had rarely given him a thought.

'Everyone handles it differently,' she said. 'And unfortunately some people turn to alcohol, although that's never the answer to anything. But can we agree Ray and Hazel's relationship with Chrissie Baird is worth looking into?'

'I'd like to find out more about Chrissie's alleged affair too,' Kate said. 'She's much more likely to have had a lover than Hazel, although I can't believe the news hasn't leaked out before now.'

'We don't want to spread ourselves too thin.'

'Speak for yourself. I've never been too thin for anything.' Kate patted her stomach and grinned. 'If she was having an affair, it can't hurt to find out who it was with.'

'I don't recall anyone in the pub rushing to agree with Ray when he mentioned this. For all we know he could have made it up.'

'Why would he do that?'

'Because he's hiding something?'

Kate shrugged. 'Okay, but we should keep it in

mind when we're talking to people. Everyone's on their guard when they're being questioned by the police, but they'll speak freely to us.'

'Not necessarily.'

'In which case we'll have to draw as many conclusions from what people don't tell us as from what they do. I'm going to follow my instinct and try to nail exactly what Alice's relationship with Gregor is. Do you want to visit the Andersons and try to get to know them better?'

'They're not likely to welcome me with open arms after I set DCI Mather on them with questions about their Volvo.'

'That can be your excuse. Say you must have made a mistake and want to apologise. I suggest you do it tomorrow morning.'

'Why so soon?'

'Ray'll be off on his weekly run to the cash and carry, so you should find Hazel on her own. Your being a doctor will help. You just need to turn the conversation round to the son, which won't be difficult. His name was Duncan, by the way.'

'That seems callous.'

'As you keep on telling me, we're dealing with someone who's a lot worse than callous. Anyway, you're a doctor and a nice person, so she'll probably feel better after talking to you. She won't realise you have an ulterior motive.'

'You really are devious.'

Obviously choosing to take this as a compliment, Kate beamed. 'And you need to stop being so caring and polite. Sometimes the only way to get the truth out of people is to provoke them.'

'I'll try to remember that.' Zoe finished her drink and looked at her watch. 'Now we have a plan of action, will you take me home? My ribs have started to ache again and I forgot to bring my painkillers with me.'

As soon as Zoe got inside and locked her front door she dialed 1471; Neil had phoned ten minutes earlier. It was unlikely to have been the first time, but she hoped it would be the last, at least for tonight.

She changed into her pyjamas and sat down in front of the woodburner with Mac to think over the events of the evening. What stood out most was Alice's violent reaction to the prospect of Tom marrying Jean, which seemed to have strengthened her resolve to gain custody of the twins. Tom claimed not to know what Chrissie had planned to use against him, but Alice obviously did. His troubles had not died along with his mother-in-law.

Now Zoe faced another dilemma. She could rationalise looking into who killed the Bairds as a means of unmasking her own aggressor, but did she really want to get tangled up in the domestic disputes of others? Then again, Tom and Jean deserved some consideration. He was Kate's cousin, after all, and she was employed by the practice and had just lost her mother.

Should Zoe warn them about Alice's intentions?

TWENTY-SIX

'We're walking to the village this morning,' Zoe told Mac after breakfast as she put him on his extending lead. Despite feeling less sore than the previous day, she was not yet up to chasing him across a field.

They met no one on the way, but once on Main Street several people, most of whom Zoe did not know, approached to ask how she was feeling. She knew they meant well, but it was a relief to reach the sanctuary of the shop. Brian stood on his own behind the counter, taking money from a queue of customers buying cigarettes and snacks on their way to work. Zoe amused herself by comparing newspaper headlines about the latest political maelstrom until she and Brian were alone.

He walked along the narrow aisle, coming to a halt by her side. 'Doctor Moreland. Glad to see you up and about after your accident. Are you feeling better?'

Zoe took a step back to distance herself from the blast of garlicky breath emanating from his thin mouth. 'Yes, thank you. I'm still without a car, so I thought I'd walk. It's a lovely morning, isn't it?'

'As you're on foot, you must say if you need us to deliver anything to your house.' Brian moved to close the gap between them, forcing Zoe, who felt equally disturbed by his proximity and his halitosis, to retreat further.

'What a kind offer,' she said, bending down to pick up a packet of dog biscuits. 'In that case I'd better make it worth your while. Could you fetch me a basket please?' These were kept next to the counter, compelling Brian to withdraw from her space.

Lisa had still not appeared by the time Zoe paid for her purchases, so as Brian passed over her change she had no alternative but to ask him where his wife was.

'In the house. She's none too good these mornings, as you can imagine.' Although the counter was now between them, Brian leant forward as far as he could towards Zoe. She smelt his breath again, but more repulsive was the leer on his face. He may not want the child his wife was carrying, but that did not stop him from taking a repellent pride in having impregnated her.

Zoe hesitated. Brian thrust out his hand and held it disturbingly close to her left breast, although he looked her straight in the eye.

'I'll take whatever you've brought in for her.'

Just as she was about to hand over the envelope containing a leaflet about the Edinburgh clinic, Zoe heard a small voice call out, 'Is that Doctor Moreland?'

Brian frowned and made to snatch the envelope from Zoe's fingers. She withdrew her hand before he could reach it.

'I'll give it to her myself. Through here, is she?'

Brian looked set to place himself between Zoe and the door she was heading for, but at that moment an elderly woman came in with a large parcel, demanding to know if it would reach New Zealand in time for Christmas. Ignoring Brian's furious expression, Zoe slipped into the stockroom.

Lisa stood at the end of an avenue of metal shelving packed with jars, tins, bottles and packets. A short yellow dressing-gown accentuated her pallor and revealed a pair of skinny legs that looked hardly strong enough to support her. She was holding a piece of toast.

'Hello Lisa. How are you feeling today?'

'A bit better.'

'Here's the information I promised you.'

190

Lisa took the envelope from Zoe. 'Can I talk to you?'

'Of course, but you look cold. Is there somewhere else we can go?'

A door at the rear of the stockroom opened into a small hallway, which in turn led to a sizeable kitchen with blue walls, white tiles and wooden-fronted cupboards. The smell of burnt toast hung in the air, despite one of the windows being open.

Although they were well out of her husband's hearing, Lisa spoke in a voice so low that Zoe was forced, as usual, to strain to hear her. 'Do I need to do anything straight away?'

'Legally speaking, you have a little time, although like any surgical procedure it's better to have it done sooner than later. However – '

Lisa tried to interrupt but Zoe held up a hand to silence her. 'Please listen. This is important.' She looked hard at the girl, trying to maintain eye contact with her. 'However, if you're having second thoughts, you must take your time to reach the right decision.'

'But how do I know what that is?'

Zoe pointed at the envelope Lisa clutched in her hand. 'Those people will counsel you.'

Lisa opened her mouth, looked towards the hall, and shut it again, her complexion suddenly even paler. Turning around, Zoe saw Brian leaning against the doorframe with his arms folded and a sneer on his face. *How long had he been there?*

'Thank you for bringing this.' Lisa put the envelope into her gown pocket. 'I'll let you out of the side door, save you going back through the shop.'

As she was leaving, Zoe saw Brian move next to his wife and put an arm around her. Lisa's thin body stiffened.

The small child parked in a pushchair outside the shop began to grizzle as Zoe untied Mac and led him away. They walked towards The Rocket, giving another stranger the opportunity to stop and sympathise over her accident. She suppressed the urge to shout that it had not been an accident, that someone had tried to kill her.

They had barely moved off again when Zoe's attention was caught by a man coming out of Horseshoe Cottage. Despite his upper body being hidden behind the boxes he carried, she immediately recognised those shiny trousers. She watched Terry clumsily set his load on top of some more boxes already piled behind a parked red Fiesta, unlock the car and open its boot.

About to walk on, Zoe remembered Kate's assertion that the only way to find things out was to stop being polite and start provoking people. She crossed the road.

Terry had begun loading the boxes into the Fiesta. Zoe stood behind him and said, 'Hello, Terry. I'm Zoe Moreland. We met last night in Eyemouth, remember?'

The young man hastily withdrew from the depths of the car, banging his head in the process. He blinked hard, as though he rarely saw daylight, and grunted in recognition.

'Alice sorting out her mother's things, is she?' Zoe asked.

'Yeah.'

'Such a sad task. She's lucky to have you for support.'

'Yeah.'

'And Gregor, of course. I know he's her step-brother, which can't be the same as a blood relative, but they do seem very close.'

Terry scowled and gave a hollow laugh before bending over to pick up another box. Zoe was wondering whether to bait him further when she looked down. Mac had been sniffing around the boxes; now he was lifting his leg.

'No, Mac, don't do that! Oh. I'm so sorry.'

One of the boxes had a dark stain down its side and a yellow pool at its base.

'I do hope nothing's damaged,' Zoe said, opening the top of the box to reveal tightly-packed china, unwrapped bar a few pieces of newspaper stuffed into the gaps. 'Shouldn't we fetch a cloth and wipe it?'

Terry pushed the cardboard flaps back down and lifted the box away from her. Its contents clattered as he thrust it into the car.

Kate would probably have accomplished more from this episode, but Zoe allowed herself a brief smile as she walked on up the street. She had provoked Terry and although he had said very little, his response to her comment about Gregor was all the proof she needed. Alice's boyfriend was jealous of her step-brother.

Gaining entry to the Andersons' living quarters above The Rocket proved easier than Zoe expected. She rang the bell and immediately heard a dog barking. Shortly afterwards, Hazel Anderson appeared with a brown cocker spaniel at her heel.

'Hello,' Zoe said. Having steeled herself to meet some resistance, it was a relief when Hazel responded by making an extravagant sweeping gesture with her arm.

'Come away in.' The words were slurred.

'Will it be all right if I fasten Mac to this?' Zoe indicated a boot scraper set into a slab of concrete.

'He can come too. The more the merrier. As long as he doesn't try to play with Sukie – she's past all that now.'

Dogs and owners filed along the narrow hall and up a steep staircase. The first door on the right led into a large, airy room stretching from the front to the rear of the building, its walls a pale green, its floor covered in the same tartan carpet as the pub's dining room.

Hazel ushered Zoe across the room and pointed to one of the leather sofas arranged in front of an unlit open fire. She sat down heavily on the other sofa, reaching over to rearrange the contents of a small table, though not before Zoe spotted the whisky glass which disappeared behind a pile of magazines.

'Welcome to our humble abode,' Hazel said, again with a flamboyant wave. 'What can I do for you, Doctor? Did my husband tell you to come and see me?'

'No, he didn't. I've actually come round to apologise.'

'Apologise? What for?'

'You've had a visit from the police because I mistakenly thought I saw your car near the water meadow the morning Jimmy Baird died.'

Hazel leaned back, making the sofa squeal. 'Oh that. Don't worry about it. Life's too short.' She smacked the seat next to her and called to Sukie, who was exchanging bottom sniffs with Mac. The old dog struggled to climb up, her paws slipping on the shiny leather.

'Lovely creatures, aren't they?' Hazel said, pulling Sukie up by the scruff of the neck. 'You can always rely on a dog. How long have you had yours?'

'Only a few months, but I wouldn't be without him now.' As if endorsing the closeness of their relationship, Mac sat down at Zoe's feet and gazed up at her.

'How old is Sukie?' Zoe asked.

'She's twelve, but we've not had her all that time.'

'Did you get her from a rescue centre?'

'No. She belonged to our son, but when he couldn't look after her any more she came to live with us. Then he died.' Hazel absentmindedly stretched her hand towards the table and looked surprised when it did not find the glass.

'I'm so sorry.' Zoe already wished she had not gone along with Kate's suggestion to come here. It was all very well needling someone like Terry, but this poor woman deserved compassion not suspicion.

'We knew it was going to happen.'

'It must have been very painful for you.'

'Still is. But I don't have to tell you. You being a widow.' Forgetting or abandoning her pretence of sobriety, Hazel reached behind the magazines and brought the glass of whisky to her lips. 'This helps for a time,' she added, once the liquid had gone down her throat.

'It's not the sort of help I would recommend.'

Hazel slammed the glass down on the table. 'Ray did send you here!'

'No, Hazel, he didn't. Truly. But I'm sure he's worried about you.'

'Worried about the business, more like. Worried that having a barmy wife'll stop people coming into the pub.'

'You may feel better if you could talk things through with someone. I could put you in touch with a bereavement counsellor.'

'I've got someone to talk to,' Hazel said. 'Trouble is, Ray won't let me.' She got up and lifted a framed photograph from the mantelpiece. It was of a young man in his early twenties standing alongside a boat. He had delicate features and his mother's dark curls, and cuddled a young Sukie.

Thrusting the picture so close to Zoe's face that she could not focus properly on it, Hazel said, 'My Duncan. Handsome, isn't he?'

'Yes.'

Hazel still held the photograph up to her. 'He's the only one I want to talk to,' she said, then fell back into her seat, clutching her dead son to her breast. Tears coursed down her face and her nose ran.

'When are you expecting Ray home?' Zoe asked.

Hazel sniffed noisily. 'He's no use. As far as Ray's concerned, Duncan died a long time ago. He's over it now, and thinks I should be too.'

'We all react differently to grief. It's not unusual for men to bottle up their feelings.'

'But surely, Doctor, it's unusual for a father to be angry with his son because he gets sick and dies. I tried to tell him it wasn't Duncan's fault, but he wouldn't listen.'

'Feeling angry towards the deceased is one of the accepted stages of bereavement.' Zoe frowned, aware she sounded like one of the leaflets she was supposed to give patients to help them cope with the loss of a loved one. But she also knew from personal experience how true those words were.

Hazel had not heard. She stared at Duncan's picture, her lips moving silently, as if chanting a spell which could bring him back to life.

'I've found the one person who can help me,' she said eventually, 'only to be told I can't see him again.'

'Who's that, Hazel?'

'A lovely man in Norham. He – '

Hazel stopped speaking and looked warily at Zoe. Her face broke into a travesty of a smile. 'Oh no, you don't catch me out that easily. Ray's trying to have me put away and you're helping him.'

It was impossible to persuade her to talk further. Reluctantly, with no alternative short of refusing to leave before Ray came home and having no idea when that would be, Zoe left. Hazel made no effort to show her out, but continued to gaze at Duncan's photograph.

As she crossed the room, Zoe studied the view from the window overlooking the beer garden and fields beyond. The bonfire site, still cordoned off by police tape, was clearly visible only a short distance from the pub and the Andersons' living quarters. It would have been easy for two people, or just one strong one, to transport Chrissie Baird's body there, unobserved, after dark.

TWENTY-SEVEN

'There's a sensible-looking vehicle parked outside,' Kate said, removing her coat to reveal a baby-pink cardigan with pearly buttons over a short, black skirt. 'You'll not be wanting to keep that for long.'

'The insurance company arranged it,' Zoe said. 'They even had it delivered to the health centre yesterday afternoon. So I can't complain, although you're right, it's not the sort of car I'm used to.'

'Were you okay, getting back behind the wheel for the first time since your crash?'

'Margaret and Paul insisted on watching me drive away, so I was more worried about doing something stupid, like stalling.' The flashbacks of careering out of control into that field had only come on when Zoe was nearly home. *No one needed to hear about those.* She bit into one of the donuts Kate had brought with her, realising she had once again forgotten to have lunch.

'Mmm, that was good.' Kate licked jam off her fingers then wiped her mouth with a piece of kitchen towel.

'You missed some.' Zoe tapped her own face to show Kate where a few granules of sugar lurked on hers. 'Your text said you'd spoken to Etta about Alice and Gregor. Could she tell you anything?'

Kate shook her head. 'Mum doesn't even remember making that comment about them, so perhaps it wasn't her who said it.'

'Did you ask if she thought they might have been closer than they should be?'

'I did, although it wasn't easy raising the subject of incest with my mother, especially involving someone who used to be a member of the family.'

'If it helps, Alice and Gregor aren't blood relatives, so strictly speaking it wouldn't count as incest.'

'That may be, but Mum was still shocked at the idea. Although when she gave it some thought, she admitted those two spent what she described as "an unhealthy amount of time" together, especially as Gregor must be about fifteen years older than Alice. Don't forget they lived above The Rocket then, and Chrissie and Jimmy would have been downstairs working every evening. Plenty of opportunity for Gregor to introduce his little step-sister to all sorts of bad habits.'

'Didn't he help out in the pub too?'

'I'm glad you asked that.' Kate grinned broadly. 'Mum did remember something interesting. Gregor was once barred from the pub. By Chrissie. For picking a fight with a customer.'

'And . . . ?' Kate seemed too pleased with herself for this to be the end of the story.

'And the bloke he beat up was Alice's boyfriend. At the time – this was before she got her claws into Tom – she was going out with Gerry Hall's son, Lee. He works for his dad. You might have seen him working at the coach house.'

'Not much chance of that.'

'He's a big laddie, plays rugby. Alice was very keen on him apparently, and Chrissie obviously thought he was good son-in-law material. One night she was boasting to anyone who'd listen about him taking Alice to some fancy restaurant in Edinburgh. Gregor was working behind the bar and serving himself more than the customers. Lee came in for a drink after dropping Alice off and when he left, Gregor followed him out to the car park and beat him up.'

'Did someone call the police?'

Kate shook her head. 'Mum and Dad were having a meal there the night it happened, that's how they knew about it. They left not long after Lee, and came across him and Gregor fighting. Dad managed to pull them apart, and handed Gregor over to his father. Then Chrissie appeared and started shouting, threatening to throw him out. Gregor was never seen in the bar again, either drinking or serving.'

'And you think he picked a fight with Lee out of jealousy?'

'That must be a strong possibility.'

'What does your Mum say?'

'She's never heard anyone mention the episode since it happened, so she has no idea what was behind it. But now I've started her thinking, she may remember something else useful.'

'You took care not to arouse her suspicions about why you were asking, didn't you?'

Kate looked affronted. 'Zoe, this is my mother we're talking about. She and I gossip all the time. You should hear the questions she asks me about you and Neil.'

'Please tell me you're not exchanging titbits about my private life for the lowdown on the Bairds.'

'Certainly not. I've told her you value your privacy and she must respect that.' Kate's assertion would have been more convincing if she had not abruptly changed the subject. 'Anyway, before you tell me what you've been up to, I've got something else to report. I took a diversion on my way here to stop and peer in through the front window of Horseshoe Cottage. It's an absolute mess – you'd think it had been ransacked by burglars. I can't believe the police would have left it like that.'

'They didn't. It was Alice.' Zoe told Kate about her encounter with Terry the previous day and they put their sugary plates down to Mac as a reward for the part he played in it.

'The Fiesta must be Terry's,' Kate said. 'I don't think Alice can even drive. So, the vultures have descended already – and what a state they've left the place in. Do you think they were looking for something? Like a will, maybe.'

'I don't know the answer to that, but thanks to Mac, I can tell you they aren't only sorting out clothes to take to the charity shop. The box I peeked into was full of good-quality china, although as far as I could make out there was nothing of great value.'

'Jimmy wasn't the type to let his wife spend his hard-earned cash on expensive antiques.'

'That's not the first time you've suggested he was tight-fisted. Maybe people were unfair to assume Chrissie only married him for his money.'

'He might not have been rich, but he offered her security. Though who can blame her for wanting that? It's not easy being a single mother. And whatever her motives, she worked hard to make the pub a success. Not everyone is cut out for it.'

'That's true. I would make a terrible pub landlady,' Zoe said, and they both laughed at the very idea.

'Speaking of landladies,' Kate said, 'how did it go with Hazel?'

Zoe briefly ran through her visit to the flat above the pub. She purposely left out any mention of Hazel seeking solace in a glass of whisky, but her diplomacy was wasted.

'Was she already drunk?' Kate asked. 'I bet she was.'

'Um, maybe a bit.'

'That shows what a state she's in. No wonder Ray never lets her behind the bar during opening hours any more. Have you noticed how she doesn't pour drinks for people in the dining room herself, but asks Ray for them?'

'Now you mention it, I have. But we should feel sorry for the poor woman, not condemn her.'

'Next you're going to tell me you never got round to talking about Chrissie.'

'I wouldn't make a good detective either, would I? Hazel was so distressed, I didn't even mention her.'

'What are you like?' Kate said. 'You never want to upset anyone. In fact, it's more than that. You feel responsible for them and want to make their troubles go away. Did becoming a doctor make you so compassionate, or was it the other way round?'

'You can't be a doctor without wanting to help people, although I may take it a little more seriously than some of my colleagues.'

'Like Walter Hopkins, you mean.'

They exchanged knowing looks.

'Call me naive,' Zoe continued, 'but I think you get more out of people by being kind to them.'

'Well you've got the ideal excuse for seeing Hazel again. You can say you hated leaving her in such a bad way and wanted to check she was alright.'

'You're a schemer, Kate. Have you always been one or did you have to work at it?'

Kate laughed. 'I guess I asked for that. But seriously, now you've earned Hazel's trust it would be a pity to waste it. She may be more forthcoming about Chrissie when you go back than she would have been if you'd broached the subject on your first visit.'

'I got her to mention this mysterious man in Norham before she clammed up. That could be important. Where is Norham, by the way?'

'It's the first village on the English side if you follow the road Hazel was on when she passed you that morning in her Volvo.'

'You still think she couldn't have a lover?'

'It looks like I may be wrong on that count. Who else would a husband forbid his wife to see?'

201

'If he does exist, he's probably a red herring,' Zoe said. 'If Ray already knew Hazel was having an affair, she'd have no reason to kill Chrissie to keep it a secret.' She gathered up their plates and mugs to put them in the sink. 'I think I'd rather run a pub than be a policeman. We're making no progress at all.'

'Cheer up, it's early days. Let's talk about our next moves. Have you spoken to Erskine recently?'

'No, I've not heard from him.'

'Let me know if he arranges to come and see you again. Only because he might tell us something useful.'

'If you say so. And apart from pumping an old flame for information, what are your plans?'

'Even though I refuse to consider the possibility of Tom being the murderer, he was married to Alice and probably knows more than anyone about her relationship with Gregor. So I'm away to see him and Jean. I really should get to know her, if she's marrying into the family. Want to come too?'

'When?'

Kate looked at her watch. 'About ten minutes ago, actually. I recently had a big sort-out and found lots of my girls' things which would be perfect for Tom's twins. Mum arranged for me to drop them round to Jean today, and when I do I'm sure she'll invite us in . . .'

TWENTY-EIGHT

Zoe had last seen Jean the day her mother died, and was shocked by how much weight the young woman had lost since then. As Kate predicted, they were immediately invited in for a cup of tea.

'I heard about your accident, Doctor Zoe,' Jean said. 'What a terrible thing to happen.'

'I'm sorry it meant I couldn't make your mother's funeral.'

Explaining that Tom was working and the twins were at a birthday party and due to be dropped off by a friend's mother very soon, Jean stowed the two large bags of clothes Kate gave her into a cupboard.

'Thank you so much. Angie and Maddy will be tired when they get home, so I'll save the clothes for another day. They'll have such fun – they love dressing up.'

The doorbell rang.

'This must be them. You haven't seen them for a while, Kate, so you'll be surprised how much they've changed. They're very grown-up now.'

But it wasn't the twins at the door. It was their mother, Alice. And Zoe could tell by her expression this was no social visit.

In defiance of the cold weather, Alice wore a short denim skirt and no tights. Hands on hips, she met Jean's startled greeting with, 'I've come to see my girls. Where are they?'

'They've gone to a birthday party,' Jean said. 'I'm expecting them home any minute. Do you want to wait?'

Alice slammed the front door shut behind her, pushed past Kate and Zoe, and strode to the lounge. After a cursory glance around the room she turned to face Jean again. 'When will they be back?'

'I told you – any time now.'

'Why don't we all have a cup of tea and wait for them?' Kate suggested.

Alice rounded on her. 'You don't need to stay. They're my daughters.'

'And we've come to see Jean,' Kate said. 'Jean, do you want Zoe and me to stay?'

'Yes please.'

Alice stood glowering, Kate looked back at her defiantly, Jean stared at the floor. *Stalemate.*

Spending time with your future husband's first wife can never be easy, and given Jean's submissive nature and the fact that Alice was patently spoiling for a fight, Zoe knew who would come off worse if the women were left alone. However, Jean confounded expectations by raising her head and fixing her gaze on Alice's face.

'I'm sorry about your mother. I know how painful that is – mine passed away recently too.' Jean's voice trembled but she carried on. 'But it doesn't matter how upset you are, you've no right to come barging into my home and being rude to my friends.'

Alice may have wanted to interrupt, but Jean, her voice growing steadier the more she spoke, was not going to let her. 'I expect you're worried that when Tom and me are married he'll try to stop you seeing Angie and Maddy. Well, I wouldn't let him do that, even if he wanted to, which he doesn't. You're their mother, and they need to grow up knowing you. For their sakes we all have to get on.'

Zoe's eyes met Kate's, then they both looked at Alice. Their hopes she would be affected by Jean's obvious sincerity were dashed when she raised her hands and started to clap slowly.

'What a bonny speech. How long have you been practicing that one? Too right I'm their mother. You'll never be, and you'd do well to mind it.'

Jean's courage evaporated in the face of such malice. 'We only want what's best for Angie and Maddy,' she whispered, looking down at the floor again. Kate frowned, no longer able to read her lips.

'Which is why I'm after taking them away from their pervy father.' The triumph in Alice's voice made it obvious that saying this had been the aim of her visit all along.

'What do you mean?' Jean said.

'You really don't know what he gets up to when your back's turned, do you? Even a sad creature like you wouldn't stick around if you did.'

Jean looked at Kate and Zoe, her face imploring them to help make sense of what Alice was saying, and now Zoe wished she had warned Tom this might happen. Even on the strength of one encounter she should have known Alice would be unable to resist hurting Jean.

'Mum had proof, so don't think you can stop me.'

Kate put her arm round Jean's narrow shoulders. 'If you've got something to say, Alice, why don't you just come out with it?'

Alice tossed her hair back and sneered at Kate. 'I'll say this slowly so you get it first time. You and your family can't tell me what to do anymore.'

The bell rang. Jean took a deep breath and went to open the front door. Two little girls in matching blue party-frocks hurtled inside.

'Look what I made.'

'I made one too.'

A dark-haired woman stood on the step. 'They're a bit over-excited, I'm afraid.'

Jean thanked her for bringing the twins back and

closed the door. Angie and Maddy noisily vied for her attention.

'Look, girls, we've got visitors.' Jean glanced at Alice. 'And you've got one very special visitor. It's your mummy.'

The girls slowly turned to look in Alice's direction, then hid their faces in Jean's skirt. A look of satisfaction passed over Jean's face, quickly replaced by anxiety.

'Come on girls, don't be silly. Mummy's come to see you. Say hello.'

The girls peered out from the safety of Jean's skirt, but it took a lot of coaxing to persuade them to approach their mother. Eventually, holding Jean's hands, they went up to Alice and shyly offered her their creations, small paper plates adorned with pieces of coloured paper and dried pasta roughly in the shape of faces.

'This is Daddy.'

'My one's Jean.'

Alice took the plates, gave them a cursory glance, and put them on the hall table. 'Do you like hamburgers?' she asked the girls. 'Want to come to McDonalds with me and my friend?'

The girls nodded enthusiastically, then looked up at Jean.

'I don't think so,' Jean said. 'They've been to a party and probably eaten more than enough already.'

'It's only a hamburger, for chrissakes,' Alice said.

'Girls, take Mummy into the lounge,' Jean said. 'You can show her your toys.' Giving Alice no chance to argue, she turned and went into the kitchen. Kate and Zoe followed.

Jean sat down on a stool, biting back tears.

'Is there anything we can do?' Zoe asked.

'I need to speak to Tom.' Jean reached for the phone on the kitchen wall. At the end of a brief conversation, she told Tom to be quick and put the phone down. 'He's just finishing off at the Auld Manse, so it won't take him long to drive home. Will you help me stop her from taking them away until then?'

'Of course,' Kate said. 'Why don't you put the kettle on and I'll go and suggest the girls change out of their party frocks. It'll take a while if they're anything like mine were at that age.'

Alice declined the offer of tea and said there was no need for the girls to change. She got up from the sofa and said, 'Come on you two.'

The twins obediently put down the identical dolls they had been showing their mother and followed her into the hall.

'Tom's coming home,' Zoe said. 'He wants to see you.'

'I bet he does. I'll see him when we get back. Terry's been waiting out in the car for long enough.'

One of the girls – Zoe guessed it was Maddy – asked if Jean could come too. Their mother's curt reply did nothing to reassure them, and when Jean came out of the kitchen a moment later they ran to her.

Alice glared at Jean. 'Come on kids, let's go. Terry's waiting for us. You'll like him.' When neither twin moved, the forced jocularity in her voice vanished. 'I said come on!'

Too young to understand their mother's anger was not directed at themselves, Angie and Maddy burst into tears simultaneously and clung more tightly to Jean.

Tom took in this scene as he entered the house seconds later. While doing his best to combine greeting his daughters with keeping them clear of his dirty work clothes, he fixed Alice with a stare from a pair of eyes that glowed pale out of a face black with soot.

'We'll talk about this outside. Now.'

Jean went to the hall cupboard and pulled out the bags of clothes she had put in there earlier. 'Look girls. See what Auntie Kate's brought for you. New clothes.'

The mood in the house quickly lifted with Alice gone. Zoe sat in the lounge drinking tea, watching Kate and Jean help the twins try on assorted dresses, T-shirts and trousers, fastening buttons and doing up zips, then unfastening and undoing them. It was nearly dark, but when she got up to look out of the window she saw a light above the front door was illuminating the confrontation taking place in the garden. Halfway down the path, Tom sat on a low stone wall and looked up at his ex-wife as she stood over him, wagging a finger.

Kate's lip-reading skills would have been useful, but Zoe did not need to know the actual words passing between them to realise Alice had the upper hand. Tom looked defeated and at one point held his head in his hands. Whatever it was Alice had learnt from her mother and was now threatening him with must be very serious indeed.

Jean came alongside Zoe and peered anxiously out of the window. 'Can you see them? Is Tom all right?'

'He's coming in now. And she's leaving.'

As Jean dashed out to the hall, Zoe rejoined Kate, who was explaining to the twins what being deaf meant. They listened intently then returned to trying on clothes, but Zoe noticed how they subsequently made a point of touching Kate lightly on the hand before speaking to her.

Jean reappeared a few minutes later followed by Tom, who had changed into a navy blue towelling gown.

'She doesn't like me walking around in my work gear,' he said. 'I'll have a shower in a minute.'

'We'd better be going.' Zoe got to her feet.

'What did Alice say?' Kate asked.

Everyone turned to look at the girls playing on the floor.

'I'm seeing her tomorrow,' Tom said quietly. 'At my house. To have a proper talk.'

'Don't let her bully you,' Kate said.

'You may want to take legal advice before

agreeing to anything,' Zoe said.

It was clear Tom's thoughts were elsewhere. He nodded absently and left the room without saying goodbye.

Kate and Zoe were not far from Keeper's Cottage when a vehicle coming towards them flashed its headlights several times for no apparent reason.

'Bloody idiot,' Kate said as it went slowly past them. She looked in her rear-view mirror. 'He's stopped. And now he's turning.'

Zoe twisted herself round in her seat to see out of the back window. She could not have done that the day before, although the manoeuvre still hurt a little. 'I think it's Neil.'

Kate looked at her. 'It's Neil,' Zoe repeated.

'Well I'm not stopping. He'll have to follow us back to your place.'

Minutes later, Kate brought her car to a halt on the road outside Keeper's Cottage and Neil's Land Rover pulled in behind them.

'I'll leave you to deal with him,' Kate said as Zoe climbed out. 'Sorry, but I'm already late collecting the bairns.' She drove off.

Zoe folded her arms and watched Neil approach.

'Hi,' he said.

'Hello.'

'Can we go in? It's cold out here. Although from the look on your face it won't be much warmer indoors.'

Zoe unlocked the front door and gained irrational satisfaction at seeing Mac give Neil no more than a cursory sniff before throwing himself at her.

'Did you think you'd never see me again?' she said to the dog, hugging him. 'Let's go through into the sitting room,' she told Neil, without looking at him.

The fire was down to its final embers, so Zoe busied herself adding some kindling and opening up the woodburner's air flow. Then she turned to Neil. He had sat down, but jumped up again as soon as he saw her face, putting his hands out in what was now a familiar gesture of capitulation.

'I can only think I've incurred your wrath this time by phoning the health centre and asking Margaret how you were.'

'Don't you know the meaning of the word "discretion"?'

'I wanted to check you were okay.'

'That was considerate of you, but was it necessary to virtually tell her you'd stayed here overnight?'

'Does it matter? You know Margaret can be trusted – she works for you.'

Zoe groaned in frustration. 'That's my point.' She swept back a lock of hair which had escaped from her ponytail. 'I've given up on you ever understanding, but I don't want the rest of the world knowing about my personal life. If this relationship stands any chance, it has to develop quietly and slowly.'

'I'm not a quiet, slow person.'

'That's obvious. But if you can't respect my most basic need for privacy it isn't going to happen at all.'

Neil reached out and gently took hold of Zoe's upper arms. Receiving no reprimand, he pulled her a little closer. 'I promise I'll try harder,' he said. 'But do one thing for me, will you? Next time I annoy you – and we both know there will be a next time – tell me to my face. Don't just keep avoiding me.'

'I haven't been avoiding you.'

'So I've been unlucky every time I phoned and each time I dropped by?'

'Of course. Where did you think I was – hiding behind the bookcase?'

'I knew you weren't doing that. I peered in through the window.'

Despite her best efforts to stay stern-faced, Zoe

smiled. 'You must have sent poor Mac crazy.' She disengaged herself from Neil's grasp. 'I suppose I'd better get us both a drink.'

'Thanks, but I've arranged to meet some mates. I just wanted to check we're still on for next Saturday night. I've booked a table.'

'As long as you don't go around telling everyone.'

'So you want me to cancel the ad I've taken out in the *Berwickshire News*?'

'What time?'

'I'll collect you at seven.' Neil pulled on his hat. Zoe was startled at how much this changed his appearance, and wondered what he looked like with a full head of hair. Maybe she would get to see a photograph one day.

'Can I ask one final thing before I go?'

'What?' Zoe asked warily.

'Please will you give me your mobile number?'

'You're determined to track me down wherever I go, aren't you?'

'No. You'll still have the option not to take my calls, but at least I can leave a message. It's not much to ask from a man who's going to buy you a slap-up meal, is it?'

TWENTY-NINE

Monday morning was the coldest yet of Zoe's first Scottish winter. She found a layer of ice on the inside of the bathroom window and spotted the cat slinking into the living room to curl up on Mac's armchair. *He wasn't going to like that.*

Despite energetically working the lever which sent ash tumbling into the pan below, she could not persuade the woodburner to perform with its usual gusto and resolved to call Tom later, once she got his number from the business card display in the shop's window. However, stopping there would have to wait until lunchtime. Mac's morning walk started later every day, now that it got light so much later, and she was already running behind schedule.

She had not put the hire car away, so its windscreen had iced up overnight. It might be a safe, sensible drive, but it did not come equipped with a scraper or a de-icing spray, so she was further delayed by having to turn on the engine and wait for the windows to defrost from the inside.

Walter was standing at the reception desk talking to Margaret when Zoe rushed in. He broke off their conversation to look pointedly at his watch.

'Sorry I'm late,' Zoe said.

Walter tutted. At first she thought he was joking, but he continued to frown.

'It's only five minutes.'

'What would happen if we were all only five minutes late?' Walter glanced towards Margaret for support, but she stared at her computer screen.

'I've got a little time before my surgery starts.'

'Your first patient is already here.'

'Then he's early. He can't have had to scrape ice off his car.'

'You're living in Scotland now. You must allow for that sort of thing.'

Her face reddening, Zoe turned and strode to her consulting room.

After that discouraging start, the morning rolled by surprisingly quickly, despite some patients still seeming keener to enquire about her health than discuss what was wrong with their own. By the time surgery finished she was almost able to remember why she trained to be a doctor in the first place.

Then Walter came in and stood stiffly in front of her desk.

'I'd ask you not to argue with me in front of the clerical staff,' he said. 'Please remember I'm a partner in this practice.'

Resisting the urge to shout, 'You started it,' Zoe swallowed hard. When she trusted herself to speak, she said, 'Walter, I'm well aware that you're a partner and I'm not. But the same principle applies when you wish to reprimand me. I'd prefer you did it behind closed doors.'

Walter studied her in silence, then stomped from the room. Dropping the pen onto her desk, Zoe slumped in her chair and groaned. She couldn't go on like this.

Leaving the health centre a few minutes later, she drove the short distance to the shop, trying to take her mind off Walter by listening to the radio. For the first time in ages, Radio Borders made no mention of Westerlea in its news bulletin.

She had not been to the shop since giving Lisa the contact details of the abortion clinic, and was anxious to know if the young woman had done anything with this information. However, after her earlier brush with Walter, the last thing she needed was a run-in with Brian, so she bypassed the shop's front door and stopped at the window displaying business cards and For Sale notices.

'Not coming in today?'

Startled, Zoe looked up from her mobile. 'My chimney needs sweeping,' she said. 'I'm just taking down Tom Watson's number.'

Brian stood at the shop door, arms folded. 'Or maybe you saw I was here.'

'No surprise there. It's your shop.'

'I know what you're up to, Doctor.'

Zoe looked around. Luckily, no one was nearby. She did not want to be seen arguing out on the pavement. 'You've misunderstood my intentions.'

'I don't think so.' Brian took a few steps forward, delivering a blast of bad breath which reminded Zoe of their encounter some days earlier. 'I've only got one thing to say to you.'

'And what's that?'

'Stop interfering in other people's lives.'

'I'm a doctor, Brian. If someone asks for my advice on a medical matter, I'll try to help them. That may mean prescribing a course of medication or perhaps referring them to a specialist. But there are instances when only the patient can decide what course of action is best for them.'

'She's not your bloody patient.'

Zoe bowed her head in acknowledgement of this fact. 'I'm only trying to help Lisa reach an informed decision.'

'Oh really?' Brian's voice was mocking.

'Why are you so keen for your wife to have an abortion?'

'I don't have to tell you. The girl knows what she needs to do. She's always done what she's told and I don't intend to let some do-good pro-lifer change that.'

'I have no personal axe to grind on the subject of abortion. I merely believe that Lisa is right to be considering all the options. You should be supporting her.'

'Don't tell me what I should be doing. I'm not your patient either. I could report you to the authorities for misconduct, I could.'

'In which case there's nothing more to be said.'

'Just remember, I don't want you talking to my Lisa again.' Brian thrust his face up close to Zoe's. 'Not here, not at the health centre, not at your place. I've told her and now I'm telling you.'

'If Lisa comes to see me, I won't turn her away.'

'She won't be coming anywhere near you again. I'll see to that.' Brian turned and went inside.

Zoe got into her car. *What a creep that man was.* Now she would have to be more organised and do a weekly shop somewhere else. Or order what she needed online, like she used to.

Given Brian's hostility, it was a relief to speak with Tom, who sounded genuinely pleased to hear from her. He apologised that the first appointment he could offer her was Wednesday morning, far sooner than Zoe had expected.

THIRTY

As promised, Tom arrived not long after breakfast on Wednesday. He turned down the offer of tea or coffee until he was finished, and before long the fireplace was swathed in sheeting except for a gap at the woodburner's front, like a patient prepped for surgery. Zoe asked how Jean was.

Tom looked up from taping the sheet's edge to the hearth. 'She's behaving like everything's back to normal, but I think that's just putting on a brave face for me and the girls.'

'We all grieve in different ways.'

'Aye. It's always been Jean's way to keep busy, but I don't think she should be sorting out her Mum's things so soon. I found her in floods of tears yesterday because some of Bonnie's bits and pieces have gone missing.'

'Anything valuable?'

'No, mainly junk. A brooch, a key ring, a few photos. You ken the sort of things old folk hang on to.'

Zoe glanced down at the diamond-chip eternity ring she always wore. It had little monetary worth but she cherished it because her gran had made her accept it a few days before she died.

'Losing Bonnie so suddenly would've been bad enough, but now I've brought all this extra worry into her life. She doesn't deserve it, not Jeanie. She's never hurt anyone.'

'It's not your fault either.'

Tom didn't reply. He opened the metre-long tube he had brought with him and pulled out several plastic rods. Zoe watched as he attached a brush to the first one, inserted it into the woodburner then pushed it upwards. As this disappeared up the chimney, Tom screwed on another rod, then another and another. After using six rods he turned to Zoe.

'Will you go outside and chap on the window when you see the brush come out of the pot?'

After standing in the cold for several minutes, looking up at the cottage's chimney, Zoe was relieved to see Tom's brush appear. She knocked on the window and gave him a thumbs-up, then hurried back in to put on the kettle.

'That needed done,' Tom said as they sipped coffee a few minutes later. 'You're lucky the chimney hasn't gone on fire by now.'

Zoe took a deep breath. He might tell her to mind her own business, but she would risk it. 'Tom, what's happening with Alice?' she asked.

'I talked to her again the day after you and Kate came round, offered her the chance to see the twins whenever she's up here. I even said they could maybe visit her in Newcastle when they got used to her.'

'Is she happy with that arrangement?'

Tom rubbed at a smudge of soot on his cheek. 'She's threatening to go to a solicitor. She can afford one now. And he'll make me give up the twins completely.'

'But you've looked after them brilliantly on your own – everyone says so. And you and Jean getting married can only help.'

'It's a problem of my own making. I must thole it.'

This was a new expression to Zoe, but she got the gist. 'You aren't the only one who'd suffer. Do you really think Angie and Maddy would be better off with their mother?'

'No. But if I fight her she'll get them anyway, and I'll lose Jean too.'

'Why would that happen? Jean's devoted to you.'

As Tom stared out of the window and chewed on a fingernail, Zoe could sense the battle raging inside him, the need to share his dilemma versus the fear of revealing the hold Chrissie Baird – and now her daughter – had over him.

'Whatever it is, I promise you I've heard worse.'

He turned back to her and for an instant it looked as if he was about to tell all. But instead he put down his mug and lifted the tube holding his rods and brush. 'I should go. I've got a lot of customers to see. It's always the same after a cold snap.'

Once outside, he withdrew his cigarettes and a matchbook from his overalls. The matchbook must have been empty because he stared at it, made a face, then returned it to his pocket and brought out a lighter. He trudged to the small white van and flung his tools in the back.

In an attempt to shrug off the downcast mood she was in after Tom's visit, Zoe decided to push her own and other people's problems out of her mind by visiting Kelso. She had got into the habit of going there nearly every week, but had not made the trip since her car crash.

The waitress at the café smiled in recognition and invited her to sit at what Zoe now considered 'her' table, overlooking the cobbled square and the pleasingly symmetrical town hall built of pale stone. She had enjoyed a cheese scone and was pouring the remainder of the coffee into her cup when her mobile rang. It was Neil.

'Made your mind up yet?'

'I thought I'd already accepted your invitation for Saturday.'

'No, not that. Your kitchen. We need to start working on it soon if it's to be done and fitted by Christmas.'

'Oh. You mean this is one of those kitchen-company sales calls.'

'I didn't think you'd appreciate me ringing simply to tell you how much I'm looking forward to our date.'

'Well you're wrong. I've managed to upset so many people this week it's nice to hear a friendly voice.'

'That doesn't sound like you. What's happened?'

'It's too complicated to go into.'

There was a brief silence; Zoe wondered if she had lost reception. Then Neil said, 'I was beginning to think I'd got the hang of this courting lark but now you've clammed up on me again.'

'Please don't let's argue. I'm looking forward to Saturday too.'

After he rang off, Zoe sat looking out at the people walking past the café window. She saw no familiar faces and try as she might, she didn't feel at home here. Perhaps she had expected too much.

The rest of the week dragged by, although Zoe was kept busy working additional sessions to cover for Walter, who had taken a few days off to visit his mother in Wales. She also paid daily visits to the coach house where Gerry Hall's men were at last making headway on the conversion. During one of those trips, on impulse, she walked up to Larimer Hall. There was no sign of Neil but Peter took her through to the showroom and left her to wander around the kitchen displays, trying to choose between natural wood and a hand-painted Shaker style.

Although they exchanged numerous texts, she saw little of Kate, who was spending much of her time in Edinburgh, looking up records at the ScotlandsPeople ancestry centre. She tried to persuade Zoe to join her one day, but despite the temptation of lunch at Harvey Nichols and shopping for a new outfit, Zoe declined. Saturday night was, after all, only a meal with a friend at a local restaurant. There was no need to buy special clothes for it.

However, she regretted that decision when Saturday came, as none of her existing outfits seemed to fit the occasion. After trying on endless combinations of skirts and tops, she settled on a pair of black trousers with a red silk blouse. She brushed her hair for a long time then let it swing loose.

At seven-fifteen, she realised she did not know Neil well enough to judge whether his being a quarter of an hour late was usual. At seven-thirty she rang Larimer Hall and got no reply, and a subsequent call to Neil's mobile went straight to voicemail. By eight o'clock, she could not stay still or concentrate on a book, due to extreme annoyance combined with a similar degree of worry.

Just as she decided she had been stood up, Mac started to bark. Zoe checked her reflection in the mirror above the bookcase then peered out of the sitting room window.

Constable Geddes was approaching her front door.

THIRTY-ONE

The young policeman walked slowly, an apprehensive look on his face. Zoe raced to the front door and flung it open, heart pounding.

'What's happened?'

'DCI Mather sent me to fetch you.'

'Why?'

'There's been an incident. In the village.'

'Oh my God. Is it Neil – Mr Pengelly? I was expecting him over an hour ago.'

'You'll see him when you get there.'

'But is he all right? I'm not going anywhere until I know.'

'He's unhurt.'

They drove the short distance to the village in silence. Geddes had obviously been told not to discuss anything with Zoe so she did not press him, but the journey felt longer than it ever had before.

Several police vehicles were parked along Main Street and an ambulance stood with its doors open. A uniformed constable restrained a small group of people gathered on the pavement opposite. Neil's Land Rover was parked directly outside the shop, its owner leant against the bonnet smoking a cigarette and staring at the ground, watched by a policewoman who stood a short distance away from him.

As soon as Geddes stopped the car, Zoe leapt out and ran across the road to Neil. He was wearing a leather jacket she had never seen before over a pale shirt with some sort of dark pattern down the front. As she got closer, the pattern started to look like bloodstains.

'Neil!'

He looked up and attempted a smile. 'Hi.' The hand holding his cigarette shook.

'What's happened?'

'She's killed him.'

Zoe thought she had misheard. 'What did you say?'

The policewoman stepped towards them.

Neil ground his cigarette into the road with a heel. 'Lisa's killed Brian. Stabbed him.'

'Mr Pengelly, you were asked not to discuss the matter with anyone.' The policewoman turned her attention to Zoe. 'Are you Doctor Moreland?'

'Yes.'

'Please come with me.'

'I need to talk to Mr Pengelly.'

'I'm to take you to DCI Mather straightaway.'

Lisa's killed Brian. Zoe tried to concentrate on what was being said to her, but those words filled her head. *Lisa's killed Brian.*

'I wanted to bring you flowers,' Neil said. 'But the shop was closed, so I went round to the house door. They've opened up before, when we've run out of things. And –'

'Mr Pengelly!' The policewoman took Zoe by the arm and led her towards the shop's entrance. 'Stay there,' she called to Neil over her shoulder.

Once inside, Zoe had to retreat into one of the aisles to allow several police officers to pass by. No one spoke. Her escort positioned her in front of the delicatessen counter and disappeared through the door into the stockroom, returning seconds later.

'The DCI will be with you shortly.'

Instead of his usual patent-leather shoes and

stylish suit, Mather wore a pair of chunky suede boots, black corduroy trousers and a thick burgundy sweater.

'Thank you for coming, Doctor Moreland.'

'Why am I here?'

'What have you been told?

'Lisa's killed Brian. That's all I know.'

'That's how it appears. Mrs Humphreys has been asking for you. She refuses to speak to anyone else. Is she your patient?'

'No, not really.'

Mather raised his eyebrows.

'I mean, she's not registered with us, but I've been advising her.'

'On a medical matter?'

'I'd rather not say.'

'It may help her.'

'Can't I see her first?'

The policeman nodded. 'As far as we can ascertain she isn't injured, but she won't let a paramedic near her to check.'

'I haven't brought my bag, so I can't give her any medication, if that's what you want.'

'I just want you to talk to her, calm her down.'

Lisa's killed Brian.

Zoe glanced into the kitchen as she was escorted along the hall. Several people dressed in white coveralls stood talking in muted voices on either side of a hotchpotch of bloody footprints at the doorway. Further inside the room, a pair of bare legs lay on the floor, one foot clad in a leather slipper. The rest of Brian's body was hidden from view by a run of cupboards.

Mather touched her arm, guiding her forward. 'Constable Gray will stay with you,' he said, as they halted outside a closed door.

'Can't I talk to her alone?' Zoe asked.

'It's for both your sakes.'

He pushed the door open and Zoe stepped into a

narrow sitting-room lit by a single table lamp. High-pitched keening came from a figure rocking backwards and forwards in an armchair.

Lisa looked up when Zoe spoke her name. Her face was streaked with blood, which also had also soaked the front of her clothes, turning much of the yellow blouse orange and her jeans a dark purple.

Zoe turned to the constable standing beside the door. 'Can't she at least be allowed to wash and put on clean clothes?'

'Not until she's been examined. Evidence.'

The room was suddenly quiet. Zoe went over and placed a hand on the girl's back. 'Don't be frightened, Lisa. I'm here now to look after you.'

The rocking stopped and Lisa turned to face Zoe, squinting through swollen eyelids. 'What's going to happen to me, Doctor Moreland?'

Zoe knelt down beside the armchair. 'We're going to sit here until you're feeling a bit better, and then we'll go and get you cleaned up.'

'He's dead, isn't he?'

'Yes, I'm afraid he is.'

'I had to do it, or he would have killed my baby.'

Zoe glanced towards the policeman watching them. 'Shush, there's no need to talk about that now.'

'You understand, don't you, Doctor? You know what he was trying to make me do.'

'Yes, I know.'

'You'll tell them why I had to do it, won't you? They'll believe you.'

'I'll make sure they understand. I promise.'

It had not taken long for the press to arrive; several cameras flashed as Zoe and Lisa were led outside. Once in the car that would take them to police headquarters at Hawick, Lisa leaned against Zoe, quiet now. They passed few other vehicles on the road, and an aura of unreality descended in the silence and darkness. It felt as if they would be in that car forever, travelling but never arriving. Then they slowed right down and Zoe was brought back to reality by a blaze of flashlights from several more cameras. They had reached their destination.

Zoe promised Lisa she would see her again after Lisa's examination by the police doctor, then a middle-aged policewoman led her away. Zoe was escorted to an interview room and told she would not be kept long. Mather arrived a few minutes later carrying an A4 pad and a pen. He had removed his sweater to reveal a blue paisley-patterned shirt. She doubted he owned a T-shirt.

'Thank you for helping with Mrs Humphreys. She obviously trusts you.'

'I don't know Lisa very well, but as I said, I've been advising her recently.'

'About her pregnancy?'

'How do you know about that?'

'One of the few things she would say was that she had to "keep the baby safe", but there wasn't a child on the premises. It's one of the reasons why I went along with her insistence that we fetch you.'

'She's not much more than a child herself. I hope she's being treated properly.'

'She's being well looked after.'

'When will you question her?'

'We're waiting for the police doctor to confirm she's fit to be interviewed. But probably not until tomorrow now.'

'She must have a solicitor.'

'She almost certainly doesn't have her own, so a duty solicitor will be assigned to her. Please, Doctor, you have to trust us to do our job.'

'I'm only trying to look after Lisa's interests.'

'I realise that,' Mather said. 'And right now you can help her by answering my questions.'

'If you insist.'

225

'How well did you know Mr Humphreys?'

'Only superficially. He was the shopkeeper, I was a customer.'

'Did he get involved in your conversations with his wife about her pregnancy?'

Despite her earlier promise to Lisa, Zoe was unsure how much she should tell the police at this stage. She hesitated and Mather seized on this.

'You've already told me these people are not your patients. And the girl is in a very serious situation –'

'Do you think I don't realise that?'

'You can influence what happens to her. Now and in the future.'

He was right. Zoe sighed. 'Lisa came to see me alone, although I think Brian knew. He was insisting that she should have an abortion.'

'Did she tell you why?'

'I couldn't find that out from either of them. I gave her the details of a clinic in Edinburgh, but I think she was starting to have second thoughts. I saw Brian earlier this week and he warned me not to contact her again.'

'Did he threaten you?'

Zoe could almost smell Brian's breath again as she recalled her brush with him outside the shop on Monday. 'Not physically. He was unpleasant, but he didn't scare me.'

'And how did you leave things?'

'I told him I wouldn't turn Lisa away if she asked for my help. Afterwards, I agonised over whether to force the issue and go round to see her. Now I wish I had.'

'Do you have any theories as to why Mr Humphreys was so keen for his wife to have an abortion? Is it possible, for example, that the child isn't his?'

'I wondered that myself, but it's unlikely. They lived and worked together, so for a start I can't see what opportunity she'd have for a relationship with anyone else. My gut feeling is there's another reason. I can't explain why, except that his anger seemed directed at me for interfering rather than at Lisa for betraying him.'

'So what was his attitude towards his wife?'

'He behaved as though he owned her. Of course there was a big difference in their ages, which may explain why he took charge all the time, but it was more than that. As well as telling her what to do, he'd paw at her in front of customers, as though to prove he could do anything he wanted with her.'

'In a sexual way?'

'Yes. He couldn't keep his hands off her and she never told him to stop, though she didn't appear to enjoy it.'

Mather considered this for a moment or two, then asked if Zoe knew where the couple had come from. 'I believe they're relative newcomers to the area.'

'All I ever got out of Lisa was they'd lived somewhere in England.'

Looking at his watch, Mather said, 'Mr Pengelly will be ready to leave soon. I'll arrange for a car to take you both back to Westerlea.'

'Neil's here? Why?'

'To help us with evidence gathering. We needed to take his fingerprints, examine the blood on his shirt, that kind of thing. As well as taking a formal statement.'

'You can't think he had anything to do with it.'

'We have to check his version of events against the physical evidence.'

'This is unbelievable. He was the one who found them.'

'You mustn't misinterpret what we're doing. Mr Pengelly states he was first on the scene after a crime had been committed. We're not seeking to disprove what he says happened, but to prove it.'

'I'm glad to hear that.'

'However, by his own admission, he didn't actually see Brian Humphreys being stabbed. He came in on the aftermath, so we need to establish the course of events before he arrived.'

'But you are working on the presumption that Lisa killed Brian?'

Ignoring her question, Mather stood up and said, 'I'll find out if Mr Pengelly is ready.'

'I promised Lisa I wouldn't go without seeing her first.'

'You've done your best for her, but now you have to leave things to us.'

'Can I visit her tomorrow?'

'Call me in the morning.'

After a short wait, Zoe was led back to the building's entrance by the policewoman who had taken Lisa away earlier, then a young, male constable escorted her to an unmarked car. She slid on to the back seat; Neil was already there.

'You're wearing your hair down,' he said. 'Was that for me?'

'Yes.'

He put his arm round her shoulders and held her close all the way back to Westerlea. Neither of them spoke. The car dropped them off at the shop, where lights still blazed although the ambulance and all but one of the police cars had left.

'So much for me showing you a good time,' Neil said, starting up his Land Rover.

'What we've gone through can't compare with Lisa's experience,' Zoe said. 'Poor little thing.'

'No one forced that poor little thing to stab her husband. You didn't see Brian. Spare some sympathy for him.'

'I feel sorry for them both.'

'Why did she do it?'

'I don't want to talk about that now.'

Neither of them spoke again until Neil brought his vehicle to a halt outside Keeper's Cottage.

'I'll walk you to your door.'

'There's no need.'

'I want to.'

On the doorstep, Zoe said, 'Do you want to come in? I'll make us some tea and I think I can probably stretch to toast. We haven't eaten, remember?'

'Are you trying to look after me, Doctor?'

'It's been a difficult evening for both of us.'

Neil pulled her to him. 'So let me look after you too.'

THIRTY-TWO

'This is cosy,' Neil said. 'When do the newspapers arrive?'

He and Zoe were sat up in bed drinking tea and eating the toast they had discussed but never got round to making the night before. Mac lay between them, wolfing down crusts as fast as Zoe could feed them to him, all the while keeping his eyes on the interloper.

'I don't think we'll be getting any today,' Zoe said, 'given last night's events.'

'Sorry, I wasn't thinking.' Neil put down his mug and closed his eyes as if he was going back to sleep. After a couple of minutes he opened them again, sighed theatrically and grasped her left hand. 'You'll have to marry me now.'

'I've not managed to slow you down much, I see.'

'Was that a thinly-veiled complaint about my performance last night? Please remember I'd been through a very upsetting experience earlier in the evening which was bound to take its toll.'

Zoe smiled, then straightaway felt guilty for being in such good spirits. 'Do you want to talk about it?' she asked. 'Finding them, I mean.'

'As long as it won't upset you.'

'I'm made of sterner stuff than you think.'

'Maybe so, but not as stern as you pretend.'

'I'm a doctor, Neil.'

'But that can't mean you're untouched by what happens around you. They weren't strangers. At the very least Lisa was your patient, or else why did she want you there?'

'I thought we were talking about your experience.'

He let go of her hand. 'I've changed my mind. I'll only show you mine if you show me yours.'

'Enough of the sexual innuendo. Tell me what happened when you went to the shop last night.'

'Okay.' He took hold of her hand again. 'Did I mention I'd gone to buy you flowers?'

'Yes you did.'

'I was running late, as usual, and they were closed, so I knocked on the side door. Twice. Just as I was resigned to relying on my fascinating personality and dazzling good looks to charm you I heard this god-awful wailing noise. The door wasn't locked, so I let myself in. They were in the kitchen, Brian lying on the floor and Lisa knelt over him, crying hysterically. And blood everywhere.'

'So you didn't actually see it happen?'

'You sound like the police.'

'Sorry.'

'She'd stabbed him. I might not have seen her do it, but she'd stabbed him all right. A kitchen knife, all bloody too, lay on the floor.'

'What did you do?'

'I could tell he was dead. I dragged her away from him – which was surprisingly difficult, given how tiny she is – and took her into another room. Then I called the police. A couple of uniforms soon turned up, and then Mather arrived. Judging by the way he was dressed, he'd been on his way to a hot date too.'

'I wish they'd allowed you to fetch me,' Zoe said. 'I was so worried when Constable Geddes turned up and wouldn't tell me anything.'

'Mather wouldn't even let me go for a fag on my own. I asked him, "Do you think I did it?" but he took no notice.'

'That's how he is with everyone. If you ask him a question he doesn't want to answer, he simply ignores it.'

'Maybe that is what they think. After all, they took my fingerprints and went off with the shirt I'd bought especially for the occasion. Bet I never see that again.'

Zoe shook her head. 'He told me they're not trying to disprove your version of events but prove it.'

'Do you believe him?'

'He's okay. For a policeman. And he had no reason to lie to me.'

'He wasn't doing you any favours, dragging you into that mess last night.'

'Lisa wouldn't let anyone else near her. She may have been injured herself for all they knew.'

'Is it true she's pregnant?'

'How do you know that?'

'I overheard my police escort tell one of the plain-clothes guys.'

'Everyone will know by now, in that case.'

'Not from me, they won't. I've been otherwise occupied since leaving Hawick, remember?'

'That's not what I meant.'

'Will being pregnant help her?'

'I don't know,' Zoe said. 'I want to go back to Hawick later today and make sure they're treating her properly.'

Neil took the mug from her hand and put it on his bedside table. 'Just because other people are going through hell, it doesn't mean you have to go with them.'

'I can't help thinking I should have done something to prevent it.'

'Don't you doctors receive training in how to stay detached from patients' problems?'

'It's something you're expected to develop on the job. I admit I probably do care too much sometimes, although most people don't affect me as badly as this.'

'So why is Lisa Humphreys any different?'

Zoe had to think about this before she could put it into words. 'Awful things happen all the time, and in my experience people usually cope. Most of us are stronger than we imagine. But Lisa isn't.'

'You're behaving as though she's the victim here. She stabbed her husband, not the other way around.'

'He drove her to it. And I should have seen that coming.'

'You're not responsible for what other people do, Zoe. And you can't put things right that your patients get wrong.'

'Kate told me much the same thing. Either you're ganging up against me – not for the first time – or you're right.'

'Take it from me, we're right. Even if you do manage to see Lisa today, you must accept you won't be able to wave a magic wand and make everything better for her. She's responsible for her actions, not you.'

'I'll try to remember that.'

'Glad to hear it.' Neil gently turned Zoe's face towards him and kissed her.

She pushed him away. 'We need to talk.'

'You talk. I'll listen.'

'I'm serious. Please stop doing that.'

Two of her pyjama-top's buttons were already undone. Neil paused at the third. 'Okay, let's talk.'

'Don't think I'm getting remorseful over last night, because I don't regret it one little bit.'

'Phew. I'm glad to hear it.'

'But you must understand something. I didn't come here looking for a relationship. You've turned my life upside down.'

'And what have you done to mine? You seem to think I fall in love and propose to women I hardly know on a regular basis.'

'Propose is hardly the right word, Neil. It suggests I had a say in the matter. What you did was tell me you intended to marry me.'

'Which only goes to show how overwhelmed I am by the feelings I have for you.'

Zoe had no idea how to respond to this.

'Don't get me wrong,' Neil continued. 'Meeting you has been wonderful. Like discovering there's an old James Bond movie I've never seen. With Sean Connery as 007, of course.'

She knew him well enough now to appreciate how great a compliment he had paid her. 'What are we going to do?'

'I suggest we take it one step at a time.'

'Okay.' This sounded so out of character, she doubted he had finished. She was right.

'So I'd like to repeat what we did last night. Only much more slowly. Is there any chance I can persuade you to plan no further than that, at least for now?'

Zoe got out of bed and enticed Mac into the hall with her final crust.

Fortified by a second breakfast of cereal served up by Zoe in response to his comment that sex gave him a hell of an appetite, Neil went home around ten o'clock, after extracting a promise that she would phone him when she got back from Hawick. Mather could not take her call when she rang him shortly afterwards but had left a message saying she could see Lisa at one o'clock.

She checked her mobile and found a text from Kate: *Heard about last night. Dinner @ Mum's 5pm?*

After a moment's panic, wondering how Kate knew Neil had stayed over, Zoe reasoned she must be referring to events at the shop. She was lucky her inquisitive friend had not turned up unannounced, impatient to find out more.

Sunday dinner cooked by Etta Mackenzie was too good to miss, even though, unlike Neil, Zoe found sex an appetite suppressant. She quickly texted her acceptance.

234

THIRTY-THREE

The hire car continued to feel sluggish after her own, but Zoe still arrived early at Hawick police station. *Must stop building extra time into journeys for non-existent traffic jams.*

At exactly one o'clock, the interview room's door opened and Mather strode in. Today's suit was a charcoal grey pinstripe, setting off a silk tie in several shades of turquoise.

'Doctor Moreland, thank you for coming.'

Surprised at the intimation that she was there because he had requested her presence, Zoe muttered, 'No problem,' and looked at him expectantly. He pulled out a chair, stared at it for a moment as though fighting the urge to wipe it with his handkerchief, and sat down.

'How's Lisa?' Zoe asked.

'Still tearful, but fairly cooperative.'

'What does that mean exactly?'

'It means she's admitted killing her husband. She claims she did it because he was insisting she abort their baby.'

'As I told you.'

'As you told me. However, there are some strange elements to this case. You may be able to help us make sense of them.'

'I'm only here to help Lisa.'

'You'd be doing that too.' The policeman straightened his tie. 'As is usual, we carried out some background checks on Mr and Mrs Humphreys, to enable us to get in touch with their relatives. But in this case we can't.'

'Why not?'

'Because when we searched their home we could find nothing to support their having existed before arriving in Westerlea. No birth or marriage certificates, no passports, not even an address book.'

'What about records of their purchase of the shop? That would give you a previous address or the details of the solicitor they used, at least.'

'There's nothing of that nature at all. And the various computer records we have at our disposal have drawn a blank too. Neither of them appears to have a driving licence, for example.'

'Perhaps they keep that kind of thing in a safety deposit box at their bank. What does Lisa say?'

'That's where I'm hoping you can help. Mrs Humphreys has denied all knowledge of where her husband kept their records, except for the shop accounts.'

'And you don't believe her, even though it would be symptomatic of what we know about their relationship?'

'I know she's lying because she's not very good at it.'

'So what makes you think she'll tell me? I'm not keen on doing your dirty work for you.'

'I'm sorry that's how you see it. Somewhere there are people who know the Humphreys, who would want to be informed of Brian's death. Lisa won't even give us the name of any family members.'

'Can't her solicitor help?'

'He's giving her sound legal advice, but he hasn't gained her trust like you have.'

'Is this information necessary to your investigation?'

'We need to build up a complete picture. A jigsaw puzzle, remember?'

'And what should I do if she tells me where her family is?'

'I'll leave that for to you to decide.' Mather opened the file he had brought in with him and pulled out a small, creased photograph. He slid it across the table. 'This may help. We found it in Mr Humphreys' wallet.'

Zoe picked up the photograph and studied it. 'That's Brian. I wonder how long ago this was taken?'

'If it's relevant we have people who can work that out.'

'I think these children are very relevant, don't you? This little boy is the spitting image of Brian. Here's why he was so against Lisa having a baby – he already had children from another relationship.'

The clothes Lisa had been provided with hung off her tiny frame, exaggerating her frailty. Zoe desperately wanted to give the girl a reassuring hug but they were separated by a glass partition. A policeman stood against the wall behind Lisa, staring at the back of her head.

'How are you?' Zoe asked. 'Are they treating you well?'

Lisa nodded.

'And your solicitor – how are you getting on with him?'

'He keeps trying to stop me from saying things.'

'I think you should listen to him. He's looking after your best interests.'

'But I killed Brian, so why doesn't he want me to tell them?'

'The law's very complicated. What you say now may have an effect on your, er, future,' Zoe said, shying away from words like trial and sentence.

'Doctor Moreland, I don't care how long they lock me up for. I deserve it.'

'Please don't say that. You're still in shock.'

Lisa shook her head. 'You don't understand. I

truly don't mind how long I go to prison for, as long as I can keep my baby.'

'Wouldn't you rather someone looked after it for you?'

'Have it adopted, you mean? I can't do that. It's mine.'

'No, I'm not talking about adoption. Isn't there someone – your mother or a sister perhaps – who could help you with it?'

'I don't have any family,' Lisa stared down at her hands. 'Brian was the only one. But now I'll have my baby.'

'There must be someone I can contact for you. You're only young, so I expect your grandparents are still alive. Where are they?'

'I already told the police - there's no one. Why are you all keeping on at me?' Lisa scanned the room, as if looking for a way to break out.

'Lisa, I'm only trying to help.'

'I can't stand all these questions.'

'Let's change the subject, shall we?' Zoe placated the girl by asking about her cell and what she had been given to eat. When Lisa was making eye contact again and seemed less agitated, Zoe brought out the photograph Mather had given her.

'The police found this in Brian's wallet,' she said, holding it up to the glass. 'I think I know now why he didn't want you to have his child.'

Lisa reached towards the photograph and let out a wail. 'I told him we wouldn't be able to keep it a secret.'

She fell across the table in front of her, a hand thudding against the glass partition.

THIRTY-FOUR

Zoe sprang to her feet and peered anxiously into the small room where Lisa had slid off the table on to the floor. The constable hit a panic button in the wall next to him then rushed over to the girl and gently rearranged her into the recovery position. Zoe banged on the glass partition to attract his attention.

'Let me in, please. I'm a doctor.'

After a moment's hesitation, he did what she asked. She knelt down beside Lisa and checked her pulse. Lisa moaned.

Footsteps came running into the room, but when Zoe looked up she did not see a uniform or Mather's suit. Instead, a man wearing a leather blazer and cream chinos stood over them. He carried a slim briefcase and smelt of expensive aftershave.

'What have you done to my client?' he asked.

'I'm a doctor,' Zoe said. 'She fainted.'

'I know who you are, Doctor Moreland. I am questioning whether you have any right to be speaking to Mrs Humphreys in the absence of prior reference to her legal council.'

Zoe was distracted from replying by Lisa trying to sit up. 'Stay down for a while longer, until you're feeling better,' she instructed.

Mather and Sergeant Trent appeared at the door and several other faces crowded in behind them.

'Is she all right?' Mather asked.

'I really must insist that you and I speak, Detective Chief Inspector,' the solicitor said. He looked down at Lisa with pity, as though she were a homeless person begging on the street. She tried again to sit up, this time succeeding. Sergeant Trent rushed forward and helped her back on to her chair.

'In which case, Mr Kossoff, please join me,' Mather said, turning towards the door.

'Doctor Moreland should also be there,' Kossoff said, 'as what I have to say pertains as much to her behaviour as it does to your own.'

Zoe looked at Lisa, who had regained a little colour and was taking sips of water from a plastic cup Trent had given her.

'I'll look after her,' Trent said. 'Now then, don't you go all wobbly on me, bonny lass.'

Kossoff stood back to let Zoe pass through the door into the corridor before him, then handed her a stiff, embossed business card as they followed Mather along the corridor to another interview room. Once there, the solicitor sat down, placing his briefcase on the table in front of him. Mather waited until Zoe had taken her seat before pulling out a chair for himself.

'Detective Chief Inspector, I wish to put on record my protestations at your permitting my client to be interviewed without notifying me first. And furthermore, that the interview was carried out by someone who is not even a member of your staff.'

Zoe studied Kossoff as he spoke. His eyes were a little too large for his face, while his nose was a tad too small. He sat up very straight in his chair.

Mather held up his hand. 'Mr Kossoff, we aren't in court now. There's no need for the adversarial tone.'

'I wasn't interviewing her,' Zoe said. 'She'd asked to see me and we were simply talking.'

'I had advised her to speak with no one without my being present. The police were fully cognisant of this.'

'Well I wasn't,' Zoe said.

'This is getting us nowhere,' Mather said. 'Mr Kossoff, you have my assurance we let Doctor Moreland see your client because that was what Mrs Humphreys wished.'

'And, I fully expect,' Kossoff said, reaching forward to open his briefcase locks loudly and simultaneously, 'because it suited your purpose to have someone else try to find out about matters you yourselves have failed to clarify.'

Zoe waited for the solicitor to produce something from the briefcase, but he did not. Instead, he ostentatiously turned it to prevent her from seeing its contents and continued berating Mather. Had he not been so officious, Zoe might have agreed with him. After all, Mather had asked for her help in uncovering the Humphreys' past.

Then Kossoff rounded on her too. 'And you, Doctor Moreland, should be ashamed. You have allowed yourself to be inveigled into taking part in the interrogation of my client when she obviously looks upon you as a trusted confidante.'

Zoe remained silent. She had already stated her case.

Once again Mather raised a hand and addressed Kossoff. 'Please, Chris, can we return to the wellbeing of your client? I'm sure that's your prime consideration. She has admitted stabbing her husband and the evidence appears to support this. However, I don't believe she's telling us everything, and more background information may influence the Procurator Fiscal's decision as to what she's actually charged with.'

Receiving no further argument from Kossoff, Mather returned his gaze to Zoe. 'Doctor Moreland, please tell us what led to Mrs Humphreys fainting. Was it something in particular?'

Kossoff scowled but allowed Zoe to respond.

'I showed her a photograph of two young children with her late husband,' she said, hoping Kossoff would not ask how she came by it. 'She cried out, muttered something about not being able to keep it secret, and keeled over.'

'What did she mean?' Kossoff asked, curiosity for once overcoming his tendency to extend sentences beyond their natural length.

'I thought the children were Brian's from a previous marriage, which might explain why he didn't want Lisa to have her baby. But her reaction was so extreme I'm not sure now.'

'In which case,' Mather said, getting to his feet, 'if your client feels well enough, I'd like to interview her again and try to get to the bottom of this. With you present, of course, and perhaps you may consider it helpful to have Doctor Moreland join us? She is a medical doctor, after all, and can advise on your client's fitness to be interviewed.'

Giving Kossoff no opportunity to object, Mather held the door open for Zoe and followed her through it, leaving the solicitor to scurry behind them.

Lisa had been taken to another room where only a table separated her from Zoe and Mather. Kossoff sat beside his client and explained she could ask at any time for the interview to cease if she felt unwell, adding that Zoe was present as an observer, not a participant, and Lisa had only to say if she did not want her there.

Mather produced the photograph, which he must have retrieved during the confusion after Lisa fainted. 'Mrs Humphreys,' he said gently, 'please tell us why this photograph upset you so much.'

Lisa chewed her lower lip and stared across the table at Zoe. 'Doctor Moreland knows,' she said eventually.

Kossoff made a gesture permitting Zoe to speak.

242

'These children,' Zoe said, 'they're Brian's, aren't they?'

Lisa nodded, tears starting to course down her face. 'Yes,' she said in a voice so low everyone else had to lean forward to hear her. 'That's me and Ben. My brother.'

THIRTY-FIVE

Zoe, Mather and Kossoff sat in silence. All three of them worked in professions which frequently exposed them to other people's transgressions and weaknesses, yet Zoe could see the men were as stunned by Lisa's revelation as she was herself.

Mather studied the back wall of the room, while Kossoff tentatively placed a hand on his client's shoulder. Zoe contemplated the photograph of Brian and his children which lay on the table. Although the round-faced, dark-haired toddler holding a bucket and spade bore only a slight resemblance to the grown-up Lisa, familiarity with this image of her much younger self had made her assume others were able to spot the likeness as easily.

Kossoff said, 'I think my client and I need to speak in private.'

'Of course,' Mather said. 'May I ask one further question?'

The solicitor spread his hands in silent acquiescence.

'Lisa, I need you to tell me something.'

She lifted her head and looked at Mather with swollen eyes.

'Was Brian Humphreys definitely the father of the child you're carrying?'

Lisa nodded and looked down at the table again. Mather and Zoe got up to leave Kossoff alone with his client.

The office Mather led Zoe to was as neat as its occupant and the top of his desk as shiny as his shoes. A computer sat on a workstation behind the desk and above this hung a large, wooden-framed map of the Scottish Borders.

He showed her to a chair. 'I'll call for some tea,' he said, adding when he saw her expression, 'Pot, not machine. Real milk.'

Their eyes met as he put the phone down.

'Bloody hell,' Zoe said.

'You had no idea?'

'Did you? Some situations are unthinkable, and this is one of them.'

'It will certainly make a difference to the outcome of the case.'

'I hope so. Lisa is obviously the victim here. She may have participated in a complex concealment of her abuse, but abuse it certainly was.' Zoe looked hard at Mather, challenging him to come to any other conclusion. She had to wait for his response while their tea was brought in and laid down on the desk by a young constable so nervous he collided with the door before managing to go back through it.

Mather poured the tea with care, putting milk and sugar in front of Zoe before returning to their conversation.

'The decision isn't mine, of course,' he said. 'Here in Scotland it's the role of the Procurator Fiscal to consider what, if any, charges are brought. But I expect that when the full story is known, and taking into account Mrs Humphreys – Lisa – being pregnant, she won't receive a custodial sentence.'

'That may be so,' Zoe said, stirring milk into her cup, 'but what will her life be like? Brian succeeded in isolating her totally, and now we know why. Having the baby will make things more difficult, not less. She just doesn't realise it yet.'

'At least we may be able to trace the rest of her family now.'

'But will they want to have anything to do with her? I've come across cases of parental abuse before, but nothing like this. That poor girl is expecting a baby by her own father. I can't imagine what the reaction of her relatives will be.'

Mather took a sip of his tea. 'It's going to be difficult for her, I agree.'

'What a mess.'

They concentrated on drinking their tea. As the need to start making polite conversation threatened, they heard a knock at the door and Kossoff was shown into Mather's office. The solicitor's previously blustering approach was now replaced by an air of quiet satisfaction. It was evident he too viewed the true extent of his client's tragedy as her salvation.

Kossoff sat down in the seat Mather indicated to him, but shook his head at the offer of tea. 'Their real name is Tipping and they originally come from a small village in Hertfordshire,' he said.

'That should be enough for us to track down the rest of her family.' Mather took an A4 pad out of his top drawer and made a brief note. 'Is there anything else you're able to share with me?'

'I have my client's permission to divulge everything she has now told me.'

Once again Kossoff noisily unlocked his briefcase, but this time he brought out a reporter's notepad, which he occasionally referred to while speaking. 'Mrs Tipping – Lisa's mother – and Lisa's brother Benjamin were killed in a car crash when the girl was eleven. Her father first had sex with her a few months later. At the age of fourteen, Lisa was taken by Brian to live in Devon. He severed all links with their previous life, and thereafter she took on the role of his wife, a deception they perpetuated when they moved to the Borders eleven months ago. She is only seventeen years of age now.'

'Brian told everyone she was twenty-three,' Zoe said. 'I remember him telling me what a lovely twenty-first birthday party he'd thrown for her.'

'In my experience,' Kossoff said, 'when people tell one big lie, they feel driven to augment it with lesser, totally unnecessary ones. And it's often the smaller lies which eventually give them away. Though not in this case, of course,' he added.

'My client does not know what precipitated their leaving Hertfordshire, but she recalls a serious altercation between Brian and her maternal grandmother about the same time. Her abiding memory of their departure for Devon is of leaving too early in the morning for anyone to be there to say goodbye.' Kossoff paused, as if to ensure the poignancy of this was not wasted on his audience.

'A year later, Brian came into some money, inherited, Lisa thinks, from an aunt. That's how he was able to buy the business in Westerlea.'

'No doubt choosing the Borders because it's a long way from Hertfordshire and Devon,' Zoe said. 'So they've been able to continue living as husband and wife with no one any the wiser.'

'Not quite.' Kossoff turned the page of his notepad. Zoe wished he would stop being so dramatic and say what he had to say.

Mather obviously felt the same, speaking for the first time since the solicitor started his narrative. 'Go on.'

'When I asked my client if she had confided in anyone in Westerlea about her situation, she said no. However, she did tell me that one of their customers had overheard an argument between herself and her father revealing their true relationship. This happened on the second of November.'

The significance of this date was wasted on no one in the room, although Zoe and Mather responded differently to it. Mather's eyebrows shot up, but he waited

247

for Kossoff to continue. Zoe, however, could not contain herself.

'That was only a few days before Chrissie Baird died,' she said. 'Was she the customer?'

Kossoff sighed, feigning reluctance to share any further information. He was blatantly enjoying his position centre stage.

'My client and her father were in the storage area between the shop and their living quarters. Mr, er, Tipping had divined some days earlier that his daughter was pregnant, but they had not discussed the matter in detail. It was past their usual closing time and Lisa was tidying up when her father came through to her and said something to the effect that naturally she would have to have an abortion. My client told him she wanted to think about what was the best thing to do. He got very angry.'

'I bet he did,' Zoe said.

'He berated her for being so stupid as to find herself in this situation,' Kossoff continued, ignoring the interruption. 'He told her she would get them both into trouble, then shouted something along the lines of, "What will you tell the child to call me – Daddy or Grandpa?" As he fell silent, they heard footsteps and the shop door open then close.'

Kossoff paused for longer than he credibly needed to catch his breath or wet his lips. Even Mather became impatient. 'Get a move on, Chris,' he muttered. 'Tell us who it was who overheard that conversation.'

The solicitor had the decency to look embarrassed. 'I have no idea,' he admitted. 'Lisa says Brian rushed through the shop and out of the front door, but claimed not to have seen anyone.'

'You use the word "claimed",' Zoe said. 'Didn't Lisa believe him?'

'That is the precise word she used. I realise it could be important, that Brian may have lied to her. However, I didn't want to question her more closely about it today. Despite everything, my client's natural tendency is still to defend her father's actions. If a link exists between that episode and what happened to Mrs Baird a few days later, I respectfully suggest it is up to you, DCI Mather, to establish it.'

Mather was about to respond when his telephone rang. He picked it up, listened, then said a few words. On finishing the call he stood up. 'I'm needed elsewhere. Thank you both for your help. I'll send someone to see you out.'

A few minutes later, having been escorted to the station's front door, Zoe asked Kossoff, 'What will happen to Lisa now?'

'Because this case is so complex there will have to be a judicial examination.'

'What does that involve?'

'Essentially, it means a meeting in chambers with the Procurator Fiscal and the Sheriff. They can question Lisa – don't worry, I'll be there with her – before a decision is reached on what she'll be charged with.'

'Will this help her case?'

'Very definitely. It's not a cross-examination, they can only ask a restricted range of questions. But we'll be able to outline her defence, the intolerable circumstances under which she found herself, and the Fiscal will be obliged to investigate these and take them into account.'

'This is your area of expertise,' Zoe said. 'So I guess I must let you get on with it. Though I really wish I could do more to help Lisa myself.'

'You have already done more than anyone else, Doctor Moreland. After all, you unlocked her deepest secret, didn't you?' Kossoff held out his hand and Zoe shook it, then the solicitor strode away to his car.

THIRTY-SIX

Back at Keeper's Cottage, Zoe tried to reach Neil on his mobile. It went straight to voicemail so she left a brief message telling him she would call again later. Then she led Mac out to the hire car for the short drive to Tolbyres.

Etta Mackenzie's kitchen at Tolbyres Farmhouse was an expanded version of her daughter's and must have been a major undertaking for Peter and Neil to fit out. The Aga – seemingly mandatory in the Scottish Borders – was half as wide again as Kate's, and there was an additional full-size sink. Above the highly-polished dining table, which could seat up to fourteen, hung photographs of Kate and her brothers at their respective weddings and a montage of images of their children.

Zoe sat down, her offer to help Etta with her preparations for the meal having been refused. As usual, Kate and her mother were better informed than they ought to be. News had leaked out about Lisa's pregnancy and they knew Zoe had been to Hawick that afternoon to see her. Ignoring Brian's fate, what they wanted to know was how Lisa was holding up.

'She's as well as can be expected.' Zoe waited to be challenged on this noncommittal reply, but Etta was crumbling a stock cube into a saucepan and Kate's grasshopper mind had already moved on.

'You may find this hard to believe,' she said, 'but until recent events there hadn't been a murder in Westerlea since July 1899, when the blacksmith flew into a jealous rage and smothered his wife with her own shawl.'

'Let's hope this is the last one the village ever sees,' Zoe said.

'At least there's no way Lisa killing Brian can be linked to what happened to the Bairds,' Kate said.

Zoe did not trust herself to comment. Since leaving Hawick, she had been unable to stop thinking about the possibility that these events were connected. It might simplify matters if Brian was responsible for Chrissie Baird's death. On the other hand, if she was the mystery person who overheard him shouting at Lisa in the stockroom and he killed her as a result, would the police ever find sufficient evidence of this to close the case? And how did that explain Jimmy's death and the attempt on Zoe's own life?

Etta looked up from stirring a saucepan of gravy. Her face was very red. 'I feel so bad for the poor wee thing. She needed help. I should have done something.'

'No one could have predicted it would go that far, Mum,' Kate said. 'Not even Zoe, and she knew about the baby.'

Zoe nodded. That at least was true.

'Lisa's lucky to have Chris Kossoff representing her. Remember, Mum, how he helped out Aline Morton's son with that spot of bother last year?'

'Even so, I wish . . . '

Etta's voice trailed off. She bent down to open an oven door, and the smell of garlic, rosemary and lamb billowed into the room.

'Is there anyone in the Borders you two don't know?' Zoe asked, wanting to move the conversation on from Lisa and Brian. When the full story came out, as it must, Kate was going to give her a hard time for not sharing all the facts.

'There's a young couple who moved down from Edinburgh to Duns last week,' Kate said. 'Mum's still trying to find out about them, but give her time.'

'Don't forget it was you who told me first about Saturday night's goings-on,' Etta said, walking to the sink. Her face disappeared in a cloud of steam as she tipped a large quantity of potatoes into a colander, then returned them to the saucepan.

Splashes of colour appeared on Kate's face. 'I only knew that something had happened at the shop. You got the gory details from Auntie Phil, remember?'

At that moment, the door opened and Eva rushed in, stopping Zoe from pressing Kate about the source of her information. Although she already had her suspicions.

'How long will dinner be?' Eva asked. 'We're starving, and so's Mac.'

'Not long now,' Etta said. 'Ask Granddad to come through and champ the tatties for me, will you? Then you can all wash your hands and sit down.'

Eva ran out of the room, shouting to Mac that he must wash his paws.

'We've done well to get this long without them,' Kate said. She started to lay the table.

'Will you be coming to the Bairds' funeral on Tuesday, Zoe?' Etta asked as she stirred the steaming saucepan of gravy. 'It'll likely be a good turnout, although most people will be there to pay their respects to Jimmy rather than Chrissie.'

'Do you think I should? I didn't really know them.'

'It's expected of you.'

The children and their grandfather arrived and took their seats around the dining table. Mac sat under it.

Once everyone had been served their food, Frankie turned to Zoe. 'Did you see the body?' he asked.

'Frankie!' his mother scolded.

'We all know Lisa killed Brian,' Frankie said. 'Why can't we ask Zoe about it? She was there.'

Ranald Mackenzie looked up from the heaped plate his wife had put in front of him. 'It's not a suitable topic for the dinner table.'

'So will you let her tell us about it when we've finished eating?'

'Frankie, be more thoughtful. Zoe probably wants to forget about it,' Etta said.

'Mum's always telling us it's better to talk things through than bottle them up. I bet you've all been asking her about it. And she's a doctor so she's used to dead people.' Frankie fell silent when he saw the look on his mother's face.

'What have you been doing this weekend?' Zoe asked Eva, who was sitting next to her.

'We went swimming yesterday,' Eva said. 'And then –'

'I can float without arm-bands now,' Mhairi said proudly. 'Can you, Zoe?'

'Of course she can, she's grown-up,' her sister said. 'And then that nice man came to see us.'

'What nice man was that, Kate?' Zoe asked.

Kate's face took on the hue of her pink sweater. 'Erskine Mather,' she said. 'He just dropped by to say I mustn't feel obliged to go and see Bette, if I'd rather not.'

'So that's how he got to the shop so quickly,' Zoe said.

'Yes, he was with me when the call came in.'

Ranald put down his cutlery with a clatter. 'You hadn't mentioned you were seeing him again.'

'Because I'm not, Dad.'

'Etta, did you know about this?'

'Oh, Ranald, don't go on. She's a grown woman, she knows what she's doing.' Etta set down the gravy jug with such force that it banged on the table, startling everyone except Kate.

'Your mother seems very upset about Lisa,' Zoe said as she prepared to go home later. Despite arriving at Tolbyres with no appetite, she had eaten so much she was surprised her coat would button up.

'We all are. It's another thing that's been happening under our noses and we didn't realise. How dreadful to have a husband who doesn't want the child you're carrying.' Kate passed over the half-dozen eggs Etta had boxed up for Zoe. 'I'll see you on Tuesday. The funeral's at eleven, so I'll pick you up about twenty to.'

'Do I really need to go?'

'Of course. Everyone'll be there. And it may be our last chance to observe Gregor and Alice together before they disappear back to Newcastle with their ill-gotten gains.'

Zoe checked her mobile as she walked to the car. No message yet from Neil, which was probably a good thing. He would expect a blow-by-blow account of her time in Hawick with Lisa, yet despite their new-found intimacy she could share nothing with him either. Whatever he and Kate believed, knowing other people's secrets was a burden not a blessing.

The weekend could not have turned out more unlike the one she had planned. To start with, there was no way she would have slept with Neil so soon under normal circumstances. And instead of moving closer to solving the mystery surrounding her car crash, she felt even further away from it.

THIRTY-SEVEN

Zoe had always assumed the small scale of The Rocket exaggerated the size of her final patient on Monday morning. Yet, even in the airy space of the health centre, Ray Anderson towered above her and his hefty thighs spilled over the sides of the chair when he sat down.

Around six-and-a-half feet tall, he was solidly built rather than fat, although the tautness of the shirt across his stomach suggested recent weight gain. His medical history revealed he was approaching sixty, which was surprising, and a history of hypertension, which was not. At no time had Zoe seen him drink anything stronger than lemonade, but the publican was never far from an open packet of fatty snacks. She would recommend an appointment with the practice nurse for a cholesterol test and advice about a healthy diet.

Until he spoke, Ray's demeanour appeared as relaxed as it usually was in The Rocket, and he smiled at Zoe as she sat down. But his mood changed rapidly when she asked what she could do for him.

'You've got to help me, Doctor. Please.' He wrung his hands and sounded close to tears.

Zoe shifted her voice to a softer tone. 'What's wrong, Ray?'

The big man closed his eyes briefly as if to stop them brimming over, and took a deep breath. 'It's Hazel.'

'Has something happened?'

'You've seen her. You know how she is.'

'I know she hasn't yet come to terms with your son's death. Have you?'

'I'm fine. This isn't about me.'

'What do you want me to do?'

'Can't you give her something?'

'Hazel needs to make an appointment to see me or one of the other doctors. Then we can assess how best to help her.'

Ray ran a huge hand through his thinning hair and stared at Zoe. 'But you came to the flat. Don't tell me that was just a social call.'

Zoe winced. She had imposed herself on a vulnerable woman, albeit one who may have been involved in Chrissie Baird's death, to pump her for information. And now that woman's husband was giving her credit for a far more noble motive. 'I take it she doesn't know you're here.'

'She won't come herself. Won't even admit there's anything wrong.'

'I can't treat her with you acting as go-between.'

'If you prescribe something to help her snap out of this depression, I'll make sure she takes it.'

'Taking drugs isn't necessarily the answer. She may benefit more from talking to a trained bereavement counsellor.'

'Talk? She doesn't need to talk, she needs medication.'

Zoe again told Ray she could not give him a prescription for his wife. Once more he insisted that she must. Eventually, backed into a corner, she offered to call round to see Hazel again that afternoon.

'Then you'll put her on anti-depressants?'

'Not necessarily.'

'Well what about me?' Ray no longer looked Zoe in the eye but stared down at his hands. 'Will you prescribe anti-depressants for me?'

'Not if I think you intend to pass them on to

someone else.'

'In that case I'll ask one of the other doctors for some.'

'They'll say exactly the same thing. Let's talk again once I've seen Hazel, shall we?'

Ray sniffed loudly and got up. Zoe watched him trudge from the room, his long arms and massive hands hanging dejectedly by his sides, then typed a brief note into his records in case he tried to obtain drugs for Hazel from anyone else.

Paul and Walter had their heads bowed over a magazine when Zoe entered the kitchen. They sprang apart like schoolboys caught sharing their first taste of porn. Walter got up and switched the kettle on.

'What do you think of this?' Paul asked, waving the magazine in Zoe's direction.

She scanned the open page then looked up. 'From whose point of view – a doctor's or a woman's? That might influence my response.'

Paul laughed and Walter looked as though he was trying not to.

'I'm sorry, my dear, I should have explained,' Paul said. 'I was wondering if this article would be reassuring to our male patients who have concerns about their own, um, assets.'

Zoe flicked over the page, then checked out the magazine's front cover. 'I wouldn't have had you down as a reader of this sort of thing, Paul.'

'Alasdair was home over the weekend and suggested I might find it useful. He and his friends read magazines like this all the time, apparently. His mother used to enjoy Cosmopolitan, but I've never been a great one for reading.'

'In which case, my answer to your question is yes, it definitely conveys the message that male genitalia come in an infinite variety of sizes and shapes.'

Walter returned to the table with a cup of coffee and placed it in front of Zoe. She smiled her appreciation but he didn't smile back.

'I doubt Zoe's male patients confide in her about such matters,' Walter said.

Zoe agreed, but balked at giving him the satisfaction of saying so. *He wasn't the only one who could be offhand.*

Paul looked at her over the top of his glasses. 'Do you want to talk about what happened at the weekend? It must have been very distressing, getting involved in such unpleasantness.' The word 'again' remained unsaid but hung in the room.

The two men listened as Zoe told them about the events of Saturday night and the following afternoon. It was a relief being able to reveal the true relationship between Brian and Lisa, secure in the knowledge that it would go no further.

'Oh my Lord,' Walter said.

Paul heaved a sigh. 'What a wicked world this is.' He was about to say something else when there was a knock on the door. It opened seconds later.

'Excuse me, Doctors, I was told to come through and find you,' Mather said.

'Come on in, Detective Chief Inspector,' Paul said. 'I expect you're here to see Zoe. Walter and I will leave you in peace.' He picked up the magazine, though not before Mather's eyes alighted briefly on it.

'Please stay. Some of what I have to say concerns you all.' Mather continued to stand, despite Walter's gesture towards the fourth chair at the table. 'Firstly, I have a question about the late Mrs Baird.'

'Ask away,' Paul said.

'Was she a smoker?'

'Can't you tell that from the post mortem?' Zoe asked.

Mather ignored her.

'Perhaps before she moved here, but certainly not while I knew her,' Paul said. 'In fact she used to be concerned about the amount of second-hand smoke she and Jimmy inhaled at the pub. She welcomed the smoking ban when it came in, unlike a lot of their customers.'

All three doctors waited for Mather to explain his question. He did not. Instead he turned to Zoe and said, 'I'm afraid I have bad news about the young woman you know as Lisa Humphreys.'

'What's happened?'

'She became unwell while being questioned by the Fiscal first thing this morning. An ambulance took her to Borders General, but despite the best efforts of the staff they couldn't save the baby.'

'Oh no,' Zoe said, shocked at such a cruel outcome when Lisa had gone to such desperate lengths to save her child.

'What about the poor girl herself?' Paul asked. 'Zoe has made us aware of the circumstances behind Saturday night's tragedy.'

'I'm told she'll be fine.' Looking embarrassed at how inappropriate that may have sounded, Mather added, 'In the circumstances.'

'Physically, maybe,' Zoe said. 'But I wonder how she'll cope emotionally with losing the baby on top of everything else.'

'Perhaps it's for the best,' Walter said. 'In the circumstances.'

The room fell silent. Zoe was about to ask Mather if he had any other news when the policeman said, 'While I have all of you here, there is one more thing I need to say. I hope you'll take it in the spirit it's intended.' He paused, unnecessarily Zoe thought, like he had been taking lessons from Chris Kossoff.

'I realise as doctors you feel bound by confidentiality, but you obviously discuss matters between yourselves that you wouldn't share with anyone else. By all means debate what you can and cannot tell the police, but don't forget that we're looking for a killer. Doctor Moreland nearly became another victim.'

Paul turned to Zoe. 'Is this true? You told us it was an accident.'

Walter said nothing.

'I didn't want to worry you,' Zoe said, her face burning.

Walter stood up and put on his jacket. 'I for one, DCI Mather, would never keep back anything that could be useful to your investigation. And I'm certain Doctor Ryder feels the same. Are you coming, Paul? We're expected in Melrose at twelve-thirty.'

Despite Paul's obvious reluctance to leave, he said goodbye and followed Walter out of the room.

'Was that a medical textbook Doctor Ryder was trying to hide from me?' Mather asked Zoe when they were alone.

Hearing him joke shocked Zoe almost as much as the one time she overheard Gran swear. Before she could think of a reply, he pulled an envelope from his breast pocket and handed it to her.

'What's this?'

'Official notification that your car has been retained as evidence. It can't be released until the conclusion of any court proceedings, so your insurance company will probably write the vehicle off now, even if it is salvageable. You'll be able to go out and buy yourself another one.'

'I didn't know that's what happened.'

'Not many people do.'

As Mather moved towards the door, Zoe asked, 'Can I go and visit Lisa?'

'She's still in the BGH but I don't know how long for. Once she's physically stable she'll be taken somewhere less open.'

'To prison? After all she's been through? That

would be cruel.'

'It's out of my hands. But I'll let you know if I hear anything.'

Mather turned and was halfway out of the room when Zoe asked, 'Why are you so interested in whether Chrissie Baird smoked?'

'Goodbye, Doctor.'

At a little after two o'clock, Zoe paused outside the shop on her way to see Hazel. The 'closed' sign on its door contradicted the neatly-written opening hours displayed below it, and a cluster of smudges on the glass told of attempts to see inside past the pulled-down blind. She wondered what would happen to the business Brian and Lisa had worked so hard to build up. *Would being a murder scene attract or repulse potential buyers?* Judging by what she knew of human nature, it could go either way.

Arriving at the entrance to the flat above the pub, Zoe knocked twice and had her hand raised to try for a third and final time when she heard footsteps. Hazel opened the door, but it was obvious she had not been expecting Zoe and was on her way out, car keys in one hand and a plastic bag weighed down with something soft and heavy in the other.

'Hello Hazel. Didn't Ray tell you to expect me?'

'Ray? He's away shooting with his farmer pals. Won't be home 'til opening time.' Hazel swayed slightly and her eyes were unfocused.

'Oh. Where are you off to?' Zoe spoke cheerfully, trying to hide her concern. She wanted to avoid having to wrestle Hazel's keys away from her.

The older woman's eyes narrowed with suspicion. 'Did Ray send you to stop me?'

'No, of course not. In fact, I'd like to come with you.'

Hazel nodded. 'Okay.'

'Shall we take my car?'

'You don't know the way.'

'You can show me.' Zoe guided Hazel to where the hire car was parked.

They passed the entrance to the Larimer Park estate and the water meadow where Jimmy Baird died. Hazel, clutching the plastic bag to her chest, stayed silent throughout the journey, except to issue directions. Now they were in an enclosed space, Zoe detected a sour odour not entirely masked by her passenger's lavishly-applied perfume.

Just after they crossed the Tweed via a narrow stone bridge, their arrival in England was announced by an inconspicuous sign. A minute or so later, they were in Norham. Zoe drove along a wide street lined with terraced houses, past a pub on one side, a gunsmith's shop on the other, until Hazel guided her to a single-storey cottage with a brown front door and window frames painted to match.

A short, tubby man in his sixties appeared on the doorstep as Zoe got out of the car. He wore cream trousers, a checked shirt and a moss-green jacket. Some sort of military medal was pinned to his lapel.

'Mrs Anderson, how nice to see you. And you've brought a friend.' He held his hand out to Zoe.

'Colonel Stevens, this is Doctor Moreland. She's suffered a loss too.'

The Colonel withdrew his hand before Zoe could shake it. 'What sort of doctor?'

'I'm a GP.'

'Her husband passed a few months ago.' Hazel patted Zoe's arm.

'I see.' The Colonel did not offer his hand again, instead he stared at Zoe as though trying to read her mind.

She forced a smile, despite the unease this scrutiny provoked. 'Hazel suggested I come with her. She thought you could help me too.'

'I doubt that. People in your profession have such

closed minds. But you can sit and wait while I consult with Mrs Anderson.'

Once inside, Zoe sat down on a low, uncomfortable sofa the Colonel pointed to before he led Hazel away.

THIRTY-EIGHT

Colonel Lucas C Stevens is a fully accredited psychic medium with many years experience. He brings comfort and reassurance to the bereaved by acting as a channel between them and the spirits of their loved ones. Money back guarantee if not completely satisfied.

Zoe put down the flimsy leaflet with a grunt of disgust. No wonder Ray had tried to prevent Hazel from wasting her money on this charlatan. The military rank was probably invented too.

She sat for half an hour in the stuffy little room, flicking through a pile of magazines, none of them less than five years old, and checking her mobile for calls. At last the door opened and Hazel came in, followed by Colonel Stevens.

Hazel wore a hippyish smile. 'Duncan's at peace,' she told Zoe. 'He's happy and he forgives his father for everything.'

'I'm glad to hear it.' Zoe got out her car keys. 'We'd better be going.'

'But it's your turn now. That's why you came, isn't it?'

Colonel Stevens stepped between them. 'I don't think she's quite ready for my ministrations, are you Doctor?'

'Oh dear,' Hazel said, putting her hand to her mouth. 'I forgot to tell her she'd need to bring something belonging to her loved one.' She held up the plastic bag; a piece of tartan material hung out of the top of it. Duncan's kilt, Zoe guessed.

Colonel Stevens peered up at Zoe. 'Sometimes it's possible to make contact unaided with those in the ongoing life, if the spirit is strong enough,' he said. 'Your late husband is most anxious to put things right between you, Doctor, before it's too late.'

'He's dead. In my book that makes it too late for anything.'

Zoe grasped Hazel's arm and steered her out through the front door. During their drive back to Westerlea, she hesitantly suggested they could meet the following day for a chat at the surgery, but the continuing euphoria from her session with Colonel Stevens made Hazel unresponsive to any conversation that did not centre around Duncan.

After dropping Hazel off at the pub, Zoe continued on to Keeper's Cottage beset by worry that she should have done more. However elated that so-called Colonel made Hazel feel now, the effects would wear off eventually. And when they did, Hazel was certain to plunge even deeper into depression.

Zoe felt like a teenager, trying – and, to her own ears, failing – to sound casual. 'Hi, it's me again. Call me when you can. Hope you're okay.'

It was the third message she had left for Neil. Although only thirty-six hours had passed since he got out of her bed and went home, not hearing from him testified yet again to how little she knew about him. *Was he demonstrating a casual attitude towards relationships in general or did it mean he was having second thoughts about theirs in particular?*

After Russell, she had doubted anyone could wound her again. Yet the anxious feeling in the pit of her stomach and the voice in her head murmuring, *He's lost interest now you've slept with him,* told a different story.

She typed a text to Kate, giving her a brief account of the trip to Norham, but a last-minute thought stopped her from pressing send. She had gone to see Hazel in her capacity as a doctor, so maybe that made the encounter she subsequently observed between Hazel and Colonel Stevens confidential. True, none of it had happened in her consulting room, but she heard again Paul quoting the GMC guidelines: 'Confidentiality is central to the trust between doctors and patients.'

Zoe deleted the text.

THIRTY-NINE

As Zoe and Kate strode up the path towards the open door of Westerlea's church, Zoe said, 'You're looking suitably funereal. No pink today?'

Kate grinned and thrust a hand down behind her black skirt's waistband. She brought it out holding the elasticated top of a pair of pink panties trimmed with cream lace.

Both women were still suppressing giggles as they entered the church. It was roomier than it appeared from the outside, yet most of the pews were full and Zoe was thankful Kate's parents had saved them seats.

'Whatever you do, try not to chat with Kate during the service,' Etta said as Zoe sat down next to her. 'She doesn't whisper well.'

Coffins always look too small. Zoe had wanted to stop her mother's burial, to shout out there was no way such a vigorous woman would have allowed herself to be crammed into so tiny a box. More recently, she had been shocked by the ease with which Russell's friends lifted his coffin on to their shoulders. And here she was again, this time with no emotional investment in the deceased but still startled by the inadequate-looking coffins which arrived in tandem.

Dragged from her reverie by the sound of singing, she flicked through the pages of her hymn book to catch up. Kate sat in silence, looking straight ahead. Despite being for two people, the service was brief, the young minister expressing regret that he had not tended this, his first flock, long enough to get to know either of the deceased. When it was over, the mourners trooped out and stood around in groups. Much handshaking ensued.

'You're the doctor lassie from England who found them, eh?' Like nearly everyone Etta introduced her to, the elderly man with a walking frame knew exactly who Zoe was. She quickly learned all she had to do was smile; they had little interest in anything she had to say. The succession of strangers passed by in a blur of faces and names she would never remember.

She saw some familiar faces as well, although she was not surprised to observe that Neil and Peter were not among them. Sergeant Trent stood alone, half-hidden behind a yew tree, and when his eyes met Zoe's he nodded in acknowledgement. Then she spotted Gregor and Alice moving quickly through the throng, barely stopping to speak to anyone. He wore mismatched dark trousers and jacket, she had on an old-fashioned black coat that swamped her. They climbed into a maroon Jaguar which set off slowly behind the hearse carrying their parents' coffins.

Tom and Jean appeared straight after, as if they had been waiting for his ex-wife to leave before venturing out, with Angie and Maddy in matching coats walking between them. They too bypassed several well-wishers, only pausing at the church gate for Jean to fasten the twins' coats while Tom lit a cigarette. Then they crossed the road, Jean and the girls got into a silver Peugeot, and Tom inhaled deeply on his cigarette before throwing it into the verge and joining them.

Something niggled at Zoe about what she had just observed. It reminded her of the day Tom came round to sweep her chimney, but she could not figure out why. Before she could give the matter any more thought, her attention was caught by the sound of someone calling her name. She hardly recognised Paul, whose wardrobe she had imagined consisted solely of baggy chinos and tartan ties. Today, however, he looked dapper in a navy suit, and was accompanied by an equally stylish Margaret, whose black outfit was topped off with a matching pillbox hat. Zoe exchanged a few words with them, then joined Kate and her parents in the procession of mourners walking to the cemetery.

Traffic through Westerlea, including the postman in his van, was stopped for several minutes to allow the mourners to pass. Ranald Mackenzie had refused all offers of a lift and insisted on going by foot like everyone else, his only concession to ill-health being the use of a stick. Zoe, Kate and Etta moved at his pace, and as a result they were nearly the last to arrive.

Preparations were still taking place for the actual interments, so Zoe slipped away as Kate and her parents chatted with a woman who looked like an older version of Etta. Despite the buzz of human voices, the cemetery felt peaceful. Even the wind, which when they left the heat of the church had made Zoe long for her woolly hat, was not blowing here. She walked along a grass path between the serried rows of graves, stopping occasionally to read an inscription that grabbed her attention. The same names – Jardine, Dixon and, of course, Mackenzie – cropped up time and time again.

She sat down on a wooden bench under the beech hedge, closed her eyes and was immediately transported back to Russell's funeral. Even though surrounded by dozens of people, she had felt as alone then as she did now. The hot, humid day had brought out a profusion of insects, and she remembered standing at the graveside, trying to keep her composure by watching a butterfly feed on a wreath of purple and cream flowers. When she had eventually looked up, hardly any of the other mourners had met her gaze.

A soft voice brought her back to the present. 'They say the first year's the worst. Your first Christmas or anniversary without them, the day that would have been their birthday.' Etta sat down beside her. 'I can't imagine how difficult coming here must be for you.'

'It's not easy,' Zoe said.

'You can never escape your memories. If it's any consolation, eventually you won't want to.'

That seemed unlikely, but Zoe agreed anyway. She pulled her coat around her, preparing to get up.

'Don't go, please,' Etta said. 'I need to talk to you about something that's been worrying me dreadfully.'

Etta's role within the Mackenzie family being counsellor-cum-peacemaker with a big helping of oracle thrown in, the problem had to be serious for her to confide in someone she had met only a few times. Zoe asked, 'How can I help?' but her question went unanswered. Following Etta's gaze, she saw Kate approaching.

'Dad sent me. They're ready to bury them now. Are you two coming over?'

Zoe walked with Kate and her mother back to the Bairds' burial site. Jimmy was first to be put into the ground, the cords lowering his coffin held by his son and five much older men, one of whom Zoe recognised from the pub as the first Mrs Baird's brother. The task of lowering Chrissie's remains – for the first time in days, the image of that blackened form stirred in Zoe's mind – was undertaken by Gregor again, aided by the funeral director's team.

When the time came for handfuls of earth to be scattered on Chrissie's coffin, Tom stepped forward with one of his daughters, who picked up a few grains of dirt and flung them towards the open grave. Alice then attempted to follow suit with the other twin. This little girl hung back, started to cry, and ran to Jean. Her sister joined in with her own tears.

Alice turned to Tom and pointed a finger at him. 'You told them to do this, didn't you?'

Some of the mourners walked away in

embarrassment, while others stood their ground, watching to see what would happen next.

'I warned you they were too young,' Tom said.

'She was their granny. I want them to say goodbye to her.'

'So do I, but we should have done what Jean suggested and brought them here another day.'

Alice strode over to Jean, who was holding a handkerchief while one of the twins blew her nose into it. 'This is all your fault,' she said. 'You're desperate to show off what a great mother you think you are to my kids.'

Jean said nothing but looked as though she wanted to start crying herself. Tom rushed to her side.

'Leave her alone,' he told Alice. 'Why are you doing this? I'm giving you everything you want, aren't I?'

'Not got much choice, have you?' His ex-wife turned away from him and linked arms with Gregor, who had come up behind her. The crowd of onlookers parted, allowing the pair to walk to where their car was waiting. Everyone watched silently as they got in and were driven away.

As soon as they had gone, people started talking again. Tom lifted one of the girls up on to his hip and laid his hand on the other's head. Jean fiddled with the crucifix hanging round her neck.

'That was unseemly,' Kate said. 'Fancy making a scene at your own mother's funeral.'

'Grief does strange things to people,' Etta said.

'I can't believe you're making excuses for her, Mum. You'd never tolerate any of us behaving that way in public. Or in private.'

'All I'm saying is that Alice is obviously a very unhappy young woman.'

'She chose to run off and leave Tom with the twins. Why is it only now she's after getting them back?'

'Perhaps she's scared. Suddenly she has no other living relative.' Etta put her arm round Kate's shoulders.

'Imagine how you'd feel if that happened to you. No brothers, no parents, your children being brought up by somebody else.'

Kate leaned into her mother and Zoe felt a pang of envy at the closeness the two women shared. She chased this away by puzzling over what Etta could possibly need her advice about.

Sherry, which Zoe detested, was being served half an hour later to the mourners who had chosen to go back to The Rocket for lunch. Hazel reacted to Zoe's expression when offered a schooner of the stuff by saying, 'There's a bottle of whisky put aside for them that wants it. Or beer. Ray's in charge of those.'

'She looks in fine fettle today,' Kate said after Hazel left them to continue her circuit of the pub. 'I wonder what's caused that. Did you get to see her again?'

'Yes,' Zoe said. She was going to have to pick her words very carefully. 'But only briefly.'

'And?'

'And nothing. Except I don't think the man in Norham is Hazel's lover.'

'How do you know?'

Zoe shrugged.

Kate frowned. 'I see you're wearing your doctor's hat again.'

'What more do you want me to say? Surely the important thing is what we find out, not how?'

Now it was Kate's turn to say nothing, although she made it obvious from her expression that she was not appeased.

'This is good news,' Zoe said. 'Now we know the argument I overheard between Ray and Hazel the night after Jimmy was found dead wasn't about her having an affair.'

'So you're ruling them out as suspects?'

'On the contrary. It makes them more interesting,

not less, because there's definitely another reason why Ray said they could get into trouble if they didn't keep their heads down. And don't forget what your friend Mather told us about the pub being the last place Chrissie was seen on the day she disappeared.'

'That doesn't get us any further forward.'

'The police don't seem to be making much progress either.'

'I think we need to shake things up a bit.'

'Oh God, Kate, what are you going to do?'

'I don't know yet.'

At that moment, Westerlea's young minister came up to them. After complimenting him on the service, Zoe left him talking to Kate and wandered through to the dining room. It was twice the size of the bar and usually crammed with tables, but today most of these had been gathered at one end to free up space. She hoped to catch Etta and continue their conversation which had started in the graveyard, but could not find her. Instead, she saw Paul and Margaret talking with a ginger-haired woman she remembered standing apart from all the other mourners at the cemetery. Hazel went up to them with her tray of sherries, then moved away to another small group nearby. Margaret sipped at her drink, saw Zoe and beckoned her over.

'You must meet Chrissie's friend who's travelled down especially for the funeral.'

Zoe shook hands with the woman, who introduced herself as Fiona MacBride. She wore spectacles with red frames, and had removed her dark coat to reveal a suit of dazzling red tartan.

'I'm so glad to meet you, Doctor Moreland, even though it's under such sad circumstances. As I was saying to Doctor Ryder and Margaret here, I'm in the same line of business as you all. I started off as a receptionist and now I'm practice manager.'

While Zoe searched for suitably complimentary words, Fiona chattered on. 'I'm distraught, absolutely distraught, about what happened to poor Chrissie. What a terrible thing.'

'Had you known her long?'

'Oh, forever. We met when Alice was only tiny. She used to called me Aunty Fee. Still does. She was a beautiful child, it's good to see her daughters are equally bonny. Of course poor Chrissie was saddened by Alice's marriage not working out, but she doted on those little girls, would have done anything for them.'

'I'd heard that,' Zoe said. Paul and Margaret had wandered off towards the buffet, and she was already tiring of this woman's gushing. Then she saw Kate looking in their direction and gesticulated to her to join them.

'This is Fiona MacBride. She was a good friend of Chrissie's, since before she even came to Westerlea.'

Kate gave Fiona her warmest smile and after explaining about being deaf, led her to some seats which had just been vacated. Behind them, having finished taking round the complimentary drinks, Hazel was clearing away empty and abandoned glasses.

'This must be a very sad day for you,' Kate said. 'Chrissie never spoke much about her time in – where was it you met?'

'Oban,' Fiona said. 'Do you know it?'

'Mum and Dad took us there on holiday once, but I was only wee.' Kate turned to Zoe. 'I don't suppose you've ever been there, have you?'

'I'm afraid I don't even know where it is,' Zoe said. 'Edinburgh's the furthest north I've travelled so far.'

'Oban's a lovely town on the west coast,' Fiona said. 'You really should visit it. You can take the ferry to lots of the islands from there too.'

Zoe began to say she would try to see Oban one day, but her words went unheard. A crashing noise caused everyone, except Kate, to look round in surprise.

This time, Hazel had not accidentally dropped something. Instead, she had slammed the tray of sherry schooners down on a table, from where the glasses had bounced and clattered against one another and on to the floor.

Everyone watched as she stood motionless for a few seconds, clutching the sides of the tray, her knuckles white. Then she let go of the tray and plucked a pint glass nearly full of beer from a mourner's hand. Holding this out in front of her, she walked over to Zoe's table.

'How dare you come in here!' she shouted. And threw the beer in Fiona MacBride's face.

FORTY

Hazel placed the empty pint glass on a table, turned and marched out of the room, brushing past Ray who had come from the public bar in time to witness the entire episode. He looked as shocked as all the other bystanders. No one said a word.

Fiona MacBride sat motionless, beer streaking her spectacles and dripping off her nose and chin. She scarcely reacted when Kate and Zoe set about mopping up the worst of the liquid with a bar towel and some paper napkins. Then the room abruptly filled with the sound of voices, as if a radio had been turned on. Someone must have gone to fetch Alice, because she arrived shortly afterwards and rushed Fiona out of the pub and across the road to Horseshoe Cottage.

Zoe wondered if she should go to check on Hazel but decided against it. There was no sign of Ray now, so he must be with her.

Half an hour later, the food eaten and the excitement over, only a handful of mourners remained in The Rocket, so Zoe and Kate moved back to the public bar. Ray had returned, although Hazel was still absent. Gregor sat on a stool by the fire, sipping a glass of whisky, deep in conversation with his uncle.

'This funeral's turning out to be very lively,' Kate said as she slid into the seat next to Zoe. 'Poor old Aunty Fee. I wonder what that was about?'

'Your guess is as good as mine,' Zoe said. 'There

was no hint those two even knew each other until Hazel came over and started shouting.'

'I'd noticed she was listening in on our conversation with Fiona. What were we talking about immediately before it happened?'

'Fiona was doing her best to sell Oban as the perfect holiday destination, I think. It's all a bit of a blur now.'

'Hardly reason for Hazel to cause such a stushie.'

'Could it be connected with Chrissie's death?' Zoe took a sip of orange juice.

'I don't know. If only Hazel had given me time to find out about Chrissie's first husband.'

'You don't think he had anything to do with her death, do you?'

'No, but I'm curious.'

'Perhaps she wasn't even married before she came here.'

Kate affected a look of shock.

'Being a single parent's not a recent phenomenon,' Zoe said. 'My mother never married.'

'You haven't mentioned this before.'

'I rest my case. It's irrelevant.'

'But don't you realise the significance of your telling me?' Kate's voice rose and Gregor cast a hostile look across the room at her. 'It's the first time you've ever volunteered any personal information. Usually I have to force it out of you.'

'Put that down to the whisky I drank earlier.' Zoe inclined her head towards the front door. 'You'll think I'm trying to change the subject, but Alice is back. And she seems in far better spirits than you'd expect from a woman who's just buried her mother.'

Back to wearing her usual T-shirt and denim skirt, Alice stood at the pub's doorway, her body jiggling with barely suppressed excitement. She spotted Gregor and rushed over to him, and shortly afterwards his uncle gave

277

up his stool to her and moved away. Once seated, she yanked an envelope from her pocket and shoved it under her step-brother's nose.

'I wish I knew what they're talking about,' Zoe said.

Kate did not reply. She was watching the pair intently.

Gregor slid a single sheet of paper out of the envelope and unfolded it. Alice watched as he did that thing middle-aged people do when they need glasses but refuse to admit it, holding the page up close to his face and moving it away again. At last he seemed to be reading, then he looked up with a mystified expression. Alice snatched the page away from him and jabbed her finger at a point about halfway down. A whispered discussion followed, at the end of which Gregor gulped down the remains of his drink. They both got up to leave.

Kate plucked at Zoe's sleeve. 'As soon as they've gone, we need to get out of here. I've got something amazing to tell you.'

The door into The Rocket opened before Alice and Gregor were halfway across the room. Given the scene at the graveyard, no one had expressed surprise at Tom and his family giving lunch at The Rocket a miss, but he was here now.

'What do you want?' Alice demanded.

'To talk.' Tom walked up to her until their faces were only inches apart. 'Ideally without it ending in a shouting match.'

'Who's shouting?' Alice said. 'I told you what I wanted, and I thought you'd agreed.'

'We have to do what's best for Angie and Maddy. Taking them away from everything they know isn't the answer. Surely what happened earlier proved that.'

Alice turned to Gregor. 'Can you believe him?' she said. 'Today of all days.'

'This'll have t'wait. She's jus' buried her mother.'

The whisky Zoe had watched Gregor finish in a hurry must have been the last of several.

'You stay out of this,' Tom said. His voice was quiet but he took a step towards Gregor.

The relief Zoe felt as Gregor retreated was replaced by alarm when she realised he was doing this to get a better aim. He felled Tom with a single punch, sending him sprawling backwards on to the floor, blood pouring from his nose.

Ray moved quickly from behind the bar, putting himself between the two men. 'Out of here, now!' he commanded. Alice scowled at him then grabbed Gregor by the arm and pulled him through the front door.

Zoe dashed over to Tom and helped him sit up. 'No, don't put your head back, you'll end up swallowing blood. Ray, I need some ice wrapped up in a towel. And an empty bowl, if you've got one.'

A murmur of, 'She's a doctor,' circulated among the pub's few remaining customers, who seemed content to watch Zoe take charge. She showed Tom where to pinch the bridge of his nose and directed him to lean forward over an old washing-up bowl Ray found. When the bleeding stopped, she guided Tom to a seat and pressed the improvised ice pack on his face.

'Should I call an ambulance?' Ray asked.

Zoe looked up and was surprised to find the pub empty apart from herself, Ray, Tom and Kate. 'No. He's not bleeding any more.'

'But won't he need an X-ray or something?'

'Fractures of the nose don't usually show up on X-rays. We'll have to wait until the swelling goes down to see the extent of the damage.'

'In that case I'll bring the car round and drive him to his girlfriend's house,' Ray said.

Zoe studied Tom. He looked a sight. His nose had started to swell asymmetrically, a dark bruise was already emerging under his left eye, and blood was encrusted round both nostrils and on his chin. He would terrify the twins and distress Jean if they saw him like this.

'I need to clean him up a bit first.' Zoe turned to Kate. 'Will you take us to the health centre?'

'As long as I can get back before the bairns come home from school.' Kate rummaged in her handbag for her car keys.

'Doh,' Tom said. He tried to stand up but his cousin shushed him, and he slumped back in his seat.

In the pub's car park a few minutes later, Zoe saw Tom reach inside his pocket and pull out a packet of cigarettes and a disposable lighter. 'Oh no, you don't,' she said. 'Sorry, but that's the last thing you need at present.'

Tom returned the cigarettes and lighter to his pocket, that straightforward action suddenly triggering memories of other times Zoe had watched him do almost the same thing. She stared at him, realising now the hold Chrissie had over him and why Alice turned Horseshoe Cottage upside down as soon as she gained access to it. Claiming her mother's possessions was secondary; she had been searching for something.

And Zoe knew what that something must be.

When they reached the health centre, Zoe promised Kate they would be no more than ten minutes and led Tom to the practice treatment room after checking it was unoccupied. She helped him remove his sweater without catching it on his nose and swabbed his face free of blood.

'That's the best I can do,' she said, washing her hands and drying them on a paper towel. 'I'm afraid it'll get worse before it gets better, both in terms of pain and appearance.'

'It won't show under the soot,' Tom replied nasally.

'I'd tell you to stay away from chimneys for a day or two, but I don't suppose you'll take any notice.'

'Can't afford to.'

'Well don't blow your nose too hard, and if there's any significant bleeding again you must come and see me or one of the other doctors immediately.'

'Thanks.' Tom got up.

'Before we go,' Zoe said, 'there's something I want to discuss with you.'

Tom sat down again, looking worried.

'I think I've worked out what Alice is using to make you give up the girls.'

'I told you before, I can handle it.'

'By picking fights with Gregor? That won't do anyone any good.'

'He hit me.'

Men could be so childish sometimes.

'I don't want to argue with you. Please, Tom, let me say what I think the problem is. If I'm right, maybe I can help you find a way round it.' Taking his silence as acquiescence, Zoe continued. 'I noticed earlier today you were carrying a disposable cigarette lighter, rather than the free matchbooks I used to see you with.'

'Run out, haven't I?'

'No, I don't think that's the reason. I think you're not using matchbooks any more because they're a reminder that Chrissie caught you with one from somewhere you shouldn't have been. Somewhere she disapproved of.'

Tom studied the nails of his right hand.

'Honestly, if that's all there is to it, you've nothing to fear. I know the Borders is a more traditional place than where I've come from, but there's no way you'd lose custody of your children over something as inconsequential as that.'

Tom rubbed his nose hard, as though deliberately trying to make it hurt more. A trickle of blood ran out of one nostril but he ignored it. In a monotone he said, 'I went up to Edinburgh with a few mates for a night out. The bairns had a sitter, Hannah. She's fifteen, lives in the

Auld Smiddy with her parents. Chrissie usually babysat but she was going somewhere with the Rural.

'We went to a club, the TipTop, in Leith. I hadn't realised what sort of place it was, honestly. There was lap dancing, and private rooms too, upstairs, where they did more than just dance for you. I got drunk – we all did – and made a night of it. I can't mind exactly what happened.'

Tom blushed as he claimed this loss of memory. *He wasn't being entirely truthful, but did that make the rest of his story a lie?*

'When I didn't come home by one o'clock, Hannah got worried and called her parents. They were angry I'd left her and the twins so long, and went round to fetch Chrissie. She was at my house when I got back the next morning. I told her Mikey's car broke down and we had to sleep in it in a lay-by on Soutra Hill. I even smeared oil on my jacket to prove we'd tried to fix it. Chrissie gave me a row for not calling her, but said no more after that. I should've known she wouldn't let it rest.'

'So how did she find out the truth?' Zoe asked.

Tom gave a long sigh. 'I came home one day a few weeks ago to find her and the twins playing a new game. Flitting, they called it.' Seeing the puzzled look on Zoe's face, he added, 'That's how folk in these parts describe moving house.'

Zoe nodded.

'She'd got them carrying all my clothes to the spare room and putting their own in my drawers and cupboards. Which gave her the chance to poke about and go through my pockets.'

'And she found a TipTop match book?'

'Aye, in the jacket with oil down the front. She knew I couldn't have worn it since that night, because it's ruined. Now I wish I'd thrown it out.'

'But how did she know what sort of place the TipTop is?'

'The match book had the club's name and phone number, so she looked it up on the Internet. That was all the proof she needed. As far as Chrissie was concerned, I'd spent the night in a brothel. She said any court that heard I'd left my children with a girl not even sixteen herself to go to a place like that and not come home until morning would give the twins back to their mother straightaway. And she threatened to tell Jean.'

'Would Jean really care what you got up to before you started going out with her?'

Tom's voice cracked as he said, 'It was this July. We'd already been together for almost a year.'

'Oh Tom.' Zoe's attempt to sound sympathetic came out more like a reprimand.

'Aye, it was an awful thing to do and she'd never forgive me if she found out. You know Jean, she was brought up with all that religious stuff. She wouldn't even agree to us living together until we got engaged. Said she wasn't going to be anyone's bidie-in.'

'When did Chrissie tell you what she'd found?'

'A few days before she disappeared.'

Their eyes met. *Bad timing.*

'I should've known she'd tell Alice the first chance she got.'

'Do the police know about this?'

'Of course not.'

'And what makes you think Alice won't tell them?'

'If she did, she wouldn't have a hold over me any more.'

Zoe considered what to say next. Any advice she gave Tom could affect a lot of people, not least two innocent little girls. Slumped and defeated, he reminded her of a patient who had arrived for a consultation expecting bad news – and got it. With this thought, a solution came to her: why not do what she always did when faced with a medical problem that went beyond her remit?

'I need to fetch something from my consulting room. Don't go away.'

Tom looked puzzled but didn't move. He started to speak as Zoe came back into the room a minute or so later, but went silent as he looked down at the business card she handed him.

'Go and see Chris Kossoff,' she said. 'Tell him what you've told me, all of it. He'll be able to give you much better advice than I can.'

'I can't afford to hire someone like him.' Tom tried to pass the solicitor's card back to her.

'You can't afford not to. You're in a hell of a mess, and frankly Jean leaving you may be the least of your worries. Think about the girls. What use will you be to them if you're in prison for murder?'

'I didn't kill Chrissie.'

'So make an appointment to see Kossoff tomorrow and tell him that. Then worry about how much it'll cost.'

Tom slipped Kossoff's card into his pocket and followed Zoe back outside to where Kate was waiting for them in her car.

The first thing Zoe did after Kate dropped her off and drove away with Tom was telephone Jean to forewarn her of the state her man was in. Jean sounded unfazed by news of Tom's scuffle with Gregor. 'I imagined something much worse when he was gone for so long.'

Later, during Mac's last walk of the day, Zoe got a text from Kate. *Couldn't talk earlier. Need to meet asap re A & G. Innocent?!*

FORTY-ONE

'They were sitting at an angle to me, so I couldn't see everything they said. But I got the gist.' Kate stood in Zoe's hall, unwinding her pink scarf as she spoke.

In the two days since the Bairds' funeral, Zoe had worked extra sessions, filling in for Walter who was back in Wales moving his mother into a nursing home. She stayed away from the coach house, Neil's failure to get in touch making it obvious he did not want to take their relationship any further. Meanwhile, Kate's research into her client's Scottish roots had sent her to Edinburgh again. As a result, this was their first opportunity to discuss the conversation Kate had observed between Gregor and Alice after their parents' funeral.

Zoe led her friend through to the kitchen and persuaded her to sit down. For once, Kate ignored the food Zoe put in front of her.

'That letter Alice came rushing in to show Gregor was her mother's credit card statement.'

Zoe recalled the sceptical voice at the other end of the telephone when she tried to cancel a safari in South Africa which Russell had booked for them. She had known nothing about it until the arrival of a demand for the balance owed, long after his death. 'It can take ages to tidy up a dead person's affairs.'

'It showed a charge for November the fourth. That's when Chrissie told everyone she was driving down to stay with Alice in Newcastle. And although I thought

Alice was lying when she claimed she didn't expect her mum until the day after, I believe her now.'

'What's changed your mind?'

At last, Kate picked up a sandwich and waved it around as she continued to speak. 'Chrissie had booked to be somewhere else on the night of the fourth.'

'A hotel or restaurant, you mean?'

'I missed exactly where, but it must be one of those, probably a hotel. They take your credit card details when you make a booking, so they can clobber you for any lost revenue if you don't cancel in good time. Chrissie didn't turn up but they still put a charge through on her card.'

'If it was a hotel,' Zoe said, 'I'd give anything to know if she'd booked a single or a double room.'

'When you lie about your movements to cover up the fact you're spending a night in a hotel, you're not planning to stay there on your own, are you? She must have had an assignation with her secret lover. Whoever he is.' A piece of lettuce fell out of the sandwich Kate was brandishing. She picked it up, jammed it back in and took a bite.

'This could put Alice and Gregor in the clear,' Zoe said.

'Alice certainly thinks so. She's probably been over to Hawick already, telling the police.'

'I don't think DCI Mather will be as impressed by this new piece of evidence as we are.'

'Why not?'

'He wasn't there when Alice came into the pub to tell Gregor. As far as he knows, it could be part of an elaborate ruse to reinforce her story. Only you and your lip-reading skills can attest to their surprise at the bill's arrival.'

'Are you saying that because I eavesdropped on their conversation, I could help those two stay out of trouble with the police?'

'Ironic, isn't it?' Zoe poured tea into their mugs then looked up to add, 'Although, if we stop assuming they worked together to dispose of their parents, either of them could still be in the running. If Gregor is the murderer, he could easily have killed Chrissie without knowing she was due to be somewhere else later that day.'

'I'm sure his surprise was genuine. He was a bit slow on the uptake and Alice had to explain why the charge on the statement was so significant.'

'But that doesn't mean he didn't kill Chrissie.'

'You're crediting him with being cleverer than he actually is. It's not his brain that Gregor Baird's known for.'

'So Margaret tells me. But while he's not particularly clever, he strikes me as cunning enough to think up a ruse like that.'

'I really thought we were getting somewhere.' Kate took a gulp of tea. 'But you've shot me down in flames again.'

'I'm sorry. That wasn't my intention.'

'You're so unemotional, Zoe. Anyone would think you don't care who the killer is.'

'Of course I care. I came close to losing my own life, remember? But we all cope with things differently.'

Kate picked up another sandwich and bit a chunk out of it. She did not seem appeased.

'Look on the bright side,' Zoe said, hoping to jolly her friend out of the uncharacteristically grouchy mood she was in. 'You've got a good excuse to see Mather again.'

'I don't need an excuse to see him, thank you very much. And I'm hardly going to do anything to help Alice after the way she's treated Tom, am I?'

'You did agree we'd tell the police if we found out anything important.'

'I don't see why I should.' Kate adopted the expression she called a petted lip and often scolded her children for wearing when they did not get their own way.

'Give Mather the facts and let him do whatever he wants with them.'

'I think I might tell Alice first. Perhaps she'll agree to easing up on her demands about the twins.'

'Kate, that sounds horribly like blackmail.'

'If it stops Tom's children being taken away from him and the rest of the family, I'm prepared to do it.'

'You may not have to.'

Zoe had planned to tell Kate some, though not all, of her conversation with Tom at the health centre, but they had been so occupied discussing Alice and Gregor that the opportunity had not arisen. Now it was too late for Kate to be anything but more riled with her.

'What do you mean?'

'I think I may have convinced Tom to get help from Chris Kossoff to stand up to Alice and deal with the police on his behalf.'

'And when were you going to tell me this?'

'I'm telling you now.'

'He's my cousin, Zoe. I think I have a right to know when you've persuaded him to do something that could affect the whole family.'

'I haven't had a chance.'

'You're only telling me now to stop me from going to see Alice.' Kate's voice rose as she pulled her car keys out of her handbag. 'By the way, the full story about Brian being Lisa's dad is out at last. I suppose you were going to tell me that too, eventually. Mum's extremely upset. It would have been much better if she'd heard it from me.'

'Please don't be angry. I found out at the police station and couldn't say anything.'

Kate stood up. 'Zoe, you've got to learn to trust someone. Maybe not me, but someone.'

The front door banged as she left the cottage.

No longer hungry, Zoe stared down at the sandwich on her plate. She was so sick of keeping secrets. She had enough of her own without everyone else's too.

Even a visit to the coach house, where both bathrooms had been fitted since she was last there, did little to raise Zoe's spirits that afternoon. She trudged up the stairs to the tower room and stood staring across at Larimer Hall.

First Neil and now Kate had turned their backs on her. This was why she avoided getting close to people. *Sooner or later, they always let you down.*

Gerry Hall arrived as she was about to leave. After soliciting praise for the work done so far, he asked if she had chosen a kitchen yet.

'I know you're getting our mutual friend to make it for you, but we need a plan to show where you're wanting the plumbing and power points. Aye, a plan.'

'Neil was working on it. I'll chase him up.'

Zoe's stomach lurched. There was no avoiding it. She had to go to Larimer Hall and seek out Neil, which would be both disturbing and embarrassing. *Her own fault for mixing business with pleasure.*

As soon as Gerry Hall was gone, Zoe secured her property and drove slowly up the drive. She could feel the tension across her shoulders as she rang the bell. When Peter opened the door and looked past her, she realised he always greeted Mac when they met, not her. She had left the dog at Keeper's Cottage today.

'Is Neil around? I need to talk to him about my kitchen.'

Peter shook his head. 'He's out seeing a customer in Berwick. Won't be back till teatime.'

'Oh. It's Gerry Hall, you see. He needs a plan for the plumbing and electrics. I was wondering how far Neil's got with my drawing. I said I'd chase him up and let Gerry know when it'll be ready. If it's not too much trouble, could you –'

'He's finished. It's in the workshop.'

Humiliated by her own babbling, Zoe followed Peter in silence through the hall and down the stone staircase. The cats were in their usual place, in front of the Aga. The workshop smelt familiar, an agreeable fusion of wood and oil, like Neil without the cigarettes. She felt a pang of regret. *They wouldn't even be friends now.*

Peter lifted a buff folder from the desk and took out several pieces of paper. He gave them to Zoe without a word.

She unfolded the uppermost plan. Produced on a computer, it laid out her entire kitchen, complete with storage and work areas, an Aga – of course – and a huge island in the middle. Other sheets were hand-drawn representations of sections of the room, showing different features and finishes.

'It looks beautiful,' she said.

'You've got the measurements for everything on there. So now you can go off and buy a flat-pack from one of the DIY sheds.'

Zoe laughed, then saw the look on Peter's face. *He wasn't joking.*

'Why would I want to do that?' she asked.

'It would mean you'd stay away from Neil.'

'Maybe I don't want to stay away from him.'

'That's obvious.'

'Are you telling me to stop seeing your brother? If so, I want to hear what he's got to say about it.'

'You're making a big mistake if you take him seriously. You'll only get hurt.'

'My relationship with Neil is none of your business.'

Zoe returned the plans to the desk, hoping he could not see her hand shaking. 'Please tell him I stopped by and ask him to phone me.' She started to walk towards the door.

Peter grabbed her arm.

'Let go.' Zoe tried to pull herself free. 'Ow, you're hurting me.'

He stared at her, jaw clenched, then thrust her arm away from him. 'It's for your own good,' he said, and turned his back on her.

Zoe slipped twice going up the stone steps in her hurry to reach Larimer Hall's front door. Once in the car, she took several deep breaths and rubbed at the red mark on her arm.

What just happened?

She wondered if she had overreacted, misinterpreting Peter's warning about Neil as a threat. He was reserved, happy to play second fiddle to his boisterous elder brother; she had never seen him get cross with anyone. Maybe he knew Neil was giving her the run-around and this was his clumsy attempt to tell Zoe what Neil would not: she had been dumped. *Yes, that must be it.* She did not want to consider the alternative, that Peter resented her relationship with Neil, that he had caused her car crash.

For the first time, she allowed herself to think the unthinkable: coming to the Borders had been a mistake. *What was it Neil said? Some incomers can't hack it and soon leave. Was she one of those?*

As she approached Keeper's Cottage, she saw a vehicle parked outside the front door: Kate's Volvo. She nearly drove on, unable to face another argument today. But that would be ridiculous. This was still her home, even if not for much longer.

Kate walked towards the garage as Zoe swung the hire car into it, and stood waiting at the door. As soon as Zoe got out she rushed up to her.

'I'm so sorry for what I said.'

Not knowing how to respond, Zoe stood with the car door open, her handbag still on the passenger seat.

'I felt so awful about how things were left between us that I dumped the bairns on Mum as soon as they got home from school and came round to see you rather than texting.' Kate hugged Zoe tightly.

'It's okay,' Zoe said into Kate's hair, then pulled back so her friend could see her face. 'It's okay,' she repeated. 'You were right. I do have to trust someone. And there's nobody I'd rather confide in than you.'

She took a deep breath. 'So why don't you come inside and I'll tell you about Russell and how he died.'

FORTY-TWO

Kate and Zoe stood in the hundred-watt brilliance of the cottage's hallway, taking their coats off.

'You're as white as a sheet,' Kate said. 'What's happened?'

'It's this light – I really must buy a shade.' Zoe bent down to pet Mac, who had rushed into the hall to greet them.

Kate's silence indicated the huge effort she was making not to press for the truth.

Zoe went to make tea, leaving Kate curled up in Mac's chair and stroking the dog's head. While she waited for the kettle, she rooted about in the Pickfords' box in the hall, finding what she was searching for just as the water came to the boil.

Kate barely noticed the mug of tea being set down next to her as she stared at the photo album under Zoe's arm. Zoe sat in her own chair, flicked through a few pages then handed the open album to Kate.

'That's Russell and me the day we got married.'

Kate studied the photograph and a confused expression spread across her face. 'But he's –'

'In a wheelchair. Yes.' *Maybe it was unkind to spring it on her in this way.* 'He was injured playing rugby.'

'Oh Zoe, that's terrible. For both of you.'

'It happened before I knew him. As you can see, he was quite a bit older than me.'

'But you still married him.'

'I can't believe you said that, Kate. You of all people.'

'You know what I mean. It must have been a lot to take on.'

Zoe shrugged. 'It was part and parcel of who he was.'

'Even so . . . '

'He was a man. They're never easy to live with. I don't need to tell you that.'

Passing up this opportunity to disparage her ex-husband, Kate asked, 'How long were you married?'

'Eight years. But we were together a long time before that.' Zoe tensed as the inevitable question drew nearer, wishing she had kept her mouth shut.

'His death . . .' Kate hesitated.

Here it comes.

'Was it because of his disability?'

'No.'

Kate stayed silent.

'No,' Zoe repeated. 'He killed himself. After I left him.'

'Oh my God!' Kate's hand flew to her mouth.

'You're always saying you hate how people only see you in terms of your disability. I haven't been able to tell you before how much I agree. Because he was unable to walk, Russell had to be a nice guy. And me? I was a saint for marrying him. We couldn't simply be a normal couple with normal problems.'

'So it wasn't a happy marriage?'

'I wouldn't say that. Most of the time we got along fine. But then I– '

Zoe's mobile rang. She paused and said, 'Phone,' to Kate, but didn't move. When it stopped, she went on. 'I started to realise I'd been too inexperienced to marry. And his feelings had changed as well, although he wouldn't admit it.'

'Did you meet someone else?'

Unused to confiding in anyone like this, Zoe felt grateful for her friend's prompting. 'No. He did.'

'Oh.'

'See what I mean about people's expectations? You're surprised it was that way round, aren't you?'

Kate nodded.

'He said it wasn't serious, and knowing the woman – or, more accurately, girl – he got involved with, I believed him. I suspect she slept with him out of curiosity rather than anything else. If I'm honest, it wasn't the end of the world, but it gave me the excuse I needed.'

'So you moved out?'

'Only after we'd sat down and discussed the situation. I thought we were handling it an adult way. We told everyone it was a trial separation, though I knew our marriage was over and I thought he did too.

'But he didn't?'

'I should have spelt it out, made sure he felt the same. But it turned out he thought my leaving was a knee-jerk reaction to him being unfaithful. He expected me to move back in once I got over the initial shock.'

Kate snorted. 'Typical man.'

As she failed to leap to Russell's defence, Zoe realised she was finally coming to terms with what happened. It wasn't entirely her fault, regardless of their friends and his family thinking otherwise.

'I only found this out when I tried to raise the subject of how to divide our possessions.' She spread her hands in a gesture of helplessness. 'He was angry at first, then he calmed down and started begging me to give him another chance. And when that didn't work he got nasty, called me names and told me to get out of the house. We never spoke again.'

'Oh Zoe, you've told me enough. Stop now and I'll make us some more tea.'

Zoe clasped her hand round her mug. It was half-full and stone-cold. 'That would be nice, thanks. But I haven't finished yet.'

'We both need a break.' Kate picked up their mugs and made for the kitchen. While she was out of the room, Zoe retrieved her mobile from the bookcase. The missed call was from Neil, no message left. *Typically bad timing.*

The sound of cupboard doors opening and shutting was explained when Kate returned with their tea and a plate of shortbread. 'Hope you don't mind,' she said, dunking a piece into her mug.

'Of course not.'

'Are you sure you want to go on?'

Zoe rushed to continue, scared she would lose her nerve if she didn't. 'I couldn't leave things unresolved, so I went back to the house a couple of days later. I had to let myself in. Russell was dead. From an overdose.'

'Shit,' Kate said, sending out a spray of buttery crumbs.

'To make matters worse, the coroner recorded an open verdict at the inquest.'

'Why?'

'Because the police weren't convinced it was suicide.'

'Didn't he leave a note?'

'Yes, but – '

Zoe took a sip of her tea.

'But what?' Kate asked.

'It was addressed to me and said such hurtful things that I destroyed it. Stupid or what? It's not like I didn't know the police would need it.'

'But if he didn't kill himself, what did they think had happened?'

Zoe drank her tea, watching Kate over the top of her mug. She caught on after a few seconds.

'Oh my God, Zoe, they thought you'd killed him.'

'I was the wronged wife and a doctor with access to drugs. The clincher was the fact I'd been the one to move out. The house was adapted for Russell's needs, you see, so it made sense for him to stay put. But the police interpreted this as me being forced to give up my home. So I had means, motive and – as I was the last person to see him alive – opportunity.'

'That's crazy.'

'I tried to tell them, but they wouldn't listen. Claiming he'd left a note but not being able to produce it made matters worse.'

'Now I can see why you didn't want to get involved with finding Chrissie's killer,' Kate said. 'What an ordeal it must have been for you.'

'I have more sympathy now for people who make confessions they later retract. I knew I didn't give Russell those drugs, but at one point I nearly said I had, just to get it over with.'

'What eventually persuaded them you didn't do it?'

'My solicitor. I was like Tom to begin with, believing only a guilty person would need one. But then a friend, one of the few I had left, put me in touch with his. She's in her sixties, has long grey hair tied up in a bun, speaks better English than the Queen – and is probably the scariest person I've ever met.'

'And she got the police to leave you alone?'

'Yes.'

'How?'

'Sheer force of character, or so it seemed at the time. There was probably more to it. She challenged them to come up with firm evidence and charge me, or else admit it was suicide. Two days later someone rang to tell me I had access into the house again. I never heard anything more.'

'So they didn't admit they got it wrong?'

'For all I know, I could still be under suspicion and they're biding their time until I give them an excuse to come after me again.'

Kate pulled a tissue out of her pocket and scrubbed at the shortbread crumbs stuck around her mouth. 'It must have been a terrible experience. No wonder you came up here to escape from all that.'

Zoe hesitated. This would be the ideal opportunity to share more, to unburden herself completely. But she could not do it.

'So now you know,' she said. 'Believe it or not, I feel better having told you.'

'And you're not to worry about me breaking your confidence. It'll go no further.'

'That's not why I didn't want to tell you. I'm just not good at sharing personal stuff.'

Kate feigned a look of surprise. 'You don't say?'

'Maybe it's because I'm an only child. My grandmother used to tell me off for living too much in my own head.'

'She was probably right. But we can't help how we were brought up. Just remember you're not alone any more.' Kate leaned over and patted Zoe's hand. 'Let's change the subject. How are things going between you and Neil?'

'We haven't spoken for a while. That was him on my mobile a few minutes ago.' Zoe forced a casual expression. 'I'll ring him later.'

'So he's broken down your defences and you two are an item now?'

'No, not at all. We were supposed to be going out on our first proper date last Saturday. His coming across Brian stabbed to dead put paid to that.'

'You haven't mentioned this before.'

'It was why he went to the shop. To buy me flowers.'

'How romantic.'

'His experience will put him off such gestures in the future.'

'I doubt it. He's well and truly smitten with you.'

'How can you tell?'

'He's had a few girlfriends since I've known him, but nothing serious. And you've not exactly encouraged him, have you? Yet despite that, he hasn't given up.'

'Some men love the thrill of the chase and lose interest as soon as they get what they want.' This was the closest to admitting Neil's hurtful behaviour that Zoe felt able to come. She had done enough soul-baring for one day.

'That's a very old-fashioned attitude, if you don't mind me saying. And I'm sure it doesn't apply to Neil.'

Kate looked at her watch. 'Sorry, I need to get back. I told Mum I'd only be gone for half an hour. She's got the Rural this evening.'

'Blame me for talking too much.'

'She'll never believe that.'

It would be a pity to spoil things now they were back on good terms, but out in the hall Zoe felt compelled to ask Kate if she had carried out her threat to go and see Alice.

'No, though I still want to, even if Tom has got Chris Kossoff sorting her out. She's holed up in Horseshoe Cottage, Mum says.'

'It probably belongs to her now, remember.'

Kate's face showed what she thought of that. 'Why don't you come with me? Then you'll know I'm behaving myself.'

'I don't think she likes me.'

'Who cares? No one likes her.'

'I'm working tomorrow morning.'

'No problem. You finish about one, don't you? I'll pick you up from here the back of two.'

As soon as Kate had left, Zoe sat down and stared at her mobile. *Should she call Neil back?*

Mac's barking made her jump. Someone was at the front door.

'Have you been lurking outside, waiting for Kate to leave?' Zoe asked when she saw who her visitor was.

Neil's brow furrowed and he juggled his keys from hand to hand. 'Can I come in? We need to talk.'

FORTY-THREE

Neil stood watching Zoe until she moved aside to let him in. He pulled off his hat and coat and hung both on a spare hook. Light from the naked bulb bounced off his head.

Seconds later, after resolving to sidestep any attempt he might make to touch her, Zoe was leant against him, feeling his chest rise and fall. But she pulled away as his face neared hers, drawing the line at kissing him. *For now.*

'Come through to the warmth.'

He reached into his coat pocket and brought out a bottle of red wine. 'Can I fetch a couple of glasses first?' Without waiting for an answer he went towards the kitchen, while Zoe returned to the sitting room and squeezed another log into the woodburner.

'Time was,' Neil said, opening the bottle a few minutes later, 'when no wine worth drinking came in a screw-top bottle. Things have changed.' He poured them a glass each and they sat down.

Zoe waited to hear what he had to say.

Neil swept a hand over his head. 'You're angry with me, aren't you?'

'I hate it when people don't return my calls.'

'Sorry about that. I've been busy.'

'Me too. With work, the coach house, a funeral and an encounter with a psychic. Not to mention a row with your brother.'

'Ah, that.' Neil put his glass down. 'I'm curious to

hear about the psychic, but let's deal with Pete first. He's really sorry he mouthed off at you. He says he didn't mean anything by it.'

'And you believe him?'

'Yes. Of course. He was being a bit childish, that's all. Pete hates change, always has. You and me getting together means things will be different for him too. He'll be living on his own, for a start.'

'Not necessarily.'

'Eventually.'

Zoe let that one pass. She had already wasted enough time trying to convince Neil she would never marry him.

'He spoke out of turn and he'll apologise next time he sees you. Can't you leave it at that?'

'Another interpretation could be that Peter was warning me to stop seeing you because he knows something I don't. His exact words were, "It's for your own good".'

'You're reading far too much into this.'

'I don't think I am. Look at it from my point of view. I have no idea how you've treated other women in the past, if you've ever been married, or even how many serious relationships you've been in.'

Neil leaned back in his chair. 'My life's an open book. Ask me anything you want and I promise to tell you the truth.'

Zoe studied him, trying to disentangle the complicated feelings he stirred in her. She had known Russell for so long before agreeing to marry him, she could not remember when and how they had revealed the important things about themselves to each other. Neil, on the other hand, seemed intent on conducting their relationship backwards, ignoring the natural order of things. A stilted question-and-answer session would scarcely help. *But maybe it was better than nothing.*

'What other brothers and sisters do you have?' she asked eventually.

Neil looked surprised; wherever he had expected her to start, this was not it. 'We had a sister, Louise.'

'Had?'

'She died from a drugs overdose when she was twenty-two. We don't know if it was on purpose or an accident. She'd been clean for six months.'

'I'm sorry.'

'Me too. It was a waste.'

They sipped their wine.

'Well, have you ever been married?' Zoe asked.

'No. Though I was engaged once.'

'What happened?'

'She broke it off. Don't ask me why. She said – and I quote – "I can't go through with it". Like it was a some sort of operation.'

'Were you both very young?'

'Not particularly. It was before Pete and I moved up here.'

'But not why you moved here?'

He smiled one of those annoying smiles people use when they know something you don't. 'Hardly.'

'And since then, has there been anyone else?'

Before Zoe realised what he was doing, Neil put his glass on the table and fell to his knees in front of her. 'No one. Until you.'

'Can we please have fewer dramatic gestures and more talking?' Zoe motioned to him to stand up, but he took no notice. 'I have it on good authority you've not exactly led a monk's life since you came to the Borders.'

'I thought we were talking about serious relationships.' Neil sat back on his haunches, all the time keeping his eyes fixed on Zoe's. 'I admit I've played the field. There's a shortage of eligible young men round here, or hadn't you noticed? But I've never led anyone on with false promises.'

Before Zoe could respond, her attention was caught by Mac, who walked over to Neil and sat down beside him. She looked from man to dog and back again, then burst out laughing. The similarity between them, both in posture and facial expression, was striking.

'Woof!' Neil said. 'Now you have two faithful mutts.' He scrambled to his feet, took hold of Zoe's hands and pulled her out of her chair. 'Although I do have some advantages over your funny-looking roommate.'

He kissed her on the lips, and after a moment's hesitation, Zoe responded. As his mouth moved slowly down her neck he started to undo the buttons on her blouse. His head felt more like silk than velvet; he must have shaved before coming to see her.

The doorbell rang. Mac raced into the hall, barking.

'Leave it. Please.' Neil's breath was hot against Zoe's skin.

'Sorry.' She freed herself from his grasp and struggled to do up her blouse with uncooperative fingers. 'I'd ignore the phone, but I can't leave someone standing outside.'

Paul Ryder was straightening his tie as she opened the front door.

'My dear, I wasn't far away, so I thought I'd drop in rather than telephone. I hope this isn't an inconvenient time.'

'Of course not. Come in.' She pushed away some strands of hair that had come loose from her plait.

Neil stood up when he saw Zoe was not alone.

'I expect you know each other,' Zoe said.

'No.' Paul approached Neil with his hand outstretched. 'Paul Ryder.'

'Neil Pengelly.'

'I've heard very good things about your kitchens,' Paul said. 'Sadly, I don't cook enough to justify one.'

Neil smiled politely, then looked at his watch. 'I'll

be on my way, now we've got that misunderstanding sorted out, Zoe.' And despite Paul's protestations and Zoe's offer of supper, he left.

Paul looked embarrassed, pulling at the waistband of his trousers as if they were in danger of falling down. 'I'm so sorry, my dear. I should have phoned first.'

'No, Paul, your timing was perfect. Can I get you a drink?'

'Thank you, but no. I've got a couple of things to tell you and then I plan to pop in on old Mrs Gardner on my way home.'

'Sit down at least.'

Paul sat, crossing his legs to reveal one blue sock and one brown. 'Walter's back. He wants us all to meet at four o'clock tomorrow. Can you work in the afternoon rather than the morning?'

'No problem.' Zoe waited for him to tell her what the meeting was about, but instead he changed the subject.

'I was in the BGH earlier, seeing how one of my old ladies is doing after her hip operation. Young Lisa is still there.'

'They've kept her in this long?' Zoe felt a pang of guilt. With everything that was happening, she had forgotten to check on Lisa's progress.

'They did a D and C after her miscarriage. She's recovered sufficiently, physically anyway, to be discharged, but I think the police would rather she stayed in hospital while a decision is made about what to do with her.'

'Can't she be released on bail?'

'Where would she go? The poor girl has no friends, no relatives. She's being well cared for at the BGH, getting the kindness she needs. It has to be better than being kept somewhere under lock and key.'

'Now I'm not working 'til later, I could go to see her tomorrow morning.'

'That's what I was hoping you would say.' Paul rose, accidentally kicking Mac. The dog looked up, perceived no threat and put his head back between his front paws with a sigh.

After seeing Paul out, Zoe returned to the sitting room and texted Kate, postponing their trip to see Alice. Maybe if it was put back often enough she would abandon the idea altogether.

FORTY-FOUR

Her only previous experience of Borders General Hospital having been as a patient, Zoe was glad to arrive this time by car rather than ambulance. She walked past the information desk and coffee shop up the stairs to the gynae ward, and half-expected a policeman to be stationed outside the room she was directed to. Instead, the only uniforms in sight were those worn by nurses.

She was not Lisa's only visitor. Two women, one on either side of the bed, looked up as she entered the room. The one on the left, holding Lisa's hand, had cropped black hair and the lean body of an athlete.

'Hello, Doctor.' Lisa's habitual pallor was still evident, even against the white of the pillows propping her up. *How had they all been fooled into believing this tiny creature was in her twenties?*

'Hello, Zoe.' Lisa's other visitor was Etta Mackenzie.

The stranger offered Zoe her hand. 'You're Doctor Moreland? We have a lot to thank you for, I believe.'

'This is Lisa's Auntie Anne,' Etta said. 'She's come up from London.'

'My sister Jane was Lisa's mother.' Anne pumped Zoe's hand. 'When the police got in touch, I came up as soon as I could. It was a terrible shock, hearing what's happened, but I've been so desperate for news about Lisa that it was a relief too.'

'I'm glad the police were able to find you. Are you staying long?'

'As long as it takes,' Anne said. 'I'm not going home without her.'

Zoe turned to Lisa. 'I was sorry to hear about your baby. How are you feeling now?'

'It was probably for the best.' Lisa's words were all the more sad because they so obviously echoed everyone else's reaction to her miscarriage. She was unlikely to believe it herself.

'You've been through such a lot, sweetheart.' Anne said, and hugged her. 'You'll feel better when you're back home with me.'

'I must go,' Etta said, getting up. 'I'm so pleased to have met you, Anne. Don't forget now – you have my number, and if there's anything I can do to help, please phone me. I mean it.'

'Everyone's being so kind. Thank you.' Anne embraced Etta.

'I'll walk out with you,' Zoe said. 'Can I get you anything from the hospital shop, Lisa?'

Lisa shook her head and sank deeper into the pillows, closing her eyes. Anne sat down beside her again.

As they walked along the corridor, Zoe asked Etta how she had known Lisa was still in hospital. Unsurprisingly, it turned out one of the Mackenzie cousins was a nurse on the gynae ward.

'Kate didn't mention you were coming over. I could have given you a lift.'

'I haven't told her. She'd only ask why I've come all this way to visit someone I hardly know.'

Zoe came to a halt in front of the cafe. 'Why did you?' she asked.

Etta did not answer.

'It was you, wasn't it?' Zoe said. 'You overheard Lisa and Brian in the shop that evening. That's what you've been so upset about, not the Bairds' deaths. And why you tried to talk to me alone in the churchyard.'

'It was dreadful,' Etta said. 'Brian was the lassie's father and he'd got her pregnant? I tried to convince myself I was mistaken but I couldn't get it out of my mind.'

'And then you heard she'd killed him.'

'I feel so guilty. If I'd done something, Brian might still be alive and poor Lisa wouldn't be in such trouble.'

'It's not your fault. Even if you had confronted him, a man prepared to do what he did to his own daughter would never have listened to you.'

'But I should have told someone.'

'You certainly need to now.'

'Why? It's too late.'

'Lisa mentioned someone had overheard her and Brian talking about the baby just before Chrissie Baird died. DCI Mather is wondering if the two things are connected.'

'Oh no!'

Alarmed at how pale the older woman had suddenly become, Zoe linked arms with her and led her to a nearby table. 'Sit down and I'll buy us both a coffee.' She walked towards the counter without giving Etta a chance to argue.

'Please don't tell Kate any of this,' Etta said when Zoe rejoined her a few minutes later. 'She'll only worry.'

'Of course, if you don't want me to.'

'Why can't they use proper milk?' Etta struggled to open a tiny plastic container. 'I'm the daughter of a dairy farmer. This smells and tastes nothing like the real thing.'

'Is your family from the Borders too?' Zoe asked, keen to chat about less emotive subjects for a while.

'A few miles the other side of Galashiels.'

'How did you meet Mr Mackenzie?'

'At a Young Farmers ceilidh. I was only seventeen and he swept me off my feet. I expect you'll find that hard to believe.'

'Not at all.'

'We married a year later, and Richard came along a year after that.'

'Then Robert, Douglas and finally Kate – have I got that right?'

'Yes. I was determined to keep going until I had a girl.'

'Seriously?'

'Of course. The relationship between a mother and her daughter is so special.' Etta took a sip of coffee and made a face. 'I lost my mother at about the same age you lost yours. I've tried to be as good a mother as she was.'

'You've succeeded. Anyone can tell how close you and Kate are.'

'It wasn't always that way. I thought we'd lost her, when she told us she planned to marry Kenneth and go to live down in London. We were so relieved she had the sense to come home when things didn't work out.'

'She was lucky to have you to come back to.'

'Do you miss having a family, Zoe?'

'I sometimes wonder what it would be like.'

'Perhaps you'll marry into a big family next time.'

'Perhaps.'

'Kate tells me you aren't just buying a kitchen from Neil Pengelly.' Etta spoke nonchalantly, but Zoe got the feeling she had been hoping to manoeuvre their conversation around to this.

'It's early days. I doubt it'll come to anything.'

'How do you get on with his brother?' Still the offhand tone, but Etta had started to tap her empty milk container on the table.

'Peter? All right I suppose. Why do you ask?'

Tap, tap, tap. 'You'll think I'm interfering.'

'No I won't. What do you want to tell me?'

Tap, tap, tap. 'My friend Nancy stays in Berwick and has a daughter, Ellie. She's a wee bit younger than you, and went out with Neil last year. Don't misunderstand me, he treated her well and she was head over heels in love with him although I don't think he took it as seriously. Then, all of a sudden, she ended it.'

Zoe felt a prickling sensation at the back of her neck. 'Why did she do that?'

Tap, tap. 'Try as she might, Nancy couldn't find out. All she knew was that the last time Elly came home from Larimer Hall, as well as being very upset she seemed frightened.'

FORTY-FIVE

Although Keeper's Cottage was merely a stopgap until Zoe could move into the coach house, it had started to feel like home, despite its dodgy heating and feline squatter. Today, though, closing the front door was not enough to keep away the unease she had felt since her conversation with Kate's mother in the hospital café. On the way back, she nearly convinced herself there was a simple explanation for one of Neil's previous girlfriends suddenly not wanting to see him any more, but once she was inside, Etta's words surged through her mind again.

Did Peter warn off young Ellie too?

Zoe had no appetite for lunch, so thought she might as well go into work early and catch up on some paperwork. Yet more insurance forms had magically appeared on her desk shortly before Walter took off for Wales again. Finishing those would give him one less thing to complain about this afternoon.

As she neared the health centre, apprehension about Walter's hastily convened meeting took centre stage in Zoe's mind. Even following a vehicle whose spare-tyre cover boasted that its driver had been 'Spreading Muck in the Borders for 25 Years' failed to make her smile. Unlike those who found solace in their domestic lives, Zoe had always relied on work as a diversion during troubled times. Her morale already battered on several fronts, she feared she might be driving home later without even the comfort of a job.

Margaret waved from reception without interrupting her telephone conversation. The waiting room was empty and in a side office further along the corridor, Jean was bending down at the stationery cupboard. She did not look up when Zoe called out a greeting. There was no sign of Paul or Walter.

Concentrating on filling in a too-small box on a patient's critical-illness insurance claim, Zoe only realised someone else was in the room when a heap of repeat prescription forms was placed on the corner of her desk. She looked up.

'Hello Jean. How are you?'

Jean grasped the crucifix hanging around her neck, ran it back and forth along its chain and stared at the floor. 'Not very good, Doctor, if you must know.'

'What's wrong?'

'Tom's moved out.' The girl raised her head, revealing eyes swollen from crying. 'We won't be getting married now.'

'Oh Jean, I'm so sorry.'

'You shouldn't be surprised. Seeing as it was you who sent him to that horrible man.'

Shocked at Jean's bitter tone, Zoe asked, 'Do you mean Chris Kossoff?'

'Both of you wanted Tom to tell me what happened when he went to Edinburgh that night. So he did. And now I can't bear to look at him.'

'Here,' Zoe indicated the chair on the other side of her desk, 'sit down. Let's talk about this. I've got time before surgery starts.'

'No. Thank you.' Jean stood immobile, the crucifix still gripped between her right thumb and forefinger. 'When Tom got arrested and Mum died, I thought things couldn't get any worse. But they have.' She let out a sob and fled from the room.

Rising to go after her, Zoe heard Margaret's voice out in the corridor. 'There, there, hen. Come with me and

I'll make us both a nice cup of tea.'

Zoe sat down and put her head in her hands. She had only wanted to help, but instead her intervention had made things far worse. *Poor Jean. It was never a good idea to think you had reached rock bottom. There was always some way to go.*

Looking up again, she slid the insurance form to one side and tried to focus on the list of patients she was due to see that afternoon. Her eyes were immediately drawn to one name: Gregor Baird. He probably wanted more of the medication she had prescribed to help him sleep.

Two patients mentioned seeing Zoe at the Bairds' funeral, but for the first surgery in a long time most of the people who came through her door were more intent on describing their ailments than trying to engage her in conversation. Being worried tended to make her impatient, so she consciously fought the urge to hurry things along and gave everyone as much time as they wanted. As a result, she was a few minutes late fetching Gregor from the waiting room.

He wore a white T-shirt over black trousers, topped off with a faded denim jacket. As before, the scent of freshly laundered clothes hung about him.

Zoe did her best to summon up a smile. 'What can I do for you today?'

'More of those pills would be good.'

Despite their fetching colour, the stare from his blue eyes made Zoe uncomfortable. She tried to hold Gregor's gaze, but eventually looked away, pretending to read what was on her computer screen.

'Have they helped the problem at all?'

'You mean the problem of people like you thinking me 'n' Alice killed our parents?'

'No, I mean not being able to sleep.'

'If they had, why would I be here?'

Zoe felt in no mood to play games. 'I don't know. Is there something else you want?'

Gregor sat back in his chair and folded his arms. 'You think you're so clever, don't you?'

This time Zoe did not retaliate. She had learned early in her career that the best way to handle insults from a patient is silence. However much they huffed and puffed, eventually they blew themselves out.

'Sticking your nose in where it's not wanted.'

Still she said nothing.

'Sending that numpty Tom to your smart-arse solicitor.'

Zoe pursed her lips. *If he wanted an argument, he could have one.*

'You and Alice aren't happy that Tom's called her bluff, are you? And with you both suspects in your parents' murders, she doesn't stand a chance of taking the twins away from him now he has Chris Kossoff on his side.'

'You're not as clever as you think. The police know we didn't kill them. There's proof.'

'You mean the credit card statement showing where Chrissie was going the day she disappeared?'

Gregor scowled, those blue eyes narrowed. 'I knew that deaf bint was watching us. It's creepy how she snoops around lip-reading people's private conversations. No, the police had already sussed out where Chrissie was supposed to be.'

'How?'

'Her phone records, of course. And the cash they found in the car.'

'Cash?'

His tongue loosened by triumph at knowing more than Zoe, Gregor rushed to answer. 'Three hundred and fifty pounds – to pay for the spa break she'd booked at some poncey hotel in Durham. The old man must've been slipping to let her stash that much away.'

Zoe stared at the screen in front of her, seeing nothing.

A spa break. That's all it was? No secret lover, just Chrissie getting away for a bit of pampering?

Gregor's voice brought her back.

'Like a priest, aren't you? You can't pass on what I say. So here's something for you to chew on.' His eyes challenged Zoe to try to stop him.

She would not give him the satisfaction.

'I know the dirty-minded people round here reckon me 'n Alice are more than brother and sister. I bet you do too. Well you're all wrong.' He paused; Zoe remained silent. 'It was her mother I was shagging. Almost since the day she arrived here. We used to really enjoy putting on a show, making folk think we hated each other.'

He smirked, but then his expression shifted briefly to sadness, revealing the true reason why he could not sleep. Gregor Baird was mourning the woman he had secretly loved for years.

Zoe printed off a prescription, signed it and slid it across the desk. Gregor stuffed it into his jacket pocket.

Halfway out of the door he turned back to face Zoe and put his forefinger up to his lips. 'Shush.'

The compassion she had begun to feel for him vanished.

Zoe reached the end of surgery without mishap, although five minutes later she could not have named any of the patients who came in after Gregor Baird. Her mind replayed their conversation over and over again.

She had been right: he was much cleverer than people realised. The gossip that Chrissie was having an affair did not go far enough. Her stepson had been her lover, and the pair had succeeded in keeping their long relationship a secret from everyone.

Even more intriguing was the money Chrissie had evidently planned to spend on that spa break. *If neither her husband nor her lover gave it to her, where had it come from?*

Paul put his head round Zoe's door. 'It's four o'clock. We're in Walter's room.'

FORTY-SIX

Walter raised his head and nodded as Zoe entered his consulting room without making eye contact with her. Paul jumped up to move an unoccupied chair a few inches to the left and patted its seat. She sat down and waited for one of them to speak.

Finally, Walter addressed Paul. 'As you know, I've been home to Cardiff again. As well as helping Mother move into her nursing home, I went there to think about the future. My future.'

Paul examined a stain on his tie. After a few moments' silence he looked up, as if surprised it was his turn to speak. 'What conclusion did you reach?'

'I've not been happy with certain aspects of the practice for a while. Decisions have been made that I couldn't agree with and I feel as though I'm being edged out.'

'My dear fellow, that's not the case at all and you know it.'

'I beg to differ. Which is why I've decided to return to Wales. For good.'

Paul sat up straighter in his chair. 'Is there anything I can do to make you change your mind?'

'No, there isn't.' Walter glanced towards Zoe for the first time, and in spite of those unambiguous words, his message clear. Paul could stop him from carrying out his threat to leave simply by getting rid of her.

Paul looked at Zoe. 'I'm so sorry.'

Zoe's stomach lurched. *He was going to give in. Just like that.* She concentrated so hard on not crying out in protest, she nearly missed what Paul said next.

'It's because I decided to appoint Zoe to the practice, isn't it?'

'Of course not.' At least Walter had the grace to look embarrassed at this unconvincing denial. 'But I don't think she's fitted in as well as we all hoped. With hindsight, I can see we should have recruited someone who knew the area and was more settled in their personal life.'

'You of all people should realise it takes time to make somewhere your home. You have to get to know people, make friends, put down roots.'

'Paying little heed to the wishes of one's employer in the meantime?'

'Now you're being unfair. Zoe has had difficulties recently – none of her own making – but she's always behaved professionally and the patients have taken to her.'

Zoe could not keep quiet any longer. 'I am here, you know. And thanks, Paul, but I can stand up for myself. I'm sorry if things haven't turned out as you expected, Walter. The last month or so hasn't been a bundle of laughs for me either.' She crossed her arms to hide her shaking hands. *Did that make her look defensive?* She uncrossed them.

'You don't need to apologise, my dear,' Paul said. 'No one is blaming you for what has happened.'

'That's not how it sounds.'

'You must admit you've been distracted,' Walter said. 'As well as your problems with Gerry Hall and that unfortunate accident in your car, you've become much too involved with helping the police investigate the Bairds' deaths.'

Zoe tried, unsuccessfully, to stifle a bitter laugh. 'I assure you I'm the last person who would choose to get tangled up with the police.'

'Then why did you consider breaking patient confidentiality to give them information about Gregor Baird?'

'Paul and I talked about that and I took his advice.'

'But what would you have done if Paul hadn't got involved?'

'So now I'm being criticised for something which didn't actually happen?'

'Stop it, both of you,' Paul said. 'Walter, you're forcing my hand.' He got up from his chair.

Zoe tensed. *What on earth was he going to do?* She relaxed a little when Paul lifted down the photograph of a young, dark-haired woman from a shelf of medical textbooks and waved it in front of Walter. 'You're devoted to her, aren't you?'

'Of course I am. Wouldn't any father be?'

'And Morwen's very loyal to you. Please remember that when you hear what I'm about to say.'

Walter looked puzzled.

'I admit I had doubts about your daughter coming to work with us,' Paul said. 'But after she'd been a locum here for those few weeks in the spring, I was starting to change my mind.'

'I told you she's an excellent doctor.'

'Walter, there's something you don't know and which I promised Morwen I wouldn't tell you. However, given the circumstances I'm sure she'll understand my sharing it now. Morwen didn't want a permanent job here. She was afraid of hurting your feelings, so we agreed I would say it was my decision not to offer it to her.'

'I don't believe you.'

'Ask her, why don't you? She's happy working in London, which is what she wanted all along. And when you've spoken with her, reflect on what's best for this practice. I don't want you to go back to Wales, but I'm also reluctant to sacrifice Zoe to keep you here. We must be able to work something out between us.'

Paul put the photograph down and walked out. Zoe followed, dazed at having witnessed Walter's resentment laid bare and troubled by the news that she had been Paul's second choice for her job.

'Before you ask,' Paul said a few minutes later when they were seated in his consulting room, 'I don't know why Walter insisted on your being present for that conversation. It would have been much better if he and I had spoken privately. He's an excellent doctor but he does lack some social skills.'

'Do you think he'll carry out his threat to leave?'

'Who knows?' Paul sighed. 'I often wonder how I might have felt had Alasdair been a girl. I can't imagine loving him more than I do already, but it may have manifested itself in different ways. Fathers are so protective of their girls, aren't they?'

Zoe started to murmur something non-committal, but he interrupted her, obviously remembering a conversation which had taken place during her first week at the practice.

'My dear, what an old fool I am. I apologise for being so unthinking. And also for not realising how difficult Walter has been making things for you. Not much gets past Margaret, so she was aware of the situation, but she said nothing until I asked for her advice this morning. Why did you keep it from me?'

'I'm a big girl, Paul. I should be able to fight my own battles.'

'And as senior partner I should be aware of any tensions within the practice and help sort them out. Walter expects things to go his own way all the time, and reacts badly when they don't. Which was why I agreed to go along with Morwen's little deception. We both knew it was easier than forcing him to face up to the truth.'

Zoe did her best to smile. 'If getting rid of me is what it takes for you to hang on to your partner, then of course you have to do it.'

'Let's wait and see what he decides,' Paul said. 'I'm not giving up on either of you yet.'

The smell of Heinz cream of chicken soup reminded Zoe of her grandparents, and its taste took her straight back to those first few weeks after she had moved in with them following her mother's death. She remembered eating little else then, although she must have because Gran had not been the sort to tolerate childish fads. In adulthood, she turned to this comfort food whenever she felt unable to face anything else. There was a time and a place for home-made roasted tomato soup, but this was not it.

Since leaving the health centre a couple of hours ago, she had swung between resolving to go into work on Monday morning and resigning with immediate effect and being determined to stay put and see things through, whatever Walter's decision turned out to be. To cap it all, there was Neil. She had no idea if their relationship ought to have any influence on what she chose to do. Or if, indeed, they had a relationship.

Her mobile chimed with a text from Kate: *Need to catch up. RU home?*

Zoe texted straight back: *Yes*

As soon as Kate arrived, she launched into her news. 'Things have moved on with Tom and Alice. She –'

'Let's sit down first, shall we?' Zoe steered her friend through to the sitting room.

Kate perched on the arm of Mac's chair. 'As I was saying, Alice has dropped her plan to take the girls away and, in exchange, Tom's agreed to let her spend as much time as she wants with them up here.'

Relieved this was already common knowledge, Zoe saw no need to feign ignorance. She said, 'So I've heard. Gregor came into the surgery this afternoon. He's not happy about it and blames me for putting Tom on to Chris Kossoff.'

'Take no notice of him. The Mackenzie clan is very

grateful to you. It was lucky Uncle Billy phoned Mum to tell her before I went barging in feet-first to see Alice. And you'll feel better now I don't have to use her conversation in the pub with Gregor as leverage. Though I guess I should tell Erskine in any case.'

'I don't think that's necessary any more.'

'But you insisted on it. You described it as an ideal excuse to see him.'

'Sorry about that.'

Kate grinned. 'You're useless at realising when your leg's being pulled, aren't you? Anyway, explain why I don't need to pass on this vital piece of evidence.'

Once again, Zoe was forced to decide what she could and could not tell her friend. Gregor's revelation about having been his stepmother's lover was definitely out of bounds, but she could see no harm in mentioning another piece of interesting news.

'The police have known for a while where Chrissie was due to be on the day she disappeared. According to Gregor, she'd booked herself in for an overnight spa break at a hotel near Durham. They found out through her phone records.'

'Why did Gregor tell you this?'

'He was trying to prove how you and I aren't nearly as smart as he is.'

'So, there's no mystery lover after all.' Kate looked disappointed. 'Oh well, at least it's good news about Tom and the twins.'

'Although it's sad that he and Jean have split up.' Zoe regretted her words as soon as they were out. Kate's face told her this was not yet common knowledge.

'You're kidding. How did Gregor find that out?'

'It wasn't Gregor who told me. Jean works at the health centre, remember? She's very upset.'

'They were planning to get married. What happened?'

Oh shit. Zoe had no intention of telling anyone about Tom's drunken visit to an Edinburgh nightclub.

'What happened, Zoe?'

'Ask Tom. He'll tell you if he wants you to know.'

'Remember our conversation about you having to trust people?'

'I do, but I'm adamant on this one.' Desperate to change the subject, Zoe said, 'But Gregor let slip something else you'll find interesting.'

'This had better be good.'

'It is. The police found three hundred and fifty pounds hidden in Chrissie's car.'

'So what?' Kate was not going to be so easily appeased.

'That's exactly how much her spa break was costing. She must have only used her credit card to make the booking, and never intended to settle the bill with it. But more to the point, where did she got the money from? I keep hearing how mean Jimmy was.'

'Aye, he was that. Chrissie once told Mum he'd check her shopping receipts to make sure she wasn't being extravagant.' Kate looked thoughtful. 'Could she have stolen it?'

'That was my first thought, but who from? I don't keep that much money on me. Do you?

'No, but Dad does. People of that generation are happier with cash than plastic. Sorry, Zoe, that doesn't get us anywhere.'

'There is another possibility. Want to hear my theory?'

'Of course.'

'She was blackmailing someone.'

'Why didn't I think of that?' Kate considered briefly, then nodded, looking pleased with herself. 'I know who her victims were.'

'Me too.'

'Ray and Hazel Anderson,' Kate said.

'The Andersons,' Zoe said simultaneously.

'Even if they didn't kill her,' Kate continued, 'it explains why they're so freaked out by the police asking questions. But what could Chrissie possibly know that they'd pay her to keep quiet about?'

'Everyone has secrets. What we need to find out is whether theirs is serious enough to warrant killing someone over.'

'And how do we do that?'

'I'm going to ask them, or rather, Hazel. Tomorrow morning.'

'But if Ray and Hazel killed Chrissie, that means they probably tried to kill you too.'

'I'm sure they won't hurt me. If they were responsible for Chrissie's death I doubt it was on purpose.'

'Someone tampered with your car's brakes on purpose.'

'If it makes you feel better I'll tell them from the outset that you know I've gone to see them.'

'Let me come with you.'

Zoe shook her head. 'I've gained Hazel's trust. She's more likely to open up if it's just me. I'll go to the flat first. If I time it right, Ray will be down in the pub.'

'At least let me know how you get on.'

'I'll text you.'

'Better still, why don't you come round for tea and tell me what she says?'

'What time?'

'Four-ish? I'm taking the bairns Christmas shopping in Berwick, but we'll be back by then. Let yourself in if we're not. And be careful!'

FORTY-SEVEN

The ten o'clock headlines came on as Zoe parked a little way past The Rocket on Saturday morning. She took no solace from the news that except for a spate of quad-bike thefts in the Duns area, little of note had taken place anywhere in the Borders during the past twenty-four hours. Gone was the nonchalance she had displayed to Kate last night when declaring her intention to tackle the Andersons about their relationship with Chrissie Baird. Instead, her stomach churned and Kate's warning echoed in her mind. *If Ray and Hazel killed Chrissie, that probably means they tried to kill you too.*

She got out of the car and walked to the rear of the pub. Once there, she lost her nerve and stood, hand poised, incapable of knocking on the door. The words she had prepared to explain this visit fled from her mind. *How could she hope to persuade Hazel to confide in her? And was she putting herself in danger by even trying?*

About to turn away from the building, she glimpsed movement up at the flat's window. Someone had seen her.

Zoe's trepidation vanished as soon as the door opened. As she had predicted, the comfort offered by Colonel Stevens' claim to have put Hazel in touch with her dead son had not lasted long. The Rocket's landlady pressed a trembling hand against her brow, simultaneously supporting a too-heavy head and shielding her eyes from the light. The belt of her dressing-gown was unfastened, revealing a faded blue nightie which clung to a pair of sagging breasts.

Without a word, Hazel turned to walk slowly back up the stairs. Zoe followed, and when they reached the door to the flat's living quarters she asked Hazel if she wanted to get dressed before they talked. The older woman murmured something and continued along the passageway, while Zoe entered the sitting room and crossed the tartan carpet to look out of the window. She could no longer see police tape; the area beyond the beer garden had returned to being just a field, although she could not imagine ever wanting to walk there again.

Rather than sit down and wait for Hazel, she went over to the fireplace and lifted up the photograph of the young man whose premature death was slowly but relentlessly killing his mother. It was a typical holiday shot taken in a harbour, with Duncan standing in front of a small, brightly coloured boat while in the distance another vessel, bigger and with writing along its side, was heading out to sea. A ferry.

A ferry.

At that moment, Zoe realised what Chrissie's hold over Hazel and Ray could have been. The idea appalled her, and changed entirely her attitude towards the dead woman. Nothing justified murder, but she understood now the anguish which could make it seem like the only option.

Coffee mugs rattling on a tray announced Hazel's arrival. When they were both seated, Zoe inclined her head towards the mantelpiece. 'I was admiring Duncan's photograph,' she said. 'Where was it taken?'

Spots of colour appeared on Hazel's cheeks. 'On the west coast. It was his last birthday before he got ill.'

'It was taken in Oban, wasn't it?'

'Yes.' Hazel had brushed her hair and pulled on a white T-shirt over a pair of chef's trousers, but these superficial improvements failed to mask her misery.

'I'm sorry to have to ask you this, Hazel, but what did Duncan die from?'

The only response Zoe got was a sob. She tried again, making her voice as gentle as she could. 'Hazel, please tell me. Did he die of an AIDS-related illness?'

Hazel looked up, her face shiny with tears. 'He didn't have AIDS,' she whispered. 'He was HIV-positive but the treatment was keeping him well. Then he got cancer, a horrible cancer, the sort everyone would say he brought on himself.'

'You mean anal cancer?' Zoe asked. Although caused by the same virus as cervical cancer in women, she knew how little awareness and even less sympathy surrounded this type of cancer, which affects both sexes.

Hazel winced as if she had been struck.

'Ray doesn't want anyone to know, does he?'

'I'm sure Duncan left it too late to get help because he couldn't face telling his dad.' Hazel pulled a tissue from her trouser pocket and noisily blew her nose.

'And Chrissie found out.'

'We hadn't been here long when she came knocking on the door, saying she needed to talk to us,' Hazel said, forcing back tears. 'We thought she wanted to give us advice about the pub. Instead, she warned us that some Borders people could be very narrow-minded and although she was sorry our son was dead, we shouldn't expect everyone to be as sympathetic once they knew what he'd died from.'

'She asked for money in exchange for keeping quiet?'

'Not at first. That afternoon, as she was leaving, she admired a vase on the window sill, said it would go well with the new wallpaper she'd hung in Horseshoe Cottage. Then she just stood there, waiting. And Ray gave it to her.' Hazel's face crumpled and she burst into tears again.

'You poor thing.' Zoe moved across to the other

sofa and took the mug from Hazel's hand, placing it on the table. Unused to offering more than a pat on the arm to comfort patients when they became distraught, she was taken aback when the older woman twisted around and began sobbing against her shoulder.

There was a lot more she needed to know, but her other questions would have to wait until Hazel was less emotional.

'What the hell's going on?'

Hazel sprang away from Zoe as though her husband had caught them in a lovers' embrace.

Ray loomed over them, blocking Zoe's view of the window. He stared down at his wife and demanded, 'What have you been telling her?'

Receiving no reply, he turned to Zoe. The fierce look on his normally placid face made her wish she had listened to Kate and stayed away.

FORTY-EIGHT

'You doctors are supposed to make people feel better, not worse.' Ray advanced on Zoe and the room seemed to grow darker.

Zoe's stomach contracted. This angry man bore little resemblance to the amicable landlord she knew. Forcing her voice to stay steady, she said, 'Hello, Ray. Why don't you sit down and we can talk?'

'It's my bloody home.' He leaned over, trapping her on the sofa, and brought his face to within a few inches of hers. She smelt salted peanuts on his breath. 'Don't tell me what to do.'

'Please, Ray, sit down.' Hazel had stopped crying, and her voice was subdued but steady. 'She's trying to help.'

Her husband looked like he was going to argue, then stepped back and eased himself down on to the sofa opposite them, the leather creaking under his weight. He continued to glare at Zoe, his face very red.

'She doesn't care one iota about us, love,' he said. 'I asked her to help before, but all she did was encourage you to see that con man again and ask to be put in touch with her dead husband.'

'That's not what happened,' Zoe said. 'I think he's a phoney too, and I made sure he knew it.' She turned to Hazel. 'I'm sorry. I know you're comforted by what Colonel Stevens claims to be able to do, but he isn't genuine.'

Hazel put her hands over her ears. 'I'm not listening. You both say you want what's best for me, but you don't.'

Ray's bluster had evaporated, and his face now wore an expression of helplessness. Zoe relaxed a little. *Time to get this conversation back on track.*

'I know how Duncan died,' she said. 'And that Chrissie found out.'

The only response to this was a short mew of anguish from Hazel.

'I'm guessing her friend Fiona, the red-head who came to the funeral, was employed by Duncan's GP.'

'Chrissie never let on how she knew,' Ray said. 'But when Hazel overheard that bloody woman talking to you after the funeral she worked it out.'

Hazel jumped in, 'There she was, in our pub, drinking our sherry, and all the time it was her fault.'

'She was lucky it wasn't me who made the connection. I'm not sure I'd have stopped at throwing beer over her.' Ray's clenched fists reminded Zoe of a boxer's gloved hands.

'I don't understand why you feel the need to keep something like that a secret,' she said. 'HIV and AIDS no longer carry the stigma they used to. People would have been sympathetic.'

'Oh, aye?' Ray said. 'Maybe they're used to it in big cities like the one you come from, but how many patients are you treating for it here? Anyway, AIDS didn't kill him, it was that cancer. I didn't want people knowing he'd caught something disgusting like that.'

Accepting now was not the time to challenge Ray's ignorance, Zoe said, 'You have to go to the police and tell them Chrissie was blackmailing you.'

'We didn't kill her!' Hazel cried.

'Shush, love.' Ray turned back to Zoe. 'We don't have to take orders from you. You're only a doctor.'

'If I've worked it out, how long do you think it'll be before the police do too?'

'I wanted to tell them all along,' Hazel said. 'Chrissie was the one breaking the law, not us.'

'And have them decide we killed her because of it?' Ray said. 'That's what the doctor thinks, isn't it?'

He stood up. 'Come with me.'

'Where to?' Zoe asked.

'Down in the bar. I want to show you something.'

Hazel led the way downstairs, with Zoe then Ray behind her. They walked past the back door and along the narrow corridor which connected the bar and dining room with the pub's kitchen. Zoe slowed down as they passed the kitchen, felt a hand at the small of her back urging her on, and responded by coming to an abrupt halt. Hazel continued on into the bar, unaware she was now alone.

Zoe found the prospect of entering The Rocket's empty bar intolerable, the sickly smell of stale beer which emanated from it adding to her apprehension. She hastily weighed up her options.

The building's front entrance was usually bolted until opening time; once in the bar there would be no easy way out. However, she was pretty certain Hazel had not locked the back door after letting her in. All she had to do was switch positions with Ray and make a dash for it.

Thanks to Gregor's boasting, she was better informed regarding Chrissie's private life than anyone else in Westerlea. Because of this, she had seen no point in challenging Ray to reveal who had started the rumour about the dead woman having a lover. Now, though, raising the subject might buy her some time.

She turned to look at Ray, whose face was redder than she had ever seen it. 'The night after Chrissie's body was found, you said someone told you she was having an affair. Was that true?'

Ray looked taken aback at first, then he shrugged. 'She always went about all tarted up. Don't tell me she did that for poor old Jimmy's benefit.'

'So you were lying?'

'Who cares? Anyway, I haven't got all day. Come on.'

Zoe stayed where she was, but could not help glancing towards the back door. She cursed inwardly when Ray noticed.

'Planning your getaway? You really do think we could have killed her.' He let out a rumble of humourless laughter, then called to Hazel, 'Bring me the cash tray out of the till, will you love?'

Unseen, the cash register beeped, its drawer clattered open, and coins rattled against each other. Shortly afterwards, Hazel walked back into the hall, bearing the black plastic tray of money in front of her like a joint of beef newly out of the oven. Ray squeezed past Zoe and took it from her.

Now Zoe had a clear passage to the back door. She willed herself not to look in its direction until she was ready to make her move.

'See here,' Ray said, lifting up each spring-clip in turn to demonstrate how few notes were in the tray. 'Not much is it? And last night was a good night. We're not wealthy people.'

'I don't understand the point you're trying to make.' Zoe said.

'My point is that while Chrissie Baird may have been blackmailing us, she was clever, only demanding a few hundred, never more than we could scrape together in cash. That's not enough to murder someone over.'

Was he really so naive? The news regularly reported people being killed for less.

'Did you give her money on the day she went missing?'

'Yes.'

'How much?'

Hazel spoke for the first time since they came

downstairs. 'Three hundred and fifty pounds.'

The exact cost of the spa break Chrissie had booked. The Andersons could be telling the truth. Or Ray might have tracked down Chrissie later in the day and killed her, but had not been able to find the money to retrieve it.

Ray nodded. 'We wouldn't have paid if we'd planned to kill her, would we? She left here just before we opened for Sunday lunch, alive and very pleased with herself.'

'In which case why don't you tell all this to DCI Mather?'

'Because if we don't, you will,' Ray said. 'That's what you're threatening, isn't it?'

Hazel slumped against the wall with a groan. 'It'll all come out then. Perhaps that's for the best.'

'No it isn't.' Her husband took a step towards Zoe.

The back door was only a few metres away, but Zoe estimated her chances of reaching it before Ray caught up with her to be very slim. Unless she distracted him in some way.

She reached out and pushed upwards on the base of the cash tray which Ray still held. Her hands met less resistance than she expected. A jumble of coins sprayed down the publican's front and clattered onto the wooden floor.

Zoe turned and ran. She heard the cash tray drop then the slithering of feet trying to find purchase on the uneven layer of money.

She reached the door.

It was locked.

FORTY-NINE

'Let her go, Ray.' Hazel said.

Wasting no time looking round to see if Ray was heeding his wife's plea, Zoe turned the key in the lock. Then she yanked open the door, darted outside and sprinted to her parked car, nearly colliding with the postman.

As she drove off, she saw Ray staring at her from the pavement outside The Rocket.

Keeper's Cottage had never felt more like home than when Zoe drew up outside it a few minutes later. Her heart still pounded, but she was already asking herself if her response to Ray had been too extreme. He had not come near to hurting, or even threatening, her. Even so, she remained in the car, watching through the leafless hedge for the Andersons' blue Volvo, until she felt safe enough to make for the house.

Poised, key in hand, to let herself in, she spotted what looked like small patches of ice glistening under the sitting-room window. Moving closer, she saw the ice was actually shards of glass. She rushed indoors, yelling for Mac, and relief flooded through her as he trotted into the hall, a little subdued but uninjured.

Most of the windowpane had been driven into the sitting-room and scattered across the carpet. A whinstone, small enough for Zoe to pick up with one hand, rested against the leg of Mac's chair. It looked like it came from the pile lying in her rear garden, the remains of an old wall. Anyone walking to the back of the cottage to collect this would have seen the open garage doors and known she was out. Which meant the culprit had not intended to cause her physical harm. Smashing her window was merely a childish way of expressing a grievance.

Childish.

Neil had used that exact word to describe his brother. Did Peter really resent her so much that he'd do this? And if so, was it his first act against her – or the latest? While tampering with a car's brakes could not be dismissed as childish, it shared the same cowardice, the same avoidance of actual confrontation, as tossing a stone through the window of an empty house.

She pulled up her sleeve to look at the faint bruise, testimony to the force with which he had seized her arm earlier in the week. She heard his voice again: *I'm telling you for your own good.*

Those words now sounded less like a warning and more like a threat.

She should go to the police.

And tell them what, exactly? First she thought Ray Anderson was out to get her, and now Peter Pengelly. For all his patience and courtesy, Mather would write her off as paranoid.

Zoe dropped into the nearest chair, her head spinning. All she really wanted to do was lock her front door, pull the curtains across the broken window and sit quietly with Mac until everything sorted itself out. But even as she considered this strategy, she knew it stank.

She had never been passive. Russell had often accused her of being bloody-minded. Her best course of action was unclear, but doing nothing was not an option.

After sweeping up the glass, she went out to the hire car. She had not travelled far when she saw a car coming towards her, flashing its lights. A blue Volvo. Zoe stared straight ahead and put her foot down.

FIFTY

Zoe felt absurd, skulking about in her own property with the lights off, spying on her lover and his brother. Yet despite these misgivings, she continued to peer out of the tower room's hexagonal window. Neil's Land Rover and Peter's hatchback were parked in front of Larimer Hall, as well as a large green van she had never seen before.

She should go over now and tackle Peter while Neil was there to protect her. Protect her? Was that really necessary?

She glanced at her phone – no missed calls, no new texts – and looked up in time to see Peter's car reverse out of its space and pick up speed as it tore along the drive. He was paying no heed to peacocks this afternoon.

After giving Peter five minutes to get well away, Zoe locked up and walked the short distance to Larimer Hall. Confident that Neil would be in his workshop and hear the bell, she let herself in. When she tired of waiting for him to appear, she made her way downstairs.

Bert and Tom lay curled up in their basket in front of the Aga, but the workshop and showroom were deserted and Zoe got no response to her calls. Returning to the ground floor, she heard a sound coming from above, so she climbed the next flight of stairs. Like the hall, the first-floor landing was outsized and several doors led off it. All were closed except one, and the sound – louder but still unidentifiable – was coming from that direction.

Walking around someone else's house uninvited felt wrong, even if that person had declared their intention to marry her. Zoe hesitated before going through the open doorway into a small anteroom which must have served as a gentleman's dressing room when the house was built. Its use had not much changed, judging by the presence of a wardrobe, a shoe rack and a full-length mirror.

She glanced into the mirror. What she saw reflected there made her spin round and stare at the opposite wall in disbelief.

A row of whips, canes and riding crops hung at eye level. Beneath these, a narrow shelf supported coiled lengths of chain and leather, and handcuffs: narrow ones made of metal and wider, leather ones with buckles. There were other items too; Zoe could only guess at their uses.

She stretched out a hand, pulling a thick, leather strap towards her. *Wasn't this one of the old reins from the tower room?*

The strange noise she had followed upstairs sounded again. It put her in mind of a trapped animal crying to be released, and came from behind the door on her left.

Releasing the rein, Zoe walked to the door and opened it, stepping into a bedroom many times the size of her own at Keeper's Cottage. An intricately-carved four-poster bed leaned against the nearest wall with matching bedside cabinets. An old-fashioned china pitcher and bowl sat on one cabinet, a clock radio on the other.

Looking across the room, she realised her mistake. It could not have been Peter she had seen earlier, driving his car away from Larimer Hall.

Because he was here.

He stood at the far end of the room in front of a picture window, his back to her. He was on tiptoe, his whole body stretched to its limit, due to the black leather cuff circling his left wrist and connected to a hook in the ceiling.

Red welts crisscrossed his buttocks and upper thighs, some of them oozing blood. His shoulders juddered.

The noise which had brought Zoe to this room was whimpering.

'Oh my God, what has he done to you?'

Zoe rushed forward. And stopped as Peter slowly turned to face her.

FIFTY-ONE

Peter glared at Zoe and continued to stroke his erection.

She took a step back. 'I'm sorry,' she said. 'I thought – '

What the hell had she thought? Not this. She tried to drag her eyes from Peter's naked body and its piercings. Silver hoops through his scrotum, his penis. Smaller ones through his nipples, connected by a matching chain.

With an exasperated sigh, Peter reached up to release his wrist. 'You women are all the same. Why can't you just leave us alone?'

'I was looking for Neil.'

'And found me instead. Pleased, are you, now you know our little secret?'

Our secret? Zoe recalled joking with Neil that his brother spoke sometimes as though they were an old married couple. She felt sick. 'What are you saying?'

'I didn't do this to myself.' Peter half-turned his body so she could see the whip marks again.

She looked away.

'Can't bear to see what he does to me? I warned you. But did you listen? Oh no. You kept leading him on, making him want you.'

'It wasn't like that.'

'It never is.'

Peter took a step forward. Zoe moved back.

'I don't believe Neil has anything to do with . . . this.'

'Yes you do. And because you're such a fine, upstanding member of the community, when you tell people they'll believe you.'

'I'm not going to say anything.'

'Everyone knew Chrissie Baird hated us. They might not have taken any notice of her. But you're a bigger problem.'

A band tightened around Zoe's chest, like it did the moment she discovered the police suspected her of murdering Russell. 'Oh my God,' she said. 'You killed Chrissie.'

Peter charged at her. She turned and fled into the dressing room.

Stop running. Lock the door.

Big mistake.

Peter grunted in pain as she crushed his bare foot between the door and frame. He withdrew the foot but kept on pushing, preventing Zoe from shutting the door, let alone locking it.

She gave one last shove. Made for the landing. *Nearly there.*

Her head snapped back. She almost lost her footing, but was held upright by the noose around her neck.

She plucked at the stiff, unyielding leather.

Peter pulled it tighter.

Zoe tried to bend forward, struggled to escape. Then she remembered something she learned at a self-defence class years ago.

Lean into your attacker.

Loosen the pressure.

Kick behind you.

Peter swore as her heel struck his knee. But the pressure around her throat continued to increase. The more she kicked, the tighter he squeezed.

She felt faint, saw stars.

He dragged her back into the bedroom and threw her face-down across the four-poster. The cover smelt damp and mildewy.

The rein loosened. Zoe sucked in air as Peter turned her over and straddled her. His nakedness should have made him the vulnerable one, but it didn't.

He crossed the rein beneath her chin. And started to tighten it again.

FIFTY-TWO

Zoe clawed at her neck, trying to squeeze even one finger under the rein and relieve the pressure on her windpipe. With her other hand, she pulled, punched and scratched at Peter's arm and shoulder. He was so engrossed in killing her that he failed to respond.

In desperation, she grasped the chain connecting the silver hoops through his nipples and wrenched it away from his chest.

Peter gave a roar of anger and pain as both hoops pulled at his flesh then tore themselves free of it. Continuing to hold the leather rein with his left hand, he raised his right hand and struck Zoe across the face. When she tried to shield herself from further blows, he seized her arm and slammed it against the corner of the bedside cabinet.

The wrist had to be fractured, although she felt no pain. But when she tried to make a fist, her hand refused to cooperate, flailing uselessly. Then it knocked against something cool and smooth.

On the third attempt, Zoe managed to slide her fingers through the handle. Summoning all the strength she had left, she raised the jug and swung it against the side of Peter's head.

The jug smashed. Peter's head barely moved. Zoe was left clutching a small china handle.

'Is that the best you can do?' he said scornfully. The pressure on her throat increased again.

She thrust the jagged end of the handle against Peter's neck. His expression shifted from contempt to bewilderment as blood spurted from him, some of it hitting Zoe across the face.

The rein loosened around her neck and she took a deep breath.

Peter toppled forward.

It was only when he had lain heavy and unmoving across her chest for several minutes that she felt safe enough to close her eyes.

She dreamt she was having an asthma attack, gasping for air, abandoned somewhere with the only inhaler kept in a room she was too scared to enter.

'Fuck oh fuck oh fuck!'

A weight lifted from Zoe's chest and her breathing suddenly eased. When the rein around her neck moved, she lifted her improvised weapon and stabbed at the air. A hand encircled her wrist, causing her to cry out. Fear no long anaesthetised her from pain.

She opened her eyes. Saw Neil's face.

'I'm so sorry,' he said, taking the sharp piece of china from her.

'He tried to kill me,' she said. It hurt to speak. She swallowed. That hurt too.

Neil sat down, cradled her in his arms and wiped her face with a handkerchief. Now her head was raised she could see Peter lying on the floor, partly covered by a small rug. She must have cried out again, because Neil pulled her against his chest and murmured, 'Don't look.'

Zoe closed her eyes; she so wanted to fall asleep.

'You're safe now.'

She started to shiver and tried to push him away. 'I'm going into shock. You must get help.'

'I can't do that.'

'Please. I'm so cold.'

He released her, slid off the bed and left the room.

Just when she thought he was never coming back, he did, carrying a coverless duvet.

'This'll help.' He cocooned her in the duvet. She instantly felt warmer but still could not stop shivering.

'You have to ring for an ambulance.'

'Not yet.'

'Peter killed Chrissie.'

'I know. I was there.'

'Why didn't you stop him?'

Silence.

'Tell me what happened. Please.'

Neil shook his head.

'I know it was because of . . .' Zoe struggled to find the words. 'I saw what you did to him.'

'Only because he wanted me to. You don't think it was a sexual thing for me, do you?' Neil looked appalled, endlessly running a hand over his bald head. 'Oh Zoe, I only did it to stop him going elsewhere and putting himself at the mercy of unscrupulous people. He was blackmailed once. They bled him dry. I couldn't let that happen again.'

She really wanted to believe him. 'How did Chrissie find out?'

'She turned up at the house and got in through the back door. I don't know how – we always keep it locked.'

Tom's words came back to Zoe: *Things old folk like to hang on to.* 'Jean's mum used to work here. She'd kept a key and Chrissie took it.'

Neil nodded absent-mindedly, too caught up in his recollection of that day to heed what she was saying. 'She had that stupid tray of poppies hanging round her neck. As if it would give her an excuse if we caught her snooping.'

'Did she come up here?'

'No. She went through to the workshop. I don't know what she expected to find, but it certainly wasn't Pete bent over the desk and me flogging him with his belt.'

The image burned into Zoe's brain as if she had been there herself. She suddenly felt light-headed and struggled to release a hand from the clutches of the duvet in order to support her head.

'What's wrong?'

'Feeling faint.'

Again Neil left the room, this time returning with a tumbler of water. He held it to her mouth while she took a few sips. When she was almost certain she would not black out, she told him to go on.

'Do you really want to hear this?'

No, but she had to. 'Yes.'

'We didn't even know Chrissie was there until she started to yell at us. How she was glad Alice hadn't gone out with me. How she'd enjoy telling everyone what perverts we were. How we'd be driven out of Westerlea.

'I didn't know what to do. Pete shouted back, told her she was a nosey old woman and had no right coming into our home uninvited. Then he rushed at her and she ran out into the hall. He grabbed her legs and when she fell forward, she hit her head on the stone steps. It was an accident. He didn't mean to kill her.'

'Why are you covering up for him?'

'I'm not. That's what happened.'

'Neil, Chrissie didn't die from hitting her head on a step.'

'I was there. I saw her.'

'The post mortem showed she was strangled. Mather told me.'

'I don't believe you.'

'Peter lied to you.'

'Why would he do that?'

'What happened after she fell?'

'Those stupid poppies were strewn all over the place. Pete went round picking them up while I . . . '

Neil groaned.

'What did you do?'

'He told me to go and fetch an old carpet from upstairs to wrap her in. Oh fuck. She wasn't dead, was she? She woke up while I was gone and he finished her off.'

Zoe put a hand to her throat. She felt again the pressure on her windpipe, saw again the look of concentration on Peter's face as he squeezed the life out of her.

Neil said, 'I'm sorry, Zoe'. He gently pushed away a strand of hair that had fallen over her face. 'The last thing I wanted was you to be hurt. My feelings for you were giving me the courage to break free from him.'

'It was never going to be that easy.'

'I hoped it would. That night, after we put Chrissie in the bonfire, I told him I wouldn't pander to him any more.'

'Did you tell him how you felt about me?'

'Not then. But he tackled me on the way home from coffee with you and Kate after the Guy Fawkes party. I saw no reason to deny it.'

'That's why he tampered with my car, wasn't it?'

Anger flared briefly in Neil's face. 'He said he didn't, but I always know when he's lying.'

'He told me I should stop seeing you. I didn't realise it was a threat. Then I got home earlier today and found my window smashed.'

'We had another row this morning and he stormed off. He must have done it then. I expected him to come home and apologise – that's what usually happened – but instead he was hyper. He threatened to tell you everything, bring you up here and show you his things to prove it, unless I beat him again. So I did. Afterwards I felt so disgusted with myself for giving in to him, I had to get away.'

'When Peter's car left, I was in the tower room, too high up to see the driver. I didn't realise it was you.'

'I grabbed his keys on the way out by mistake. It

was easier to take his car than go back in for mine.'

'Where did you go?'

'Where do you think? To the cottage to find you. Instead I found that smashed window. I made sure you weren't inside, then came back here to tell Pete I was going to wind up the business and start over somewhere else. Without him.'

Zoe yawned, fighting to stay awake. Which made no sense, given how scared she felt. 'What about Jimmy? Why did Peter kill him?'

'He had nothing to do with that.'

'Are you sure?'

'Why would he want to harm Jimmy? It must have been an accident.'

An accident. No one killed Jimmy. That was good . . .

Zoe yawned again. Her body was shutting down. 'Neil, please, you have to call for help.'

'Not yet.'

'What are you waiting for?'

Neil got up and walked out again. He could only have gone as far as the dressing room because he returned almost immediately, holding a pair of metal handcuffs.

Desperate to summon up enough strength to get away, Zoe tried swinging her legs over the side of the bed. They were too weak even to kick off the duvet.

'Stay still. I'm not going to hurt you.' Neil lifted her hand, kissed it, then closed a cuff around her uninjured wrist. He secured the other cuff to one of the bedposts, then sat back down beside her. 'We need to get our story straight.'

'What story?'

'You must tell them that Pete attacked you and I killed him to save you.'

'But I killed him in self-defence. Look, I'm covered in his blood.'

'Please, Zoe, do what I say for once.'

'What happened isn't your fault.'

'Yes it is. I'm the eldest. I should have stopped it.'

'They won't believe me.'

'Of course they will. You'd have no reason to lie.'

Zoe tugged feebly at the handcuff attaching her to the bed. 'Why have you put me in this?'

'To make it more convincing. I don't want there to be any doubt that you're not to blame.'

'Where will you go?'

'Don't worry about me.'

'They'll find you.'

'I'll take my chances. They'll be looking for a bald man and I won't be that for long.'

'This isn't one of your films, Neil. People can't simply disappear in real life.'

'I'll be okay. Trust me.'

She wanted to shout at him, make him see sense, but did not have the strength. All she could do now was play along with him. She didn't have to take part in his crazy plan once he was gone.

The pain in her wrist was agonizing, but she could still move her hand enough to reach inside her trouser pocket to pull out her keys. 'Take the hire car. It's parked at the coach house. It isn't as fast as mine, but – '

Neil held up his hand. 'Can you hear something?'

Zoe listened. At first she could only hear the rasp of her own breathing, then a voice from downstairs called her name.

'It's Kate. I'm supposed to be having tea with her.' Zoe looked towards the window; it was dark outside.

'Shit.'

'If you really are going, you must do it now. Before it's too late,' Zoe said. 'Hide in one of the other rooms and leave once you see her come in here.'

'Zoe, I'm so sorry. If only – '

'There's no time. Look after yourself.'

Neil took the keys and kissed her. *For the last time.*

Zoe felt overwhelmed by emotions she could not have named.

A few minutes later, she could at last close her eyes, while Kate texted Mather to come quickly and bring an ambulance.

Just before losing consciousness, she thought she heard the front door slam.

FIFTY-THREE

Zoe unlocked the Jeep and leaned in to put her briefcase on the passenger seat. She could not have chosen a vehicle less like her beloved sports car, but buying it had felt like an affirmation that she planned to stay in the Borders. *Despite everything.*

A voice came from behind her. 'Doctor Moreland?'

She frowned. At this rate she would be late for her appointment with the estate agent handling the sale of the coach house. They were due to meet at Keeper's Cottage in about ten minutes, where he would also advise her on the market value of that property. When Douglas Mackenzie first offered to sell it to her she had rejected the suggestion, but given time to consider and coaxing from Kate, she was coming round to the idea.

The tall, slightly stooped man in his sixties looked vaguely familiar, so perhaps they had already met. It was hard to tell these days. Everyone behaved as though they knew her, thanks to the photographs the local and national newspapers had splashed across their front pages.

'I'm sorry,' she said, 'surgery's finished. If you'd like to call in at reception they'll fix you up with an appointment.'

'It's you I need to talk to. On a personal matter.' The man was well spoken, with just a trace of a Borders accent. He stared at her, though not at her neck like they usually did. Instead, he explored her whole face, as though trying to memorise every feature.

'What do you want?'

'Forgive me. This is probably not the right way to go about things.'

'What do you want?' Zoe repeated, massaging her wrist. Its plaster had only come off a few days earlier.

'I knew your mother. You look very much like her.'

She took a step back. 'Really?'

'May I ask you a question?'

'All right.'

'Your middle initial,' the man said, gesturing towards the health centre's front door where the brass plate continued to display Zoe's name and qualifications, 'does it stand for "Kelso"?'

Zoe put her hand out to the Jeep for support. 'Why do you want to know?'

'Because if it does, I think you're my daughter.'

THE END

THANK YOU FOR READING

If you have enjoyed this novel, please consider leaving a review on Amazon. If you think a friend or relative would enjoy it, why not buy them a copy? It's available as an e-book too.

Due to the wonders of modern technology, you can contact me direct to tell me what you thought of *No Stranger to Death* and keep up the pressure on me to finish its sequel.

- Tweet me: I'm @JanetOKane
- Post on my Facebook page:
www.facebook.com/JanetOKaneAuthor
- Email me via my blog: www.janetokane.blogspot.co.uk

AUTHOR'S NOTE

This book is a work of fiction. Any resemblance to actual people, living or dead, is coincidental. While many of the Borders locations I describe are real, the village of Westerlea is not.

ACKNOWLEDGEMENTS

This novel may have my name on it, but a host of other people helped make it the book you have just read.

I received invaluable advice from many knowledgeable individuals in my efforts to get my facts right, in particular, Dr Petrina Moralee and Phil O'Kane. Any factual errors in this book are mine.

The term 'self-publishing' is a misnomer in my case. I and my book have benefited greatly from the professional services of Kim McGillivray, who designed the splendid cover; Caroline Smailes at BubbleCow, whose editing was both insightful and encouraging; and Jo Harrison from Writer's Block Admin Services who saved me considerable stress by taking on some of the essential IT tasks.

Without the camaraderie of co-workers and away from the beady eye of a boss, a writer's life can feel solitary and unproductive. So I want to thank my friends – those in real life and those I've so far only met on Twitter but who are no less real – for their patience and encouragement during the writing of this novel.

And finally, reaching the top of my list of supporters, I pay tribute to my lovely husband John. It was he who threw down the challenge, 'Write it then!' when we stood in front of a bonfire one Guy Fawkes night and I suggested that would be an excellent way to dispose of a human corpse. He has always believed, perhaps more than I dared to myself, that *No Stranger to Death* would be published. I'm delighted to have proved him right.